DETECTING THE SOUTH
IN FICTION, FILM, & TELEVISION

Southern Literary Studies

SCOTT ROMINE, SERIES EDITOR

DETECTING THE SOUTH

IN FICTION, FILM & TELEVISION

EDITED BY DEBORAH E. BARKER
& THERESA STARKEY

Louisiana State University Press ▐▐ Baton Rouge

Published by Louisiana State University Press
Copyright © 2019 by Louisiana State University Press
All rights reserved
Manufactured in the United States of America
First printing

Designer: Michelle A. Neustrom
Typefaces: Whitman, text; Trade Gothic, display
Printer and binder: Sheridan Books, Inc.

Library of Congress Cataloging-in-Publication Data

Names: Barker, Deborah, 1956– editor. | Starkey, Theresa, editor.
Title: Detecting the South in fiction, film, and television / edited by Deborah E. Barker and
    Theresa Starkey.
Description: Baton Rouge : Louisiana State University Press, [2019] | Series: Southern literary
    studies | Includes bibliographical references and index.
Identifiers: LCCN 2019018887 | ISBN 978-0-8071-7165-3 (cloth) | ISBN 978-08071-7269-8
    (epub) | ISBN 978-0-8071-7268-1 (pdf)
Subjects: LCSH: Detective and mystery stories, American—History and criticism. | Noir
    fiction, American—History and criticism. | Detective and mystery films—History and
    criticism. | Film noir—United States—History and criticism. | Detective and mystery
    television programs—History and criticism. | Southern States—In literature. |
    Southern States—In motion pictures. | Southern States—On televison.
Classification: LCC PS374.D4 D47 2019 | DDC 813/.8720975—dc23
LC record available at https://lccn.loc.gov/2019018887

CONTENTS

1   Introduction
DEBORAH E. BARKER & THERESA STARKEY

PART I: DETECTING SOUTHERN NOIR

17   Exploring the Noir Landscape of the New South
ACE ATKINS

22   The Beautiful Mysterious: The Case of William Eggleston
MEGAN ABBOTT

26   *Sanctuary* and "the Broken and Myriad Reflection of" Noir
BOB HODGES

40   Southern Gothic and Film Noir: The Commingling of Genre
and Cinematic Stylistics
R. BRUCE BRASELL

50   A Mountainoir: The Arrival of Country Noir and Frank Borzage's
Moonrise (1948) in Retrospect
JACOB AGNER

64   Film Noir, Matthew McConaughey, and Queer Capital
in the Southern Imaginary
SARAH LEVENTER

81   Detecting Hollywood South: *In the Electric Mist* and
the Changing Relations of Louisiana Noir
LEIGH ANNE DUCK

96   Ace Atkins, *True Detective*, and the Mystery of the "No-Orleans"
     JAMES A. CRANK

112 The Suburban Noir Heads South: From *Desperate Housewives*
     to *Gone Girl*
     SUZANNE LEONARD

     PART II: PRIVATELY DETECTING THE SOUTH

129 Elnora May Hardin: Creating Space for a Complex Black Woman
     in Southern Noir
     DOMINIQUA DICKEY

134 Down These Mean Streets (Whose Names No One Can Pronounce)
     GREG HERREN

142 Evolving Secrets: Eudora Welty and the Mystery Genre
     HARRIET POLLACK

159 Refusing a "Single Song" of the South: The Frustrated Detective
     in Donna Tartt's *The Little Friend*
     CLAIRE COTHREN

172 A Failed Southern Strategy: Detecting Race, Gender, and Region
     on CBS's *Yancy Derringer*
     PHOEBE BRONSTEIN

186 Ecological Anarchy and Philosophical Anarchism in the Florida Crime
     Fiction of John D. MacDonald
     KRISTOPHER MECHOLSKY

     PART III: DETECTING SOUTHERN COPS

207 Sheriff Andy Taylor and the Non-Procedural in Mayberry
     THERESA STARKEY

221   Arresting Visions: Film Noir, Visual Detection, and the Invisible Corpse
      in Ron Rash's *One Foot in Eden*
      RANDALL WILHELM

237   Marcos McPeek Villatoro's *Home Killings:* Sleuthing Central American
      Identity and History in the New Latino South
      YAJAIRA M. PADILLA

252   Taking the Southern Bait: *Law & Order: Special Victims Unit* and
      the Televisual South
      GINA CAISON

PART IV: JOURNALISTS DETECTING THE SOUTH

273   The Truth Sleuth: The Detective Journalism of William Bradford Huie
      and Thulani Davis's *Everybody's Ruby*
      RICHÉ RICHARDSON

286   Whiteness Undercover: Racial Passing and/as Detection in
      Black Like Me (1964)
      JACQUELINE PINKOWITZ

301   Culture Detectives: Contemporary Journalism, Creative Nonfiction,
      and the US South
      ZACKARY VERNON

317   Works Cited

339   Contributors

345   Index

DETECTING THE SOUTH
IN FICTION, FILM, & TELEVISION

INTRODUCTION

DEBORAH E. BARKER & THERESA STARKEY

In post–World War II United States, the detective genre in literature, film, and television has been heavily influenced by hard-boiled crime fiction and film noir. The noir-inflected mean streets, dive bars, and back alleys that many of the tough guys and trench-coated detectives have gone down are so associated with urban settings (typically New York or Los Angeles) that, historically, the impact of the American South has often been overlooked or undervalued. However, southern writers, detectives, and/or settings are not new to detective narratives. After all, it was southerner Edgar Allan Poe who helped to establish the genre with his stories of ratiocination, featuring the brilliant but eccentric Auguste Dupin. The Dupin stories, set in Paris, which Terence Whalen refers to as "a genre in miniature" (226), fostered the armchair detectives of the golden age of detective mysteries, such as Sherlock Holmes, Miss Marple, and Nero Wolfe, to name only a few. Poe initiated elements that are still integral to detective fiction: the detective as outsider, as smarter than the police, as cosmopolitan; the role of the newspapers for finding and planting clues; ripped-from-the-headlines plots; the clueless sidekick; the locked-room mystery; hiding in plain sight; the MacGuffin; the political thriller; the antagonistic and often personal relationship between the detective and the criminal mastermind; and savage violence against women.

But more importantly for this collection, Poe created an early example of the detective story set in the South in "The Gold Bug" (1843), featuring William Legrand, an impoverished, reclusive New Orleans aristocrat living in rural isolation after losing the family fortune. The plot elements include issues of slavery, the loss of family honor, superstition, greed, murder, and lost treasure, elements that figure into many southern detective stories. Furthermore, some of the most canonical southern writers, such as Mark Twain and William Faulkner, have made notable contributions to the genre, especially in the form of the lawyer as detective (Van Dover and Jebb 47–65, 99–184). In *Tom Sawyer, Detective* (1896) Twain created the folksy country lawyer who uses his local knowledge to solve the crime, while in *Pudd'nhead Wilson* (1894) it is the northern lawyer who uses the science of fingerprints to uncover the mystery of racial identity. Faulkner gave us Gavin Steven, the scholarly gentleman lawyer as detective, as well as the hapless and less successful lawyer Benbow, who solves the crime, but loses his client in *Sanctuary* (1930); more recently, John Grisham has made the southern lawyer-as-detective a staple of the genre.

It was, however, the latter decades of the twentieth century that saw a burgeoning of southern detective novels and the emergence of TV series and films that often depicted a mixture of noir, southern gothic, and crime stories, including both the rural and the urban Souths. In the '80s and '90s, the popularity of police detective shows such as *Miami Vice* (1984–1990)[1]—in conjunction with FBI crime statistics that ranked five southern cities as the highest in violent crime in the nation—brought to the fore the significance of southern urban crime and violence (Van Dover and Jebb 2). During this same time the tough, independent female detective was on the rise, with best-selling series by Marcia Muller, Sue Grafton, and Sara Paretsky, whose female PIs were located in California and Chicago. However, the southern setting produced Julie Smith's New Orleans female cop, Skip Langdon, as well as variations on the detective with Sharyn McCrumb's forensic anthropologist Elizabeth MacPherson and Patricia Cornwell's Virginia medical examiner Kay Scarpetta. More recently, Karin Slaughter's *Criminal* (2012) and *CopTown* (2014) highlight the early experiences of policewomen in Atlanta, and J. T. Ellison's Nashville duo of medical examiner Samantha Owens and police lieutenant Taylor Jackson are just a few of the many southern female detectives. In addition to the urban South, the early twenty-first century saw the emergence of the Rough South, which Brian Carpenter defines as "'Grit Lit's wilder kin': mostly poor, white, rural, and unquestionably violent" (xxi). The Rough South graphically demonstrates that even the bucolic, rural South is not immune to crime and violence. In fact, the southern detective has emerged as such a recognizable trope that HBO's first (and more successful) season of *True Detective* (2014) was set in Louisiana and—after the cool critical reception of the LA-based second season—has returned to the South for the third, this time set in Arkansas.

The essays in *Detecting the South* help to flesh out the historical, political, and aesthetic contexts out of which the southern detective narrative emerges and evolves, through the examination of topics such as race, social justice, gender, genre, ecology, queer masculinity, the Global South, and neoliberalism. Although many of the contributors will interrogate elements of genre, the purpose of this collection is not to define what makes a detective narrative southern. That argument has been made, and it raises the question of whether or not the setting and/or characters and/or author must be southern. This leads us back to attempting to define the American South in general, and southern literature and film in particular, by generating arbitrary limits. For example, J. K. Van Dover and John F. Jebb, in their 1996 book on the southern detective, chose to focus on texts in which the author, detective, and setting are southern in order to capture an "insider's view of the South." However, in their definition of "the South" they conclude that "Texas is not Southern; Missouri, Kentucky, Maryland, and Delaware are. Miami-Fort Lauderdale and Tampa-St. Petersburg are Southern, not because we think they really are, but because too many really good detectives have detected there" (4, 5).

In the past few decades, critics have widely contested the ability or even the advisability of attempting to create a single definition of the South, as no single definition can encompass the diversity of the region. Nor can we fully understand the region in isolation from the country as a whole. The problem with attempting to define and limit what makes a genre "southern" is that it prevents us from discerning how the South might play a key role even in a typical New York or Los Angeles setting, which can be particularly significant for African American detectives. For example, a character's southern origins often play a key role in Walter Mosley's LA-based Easy Rawlins series (1990–) and in Chester Himes's famous Harlem Cycle (1957–69), featuring detectives Coffin Ed Johnson and Grave Digger Jones. Hime's posthumously published Plan B [1993] even goes back to an antebellum Alabama plantation.

We prefer to turn the question around: instead of defining what makes a work southern, we investigate how the southern elements shape the detective narrative. Our definition of "southern" is therefore necessarily broad, and we invoke the southern imaginary as a nuanced term that is not limited by "genre or geography" (Barker and McKee 2).[2] Detecting the South uncovers the impact of the South (even if it is only a reference to the South, a southern character, or political and historical events associated with the region) as it situates the detective as an integral figure of interrogation. In investigating the role of the southern imaginary, our authors are interested both in the specificity of how the South is employed in individual works and in the more general trends (however the region manifests within the works). In taking the southern turn, at least three general, and frequently interrelated, themes present themselves: the inclusion of race (especially as it relates to slavery, segregation, and discrimination), the role of land (as a commodity, an ecologically threatened space, and a place of seclusion for committing and/or hiding crimes), and the southern gothic (the dilapidated plantation house, the swamp, family secrets, and the presence of the occult, particularly voodoo). While these elements are not unique to the South, they are often amplified because of the racial history of slavery, the Civil War, and the civil rights movement. In the southern setting a world of unquestioned whiteness is more difficult to portray because of this legacy of racial trauma and economic exploitation of the people and the land, as well as the desire to expose or erase that history and its current manifestations.

Like "southern" our definition of "detective" is flexible and open to interpretation. Many of the contributors explore variations on the southern detective, including the southern gentleman, the lawyer, the journalist, the precocious child as amateur sleuth, a hairdresser turned detective, a music professor, as well as the more standard professional detective of the urban South and the cop (male and female, urban and rural). As our focus is on detecting, we have organized three of the four sections of the collection based on the form of detection and its relationship to the law: the detective as a private or amateur detective who can operate outside the law; as representative of the police, who must uphold the law even as they are frequently implicated in the crime as well as in the detection; and the detective as journalist, who investigates the South from an outsider's perspective. We begin, however, with a section on southern noir, a retro genre that is increasingly applied to both new and old works, as evidenced by the 2014 special edition of the *Faulkner Journal*, "Noir Faulkner."

Like noir in general (Naremore 11), southern noir is difficult to pin down. As Barry Hannah asserts, it is difficult to define the distinctions among "'hard-boiled' noir, detective, and mystery" and the "better the book, the less definition and pedantry are required" (50). Yet noir is a term that still resonates with audiences and has a marketable cachet. Of its almost 90 editions, Akashic Books's Noir Series, which began in 2004 with *Brooklyn Noir*, has included the more obvious urban southern cities New Orleans and Miami, but also Richmond, Dallas, St. Petersburg, Memphis, and St. Louis, as well as states like Mississippi. Not all southern detection is noir, yet the dark and brooding world of lust, secrets, corruption, and betrayal associated with noir has permeated many southern detective narratives. Because of the ubiquity of the noir influence, it pertains to works in all other sections, but the essays in part I address southern noir's stylistic development and permutations across multiple texts, genres, media, and/or time periods.

Southern noir overlaps with the crime stories, thrillers, and police procedurals set in the urban South, but also with rural or country noir. Erik Dussere argues that the noir tradition, as an implicit critique of mainstream American consumerism, offers a sense of "noir authenticity" and an "undefinable elsewhere to which the logic of authenticity leads" (249). However, in the national imaginary, the South, particularly the rural South, has often been that "elsewhere," seen as resisting consumer culture and modernity and offering a taste of "authenticity," even as that "authenticity" is often a marketable commodity. Daniel Woodrell helped to popularize the idea of country or rural noir in his aptly named novel, *Give Us a Kiss: A Country Noir* (1996). Instead of prohibition bootleg whiskey—a significant feature in many '30s crime narratives—in much southern noir, and in Woodrell's own writing, illegal weed (*Give Us a Kiss*) and meth (*Winter's Bone*) are the new rural cash commodities. Given the overlap between grit lit and rural/southern noir, it is not surprising that Tom Franklin, in addition to coediting *Grit Lit: A Rough South Reader* (2012), also edited *Mississippi Noir* (2016); that his work is analyzed in the recent anthology *Rough South, Rural South* (2016); and that he, along with many of the same authors, appears in all three works. The southern setting draws attention to the rural dimensions of noir, as well as to the South as a site of urban crime.

In addition to the critical essays, we begin several sections with the perspective of creative writers who are currently engaged with or have been influenced by the southern detective genre, as it is the writers who directly impact the genre. Too often writers and critics are not paired together, and this can create a one-sided conversation. But that conversation is important, as writers and critics don't necessarily view the South in the same way. Writers can offer insights into how they employ the South in terms of craft and/or inspiration, while critics analyze the text as well as generic trends and literary, historical, and cultural contexts. Together they provide a fuller picture of the southern detective. In "Part I: Detecting Southern Noir," crime and mystery authors explore the creative side of southern noir and illuminate the noir stylistic and atmospheric influences of the past as they have impacted their own fiction. In "Exploring the Noir Landscape of the New South," Ace Atkins, who has taken over Robert B. Parker's Spenser series, asserts that the crime novel isn't about "introspection," but rather "looking outward at a broken world and trying to not only find justice but deeper meaning." He draws inspiration from William Faulkner to construct Tibbehah County, Mississippi, the fictional setting for his Quinn Colson series that depicts a contemporary South beset by poverty, inequality, racism, environmental issues, and violence. In "The Beautiful Mysterious: The Case of William Eggleston," Megan Abbott, who won an Edgar award for her contribution to *Mississippi Noir* and whose novel *Dare Me* is in preproduction with USA network, reflects upon the impact that Memphian William Eggleston's photographs have had on her imagination as a crime writer. Like a noirish scene, his images disorient the viewer and create an anxious, gnawing desire to *know more*. Abbott explores how the images function as sites of aesthetic unease and mystery directly linked to ways of seeing and storytelling.

The critical essays in each section are roughly chronological. We begin with Bob Hodges's "*Sanctuary* and 'The Broken and Myriad Reflection of' Noir." *Sanctuary* (1931), William Faulkner's most overt foray into the hard-boiled style, arguably marks the beginning of southern noir. The novel, which Barry Hannah referred to as a "country and Memphis noir" (50), demonstrates the interdependence between rural and urban crime in the production and distribution of illegal goods (Prohibition-era bootleg whiskey). Though the novel predates the appellation of noir, as Hodges argues, Faulkner was not only influenced by detective fiction he in turn influenced subsequent works and helped to set the stage for a noir sensibility. Hodges asserts that Faulkner "anticipates yet playfully redeploys noir topoi." Through "racialized shadow-play" he "destabilizes" readers' attributions of race and gender in his depiction of both the gangster Popeye and the lawyer Benbow as "pathological" hard-boiled homosexuals, while hard-boiling the southern belle as femme fatale. Not surprisingly, the film adaptation of the novel, *The Story of Temple Drake*, anticipates noir cinematography, with its connections to German Expressionism. *Sanctuary* is the perfect example of the overlapping influences and integration of the southern gothic, hard-boiled crime novels, and use of shadows and chiaroscuro associated with noir stylistics.

To understand the stylistic similarities between noir and southern gothic, both retroactive genres that have contributed to the southern detective narrative, R. Bruce Brasell's "Southern Gothic and Film Noir: The Commingling of Genre and Cinematic Stylistics" compares articles on visual stylistics in *American Cinematographer*. He concludes that, from the perspective of cinematographers, "although 'southern noir' was not historically a term used to refer to these films during their initial reception, their visual stylistics indicate that they are." The interaction between gothic and noir is perhaps not surprising considering that the original *noir romans* were based on translations of English gothic novels in the eighteenth and nineteenth centuries.

Jacob Agner's "A Mountainoir: The Arrival of Country Noir and Frank Borzage's *Moonrise* (1948) in Retrospect," demonstrates that even during the classic period of film noir, rural and southern settings worked equally well as the city for depicting desire and murder. As Agner notes, when the famous noir novelist James Cain considered changing the location of his earlier West Virginia proletarian novel to California in his revision of the work as a noir novel, *The Butterfly* (1946), his wife disagreed, saying that California had nothing to compare to the West Virginia coal mines. Agner reviews the concept of "rural noir" and adds to it an even more specific form of "mountain noir" in Frank Borzage's *Moonrise* (1948), based on the novel by Theodore Strauss. Set in the Virginia mountains, the film uses noir techniques to explore the racialized stigma of "hillbilly" and how far the protagonist will go to avoid it.

While *True Detective*, as critics have noted, calls attention to the devastation of southern Louisiana from agribusiness and the oil companies, Leigh Anne Duck, in "Detecting Hollywood South: *In the Electric Mist* and the Changing Relations of Louisiana Noir," examines the impact, both economic and cultural, of the film industry in Louisiana, known as Hollywood South. Capitalizing on the well-established commodification of Louisiana as a tourist site, the state now sells itself as a movie setting. However, Duck examines a group of Louisianan noir films that have "sought settings resistant to cliché or foregrounded the production of touristic and cinematic conventions." Duck provides both a history of the state's efforts to court Hollywood (in the past and the present) and a certain self-conscious resistance to it, by examining a number of noir films set in Louisiana: *Panic in the Streets* (1950), *The Drowning Pool* (1975), *Tightrope* (1984), *The Big Easy* (1987), *Angel Heart* (1987), *Storyville* (1992). She concludes with *In the Electric Mist with Confederate Dead* (1993), based on James Lee Burke's series featuring Cajun detective Dave Robicheaux. Integral to the plot of *In the Electric Mist* is the presence of a film production, backed by mob money that comes to Robicheaux's Iberia Parish. Duck asserts that the film attempts "to reclaim classic noir's sense of dynamic, inhabited space not least by implicating film production in social change."

Individual actors have also profited from the popularity of southern noir. Sarah Leventer's "Film Noir, Matthew McConaughey, and Queer Capital in the Southern Imaginary" examines Matthew McConaughey's role in *True Detective* as a function of his established heterosexual southern persona in a series of roles that co-opt aspects of "queerness, film noir, and southernness." Leventer maintains that *True Detective: Season One* (2014) provides only a "conditional embrace" of Rust Cohle, suggesting the "privileges that come with this new era of inclusion are precarious and based on ever-narrowing parameters of whiteness, class belonging, and heteronormativity." However, *The Paperboy*, the only film in which he actually plays a gay man, makes overt the racial underpinning of "southern gothic noir" and offers a radical potential.

James A. Crank provides a different pairing by comparing the setting of New Orleans in works written before and after Katrina: Ace Atkins's Nick Travers series, focusing on *Dirty South* (2004) and *True Detective: Season One*. Crank argues in "Ace Atkins, *True Detective*, and the Mystery of the 'No-Orleans'" that detective narratives have created, and often placed at odds, two versions of New Orleans: Noir Orleans of the urban mean streets and what Crank defines as "No-Orleans," a "world of trash, waste, refuse, of what's left over after the city world has used it of its value. It's liminal space—not quite urban, not quite rural, not country, not city." In *Dirty South*'s No-Orleans, characters try to create their own sense of values and their own form of authenticity to take back with them to the city, while in *True Detective*'s No-Orleans they find a "dark, retreaded fantasy of the Gothic South." Both works examine "American anxieties over blackness, waste, reconstruction, migration, borders, and perhaps most crucially, questions over authenticity."

Another space that is not urban or rural is the suburbs, and recent crime thrillers, advanced by the popularity of Gillian Flynn's *Gone Girl* (2012), have inspired the term *chick noir* and *suburban noir*. Suzanne Leonard, in "The Suburban Noir Heads South: From *Desperate Housewives* to *Gone Girl*," argues that *Desperate Housewives* (2004–2012) serves as a precursor to *Gone Girl* in helping to establish many of the elements of suburban noir, including "the increasing visibility and potency of female revenge in postfeminist media culture." "Amazing Amy" plays on the police procedural by using the police as unwitting accomplices who "detect" the very clues she plants to enact her revenge on the men in her life. *Gone Girl*, however, demonstrates what happens when suburban noir goes South, "figuring it as a space that dispels postfeminist pretensions—particularly those born from Amy's elitist east coast upbringing—undoing them with a swift dose of economic urgency." As Amy describes her southern sojourn, she is "penniless and on the run. How fucking noir" (319).

In "Part II: Privately Detecting the South," we turn to the private and amateur detectives. Many of the works in this collection reexamine the heterosexual white male "tough guy" detectives that historically dominated the genre. Creative writers Dominiqua Dickey and Greg Herren reimagine the genre through the lens of race, gender, and sexual orientation. In "Elnora May Hardin: Creating Space for a Complex Black Woman in Southern Noir," Dickey discusses her creation of an African American hairdresser/detective set in Grenada, Mississippi, in 1939. Dickey's short story, "God's Gonna Trouble the Waters," featuring Elnora May Hardin, was published in *Mississippi Noir*, and she recently completed her novel based on the character. Like other artists discussed, she finds inspiration in popular culture and in the works of other hard-boiled writers. However, it is her own family history and personal connection to Mississippi that functions as the genesis for her storytelling, setting, and character development. With Elnora as her guide, Dickey sees herself as actively "[filling] a void" in a "genre consumed by strong, capable men." In "Down These Mean Streets (Whose Names No One Can Pronounce)," Greg Herren's creation of the first gay male detective in New Orleans, Chanse MacLeod, sprang from his own experiences as a closeted queer teen in Kansas, always in search of gay characters, and his relationship to the city of New Orleans as an outsider. For Herren, Chanse is the closeted outsider who moves to the southern city "in order to feel free enough to live as an openly gay man." Herren explains how he wanted to open up the crime genre he loved and create a space for gay men who didn't "just pop up" in stories and were never "the center."

Film noir and crime writing have not only privileged white, male tough guys, they have also privileged white male writers. While critics have increasingly recognized the noir legacy of Faulkner's use of the hard-boiled style, setting, and plots, Eudora Welty is more typically noted for her relationship to crime writer Ross Macdonald than for her own contribution to the genre. However, Harriet Pollack in "Evolving Secrets: Eudora Welty and the Mystery Genre," explores the world of violence, passion, and revenge that motivates many of the mysteries in Welty's writings over the years, including an unpublished story, "The Shadow Club." As Pollack explains, mysteries in Welty's work are seldom solved; instead they lead to further and often more devastating secrets.

Television programming of the 1950s, with its expanding southern audience, attempted a balancing act to invite a southern audience without losing its northern counterpart. In "A Failed Southern Strategy: Detecting Race, Gender, and Region on CBS's Yancy Derringer," Phoebe Bronstein analyzes *Yancy Derringer* (1958–1959). Derringer, a plantation-owning, postbellum southern gentleman, serves as an intermediary figure situated between *The Gray Ghost* (1954), which was overtly supportive of the Confederacy, and the debonair detectives of ABC's *Bourbon Street Beat* (1959–1960), which followed a more typical detective narrative. *Yancy Derringer,* by including Pahoo, a Native American sidekick, "mobiliz[ed] the Western genre to re-imagine and re-route southern racism" onto Pahoo, allowing Yancy to come to his defense against racist whites, thus "showcase[ing] a pattern and history of imagining white extra-legal male heroes as redemptive forces for a white South in the midst of the civil rights movement."

One of the most prolific of the mid-to-late century southern hard-boiled writers, John D. MacDonald, penned twenty-one novels in his Travis McGee series from 1964 to 1985, creating a not-so-crime-free view of Ft. Lauderdale, Florida. Kristopher Mecholsky's "Ecological Anarchy and Philosophical Anarchism in the Florida Crime Fiction of John D. MacDonald" analyzes MacDonald's oeuvre in the larger context of Florida crime fiction and the relationship between southern identity and the often embattled Florida ecosystem. Rather than a PI, McGee is a salvager for hire who searches for lost or stolen items, an ironic profession considering that the changing landscape of Florida is something that cannot be replaced. Mecholsky argues that McGee is a philosophical anarchist because of his distrust of human organizations and the damage they do to people and the environment, but not a nihilist, as is true of some *noir romans,* because he does believe in individual acts of sympathy and kindness.

If Welty was not fully recognized for her crime writing, southern women's contribution to the genre continues to garner critical attention. In "Refusing a 'Single Song' of the South: The Frustrated Detective in Donna Tartt's *The Little Friend,*" Claire Cothren's analysis takes Welty's strategy toward mystery a step further. While the "solution" to Welty's mysteries only suggests even darker family secrets, in *The Little Friend* (2002) the very act of detection itself can instigate a crime. Tartt's Harriet is a spunky tomboy who sets about to discover who hanged her nine-year-old brother, whose lynching is deemed a mystery, precisely because he is white. Even as we follow Harriet through her attempts to uncover the truth, we realize that because of the social hierarchies of race, class, and gender—and the assumptions they generate—Harriet ends up not only implicating an innocent lower-class white man but also pushing him to commit murder.

"Part III: Detecting Southern Cops" focuses on police officers and detectives. If television's early attempts at the southern private detective were unsuccessful, CBS found the perfect formula in the small-town sheriff of *The Andy Griffith Show* (1960–68). In "Sheriff Andy Taylor and the Non-Procedural in Mayberry," Theresa Starkey argues that despite Andy's squeaky-clean country humor, and the series' avoidance of racial issues in the South, the show still alludes to the darker side of Mayberry, and to a community that is in constant need of surveillance. As Starkey demonstrates, Mayberry's heterogeneous boundaries are patrolled by an unconventional lawman whose methods and manner subvert not only the profession but also conventional notions of manhood.

While *Andy Griffith* presented a humorous version of small-town vice in the '60s, Randall Wilhelm, in "Arresting Visions: Film Noir, Visual Detection, and the Invisible Corpse in Ron Rash's *One Foot in Eden,*" demonstrates the crossover between grit lit and noir. Wilhelm demonstrates how Ron Rash employs noir visual tropes in *One Foot in Eden* (2002) to reveal the complex relationships between land and characters, which allow them to read the crimes that are not spoken. Like many other southern noirs, the southern setting invokes gothic elements and *One Foot in Eden* (as Wilhelm points out) has been referred to as "equal parts vintage crime novel and Southern Gothic." But Wilhelm argues that Rash's use of genre codes is "more complex" and that it "challenges genre categories and codes by merging a panoply of elements culled from the detective novel, the police procedural, hard-boiled crime fiction, film noir, and the metaphysical thriller."

Racial strife in southern detective narratives typically focuses on black/white schism, but, as Yajaira M. Padilla explains in "Marcos McPeek Villatoro's *Home Killings:* Sleuthing Central American Identity and History in the New Latino South," Romilia Chacón, a Nashville police detective who grew up in Atlanta, negotiates her way as a Latina in a region often dichotomized as white and black. Romilia is hired because she speaks Spanish, but as a second generation Salvadoran American she knows that language, history, culture, and politics have significant differences based on region and country. These differences are crucial in her dealings with a Mexican American reporter and a Guatemalan American drug lord/businessman who is both a suspect and an unwelcome suitor. The real killer, however, is a white male detective, who works with the drug lord and who plants evidence to suggest the murderer is a Latino.

Our final essay in this section perfectly demonstrates the role the South can play even in a show that is thoroughly steeped in its New York City setting. In "Taking the Southern Bait: *Law & Order: Special Victims Unit* and the Televisual South," Gina Caison investigates how Detective Amanda Rollins, a petite blonde who, like Romilia, also transfers from Atlanta, is repeatedly used to "bait" criminals in the New York–based series. Caison argues that "Rollins' body creates the need for policing even while she is literally the police," a move that draws on the narrative of the assumed sexual vulnerability of the southern white woman, whether in the North or the South.

The essays in "Part IV: Journalists Detecting the South" reveal the ways journalists-as-detectives can go outside the regular channels of the law even as they, unlike the private detective, present their findings to the public. In "The Truth Sleuth: The Detective Journalism of William Bradford Huie and Thulani Davis's *Everybody's Ruby*," Riché Richardson analyzes the works of activist-journalist Huie; in particular his involvement in the lesser-known case *Ruby McCollum: Woman in the Suwannee Jail* (1956), in which he collaborated with writer/anthropologist Zora Neale Hurston. Although the partnership with Hurston was not without its tensions, Richardson argues that Huie's investigative journalism and his status as what Noel Ignatiev refers to as a "race traitor" demonstrates the need for a productive interaction between whiteness studies and southern studies in an effort to "to recognize the ideological significance of the US South within a national context, and increasingly, the role of the South in global contexts in the contemporary era."

In "Whiteness Undercover: Racial Passing and/as Detection in *Black Like Me* (1964)," Jacqueline Pinkowitz explores the film version of reporter John Howard Griffin's exposé on racial prejudice, *Black Like Me* (1961), which he researched by passing as black in the Deep South. His account was serialized in *Sepia* magazine and published as a book, *Black Like Me*, to critical acclaim. However, only three years later, the film was panned as cliché, given that proof of racial prejudice was readily found in newspapers, magazines, and the nightly news. Pinkowitz argues that the story of passing is "centrally tied up with elements of racial and regional crime, detection, and investigation." Thus it is productive to analyze the connections between the two genres and to read the film as "a racial passing detective story."

Set in opposition to grit lit fiction, which stresses insider knowledge of an exceptional "real" South, Zackary Vernon, in "Culture Detectives: Contemporary Journalism, Creative Nonfiction, and the US South," analyzes an "unacknowledged subgenre" of southern travelogue by non-southern journalists, who use their status as educated outsiders to uncover the "truth" about the South. Vernon examines the works of journalist-detectives V. S. Naipaul, John Berendt, Susan Orlean, and Gary Younge, arguing that the problem with these "cultural detectives" is that of "forced cultural synecdoche" in which they define the whole in relation to the part of the South which they uncover.

The detective genre in its exploration of crime serves as a fictional contemplation of the moral and legal limitations of the country's changing values as well as revealing its darker vices, corruptions, and perversions. As sociologist Émile Durkheim posited, "We do not condemn [an act] because it is a crime, but it is a crime because we condemn it" (Giddens 123–24). Furthermore, the detective genre responds to changes in who commits as well as who has the power to investigate those crimes, thus facilitating a discussion and critique of gender, racial, and sexual mores. Given the plethora of southern-inflected detective narratives and the diversity of the authors and characters, as well as the changing critical conversations in southern studies and concerning the detective genre, it is time to reexamine the role the southern imaginary plays in shaping our national understanding of what and whom we condemn as criminal. Because of the mutability of the genre, the critical interrogation our contributors provide is interdisciplinary and intersects with conversations taking place in the fields of southern, critical race, genre, gender, cinema, popular culture, media, and literary studies. Each of the essays in this volume provides a different aspect of southern detection, whether country noir, neo-noir, hard-boiled fiction, dark thriller, suburban noir, police procedural, amateur detective, or journalist-detective. Taken together they tease out the subtleties and explore the implications of the rich and varied uses of the South in detective narratives. We hope that this collection will be the first in an innovative series of studies on a subject area ripe for analysis.

NOTES

1. See Tatiana Mcinnis, "Miami in *Miami Vice:* Regional Ambiguity and Permeable Borders in the U.S. South," *Small-Screen Souths* (2017).

2. In *American Cinema and the Southern Imaginary,* Barker and McKee define the southern imaginary as "an amorphous and sometimes conflicting collection of images, ideas, attitudes, practices, linguistic accents, histories, and fantasies about a shifting geographic region and time." It is "not a false representation that must be stripped away to see the real South but a multifaceted, multivalent concept that informs our understanding of US culture, especially in relation to ideas about race, gender, and region (2, 3).

PART I

DETECTING SOUTHERN NOIR

EXPLORING THE NOIR LANDSCAPE OF THE NEW SOUTH

ACE ATKINS

While it seldom makes the Faulkner greatest hits lists, I am a big fan of *Intruder in the Dust* as one of the master's best works. *The Sound and the Fury* is a whirlwind of innovation in storytelling and *Absalom, Absalom!* is a tour de force in scope and grandeur, but few books tell us as much about the South and its people and society like *Intruder*. The story of a wrongly accused black man and a white teenage boy trying to exonerate him with the assistance of his uncle, small town lawyer Gavin Stevens, was published more than a decade before *To Kill A Mockingbird*, but bests that novel in complexity, philosophy, and examination of society.

Faulkner, a voracious reader of all mysteries, chose the bones of a crime novel for *Intruder*—a true whodunit with a ticking time clock and the exhumation of a body in a country graveyard to search for bullets—as the best way to confront not only vicious racism but also the paternal attitudes of well-meaning whites of his time. Lucas Beauchamp—the accused—refuses to play the victim, to take charity, or worst yet, pity, from anyone, as it's beneath him. Lucas knows his value as a man and won't stoop to groveling even if it will save his life.

A crime novel isn't as much about introspection as it is looking outward at a broken world and trying not only to find justice but a deeper meaning. This is precisely the reason I've chosen crime as my focus in all my twenty-one novels. This is where you find the best stories for your readers and a platform to go well beyond your readers' comfort zones and known world. A good crime novel is about all forms of exploration, pushing the reader out into the community and seeking the roots of society's ills. I can think of no better vehicle for the novelist. My last seven novels have focused on a single county in north Mississippi, using Faulkner as my inspiration to build a sandbox for discussing modern issues of race, gender equality, family, honor, faith, economic inequality, and environmentalism. One of the compelling reasons to write about the people of Tibbehah County—which is fictional, but all too real in its inspiration—is the way southerners handle the ugly truths. What a southerner hates more than anything is discussing an unpleasant subject. A crime novel is about all the unpleasant subjects.

The first book in my series kicks off with Quinn Colson—a little echo back to Mr. Faulkner's Compson clan—coming home to north Mississippi after being at war for nearly ten years. This could've been post-World War II, Korea, or Vietnam. But I wanted the character, the South, and the issues to be as timely as an overheard conversation at the local gas station or nearby Walmart.

We first meet Quinn as a hardened soldier rolling into Jericho, Mississippi, to attend the funeral of his beloved Uncle Hamp, the local sheriff. He soon learns his uncle killed himself, a fact that Quinn can't comprehend. The first story begins a slow unraveling of a set of events, but also whittles away at the power structure of the county, from the local politicians to a ragtag bunch of alt-right racists who might've wanted his uncle dead. Within one small county, there's a rich ecosystem of the rich and poor, class and race structure, and a complicated history that I'm still unraveling seven books into the story. The stories become much more about Quinn's family and the past than they do about him. He's our guide into the dark depths of the southern hell. Quinn is the soldier marching forward into the inner circle to drag those unspoken, nasty truths we don't want to discuss out into the light.

From that first book, I've sought out stories very true and specific to north Mississippi. I've followed that terrain into stories about human trafficking (using an actual case in New Albany), the chaos and devastation following a tornado, the mob mentality following the rape and shooting of two teenage girls, and the protection of a small-town football coach even after many knew his predilection for raping young boys. The last one brought the ire of one of my longtime fans, who thought I'd grafted the Penn State scandal onto southern high school athletics. I simply sent him the news stories about a man named Dwight Bowling, a north Mississippi high school coach who'd assaulted many young boys, most often the weakest and most vulnerable. But even as Bowling spends his golden years in federal prison, you'll find many fans of "Coach" who will offer their unwavering support. The truth too ugly to understand about a "good man" and "Christian."

My latest novel, written primarily after the 2016 presidential election, concerns a trio of bank robbers targeting small towns in the Mid-South. They wear Donald Trump masks during the heists as their calling card, stunning many working-class folks, while firing guns in the air and daring anyone to move or "I'll grab 'em by the pussy." Along the way, we see a showdown of "old-fashioned Southern values" as pushed by a county politician named Skinner, who wants to see the clock return to 1950s America. Quinn and his assistant sheriff—a woman who had to recruit Quinn back to his old job after she was forced out of an election for shining the light on the dirty little truths—butt heads about the future. Quinn is hopeful. Lillie is beaten down and realistic.

> "It's just getting good, Lil," he said. "Everything we've been fighting for. All those people who want to turn back the clock to the bad ole days. The users, the racists, the peckerheads who praise Jesus but loot our land and people. We got 'em."
> "You really think so?" Lillie said.
> "C'mon."
> "It's over, kemosabe," Lillie said. "Those fuckers had us beat before we even got started."

There was a time in the South where the road ahead appeared to be paved. Southerners looked to a New South where the old clichés and stereotypes no longer mattered. I recall being a high school football player passing over Selma's Edmund Pettus Bridge on the way to a football game—with a bus filled with mostly black teammates—thinking of the rusted metal structure as part of the events from grainy old black-and-white documentaries. It had only been twenty-two years, but the events had happened before I was born. And the attitudes, the illegality of the Jim Crow South, seemed like a bygone era. In Lee County, Alabama, I knew people who harbored racist attitudes, but most of them kept those feelings private, fearing that the greater community would shun them. Those types of remarks were for villains in white robes in Hollywood movies and for withered old people who spoke of the past with a rancid bitterness for the present. Nobody paid much attention to them.

But living in Mississippi for the last sixteen years—hell, living in America—I've seen the steady increase of those type of attitudes. An undergrowth of ugliness has been metastasizing like cancer in the internet era. Where many would have to find one another through scrawled messages in truck stop bathrooms or like-minded meets deep in the woods, they now congregate with a click of the mouse. The maligned southern male with a passion for a past that never existed, a Lost Cause, and a distaste for anyone different is all around us. But in truth, southerners have never been a homogenous bunch.

My great-great-grandfather, a poor farmer in Lowndes County, Mississippi, left his family to join the Union, as did many other southerners, no matter what you read in *Gone with the Wind* or other Old South fetishizations. He spent much of the war in a Confederate POW camp because of his political views. Generations later, many are still trying to put forth the idea that a southerner is one monolithic thing: white, conservative, straight, churchgoing, rural, gun-toting, and stuck in the past. Of course, this idea is just a reactionary kick at the reality of the South in 2017: young, multicultural, multilingual, urban and suburban, and increasingly dismissive of Confederate iconography. There's a lot of potential there for a South that embraces its diversity and natural beauty and faces its past unflinchingly while moving into the future. But these new threads of hate threaten to disrupt that potential.

What I seek to do through my Tibbehah County novels is to place these folks—the good, the bad, and the ugly—into an uncontrolled environment and see what shakes out. For me, the most unimportant part of the novel is the plot of the actual crime. The crime is just the bones to hang the body on. It's more about dialogue than danger. It's a conversation between power brokers, drug dealers, racists, preachers, politicians, and folks with no way out. After all, that's what good crime stories—noir—are all about. You have people with no way out, seeking the light switch in the darkness.

I've learned to find a little humor in the absurdity of the southerner's plight. We are such a violent culture, grown from a land settled by hardened people complicit in our country's most horrific institution. But we try to soothe things over with a thin veneer of civility. We often don't succeed. Almost daily, I can see a truck with bumper stickers touting assault weapons, a college football team, a Confederate flag, and a Bible verse—all at the same time.

The crime novel lets us explore all these things in equal parts. In *Intruder in the Dust*, Faulkner had the Gowrie brothers, a dislikable duo of loggers who treated people the same way they treated the land. Here in Mississippi, many look at environmentalism as a ridiculous notion, with state laws that are almost laughable. Forests are still classified as "crops." The Gowries' racist, vile attitudes descend into a Cain and Abel story, while the story of Lucas Beauchamp centers on his unlikely friendship with Chick Mallison, a white teenager he'd once saved from a frozen pond. In the years that followed, Chick sought to pay back Beauchamp with a variety of gifts that the proud man would never accept.

The weight of the injustice brought upon Lucas is too much for young Chick to comprehend. He sees the chance to help as time to pay the debt in full but in turn only gets a nice serving of reality down South. Chick soon learns the entrenched attitudes and beliefs have been sown long ago among a people whose lives are forever intertwined. Faulkner allegedly once said, "to understand the world, you must first understand a place like Mississippi."

The Deep South has long been ground zero for so many issues facing America that seem to never get settled. We often feel we're getting ahead, only to be dragged back in the mud by the loudest and most obnoxious of our people. But while the novel will never settle these problems or even offer solutions, it does—as any good story should—simply bring up a discussion of a topic many want to ignore. As southerners, we must admit the problems of the past aren't something for the museum case or textbooks, but a reality all around that has been bred, beaten, and coerced from generations of lies and intolerance. Some have written me letters that they don't like my portrayal of the South. But no one has ever told me my picture was inaccurate.

"Some things you must never stop refusing to bear," Gavin Stevens says in a speech in *Intruder in the Dust*. "Injustice and outrage and dishonor and shame."

THE BEAUTIFUL MYSTERIOUS

The Case of William Eggleston

MEGAN ABBOTT

I'm fairly sure the first Eggleston photo I ever saw was the first color photo he ever made: the famous one of a grocery store clerk, his hair oddly lustrous, his mouth slightly open, pushing a hard, glittery tangle of the shopping carts into the store. His palm pressed just so.

At that time, I didn't know about Eggleston's important place in the history of photography, the breakthrough of color photography, the way he's so often been positioned or narrowly labeled as a "Southern" photographer, a "regional" one. A photographer of the weird.

All I knew was when I looked at that photo, I saw a world I recognized. Part of the world I lived in: Kroger's and fluorescent lights and bright shiny wrappers and the hard and soft faces of strangers and intimates. And part the world I experienced from the inside out: FEVERED, HEAVY, MYSTERIOUS, LOADED, BEAUTIFUL.

* * *

Like so many, I was first drawn to William Eggleston's photographs long before I knew his name. I only knew how the pictures made me feel, the uncanny spell they put me under. First as a teenager when they struck me with the same force as David Lynch's neo-noir *Blue Velvet*.

They seemed alive, febrile. And later, as an aspiring writer yearning for transport. Looking for a cheat.

Maybe, I thought (still think), *if I look at this photo long enough, the back of this woman's head, her finely tended coiffure, a story will surface for me. I will know what I want to tell.*

And somehow, for me, as for countless writers, filmmakers, artists, storytellers of all kinds, the looking worked. The photograph conjured and a spell incanted.

I suppose it's a cliché to say when you look at Eggleston's photographs, they seem to tell a story. I don't even think it's true. They're not narrative images like we might see in, say, Robert Capa or Dorothea Lange. Eggleston's photos don't connect dots for us. They don't assert or announce. They don't *tell* at all.

But maybe it's more precise to say you look at them and *you make the story*.

Stories, after all, have a beginning, a middle, and end. We can see all three parts in an instant in some photos. Consider one of the most famous photographs of the last half-century, by Diane Arbus: a young boy of privilege, left alone, a toy grenade in hand. It's all there.

But with Eggleston, it's different. The photos don't offer three acts, or even a first act. Instead, the photos seem to come from the intense, hot *middle* of something. We are dropped in, immersed, sunk deep. Like Jeffrey, the amateur detective played by Kyle MacLachlan in David Lynch's Eggleston-influenced *Blue Velvet*, we find ourselves skirting the edges of a mystery and wanting, needing to know more. Looking at his photos, we all become voyeurs, trying to peer between and behind the shadows. Or, more precisely, our response to these photos demonstrates that we always already *were* voyeurs.

Eggleston has talked about trying to "creep up" on his subjects, and the photographs have that feeling. We encounter these jagged Eggleston worlds just before or just after something perilous or ecstatic has happened. Or both.

But what?

In seeking to characterize Eggleston's hold on me over the years, to get to the heart of his mystery, I return again and again to the famous Albert Einstein quote, "The most beautiful thing we can experience is the mysterious." After all, mystery lurks in every busy or barren corner of an Eggleston photograph.

That mystery can feel like pathos, like Eggleston's early black-and-white photos of a slump-shouldered man at the gas station gazing longingly at a liquor store sign gleaming darkly on the dark horizon. The loneliness of film noir without its satiny gleam.

And it can feel like menace, like his photo of the eerie eye-windows of a darkened church door.

Or it can feel like so many things at once, a sweep of terrible history, as we might see in his photograph of a white-wood Dixie sign with its comic and tragic faces looming above.

Eggleston's photographs encourage the pathetic fallacy, that old term we learned in long-ago English class: attributing human emotions to things, objects: a lonely window, a lusty pair of headlights. His photos are so shot through, so infused with mood, with feeling, they demand it. Objects are as real as living things. Sometimes more so. As Eggleston himself famously said, "I had this notion of what I called a democratic way of looking around, that nothing was more important or less important."

Or, as I have always felt and as the critic Malcolm Jones writes, "He addresses the meanest objects with unstuttering love."

Consider his subjects:

A lonely pink patio chair, squat and hopeful

A uniform starched on a clothesline, insistent and formal

A dishcloth with eyes like ghost holes

The cluttered front seat of a car, white feathers dangling glamorously from the rearview mirror, promising a world more refined than the plastic McDonald's cup, the brown paper bag shot through with light.

The soulful gaze of a young man with a twin-scoop ice cream cone, change in his hand. Even to describe these photographs in sparest terms is to begin a story, but the story is ours. And it begins with feeling, trying to untangle the feeling we feel without knowing why. The loneliness, the expectation, the wonder and longing.

This image drew me so closely the first time I saw it at the University Museum at Ole Miss. At that time, it evoked a lost frame from *The Last Picture Show*, one of my favorite movies. Every time I look at it, I feel more story, more feeling.

He's so well groomed, dressed for a date who never arrived. Or arrived with someone else.

It's my guess he's deep in thought. It's my speculation that the twin-scoop bespeaks something—a love lost or never won, a yearning. An aching disappointment.

Does his hand contain change from buying the cone or is he about to play a sad, sad song on the jukebox we see in another photograph from the show, gleaming and machine-like and substantial?

That change, he carries it as if it were Roman coins, heavy and substantial. Or maybe he's carrying them so lightly, maybe he has not a trouble in the world and the stitch in the brow I think I see is really a mere matter of *do I pick Sam the Sham or Junior Walker and the All-Stars?* Callow youth!

And why, after all, am I assuming there are coins in his hand at all? Maybe he's snapping his fingers. Maybe he's about to dance. Maybe . . . .

See how quickly we get lost? Subsumed into a narrative waist-high. And of course the story that springs from the photograph (I wonder what yours is and how different it is) could never be the young man's story. Nor Eggleston's or his magical camera's. The story is ours. The feeling is ours. Spurred, sparked, inflamed by what we see here. The spell cast. How democratic, as Eggleston himself might say.

In a 1990 interview, Eggleston says about Elvis Presley: "He fits that hole that there never was a hero for." As the journalist interviewing him points out, Eggleston could just as easily be talking about himself. *Eggleston fits that hole that there never was a hero for.*

Because there is something in these photos we need without ever knowing why. The pursuit of an investigation where the clues we find (or invent) matter far more than the solution.

"The most beautiful thing we can experience is the mysterious," asserts Mr. Einstein. "It is the source of all true art and science. He to whom this emotion is a stranger, who can no longer pause to wonder and stand rapt in awe, is as good as dead: his eyes are closed."

These photos open our eyes, drive the blood, rat-a-tat-tat the heart. They bring us into the center of something. We cannot stop looking. We try to turn away, only to look again. We close our eyes and still see them. We're forever seeing them.

Maybe it'll happen for you today. A photo you've seen before and wondered at or thought you know. Or, more likely one you're seeing for the first time. You'll look at it, wonder. Imagine something. Remember something. And by the time you leave, it'll be a part of you, and it likely always was. The solution to the mystery is not a resolution at all: it is you.

Maybe then it is not we who might come to understand these photographs, but they who've always understood us. Speaking to places deep inside we never dared to look.

Years ago, Eggleston told an interviewer, "I would love to photograph dreams." Maybe he has.

* * *

This essay was first published as "The Beautiful Mysterious: The Extraordinary Gaze of William Eggleston" in the University of Mississippi Museum Catalog, 2018.

SANCTUARY & "THE BROKEN AND MYRIAD REFLECTION OF" NOIR

BOB HODGES

Observations of noir peccadillos in William Faulkner's *Sanctuary* (1931)[1] are almost as old hat as debates about whether noir is a genre or an alternative classification, which often entails genre *sous rature*. *Sanctuary* offers an early instantiation of noir topoi, but that label fails to capture the novel's reflection and refraction of the emergent noir genre. Faulknerian style in general "merges characters and plots, repeats stories with subversive differences, dislocates chronology to question causality, and refuses to supply customary endings" (Phillips 104). In this manner, *Sanctuary* emerges with, yet playfully redeploys, noir topoi. Racialized shadow-play in its prose destabilizes readers' ascriptions of race. The unlikely juxtaposed pair at the beginning of the novel each assume attributes of the hard-boiled and "pathological" homosexual male. A narrative process hardboils Temple Drake into a femme fatale.

Sanctuary commences on a scene anticipating the delightful bathos of culture industry mash-ups of genre worlds. Carolyn Porter explains: "Like Dashiell Hammett, whose work he admired, Faulkner portrayed a sordid and violent underworld, but instead of sending in a Continental Op . . . Faulkner sent Horace Benbow, the glassblowing, impotent, and incestuous aesthete" (60). Horace, an enervated male protagonist, strolls away from family strictures and southern modernist fiction burdens to encounter Popeye, a fugitive from gangster fiction, in a still tableau over an arcadian spring. Popeye's understated threat holds Horace to the spot. Both figures pose a "broken" or "shattered reflection" in the spring, and Popeye has a Janus- or Picasso-like quality, "face squinted against the smoke [of his cigarette] like a mask carved into two simultaneous expressions" (4–5). The doubled and fractured qualities of this tableau provide an image for the novel's co-present modernist and noir topoi.[2]

SANCTUARY, EMERGENT ÉCRITS NOIRS, & NOIR'S MODERNIST VALENCES

Sanctuary coincidences with emergent écrits noirs in 1920s–'30s US pulp magazine and book publishing markets. Contes noirs first appear from Hammett in 1924, James Cain in 1928,[3] and Chester Himes in 1931,[4] as well as Kenneth Fearing's early poème noir in 1926.[5] Graham Greene interspersed his literary novels with noir entertainments from 1932, Raymond Chandler experimented with Phillip Marlowe prototypes in 1933, and in 1936 Fanny Ellsworth assumed editorship of *Black Mask* from Joseph Shaw and ran frantic, doom-laden Cornell Woolrich and Steve Fisher tales. Adaptations of these writers provide grist for 1940s Hollywood noirs. As a result, the term *noir* conjures images of cheap films about luckless detectives/saps/criminals scurrying across nocturnal cities with expressionist shadows, foreboding doom, and femmes fatales nipping at their heels.

One may object to an improper aggregation of narrative desire in hard-boiled detective fiction (and its fantasies of violent mastery) with noir's fatalist self-abnegation (Metress 155, 157–59). But a division between hard-boiled and noir overlooks their coevolution. Woolrich offers the best example: his early noir fiction bears the macho detectives, bizarre murder puzzles, gangsters, whiny insult dialogue, and whizbang violence of the hard-boiled, and his later noir fiction retained many of those, even as it emphasizes an overriding sense of doom, the law's casual sadism, deadly deadlines, betrayals, fugitives, vanishing ladies, and inescapable death (Nevins 116–18). Common themes unite texts across a hard-boiled/noir divide. A prevalent noir trope in *Sanctuary* is the specter of corruption threatening the intimacy of the subject. Noir corruption may present as moral, psychological, or social. It may manifest as the protagonist's deterministically flawed or doomed nature, as betrayals or revelations of corruption from the protagonist's intimates, or as inescapable fate occasioned by social alienation or oppression. Hammett's second fix-up novel *The Dain Curse* (1929) resembles the later *Sanctuary* with an heiress kidnapped, imprisoned, morphine-addicted. The central mystery of *Curse* revolves around the intimate Dain family conspiracy surrounding the heiress and whether or not she is a willing, corrupt participant. Another example of noir intimate corruption is Himes's "He Knew" (1933). One of the first hard-boiled black detectives must confront an O. Henry-esque closing epiphany that he and his partner killed his sons as they committed a robbery-homicide. The corruption of children also encompasses the teen narrator of Fisher's "You Always Remember Me" (1938), for he slowly reveals himself as a serial killer to his girlfriend's family and schoolmates. These three examples use the question of corruption to establish suspense or shock, but several Woolrich texts keep even the protagonist in suspense about whether or not they are a murderer, often thanks to substance abuse and devious deceptions by intimate friends or family: for example, the tales "C-Jag" (1940) and "& so to Death" (1941) and the novella *Marihuana* (1951). Noir's disillusioning discovery of intimate or social corruption also resonates with the genre's modernist overtones.

Sanctuary occupies an intersection between modernism and the contemporary emergence of écrits noirs. The haute aspirations of modernist fiction may balk at links with commercial work, yet both favor cityscapes, nonlinearity, "subjective narration," hard-boiled affect, "misogynistic eroticism," and ambivalence "about modernity and progress" (Naremore 41–45). Noir popularizes modernist pessimism from Joseph Conrad and T. S. Eliot, touchstones for Hammett, Greene, and William Lindsay Gresham (Horsley 1–2, 12). The noir vision of pervasive futility, corruption, and despair haunts *Sanctuary*. Horace faces brutal disillusionment after Temple's perjury and Lee Goodwin's conviction and weeps as sister Narcissa Benbow Sartoris drives him home. Fatalist resignation in the novel encompasses not just Horace's failure but Lee's rape and immolation by the Jefferson mob. Popeye, in a noir trope, escapes hanging for murders he committed but resigns himself to a wrongful conviction and death sentence for the murder of a small-town Alabama deputy. He meets ridiculous fate with resignation and an exasperated (blasphemously ironic) repetition, "for Christ's sake" (310, 312). Popeye's execution anticipates drifter Frank Chambers killing his lover's husband but condemned for her accidental death in Cain's *The Postman Always Rings Twice* (1934). Following Cain, Woolrich adopts this trope. Faulkner may have borrowed the motif of wrongful yet deserved execution from Hammett's conte noir "The Golden Horseshoe" (1924) (Fiedler 86; Wenska 43–44). A possible common ancestor of both Hammett and Faulkner for this motif is a 1900 tale's ending where a police-framed criminal declares, "I don't mind croakin' for anythin' I done, but I hate like hell to croak for somethin' I didn't" (Flynt and Walton 98–99). Erroneous executions later allow film noirs to skirt censorious requirements of the Hays Production Code that guilt must be punished but deflate any sense of justice with corruption and contingency.

Sanctuary's resignation extends beyond the failures of the legal system to its last lines as Temple and Judge Drake flee the dark Mississippi summer to the Jardin du Luxembourg in autumnal Paris and images of gray imprisonment. The final words have father and daughter observe onset of "the season of rain and death" (317). Overarching noir negativity resonates with Theodor Adorno's sense of negative modernism (Breu 43). Adornoan negativity renders politico-critical noir themes' threats of intimate and social corruption. The negativity of *Sanctuary* overruns with sexual, racial, and (extra)legal violence, stultifying pedestals of womanhood, arbitrary state and mob coercion, etc., but the novel extends corruption to victims of these conditions: Temple, Popeye, Lee, Ruby, and her baby. A broad indictment recalls Adorno's observation that politically committed, literary depictions of atrocities can blur "distinction between executioners and victims . . . not quite so uncomfortable for the executioners" (189). Faulkner's novel, aimed at a mass audience yet subject to committed literature's blurring tendency, appears as antithesis of Adorno's vision for autonomous modernism. However, the novel insists on autonomy via resolute fracture of the rules of the popular form and the end's adamant negativity. Horace's feeble attempts to right wrongs ends in a noir epiphany: "discovery not of evil but of the shoddy foundations of his vision of a moral and rational universe, supported and sustained by the institutions of the church, the state, and the law" (Vickery 105).

Sanctuary gives ironic roles to three main characters as noir archetypes: Horace as detective, Popeye as hard-boiled gangster, and Temple as femme fatale. Like Chandler, Faulkner passes off a search or quest as mystery, in this case Horace's search for Temple as a witness in Lee's trial (Jameson, *Chandler* 24). Another key connection of Faulkner to Chandler is how both transcend facile oppositions of the built environment to nature in depictions of the city (Jameson, *Chandler* 76). Temple's and Popeye's initial view presents the gray city of Memphis with its "smoke-grimed frame houses . . . in grassless plots, with now and then a forlorn and hardy tree of some shabby species—gaunt lop-branched magnolias, a stunted elm or a locust in grayish, cadaverous bloom" as both the buildings and trees of the cityscape combine in an eerie evocation of death (142). The ironic title of *Sanctuary* emphasizes a refusal of refuge from rape and other violence anywhere, including Memphis's nominal antitheses: the abandoned plantation or the small town of Jefferson (Lester 38, 51).

The ductility of noir narrative in *Sanctuary* playfully deploys among Horace, Popeye, and Temple noir topoi: an obsessive sense of verbal blackness; the doubling of ostensible detective and ostensible gangster, which explores associations of white hard-boiled masculinity with black masculinity, homosexuality, misogyny, and failure; and Temple's success as a femme fatale, which exceeds readings of her ruin, abasement, and perjury. These revised topoi intertwine the novel's disillusionment and fractural narrative pattern. The visual and gendered aspects of noir predate *Sanctuary* in the mass culture of the late 1920s, but Faulkner wrote before Cain, Chandler, and 1940s film noir codify them. *Sanctuary* complicates these topoi, and a trace of mass culture influence on/from Faulkner contributes to understanding his modernist experimentation.

VERBAL/VISUAL BLACKNESS

Critics often malign *The Story of Temple Drake* (1933) as an insufficient adaptation, but Deborah Barker's close reading of its cinematography suggests its visual reproduction of the novel's verbal shadow-play (80–83). *Sanctuary* is a literal *black* novel. The word or its derivatives occurs at least eighty-seven times in the text, *dark* or derivatives sixty-eight times, and *shadow* or derivatives forty-three times. Not every use is significant, and many attach to Popeye. Nonetheless, verbal shadow-play casts a noir effect over the novel's cinematic prose. An early description of Horace comes as Ruby "saw him, in faint silhouette against the sky, the lesser darkness: a thin man in shapeless clothes; a head of thinning and ill-kempt hair; and quite drunk" (16). The fragmentary, ambiguous syntax suggests Horace's figure makes the night sky appear to Ruby as "lesser darkness" with the noir iconography of a shadowed figure.

During Temple's nocturnal terrorization at the Old Frenchman Place, shadows are a frequent motif. The novel notes the tin lamp lighting Ruby's kitchen, and Temple sees a baby "distinguished only by a series of pale shadows" (62). Temple bends to inspect it, and "her shadow loomed high upon the wall, her coat shapeless, her hat tilted monstrously above a monstrous escaping of hair" (62–63). Later she panics and flees from Tommy: "Between blinks Tommy saw Temple in the path, her body slender and motionless for a moment as though she was waiting for some laggard part to catch up. Then she was gone like a shadow" (66–67). Temple's shadow looming high on the wall conjures an expressionistic film visual and recalls the dark and disheveled figure of Horace, which Ruby observed a few days prior. The image of Temple as a fleeing shadow, albeit a shadow with particular attention paid to details of her body, recurs from her first appearance: "her long legs blonde with running, in speeding silhouette against the lighted windows . . . vanishing into the shadow beside the library wall" (28).

The visual darkness enveloping Horace and Temple, and more broadly film noir's visual style, can connote shifty moral ambiguities. Yet a moralistic explanation of the novel's and its first film adaptation's expressionistic chiaroscuro appears vague. A recent trend in noir scholarship answers oversimplifications of reading noir in moralized visual terms. The blackening of a character's appearance can connote racialized corruption yet suggest an appealing visual intermediacy (Lott 544–45). Verbal shadow-play in regard to drunken Horace and sexualized and victimized Temple is ambiguous and aesthetically pleasurable while suggesting moral and racial blackness along with the danger of the Old Frenchman Place. The racialization of shadow-effects becomes more pronounced when it applies to Popeye, whose "blackness," as John Duvall notes, "is queerly positioned between figurativeness (he's really white) and literalness (other characters identify him as black)" (41). *Sanctuary* anticipates film noir's stylistic racialization, and the novel's conflation of a hard-boiled white male with blackness troubles white hard-boiled masculinities.

Hard-Boiled and Homosexual Misogyny

Readers may mistake Popeye as black on a first reading (Duvall 38–39). Description initially focuses on "soft black rubber" eyes, a face concealed by cigarette smoke, a "tight black suit," a "dead, dark [skin] pallor," and Horace's association of Popeye with "black stuff that ran out of Bovary's mouth" (4–7). Tommy clarifies Popeye is "the skeeriest durn *white* man I ever see. . . . I be dog if he ain't skeered of his own shadow" (19–20). The text plays on the myth of a bulging-eyed, superstitious, cowardly black man, as do the descriptions of Popeye's eyes as rubber and Popeye's punning name. Even Popeye as blackened rapist conjures another racist myth, one realized in Lee's lynching (Guttman 15–16).

What does blackening the hard-boiled male represent? Duvall contends that Faulkner's "white characters' 'blackness' almost always signals sexual dissonance" or the mapping of "primitivism onto nonheteronormative white masculinity" (63). The rest of this section considers the affinities between Popeye's hard-boiled characterization and Horace's similar fantasy structure to the hard-boiled male. James Polchin contextualizes *Sanctuary*'s popularity as a capitalization on the contemporary vogue for psychological explanations of homosexuality and presents Popeye and Horace as two representative types of the male homosexual (156). This explanation provides an alternative to the dominant explanation of the popularity of *Sanctuary* inhering in its repurposing of hard-boiled detective and noir tropes. However, the two popular appeals reinforce one another. Faulkner blackens the hard-boiled white male Popeye into the myth of the black rapist but twists these equations by suggesting this rapist longs to be penetrated himself, which posits the hard-boiled male as homosexual. Misogyny provides a common linkage for the hard-boiled white male and an early twentieth-century ideological image of male homosexuality. Portrayals of mid-century hard-boiled gangsters, especially psychotic one, are sometimes sexually ambiguous. Popeye recalls Rico Bandello from W. R. Burnett's *Little Caesar* (1929); each has little use for women and a dandyish concern for his hair and dress (Wenska 50). The novel presents both Popeye and Horace as misogynists; Popeye makes frequent disparaging references to Ruby and Temple as whores, and Horace's rambling, philosophical misogyny reflects on "that feminine reserve of unflagging suspicion of all peoples' actions which seems at first to be mere affinity for evil" (201). Noticing antifeminism or misogyny in the hard-boiled style approaches a critical cliché, but misogyny has also long provided a dismissive explanation for queer male desire (Woods 339).

The hard-boiled, homosexualized Popeye's persecution, rape, and subsequent imprisonment of Temple duly and dually signify. Popeye loathes and envies the association of Temple with flapper mobility and its implied potential freedom of sex and penetration. Before her rape and subsequent imprisonment the elusive, evasive Temple constantly runs, rides in cars, and remains in motion (Barker 67–69; Gray 85). Her initial encounters with Popeye and others at the Old Frenchman Place suggest conflicts over her independence; she contemptuously asks Tommy "does that black man [Popeye] think he can tell me what to do?" (42). Temple sees "Popeye watching her," and she continues to run "without stopping" (43). Temple's fear of rape curtails her mobility when she hides in the barn crib. However, the last image before the narrative cuts away from Temple's rape shows her lying on the boards "tossing and thrashing" (102). But after the rape, when Ruby sees Popeye driving away with Temple in his car, Temple appears frozen and static within the car's motion: "The face did not turn, the eyes did not wake; to the woman beside the road it was like a small, dead-colored mask drawn past her on a string and then away" (104). Popeye "sets Temple up in Miss Reba's house of ill-repute in order to control, protect, and above all watch her," and the brothel becomes a space to surveil and discipline Temple (Watson 53–54).

If Popeye is a hard-boiled homosexual, his lengths to surveil and discipline Temple and her participation in a heterosexual coupling appear odd. Reba and Minnie discover Popeye watches Temple's and Red's copulation, "hanging over the bed, moaning and slobbering like a—" with "a kind of whinnying sound" (231, 258). Duvall points out the whinnying is "nonsignifying," with no reason to presume Popeye identifies with Red in the act. (42). If anything, the novel suggests he identifies with the penetrated Temple. Reba's description to her female guests—"It's against nature. . . . There's a funny business somewhere" and "Maybe he was cheering for them. . . . The lousy son of a bitch"—recoils from Popeye and suggests more than distaste for voyeurism (255–56, 259). Given the variety of voyeurism and snooping about in the brothel from a variety of characters including Reba, Minnie, Virgil, Fonzo, and state senator Clarence Snopes, for voyeurism to so shock Reba would be odd. However, the misogynistic and homosexual overtones of imprisoning a woman so her captor can feel vicarious penetration may outrage Reba and her guests. Polchin theorizes Popeye's captivity of Temple demonstrates "further appropriation of social power by Popeye to achieve a certain status—namely heterosexuality" (153). Keeping Temple as his girl/beard/ideal ego allows Popeye status as a heterosexual sugar daddy and offers an outlet to regulate desire. If Temple is the object of Popeye's sexual identification, casting his disciplinary gaze on her keeps his desire to be penetrated secret and confined to Temple's room in the brothel. The novel presents Popeye as a hard-boiled homosexual. His desire to restrain and violate Temple is both a product of the misogyny attributed to homosexuality and hard-boiled masculinity as well as an establishment of a pliable, controllable proxy for his desires.

Popeye may be the novel's lone hard-boiled male, but he is not its lone male homosexual. Horace makes a curious double for Popeye. The tableau of Popeye and Horace at the beginning mirrors the two, and this twinning can suggest sexual interest in and kinship with one another (Irwin 222; Polchin 151–52). Horace's status as a failed husband and professional situates him in a discourse of masculinity emphasizing failure as evidencing homosexual desire. Horace fails as a detective, which Porter attributes to his idealism, to his failure to face that perennial noir theme which "Hammett's detectives always have to recognize eventually—not only the deep and constitutive corruption of the world but also their complicity in it" (60). What Porter wants from Horace is an admission similar to Phillip Marlowe's famous "Me, I was part of the nastiness now" (Chandler 764). Horace's attempts to suppress and disavow his desires resemble how Marlowe entertains then ejects sexual otherness, for example his posing as a homosexual (Abbott 48). In another notable scene, Marlowe finds his employer's younger, nymphomaniac daughter naked in his bed. He takes her home and returns his apartment where "the imprint of her head was still in the pillow, of her small corrupt body still on the sheets. I put my empty glass down and tore the bed to pieces savagely" (Chandler 709). Popeye faces his desire to substitute himself for Temple's penetrated body by creating a disciplined space for a concealed and controlled but repeated reenactment. Marlowe's response a few years later is to toy with the fantasy (he flirted with the daughter), then indignantly disavow the desire. Horace undergoes a similar process of surreptitious entertainment followed by revolted expulsion after hearing Temple's rape narrative. The endgame for Marlowe's and Horace's guilty ejection of sexual "corruption" is an eliminationist sterilization fantasy. At the end of *The Big Sleep*, Marlowe follows his famous admission about his implication in the nastiness by associating death with the possibility of redemption (Chandler 764). Likewise, Horace waxes nihilistic: "Better for her if she were dead tonight. . . . For me, too. He thought of her, Popeye, the woman, the child, Goodwin, all put into a single chamber bare, lethal, immediate and profound. . . . And I too. . . . Removed, cauterised out of the old and tragic flank of the world" (221).

Upon returning to Jefferson, Horace picks up a photograph in which "Little Belle's face dreamed with that quality of sweet chiaroscuro" (222). This image, in the context of what he has learned about Temple's rape, makes Horace nauseous, and he vomits as his thoughts merge himself, Belle, and Temple under the hand of Popeye. Vomiting may be the premiere act of expulsion, but several critics question that common reading of Horace in the lavatory. Joseph Urgo argues Horace is not vomiting in the lavatory but masturbating or desiring to, for he "has found Temple's story as erotic as it is criminal. He also has discovered a potentiality within himself which places him in collusion with a rapist" (442). Urgo contends Horace's nausea recognizes his erotic desire, but other critics suggest the language of the passage destabilizes any neat linkage between Horace's desire recognizing itself in the action of Popeye (Duvall 43; Polchin 154). The passage's shift in pronouns from masculine to feminine, the imagery of a "black tunnel" and of Horace "plung[ing] forward . . . and lean[ing] upon his braced arms," and shared sensations of Temple and Horace all suggest Horace fantasizes about taking Temple's place rather than Popeye's (223). Horace vomits upon feeling a "cup of coffee . . . lay[ing] in a hot ball on his stomach," which duplicates Temple's description of "that hot little ball inside you that screams" just before Popeye rapes her (221). Horace, like Marlowe, finds pleasure in fantasizing about succumbing to then expelling that possibility in abrupt, defensive indignation. Popeye, like his creator, is "hard-bellied," but it is Horace who participates in toying with sexual otherness and taboo desires (322). *Sanctuary* perhaps elliptically returns to Horace's rape or sexual fantasy at the end of chapter 29, and Barker seems to be the only critic to have noticed this facet of the novel's end (88). The Jefferson mob immolated Lee and greets Horace with a threat: "Do to the lawyer what we did to him. What he did to her. Only we never used a cob. We made him wish we had used a cob" (296). At this point, the narrative slides into another abstract reflection on Horace's lack of sensation. The chapter ends abruptly, and the gap offers a potential parallel to the novel's initial skip over the scene of Temple's rape. Faulkner's voluminous yet elliptical style in *Sanctuary* both encourages the reassessment of scenes like this and the language of Horace in the lavatory. Faulkner's intense, stylized elisions anticipate frantic, borderline irrational ambiguity in Woolrich's écrits noirs. For example, his shortest short story, "Waltz" (1937), limits perspective to mostly scanty, clichéd dialogue; the reader's understanding careens through multiple interpretations of the protagonist's apparent paranoiac criminality. Through both ellipses and direct implication, Faulkner links the figures and fantasies of Popeye and Horace to popular narratives of misogynistic hard-boiled masculinity and pathologized homosexuality, as well as an indirect but pervasive fear of male victimization through rape. The addition of homosexual associations with blackness compounds an already mixed character of the hard-boiled white male with racial borrowings from white conceptions of black masculinity.

Becoming the Femme Fatale; or, Hard-Boiling Temple Drake

Having examined the trajectories of the male noir protagonists, I conclude by turning to the representation of their displaced desire: Temple. Richard Gray, Scott Yarbrough, and Susan Donaldson all identify Temple as a femme fatale. Donaldson finds the effect of Temple's rape narrative on Horace to be "as powerful a preview as one could hope to find of the disordering impact of femmes fatales upon masculine authority in many of those dark films and thrillers of the 1940s and 1950" (140). Gray's and Yarbrough's conceptions of Temple as a femme fatale differ; their split mirrors a larger fissure in noir studies over the figure.

Gray stresses Temple's resemblance to lead female characters in film noirs like *Shadow of a Doubt* (1943), *Born to Kill* (1947), and *The Reckless Moment* (1949), where "a female protagonist enters the *noir* world" (85). Gray sees Faulkner's intriguing twist on the menaced woman formula as "doubling" between Popeye and his victim, both in appearances and elusiveness (87). A description of Temple quoted above describes her face as a "dead-colored mask" suggesting a similar coloring to Popeye's "dark pallor" and his face's "queer, bloodless color" (4–5, 104). Both are small (4, 89). The twinning of Popeye and Temple implies no moral equivalence for Gray, but he sees femmes fatales intertwined with victimhood. Gray's approach resembles Jans Wager's revision of the femme fatale. Wager acknowledges that traditional use of the term implies a fatal quality of the femme for a male victim but emphasizes how femme fatale "resistance" to patriarchy "almost always prove[s] fatal to her as well" (15). The femme fatale is victim of her transgressions.

Both conceptions of the femme fatale see partially empowering performance, but the older position focuses on the epistemological trouble and existential threat a femme fatale provides for males. Mary Anne Doane emphasizes the femme fatale as the *carrier* who "overrepresents the body . . . is attributed with a body which is itself given agency independently of consciousness" (2). Doane's account captures the obsessive attention to Temple's elusive yet voyeuristically detailed body, particularly legs suggesting mobility. In Yarbrough's reading Temple is not punished for being a femme fatale, she becomes a femme fatale because of victimization. Rape and imprisonment force her to recognize the power of male desire for her body, and she appropriates this power for survival. The Yarbrough/Doane femme fatale as a learned mastering of an involuntary attribute maps better onto Temple than the tragic transgression of Gray/Wager. Temple begins a flirtatious college girl. Terrorization, rape, and imprisonment condition her capability to use her body and her class position as a white southern lady to strike at one of the men responsible for her situation. The femme fatale offers the closest female equivalent to the hard-boiled male, and Temple's process of hard-boiling finds her assuming a "tough, shell-like exterior, a prophylactic toughness that was organized around the rigorous suppression of affect and was mirrored by detached, laconic utterances and instrumentalized, seemingly amoral actions" (Breu 1).

When Temple plots to escape the brothel with Red, she grips a pistol several times. She leaves the pistol behind and thinks of it "with acute regret, almost pausing, knowing that she would use it without any compunction whatever, with a kind of pleasure" (230). Temple fantasizes about the pistol and role of a hard-boiled male, free to resort to gunfire with swift pleasure. Temple arrives at the Grotto sans pistol and, unarmed, she "turns to the innate weapon of her body, the sexuality she has divorced from her true self by use of the masquerade" (Yarbrough 60). Temple attempts to seduce Red to kill Popeye; she "grind[s] against him, dragging at his head, murmuring to him in parrotlike underworld epithet" (239). Yarbrough is correct that Temple's use of her body and words fails, but it foreshadows her effect at Lee's trial.

Temple's testimony at the climax condemns Lee to death and represents Temple harnessing the power of the southern rape complex and her power as an aristo-bourgeois white lady to kill a man. Yarbrough describes Temple's perjury "in line with her conformity to the femme fatale archetype" but also "relying on the 'myth of sanctified womanhood'" (62). While Temple uses patriarchal assumptions to gain revenge for crimes against her, a couple of critics counter that Lee was also going to rape Temple and is hardly an innocent (Urgo 440; Garnier 167–69). Temple's courtroom testimony presents her as mastering the femme fatale performance and manipulates the Jefferson mob for revenge on at least one of the men who wronged her.

Despite this moment representing the most powerful point for Temple, a tendency remains to take Horace's and the rest of the courtroom audience's impression of Temple at face value and see her as a shell-shocked victim, a "ruined, defenseless child" in the words of Eustace Graham, District Attorney (288). Temple's "detached and cringing" attitude that focuses on the back of the courtroom can just as well suggest disinterest and boredom with the proceedings as shock. But Temple does not weep, faint, or use the excessive emotionalism often expected of victims, and her disinclination to spectacle suggests a hard-boiled lack of affect. Temple's dress in the courtroom scene does not suggest the tarnished, shocked virgin of the southern rape complex but a lavish femme fatale. She wears a "black hat" with "rhinestone ornament," carries "a platinum bag" her father later kicks to the side, wears her coat open "upon a shoulder knot of purple," has "her mouth painted into a savage and perfect bow," and her "long blonde legs" are visible (284). These details visualize Temple's luxury and sensuousness, and the details, along with her identification of her home as Memphis—i.e., the brothel—create a dissonant image of the stereotypical violated virgin. Given the discrepancy, it may appear strange the Jefferson mob rapes and lynches Lee to preserve her honor. One reason might be the mob's fervor overlooks minor details such as the victim's lack of resemblance to the virtuous girl expected. The more probable explanation is Temple understands an unstated premise of the southern rape complex (patriarchal control of and desire for female bodies), which a Kinston driver articulates as "[w]e got to protect our girls. Might need them ourselves" (298). Temple emphasizes her sexuality through dress to excite among the onlookers a desire to possess her and a desire to revenge her.

Most femmes fatales find themselves punished and/or killed at noirs' ends, but despite vanquishing feminine evil, most noirs end bleakly, with epiphanies about universal guilt and corruption. A paradox: a femme fatale is a prime figure of evil for noir, which implies she ought survive and thrive in such a negative world, but she dies, for the Motion Picture Production Code mandates punishment. The end of *Sanctuary* fits this schema. The epilogue presents Temple and her judge father in scenery dominated by images of grayness, imprisonment, and death. But, a final subtle fracture of noir has Temple come away from trauma changed but not destroyed. Temple's final action after yawning in boredom is to take "out a compact and open . . . it upon a face in miniature sullen and discontented and sad" (317). The emphasis on Temple's sullen boredom suggests a similar detachment to her in the courtroom. Temple achieves her fantasy of hard-boiled insulation against male violence. Temple as a character has been gazed at and fantasized about by a variety of spectators, most dramatically, the mob. The compact emblematizes Temple's necessary concern for appearance to exercise the power of her body as a femme fatale. Like Popeye's imprisonment of her in order to cultivate the appearance of heterosexuality and regulate and enact his desires, Temple's self-directed gaze demonstrates the internalization of discipline necessary for a hard-boiled or femme role. This internalization is an element in a learned process that is Temple's response to violation and discipline to which Popeye and others subject her. Temple upon close examination is not defeated or punished but masters her body for a sort of hard-boiled role, unlike her failed male counterparts.

Faulkner's relative triumph for a femme fatale impacts subsequent noirs. Temple's ambiguous survival is not copied in *The Story of Temple Drake*. But like its source, the film does not kill, punish, or purify Temple, in contrast to James Hadley Chase's rewriting of *Sanctuary* as *No Orchids for Miss Blandish* (1939) where Missouri police and vigilantes storm gangsters to rescue Miss Blandish (a drug-addled and nigh-mute Temple stand-in), but she leaps from a window, fulfilling her father's proclamation: "impossible . . . to think of her still alive and in the hands of such men" (83). Instead, Temple in *Temple* kills in self-defense Trigger (phallic renaming of Popeye) and exonerates the framed Lee in court (with Stephen [Horace] Benbow's coaching). The end of the film lacks the negativity, failed epiphany, or sense of universal corruption present in the novel but affords Temple survival, redemption, and avoidance of the conventional outcomes for "ruined" rape victims: shame or death. This unorthodox move along with the relative explicitness of the film and other early 1930s femme fatale films like *Baby Face* (1933) and *The Notorious Sophie Lang* (1934) caused an uproar that resulted in far stricter industry self-adherence to the Motion Picture Production Code (adopted in 1930 with certification begun in 1934). Among other things, the Code established a nondiegetic insurance that murderous femmes fatales in future would be punished and/or killed. Uproar occurred despite expensive post-production to bring *Temple* and *Baby Face* in-line with the Code (Balio 57; Laberge & Smith 77; Vieira 148–50). Temple's femme fatale characteristics, her power to kill, her hard-boiled detachment and control over her body, indirectly, through the film adaptation, help create a backlash that determined the more brutal, final courses for femmes fatales in the haute period of film noir.

Beyond the unappreciated importance of Temple to the genre and her archetype, what is significant about the novel's modernist fractures of an emergent noir genre? Ultimately, Faulknerian fractures in *Sanctuary* help consolidate noir topoi in fiction and film as well as develop a mass outlet for modernist obsessions and traversals of the fantasies of southern and US ideology. Whites are racialized as black, rendered as mobile criminals subject to rape and lynching. Fantasies of white mastery and detachment are intertwined with blackness and same-sex male desire. Aristo-bourgeois white womanhood transmutes from purity to cynicism. All of these traversals and elisions culminate an aesthetic mood overlaying both *Sanctuary* and its fictive and filmic successors: a sense that both social and intimate corruptions pervade.

NOTES

1. See Forter, Gelly, Gray, Malraux, Osteen, and Yarbrough. My argument recalls both Forter's and Osteen's. The former emphasizes psychoanalytic, somatic, and formal resonances of the novel's meld of hard-boiled and noir fiction while I emphasize generic and narrative aspects (7, 91–92, 233n1). The latter thoroughly catalogues film noir affinities with *Sanctuary*, while I contextualize it amidst écrits noirs and suggest its influence on film noir's development.

2. *Sanctuary* exceeds these genres and exemplifies uneven development and simultaneous competition of genres (whether dominant, residual, or emergent) within a single text (Jameson, *Political* 140–41; R. Williams 122–25). The emergent noir and dominant modernist elements of *Sanctuary* counterpoise residues of antecedent genres to noir. Naturalism evidences from the psychosexual backstory of Popeye. Moreover, Zola's *Nana* (1880) influences Temple and the grotesqueries of Miss Reba's brothel, several characters' object fetishes recall Norris's *McTeague* (1899), and Temple's urban sexual exploitation intensifies Crane's *Maggie* (1893) and Dreiser's *Sister Carrie* (1900). Debauchery and violence in a ruined plantation anticipate Caldwell's sensational rural naturalism. Per sensation novels like Collins's *The Woman in White* (1859) and Le Fanu's *Uncle Silas* (1864), *Sanctuary* offers the conspiratorial kidnapping and imprisonment of a young heiress via many short chapters from multiple perspectives. The gradual revelation of a femme fatale lurking in an aristo-bourgeois family by a moralizing, questing, and inept lawyer protagonist recalls Braddon's *Lady Audley's Secret* (1862).

3. "Pastorale" (1928), Cain's first conte noir echoes Ring Lardner humor but anticipates Caldwell's rural southern white grotesque stupidity in contrast to Cain's usual western settings.

4. Himes's first surviving published story, "His Last Day" (1932), relates the final hours of a sharp-dressing condemned man who selectively and unconvincingly maintains his innocence and composure, in marked contrast to Popeye at the end of *Sanctuary*.

5. Like Horace in *Sartoris* (1929), Fearing's "St. Agnes' Eve" (1926) reimagines a Keats poem. Haute modernism often casts itself against a feminized, consumerist mass culture of cinema and popular narratives (Forter 232 n6; Huyssen 53, 62; Rabinowitz, *Black & White,* 6). Naremore links French existentialist fascination with modernist and noir writers: Hemingway, Dos Passos, Faulkner, Hammett, Cain, Chandler, and Richard Wright (23). In the 1950s, writers marketed and packaged as backwoods hard-boiled fiction include romancier noir Jim Thompson and late modernists Faulkner and Flannery O'Connor (Earle 197).

SOUTHERN GOTHIC & FILM NOIR

The Commingling of Genre and Cinematic Stylistics

R. BRUCE BRASELL

When Tennessee Williams's *A Streetcar Named Desire* premiered on Broadway in 1947, theater critics compared his approach to that of novelist James M. Cain, the hard-boiled detective writer of *The Postman Always Rings Twice* (1934) and *Double Indemnity* (1943), both of which had recently been adapted to films and were, by the 1960s, perceived to be key works of film noir (Nathan 20; Brown 22). At the time of the release, however, film noir did not exist within the United States as a classificatory schema, whether one calls that label a genre, a cycle, a style, or a mode. Such films were conceived by Hollywood studios and filmmakers and received by American critics and audiences not as film noirs but melodramas and crime films. Film noir was a label retrospectively applied to them when they were subsequently screened, discussed, and written about several decades after their initial release. Film noir as a genre emerged through film criticism in France during the immediate post–World War II period, only entering the American lexicon during the 1960s, where its existence was perpetuated by the academy (through the introduction of film production and film studies into the curriculum) and journalism (through the introduction of film criticism that privileged film as an art form).

The 1951 filmic adaptation of *Streetcar* would decades later be called "Tennessee Williams' southern gothic masterpiece" (Anderson 59). Southern gothic similarly emerged as a classificatory schema through journalistic cultural criticism, except that in its case the formation occurred simultaneously with the release of the cultural objects in question and through the practice of book reviewing in magazines aimed at the American cultured classes. It solidified as a literary schema in the early 1940s and as a film one in the late 1950s in the wake of the media spectacle and financial success of the Tennessee Williams adaptation *Baby Doll* (Elia Kazan 1956), with a string of Broadway plays interceding between these two periods. The works that became aligned with southern gothic early on shared similar terrain with works that became aligned with film noir, at least on the level of narrative. But what about visual style? To think through the intertwining relationship of film noir and southern gothic from the perspective of their visual stylistics, I will consider articles about films aligned with these two genres published in the flagship publication of the American Society of Cinematographers (ASC), *American Cinematographer*. Although concerned with a particular aspect of making films, the ASC is an elite organization composed of a small group of practitioners who have been invited to join the organization. Their self-conception is as artists, not just technicians, and the organization sees itself with the "dual purpose of advancing the art and science of cinematography and . . . bringing cinematographers together to . . . promote the motion picture as an art form" ("About"). From the perspective of cinematographers it is the shared centrality of visually generated mood that links southern gothic and film noir, while generically they both are increasingly associated with the thriller.

Both terms derived from the cultured classes; however, the label *film noir* referred to works adapted from popular fiction for a mass audience, and its subsequent application to them endowed them with cultural validity for future generations. Although the United States was a leader in the production of popular culture, Americans associated cinematic art with European culture. So because the French label connoted artistry, it accrued a certain cultural pedigree to works labeled such. As a label *southern gothic* was applied to works created specifically for the cultural classes and—at least initially—considered "serious" works of art and engaged critically by the New York cultural intelligentsias. But because the word *gothic* was typically used as a derogatory slur, it threw the cultural worth of those works into question. As a result, many writers aligned with it fought—along with their journalistic and academic supporters—to disassociate themselves from it. So while southern gothic emerged contemporaneously and challenged the cultural validity as it transformed the works from cultured to popular, *noir* was applied retrospectively and in that subsequent classification increased the cultural prestige of those works as it transformed them from popular to cultured.

These two discursive schemas emerged out of different historical periods and contexts; yet the textual works that provided the basis for the reviewing practices that birthed them emerged out of the same historical American milieu, although from different segments of the US cultural industry. As a result, both genres embody the mood of that historical zeitgeist as will be discussed shortly. Because southern gothic emerged out of the reception of literary work, it did not materialize on the screen until after the film noirs. Therefore it is not surprising that these filmic reincarnations would borrow the visual vocabulary of film noir for their audiovisual manifestation given that they produce within viewers similar moods. However, this vocabulary was based on a black and white palate. By the time color film became the norm during the 1960s, film noirs were no longer being produced while southern gothic ones were, and it adapted their shared visual stylistics to color. Ironically, when film noirs began to reappear on the screen the following decade, they in turn borrowed southern gothic's adaptation of the classical film noir black-and-white style to color.

My concern is not with southern noir per se but rather the intersection of film noir and southern gothic; however, on a certain level that juncture can be thought of as southern noir, at least in its audiovisual form if not its written one. One of the key characteristics imputed to southern gothic by book reviewers during the 1940s was the privileging of mood over narrative. Carson McCullers's 1940 novel *The Heart Is a Lonely Hunter* was described as "not so much a novel as a projected mood" (Wright "Inner Landscape" 195) while William Goyen's 1952 book *Ghost and Flesh* was held to "create a mood rather than people" ("Southern Variety" 104). By 1961 a reviewer for *Time* magazine felt comfortable enough to make a blanket association of southern literature with the centrality of mood. Incidentally, however, all of the writers mentioned in that assessment were aligned with southern gothic. After mentioning William Faulkner, Tennessee Williams, and Carson McCullers, the reviewer mused: "As craftsmen, the Southern writers are generally sloppy; they represent the triumph of mood over matter" ("The Member of the Funeral" 118). While this mood is haunting and accentuates the horrific elements of the text, it is typically associated with another common characteristic assigned to the genre by book reviewers, a mood of existential angst and aloneness. While one could easily argue for the importance of narrative structure based on an academic analysis of the literary and stage works aligned with southern gothic, such works were perceived by cultural critics upon their initial release as privileging mood over that narrative, assigning this prioritization as one of the genre's defining characteristics. And this characteristic accrued to the cinematic reincarnations as well. But while publishing and the theater privilege the written and spoken word respectively, the visual assumes a level of importance in the formation of cinematic texts unmatched by those for the page and stage. And this becomes the big quandary for the conjurers of southern gothic cinematic reincarnations: how does one create mood through images rather than words?

Gary Gach highlights, in an *American Cinematographer* article, that "The very term 'film noir' was, in fact, an afterthought—a French term derived from the expression 'roman noir' ('dark novel') which describes English Gothic fiction of the 19th Century" (90). Without making any assumptions about whether his etymology of the phrase within French criticism is correct or not, at least for his American audience of cinematographers he presents a connection between film noir and the gothic. And of course this connection is readily visible on the American screen in the stylistic borrowing of German Expressionism by both film noir and early-1930s Universal Studio horror films about gothic characters such as Dracula and Frankenstein. By the mid-twentieth century a particular strain of southern literature was perceived by many within the American literary establishment to share similar enough terrain with the gothic to justify borrowing the label.

Within the US context, the word "noir" has come to be synonymous with "film noir," allowing its signification to easily conjoin with other words to imply use of its cinematic stylistics in a different generic context. Another popular variation of the word along with *neo-noir* is *future noir*, the science fiction film *Blade Runner* (Ridley Scott, 1982) the impetus for its critical formulation. A 2007 *American Cinematographer* article on that film and its use of future noir quotes cinematographer Jordan Cronenweth as saying: "We used contrast, backlight, smoke, rain, and lighting to give the film its personality and moods" (Williams "Forging" 36). These visual characteristics along with unusual camera angles, low-key lighting, and shafts of light define many of the key visual stylistics of film noir and, although they can still be emotionally powerful, they require skillful execution in order to avoid being perceived as clichés. Although discussing a science fiction film, Cronenweth justifies use of film noir stylistics because of its ability to create mood. Along similar lines, John Alton is quoted in a 1996 *American Cinematographer* article on his contribution to the development of the visual stylistics of film noir as proclaiming: "The mood had to be done with lighting. That's my profession—not the lighting and how to light, but bringing out the mood" (Gach 88). In other words, the primary goal of cinematography is the creation of mood. But while film noirs of the 1940s and 1950s are commonly thought of as exhibiting complicated plot structures, they are also routinely perceived as using a labyrinth structure. As a result, following on Alton's claim, one could argue that those knotty plot structures become not about the forward movement of the story per se but the establishment of a mood, the narrative experientially replicating the mood of the main character's sense of loss and isolation. So like the southern gothic authors who were writing contemporaneously with Alton's cinematographic work on films that would eventually become known as film noirs, he held the creation of mood a primary goal, except here with light rather than words, although camera angles and mise-en-scène were important components as well.

Although film adaptations of literary works aligned with southern gothic—many preceded by successful adaptations to the stage as well—occurred prior to the release of *Baby Doll* in 1956, in the wake of the success of that film, Hollywood adapted in two years as many southern gothic works as had been made in the preceding fifteen. *Baby Doll* played an important role in the film industry's subsequent embrace of southern gothic literature and in the studios' adapting them and reviewers perceiving them as a film type. Soon after the film's release, its cinematographer, Boris Kaufman, shared his experience shooting it in a 1957 *American Cinematographer* article. He began the discussion, however, by asking: "What is the main problem confronting a cinematographer starting a new picture? To me it has always been the same: to establish a style of photography most compatible with and complimentary to the theme of the story" (92). In other words, he seeks a visual form that matches the narrative content of the film. And what did he consider the subject matter of *Baby Doll?* He explains: "The story is better described, perhaps, as a tragi-comedy in which every dramatic situation is offset by a grotesque twist, and every comedy scene underscored in tragic overtones" (93). Although he used a number of different styles in the film, he delighted most in describing a particular scene that used a style recognized today as film noir, although at the time it was not known by that label. He continued that "when Archie Lee goes mad and shoots at shadows, the pictorial mood of the lighting changes to extremely low key so that shadows virtually have more body than real objects" (93). He directly links a certain style of lighting—low key, high contrast that produces distinct shadows and shafts of light—with the formation of mood. And the ability of this style of lighting to produce a certain type of mood makes it the ideal mechanism for the translation of southern gothic works from words on a page—where the assignment of imagery resides in the individual reader's imagination—to an explicit visualization of the text. Film noir provided a model for the cinematic reincarnation of southern gothic works even before film noir was known in the United States as film noir.

Boris Kaufman photographed another Tennessee Williams–derived film three years later, *The Fugitive Kind* (Sidney Lumet, 1960). As before, an *American Cinematographer* article appeared about the film, except this time, rather than being written by Kaufman about his experience, the article was instead written *about* him. The article reiterated Kaufman's earlier concern of finding a photographic style to produce a mood that corresponded with the story, a story (per the author of the article) that "unfolds in a downbeat if not degrading atmosphere" (Foster 354). The article quotes Kaufman as asserting that "The blend of the grotesque and the tragic inherent in Tennessee Williams' writing had to be stated visually" (Foster 354). The main elements mentioned in the article to describe the cinematic style included unusual camera angles, smoke, light rays, and shadows, all characteristics associated with what was already known in France as film noir and would soon be too in the United States. That the article is about a southern gothic work is connoted, just like with the *Baby Doll* article, through invocation of the word "grotesque," one of two concepts the cultured classes closely associated with the genre at the time—the other "degeneracy," also routinely alluded to with words such as "decay," "decadence," and "degraded," the latter word used to describe the mood of the film too. The genre is also invoked through the citation of Tennessee Williams's name. While his name was casually mentioned once in a throwaway fashion in the *Baby Doll* article, it was prominently displayed in the byline to *The Fugitive Kind* article as well as highlighted within the text itself. While by the early 1950s Williams had a "reputation for being an author whose texts were as sensational as they were artistic" (Palmer and Bray 125), in the aftermath of *Baby Doll* his name came to signify southern gothic similar to literary writers such as William Faulkner, Carson McCullers, Truman Capote, and Flannery O'Conner, his name was conscripted into the southern gothic family tree that cultural critics cited as the apostles of the genre.

While southern gothic as a genre had previously only been connoted in *American Cinematographer* through reference to the names of writers and dramatists from its authorial family tree and use of coded descriptive words associated with it, telling of the general trend during the mid-1960s, the magazine's feature on the filming of *Reflection in a Golden Eye* (John Huston, 1967) explicitly acknowledges a genre affiliation. So while, similar to *The Fugitive Kind* six years earlier, the byline invoked an authorial name to connote genre, it went further and used the explicit label: "New, unique desaturation process by Technicolor lends eerie mood to motion picture version of Carson McCullers novel directed by John Huston in brooding 'Southern Gothic' style" (Lightman 862). The tagline, however, refers to southern gothic as a style rather than a genre, a distinction that continues to be debated today. But placed within the context of the body of the *American Cinematographer* article, does this editorial word choice necessarily negate the claim that southern gothic is a generic classificatory schema?

Alan Lloyd-Smith holds that placing the two frameworks of genre and style in opposition, as though one negates the other, is a false dichotomy. And, fortuitously, given the topic of this article, he explores the difference between the two as they relate to the gothic through a comparison to film noir, where he observes some films are "full developed" while others only contain "episodes, or just brief scenes and images" (134–35). In other words, style and genre are not mutually exclusive frameworks. Although key differences exist, the debate over style versus genre in cultural criticism shares, on a certain level, affinity with the semantic versus syntactic distinction in film genre theory. Echoing Rick Altman's analysis of problems associated with the singular use of just semantic elements (iconic codes that produce a large body of films but little explanatory power) or syntactic elements (narrative constructions that increase explanatory power but narrows the cannon of films), Lloyd-Smith warns that emphasizing genre taxonomies "can lead to an empty kind of formalism" while privileging style can result in everything being "seen as Gothic" (134–35), the term becoming meaningless and losing any explanatory power. Altman's now-classic book *Film/Genre* introduces a third method, the pragmatic, to accompany these two methods as a way around this dilemma. And the pragmatic approach is the one I have been using here, focusing on the reading positions assumed by users, rather than an analysis of the particular texts, be they novels, plays, or films. In this particular case, that reception is of cinematographers as represented by the industry trade publication *American Cinematographer*. From such a perspective, whether one calls the result a style or a genre—or even a mode—is ultimately irrelevant because either way it is a classificatory schema for which an identifiable label was eventually acknowledged as a shorthand mechanism for referring to certain types of artistic works, some of those works closer to the phantom archetype than others.

The 1960s saw not only the importation from France of the critic-derived genre term *film noir* but also the idea of the director as the auteur of a film that had been developed the decade before by the writers-cum-future filmmakers who associated with the French film journal *Cahiers du Cinema* and became the French New Wave. So while the stylistics of *Baby Doll* and *The Fugitive Kind* were approached through the contribution of their cinematographer Boris Kaufman, *Reflections in a Golden Eye* (John Huston, 1967) was framed in *American Cinematographer*—ironically given the focus of the magazine—through its director, adopting the auteurist approach that had recently become popular in the US. Although the article focused on the film's director rather than its cinematographer, it follows the trajectory established earlier by the articles on cinematographer Boris Kaufman. It justifies Huston's choice of Technicolor's desaturation process because it "serves the mood of the film well by creating a brooding, low-key aura of unspoken (and perhaps unspeakable) psychological chaos. Without it, the haunting atmosphere which leaves the viewer vaguely disquieted long after the final fadeout might not be nearly so palpable" (Lightman 864). Once again, creating a mood that advances the thematic concerns of the film is prioritized over one that advances its narrative storytelling.

So why does adoption of the muted color pallet provided by the new Technicolor desaturation process stylistically fit the thematic of the film? Unlike the earlier *American Cinematographer* articles, this one offered an explicit definition of southern gothic, contending:

> In the shadowy, Southern-fried world of which these authors [Tennessee Williams, William Faulkner, and Carson McCullers] write, Dixie is not a sphere of joyous cotton-chopping, but rather a kind of psychological compost pit beneath the tranquil surface of which festers a turbulent humus of violence, lunacy, murder and decay—to say nothing of a spectrum of sexual aberrations that would have exhausted the imagination of Krafft-Ebing. What makes it really horrifying is that the entire putrefying mass is precariously contained within a paper-thin veneer of traditional-laced gentility." (Lightman 863)

Historically cultural critics associated southern gothic with both the grotesque and degeneracy. Although the two concepts share similarities, they are not synonyms. A quick skim of their definitions in the *Oxford English Dictionary* makes this clear. The grotesque deals with distortion or fantastical combinations while degeneracy refers to a decline from a higher to lower state. While grotesque aligns with incongruence, degeneracy invokes degradation and decay. So unlike the static state implied by the grotesque's juxtaposition, degeneracy refers to an active process of downward motion. The definition of southern gothic proffered in the article privileges the concept of degeneracy through its invocation of "compost pit," "decay," and "putrefying," making no reference to the grotesque as the earlier articles did. So why would color desaturation contribute to the creation of a mood that embodies a "psychological compost pit beneath," a "tranquil surface," and a "putrefying mass . . . precariously contained within a paper-thin veneer of traditional-laced gentility"?

Desaturation is the process of making a color less saturated, a decline from a bright vivid color to, at the extreme end, a dull gray shade. Although a decline in color intensity, the result is accomplished through an additive process rather than deductive one. In other words, one taints the purity of the color, degrade it through the introduction of a contaminant, usually gray. The film's coloration is created through a process that parallels the thematic concern of southern gothic as defined in the *American Cinematographer* article, the color on screen the result of a process similar to the one that produced the characters on screen, material degradation through contamination of the substance of a color in the former, a person in the latter. In addition, the technique muddies the colors and as a result can introduce shadowy spaces that hide areas of the screen from viewers, forming a "surface," a "veneer" that covers the "compost pit," the putrefying mass" that would have been illuminated otherwise, those shadows with more "body than real objects." The gray shadows that dull the intensity of the color on the screen produce a similar spectator affective state, an unsettling mood of a murky degenerate world. One could call the desaturated color introduced in *Reflections in a Golden Eye* "color noir" because during the 1970s, when contemporary film noirs became popular, many of the films used desaturated color to create a mood comparable to that created by the original film noirs through black and white photography. But the southern gothic film *Reflections in a Golden Eye* got there first.

Soon after southern gothic's screen presence dissipated in the late 1960s, film noir received a self-conscious resuscitation by the auteurs of the New Hollywood, the Classical Hollywood genre resurrected for a new generation of moviegoers. And as with film noir, southern gothic also experienced a regeneration. Two films from that resurgence that began in the late 1980s were written about in *American Cinematographer*: *Sister, Sister* (Bill Condo, 1987) and *The Gift* (Sam Raimi, 2000). While the article on *Reflections in a Golden Eye* dealt with matters of concern to cinematographers—film stock processing—its funneling of the discussion through the director was a temporary blip, and the focus of these subsequent articles shifted back to the films' cinematographers, as with the earlier articles. In spite of this momentary disparity, the goal of the creation of a mood through cinematographic methods remained consistent across the years, although the latter articles were more likely to express it through the concepts of the film's "feel" and "audience experience" rather than the rhetoric of "mood" per se. While the specific stylistics invoked in the articles where more elusive than those of the earlier articles, the concern with lighting and composition to create a haunting, daunting, or mysterious atmosphere remained.

The articles on these two films are telling in terms of how southern gothic in its second manifestation was stitched closer to film noir. Both films are immediately aligned in their respective articles with southern gothic, one through its very title, "Southern Gothic" (Holben 58), the other its opening sentence, which informs us, "Hollywood returns to the Gothic tradition . . . of the great southern fiction of Flannery O'Connor and Carson McCullers" (Schiller 69). But this linkage is quickly followed by another one. In southern gothic's earlier manifestation, it was perceived primarily through the lens of family melodrama. But in its revival, that perceptional vector had changed to one that closely linked it to the film noir revival, which some writers preferred to refer to instead as neo-noir, to differentiate it from the 1940s and 1950s manifestation. While crime continued to be important to film noir in its neo form, it was more commonly approached through a Hitchcockian framework of suspense and thriller. The creators of

Sister, Sister describe the film as "Eudora Welty filtered through Alfred Hitchcock" (Schiller 70). And both it and *The Gift* were explicitly described in the articles as a "thriller" entailing "mysteries" or a "mysterious" look. Although historically film noirs textually contained a family melodrama component—which one could hold is what led two theater critics in 1947 to invoke *The Postman Always Rings Twice* and *Double Indemnity* when reviewing *A Streetcar Named Desire*—and southern gothic a crime and violence textual element, the intertwining genres were rarely connected discursively during their initial Classical Hollywood manifestations. But during their New Hollywood reappearances, as a result of the introduction of the framing device of the thriller, they were. With the shift from associating southern gothic predominately with melodrama and film noir with crime to prioritizing both with the thriller, their prior shared visual vocabulary finally received a shared generic acknowledgement as well. Although "southern noir" was not historically a term used to refer to these films during their initial reception, their visual stylistics and linkage to the thriller indicate that they are.

A MOUNTAINOIR

The Arrival of Country Noir and Frank Borzage's
Moonrise *(1948) in Retrospect*

JACOB AGNER

O ver the last twenty-odd years, the tradition broadly known as *noir*—its mid-century world of mean streets, hard-boiled criminal toughs, and cities of perpetual night—has found itself as of late not on a mean street per se, but on Main Street and country roads. Since at least 1996 when Missouri Ozarks novelist Daniel Woodrell titled his fifth work *Give Us a Kiss: A Country Noir* and the Coen brothers released their acclaimed Minnesota crime film *Fargo*, trends in the chiefly urban noir category have arguably "gone country" indeed. On recent television, many popular American crime shows such as Netflix's *Ozark* (2017–) and FX's *Fargo* (2014–) not only look like direct descendants of this rural turn, but they are also expanding noir's playing field to the point where the bayous of Louisiana (HBO's *True Detective* [2014]), the hills of Kentucky (FX's *Justified* [2010–2015]), and the suburbs of New Mexico (AMC's *Breaking Bad* [2008–2013]) have become fair game. The dark cities of old, this is all to say, have found themselves increasingly complemented by a *country dark* coming out of the nation's vast and remote rural stretches.

Thus with this movement in mind, this essay proposes a subcategory of its own: the "mountainoir." In the contexts of a category known for vertical city imagery (high windows, fire escapes, circular stairwells, towering high-rises, etc.) and fate thrown in free fall, it seems reasonable to extend this logic to mountains. Mountains, to be sure, can already be found in several of noir's canonical works. In the first American hard-boiled novel, Dashiell Hammett's *Red Harvest* (1929), the story is set within the Rocky Mountains of Montana in a corrupt mining city. And in James M. Cain's *The Postman Always Rings Twice* (1934), California's craggy mountain coast serves for two lovers not just as an isolated spot for a murder, but as the very weapon with which they'll commit it. Commandeering a husband's car and sending it (with said husband) down the cliffside, Cain's murderous lovers realize, at the same time they comment on "what a hell of a looking country those mountains were," that in the morally unbounded world of noir, mountains of trouble are usually nearby (41).

Yet beyond these impactful moments, there are also works that ground themselves not just in mountains alone, but in the lives and culture of mountain *people*. Indeed as the pun in my term suggests, a "mountainoir" is not just mountain noir. It's *mountaineer* noir. The mountaineers of the upper southern United States and their rural communities also had their own important noir story to tell throughout the twentieth century's first half. Although general understandings of noir tend to locate themselves within the urban landscape of the dark city, it is important to remember that, for such nocturnal cities to ever come to be, they had to harvest many of their most crucial resources from off-site, rural places. And one of those places was, of course, Appalachia. The mountains of the US South from approximately 1880 to 1930 were at the forefront of the same kind of social conditions and historical processes that led to the formation of noir fiction and film in the 1940s and 1950s. Before the hard-boiled detective and the femme fatale, the subsistence farmer and the coal miner came into contact with the machinations and exploitative measures of the ever-multiplying world of timber barons and land capitalists as well as the tyranny of the company town.[1] And such a dark noirish history, as it turns out, was not entirely lost on noir. Among its many black-and-white works, the classic noir tradition featured a few noteworthy mountainoirs set in places like West Virginia, Virginia, and the hollows of Appalachia. And one of these mountainoirs has grown in retrospect as an important early example that predates the country noir in vogue today. This work is Frank Borzage's 1948 film noir, *Moonrise*.

Moonrise was originally written in 1945 by former *New York Times* critic Theodore Strauss. Published in serial form for *Collier's Magazine*, *Moonrise* tells the story of Danny Hawkins (played by Dane Clark in the film), a poor white from the Virginia mountains who is tormented by his family's traumatic history. When Danny was a child, his father was legally executed for committing a murder. This violence from Danny's past, unfortunately, will ultimately lead to another murder in the story's first chapter—and committed this time not by Danny's father but by Danny himself. In the aftermath of a heated fight, Danny discovers in a scene of frenzied panic that now he, like his father before him, has suddenly and accidentally become a murderer. The story's remainder, as a result, wrestles with Danny's fear that his father's violent past has somehow determined his own.

Strauss's serial story was repackaged into novel form by Viking Press in 1946. But soon after that, the story's rights were also quickly sold for Hollywood optioning. Independent producers Marshall Grant and Charles Haas came close to bringing acclaimed filmmaker (and noir artist in his own right) William A. Wellman and A-list actor John Garfield to the project, but a string of financial and

legal issues ultimately led them to sell the rights to Republic Pictures on "Poverty Row." A studio known at that time for its cheap, post-Depression B movies,
Republic gave the project to an unconventional noir artist: the fading silent-era
auteur Frank Borzage. Though an acclaimed filmmaker in his time—twenty-odd
years before *Moonrise*, Borzage was the first recipient ever of the Academy Award
for Best Director in 1927 for *7th Heaven*— by the noir 1940s Borzage's romantic
predilections for stories of young love and the redemptive power of forgiveness
in his films were falling out of fashion. Nevertheless, in order to complete his
three-picture deal with Republic (after which he would not make another movie
until a decade later), Borzage would sign on and promise his skills as a seasoned
filmmaker, cutting costs with routine efficiency.[2]

And while *Moonrise* in 1948 would receive poor domestic box office results,
Borzage's only film noir has grown significantly in stature in recent year. Jake
Hinkson writes in 2014, *Moonrise* is arguably one of the "first fully formed" "rural noirs," film noirs that present the "country without its big-city contrast" (35).
"If I had to select just a single shot to illustrate that noirs are set in rural locations," writes Jesse Schlotterbeck in 2008, "it would be the opening sequence
of *Moonrise*" (Schlotterbeck). As comments like this suggest, *Moonrise* has especially grown in consideration because of the bruising way Borzage begins it.
Moonrise begins with a mostly wordless sequence that links Danny's father's execution in the past to Danny's earliest memories. The first shot follows Danny's
faceless father (Borzage only films him from the knees down) down a dark and
rainy street. It becomes increasingly clear that this is the last day of his life. The
shot continues following his father until, as the camera takes note, a gather-
ing crowd appears nearby. While we cannot see exactly what's catching their
attention, Borzage alludes to the execution in signature noir fashion. On the
wall behind the onlookers, the camera captures the shadows of the hangman's
platform. The sequence's most disturbing moment, however, isn't its filming of
the hanging. It is, instead, at the very moment when we expect the platform to
drop, Borzage match-cuts the morbid shadows not with a dead man dangling on
a rope, but with the lifeless shadow of a doll, which hangs above Danny's crib.
This is the way we meet Danny in the film. From his earliest infancy, Borzage's
surprisingly poetic transition suggests, Danny Hawkins has been marked as the
son of a murderer, the boy with a shadowed past.

The sequence doesn't stop there, however. Borzage then jumps later into
Danny's childhood. There, through brief snatches, we realize the extent of the
social consequences Danny will have to suffer for his disgraced father's death.
Danny will not only be taken away from his home in the mountains and sent to

the small town of Woodville in Virginia, but he'll also find himself constantly tormented there by the vicious bullying of Jerry Sykes, the son of a wealthy banker in town. We see Sykes in this sequence grotesquely mimicking Danny's father's hanging, lolling his head while other boys chant, "Danny Hawkins's dad was hanged!" It is hardly surprising, then, when, by the sequence's end, the two foes run into each other in their early adulthood, the encounter quickly turns fatal. Confronting Danny on the outskirts of a party, Jerry (now played by Lloyd Bridges) viciously taunts Danny, "Did your old man have time to tell you how it feels to drop six feet at the end of a rope?" It takes little time for Danny to throw the first punch, but the course of the fight changes when Jerry picks up a rock. Suddenly enraged by a flashback to Jerry's lolling face, Danny wrests the rock from Jerry's hand and raises it above his head. As Jerry slowly falls out of frame and the music spikes, Danny slams the rock down in three deadly strikes. Suddenly, after a last-ditch effort to defend himself, Danny discovers in a few seconds' horror he's no longer just a victim of his family's circumstances. He's also now a murderer: like father, like son.

"There are many other classic *films noirs*," notes critic Lee Horsley, "in which the protagonist is wrongly accused, hounded or victimised by a society that misjudges and despises him. He is unlikely to be entirely innocent" (156). This is precisely the case in *Moonrise*. As soon as Danny realizes what he's done, he realizes the burden he now assumes. Like his father, Danny could be painted at any moment as a murderer. Danny scrambles to hide Jerry's body in the nearby swamps, but the second he returns to town, he realizes he has to put on an innocent face in order to avoid detection. In this regard, *Moonrise* has been described by Imogen Sara Smith as a good example of a "small-town noir," in which "nothing can be kept hidden for long in such a town, and nothing is forgotten" (100). Running into characters like Woodville's sheriff (Allyn Joslyn), Danny's African American friend Mose (Rex Ingram), and Danny's love interest Gilly Johnson (Gail Russell), Danny will now have to suffer under the weight of his new secret.

Beyond these small-town dynamics, however, another important element in Danny's noir tale is his past from the mountains. As his backstory explains, Danny has *always* had a precarious social status in Woodville, long before Jerry's murder. From the very day he enters town as a poor white from the mountains, Danny is spurned by his peers as an outsider. Since the time of the Greeks, scholar J. W. Williamson has pointed out, mountains and their people have been inscribed with a "deeply ingrained aversion" in Western societies, as a realm known for chaos and disorder, "where anything could happen at any moment" (19). With these contexts in mind, then, Danny can be seen not just as a typical film noir antihero, but as a tragic figure steeped in the regional and social anxiety of his mountainoir predicament. *Moonrise,* in other words, is not just about Danny's murder. It's also about Danny's fear that, like his father before him, he too is about to be railroaded in town, and not just as a killer, but as a violent "hillbilly" from the mountains.

The term *hillbilly,* like all other poor white slurs—such as *poor white trash, cracker, clay eater,* and *redneck*—speaks to the issue of white "otherness" in America.[3] Known for his proclivities for violence and poverty, illiteracy, laziness, inbreeding, and racism, the hillbilly stereotype soon came to serve as an ambiguous expression of the wider nation's dual interests in and aversion to Appalachia. Amid large-scale changes let loose by social processes and attendant fluctuations like industrial modernization, economic instability, artistic depiction, and technological innovation, the hillbilly continued to develop as an important cultural tool for the larger nation, a form of expendable whiteness through which "regular" modern Americans could examine certain less appealing aspects of themselves and their society. In essence, the hillbilly was a "safe mirror," writes Williamson, "for seeing what we could not look at otherwise" (195–96).

With some of these cultural contexts in mind, we start to get a better sense of why the hillbilly made his way in the world of noir. Writes James Naremore in *More than Night: Film Noir in Its Contexts* (1998), the "dangers that assail the protagonists in noir" are often embodied by "a variety of 'others'" like the hillbilly, a milieu of "criminals, sexually independent women, Asians, Latins, and black people" (220). The same rule of thumb also arguably applies for the mountain hillbilly. Both before and after *Moonrise* in 1948, the hillbilly can be found serving nefarious purposes throughout the noir tradition. A year before Borzage's film, James M. Cain of *Postman* fame wrote another one of his sensational hard-boiled novels, *The Butterfly* (1947), and set it exclusively in the mountain South. *The Butterfly* would not only receive significant commercial success that year and Cain would admire it as one of his best, but Cain's mountainoir in retrospect also speaks to several of the cultural problems suggested above.[4] Though *The Butterfly* begins innocently enough with a mountaineer in West Virginia greeting his long lost nineteen-year-old daughter, Cain soon enough devolves this meet-and-greet into something else entirely: the taboo of incest. Cain's mountainoir, as a result, has been read as nothing more than than a vehicle for him to exploit this Appalachian stereotype. The main character is even reduced to saying at one point, "'Shining, shooting, and shivareeing their kin, that's what they say of people that live too long on one creek'" (384). It's not, then, a California vagrant or postman that rings twice in *The Butterfly*. It's the southern hillbilly.

The villainous noir hillbilly, unfortunately, won't stop there in the tradition. Apart from the fact that *The Butterfly* would somehow find a way to receive cinematic treatment as late as 1982 in Matt Cimber's critically reviled *Butterfly*, several other mountainoirs can be found in American cinema. For example, a few years after *The Butterfly* and *Moonrise,* in 1955 Robert Mitchum would famously play a poor white serial killer roaming the river bottoms of West Virginia in Charles Laughton's *The Night of the Hunter.* And seventeen years after that, the infamous hillbilly rape scene from James Dickey's *Deliverance* (1970) would not only be adapted into a blockbuster film by John Boorman in 1972, but it would be matched a year later by similar scenes of necrophilia and murder in Cormac McCarthy's third novel, *Child of God* (1973). As many of these works suggest, the mountain holler has been depicted in America as an othered danger zone, not unlike all of noir's other Chinatown districts and Harlem alleys.

To be clear, it's not my intention to celebrate these mountainoirs and their depictions of the southern hillbilly. I bring them up here so as to shed a better light on Danny Hawkins in *Moonrise* and the crime he accidentally commits. Though Danny could be seen as a "hillbilly" villain, I want to make the opposite claim here and suggest that he is hardly the stereotype like those other works. In fact, once we place Danny beside this hillbilly lineage in the genre, we start to sense how much time and energy his noir story spends to undercut (rather than underline) these implicit prejudices around this cultural figure. In other words, a term like *hillbilly* is arguably as painful to Danny throughout the film as *murderer*. As theorist Matt Wray writes, terms like *hillbilly* and *poor white trash* can be, and very much have been, deployed, as verbal weapons, *stigmatypes* (combining *stigma* and *stereotype*) that function as "crucial markers of status and prestige" and serve as "thresholds of inclusion and respectability" within the fluctuating and ambiguous field of whiteness in America (134). Like all other slurs, being on the wrong side of "hillbilly" and "poor white trash" in America can strike boundaries as socially limiting and derisive as any other.

And such boundary-making, indeed, can be sensed throughout *Moonrise.* The most clear-cut of these exchanges occurs when a friend asks Danny a day later at the Woodville diner if he'd like to search for Jerry. Danny politely declines and says, "I reckon not," but Danny's simple response gets him in trouble. Danny's friend critiques Danny's vernacular: "When are you going to stop talking like a hillbilly, Hawkins?" Danny flinches at the remark. The slippage between Danny's guilt over the murder and his frustration in being called a "hillbilly" is telling. Each burden is piling onto the other for Danny. In the novel, Strauss suggests this point by collapsing the two into a metaphor. When you "kill a man and then you got to protect the first killing," Danny thinks, "It piles up. Pretty soon you're carrying a mountain" (168). Little does Danny realize how close to the truth he actually is.

When Danny returns to town after Jerry's death, he runs into his peers harassing another outcast in town. Their other victim this time is Billy Scripture (Harry Morgan), a deaf-mute who lives alone in their community. With a past like Danny's, it makes sense why bullying of any kind causes him to soon intervene. But in offering his hand to Billy, Danny reveals an uncomfortable similarity with the other town reject. Like Billy, whose physical disabilities keep him apart, Danny is ostracized in a similar manner because of his social background. The film seems to intuitively know this. When Danny takes Billy away and brings him into a nearby restroom, Borzage makes a visual cue that suggests their implicit brotherhood. Looking into the restroom mirror, Danny sees Billy staring back at him in place of his own reflection. This mirrored moment speaks to another subtle irony behind Danny's predicament. Not only a social outcast like Billy, Danny discovers here that he, too, to a certain degree, has come to share Billy's disability. Like Billy, Danny cannot speak of his affliction.

The stakes in this regard get raised ever higher when Danny next runs into Woodville's schoolteacher, Gilly Johnson. Unlike Billy Scripture who lives on the edge of town, Gilly is far from an unnoticed outcast. In southern culture, belles like Gilly are at the very center of the South's social organization. When a young white woman like Gilly becomes old enough for marriage, a southern town like Woodville will make sure her hand in courtship will end up with a suitor of her race, class, and social position. In this context, Danny from the mountains hardly seems the best match for her. Moments before their fatal fight, in fact, Jerry warns Danny, "Quit dancing with Gilly Johnson. I told you at that coon hunt three months ago she's out of your class." Through these additional barbs, *Moonrise* is effective at lacing its noir murder story with the strict social customs of southern culture. In "addition to his father's criminal past," writes Rose Capp, "Danny's working class, rural origins" are "consistently contrasted" in the film "with the 'new money' affluence of the Sykes banking family" (Capp). Even after his death, wealthy Jerry Sykes somehow seems a better suitor for Gilly than Danny. Gilly's highly contested hand, moreover, will further add to Danny's endangerment. Irrespective of the fact that Gilly's other suitor has just disappeared, her social interactions are still going to be held under close scrutiny by the town. When the sheriff and his wife one day, for example, see Gilly and Danny together, the sheriff's wife remarks, "Well, she sure didn't take long to tie up with another boy." The sheriff hears this. This, indeed, can be the case in the gossipy, ever-watchful South. Thus whenever Danny decides to come into contact with Gilly, he's virtually risking his neck. Though Gilly may not be a traditional noir femme fatale, her symbolic position as protected southern belle is.

Nevertheless, Gilly also stands for something else to Danny. While Danny most likely knows contact with Gilly is dangerous, he also knows that, if he were to win her hand, her value in town can counteract his criminal past. At the same time that Gilly is a figurehead for the town's watchful eyes, she is also one of Danny's best tickets to leverage his social status. Danny, then, will try in several ways to continue courting Gilly. When he first sees Gilly at the party before he kills Jerry, Danny tries to woo her with his friend's father's car. Danny hastily asks his friend if he can drive them all home that night, but Danny loses control of the vehicle and crashes it. When this plan goes up in smoke, Danny reverts next to a much older strategy—chivalry. Knowing of an abandoned plantation in the swamps outside of town, Danny invites Gilly for a secret rendezvous there. Despite its decrepit interior and its ties to the Old South, Blackwater Mansion provides a space for the couple to escape their class differences for a moment. Gilly play-acts there with Danny, taking on a southern affectation, deferring to Lady Blackwater's portrait over the mantel, and imagining Danny as a much more socially esteemed figure, a "Captain Hawkins" of the romantic antebellum South. Borzage concludes the scene with an elegant crane shot that transcends above the couple, but the moment is contradicted by the mansion's blasted interior. Less than ten years after David O. Selznick's *Gone With the Wind* (1939), *Moonrise* in 1948 literally waltzes in the ruins of this southern fantasy. By the noir 1940s, it seems, the plantation romance has withered into a broken and impossible dream.

After neither of these strategies work, Danny tries one more: he takes Gilly to the town fair. Like the plantation sequence, the scene at the fair is a loaded one. In southern studies, the carnival and the sideshow have been theorized as itinerant spaces in which southerners like Danny and Gilly can peep at, or come face to face with, transgressive or ambiguous "freak" forms of identity. Writes scholar Harriet Pollack, "Southern literature is frequently drawn to the landscape of the sideshow body," for such hybrid bodies speak to and challenge "the South's apartheid culture" and the South's social "categories based on binaries that inform systems of gender and class as well as race (151)." Such is the case in *Moonrise.* As soon as the carnival sequence begins, Borzage starts with a carnival barker announcing—while pointing his cane at exotically dressed women on a stage—that one can now see at "the county fair, your own fair, for the first time, the siren enchantresses direct from the forests of Lebanon." Nearby, Danny and

Gilly stand and stare. While it first seems as if the women on stage are the ones who are on display here, the scene slyly adds to Danny's creeping sense that it is actually him all alone who has been the town "freak" from the mountains. In his own way, in fact, Danny is the one who's been on stage throughout the film.

With this context in mind, it makes sense why Danny finally speaks about his father with Gilly at the fair. Later atop the carnival's Ferris wheel, Danny explains how his father, after a doctor refused to visit them when Danny's mother was sick, ultimately decided to kill the doctor when Danny's mother died from her lack of treatment. Then, "It took three bullets to kill [the doctor]," Danny laments, "and it took them three weeks to hang Pa." Thus as Gilly sits beside Danny and listens to his sad story, the film then reveals one of its most powerful ironies: as the Ferris wheel climbs into the sky above the carnival's "freak show," Danny tries to make his most humanizing case. He is trying to paradoxically ascend, in other words, from a past that was already on high. Indeed, like the moon in the film's title, it becomes clear in this scene that Danny is a white subject desperately trying to rise above his social rank.

This task will not be an easy one for Danny, especially after Jerry's death. In fact, while Danny tries to plead his case to Gilly, the town sheriff gets on the same ride and eyes Danny. At the very moment Danny explains away his family's violent history, the law officially begins to close in on him. Danny realizes this. Like the Ferris wheel upon which he sits, Danny's fate is now in the balance; in the future it will either rotate upwards or downwards. But the uncertainty of it all, unfortunately, is too much for Danny. Seeing the sheriff from below, Danny leaps from his seat and jumps to the ground. Borzage captures the moment's suicidal intensity with a shaky, plummeting point-of-view shot that distills the central Sisyphean dilemma at the heart of Danny's mountainoir: for every step up for Danny, the bottom is never far away.

While this public collapse will not end Danny just yet, he realizes afterward that he needs to recede from the public eye for a while. Fortunately, Danny has one other marginalized character in town to seek counsel from: Woodville's only African American character, Mose. While some critics have praised Mose as a "remarkable . . . African American part," his underlying purpose in the film also arguably adds to Danny's growing sense of anxiety (Römers). We especially gather this when, as Danny visits Mose one day and circles in conversation his killing of Jerry, Danny stops in his tracks and wonders aloud to Mose, "What if there's bad blood in me, Mose, that makes me do bad things?" Such a question between a poor white and an African American in the US South is no small issue. As lily-white Gilly's protected hand suggests, the problem of "bad blood" in the segregated South adds a distinctly racialized dimension to Danny's internal struggle. Though there does not seem to be any overt sign that Danny thinks he's an African American, the fact he speaks of "bad blood" to Mose speaks to an important intersection at work in the film between class and race. Though Danny may barely "pass" in Woodville as a poor white man, his poverty and his ties to the Appalachian hills put him dangerously close on the social ladder to black men like Mose. This racial anxiety at the bottom of Danny's social narrative is also alluded to in the film's opening sequence. In it we not only see Danny get physically beaten, but we also see a scene where Jerry smears Danny's face with a dark, viscous substance. Though it's unclear what the substance is, its opaque and unmistakable blackness suggests a racializing element to Danny's social torment.

This racial fear, moreover, is hardly a rarity in the "black film" of film noir. As Eric Lott points out in his important essay, "The Whiteness of Film Noir," many classic film noirs in their dark depictions of post-war America often aided and abetted their seedy tales with the anxiety of racial darkness. Writes Lott, the "blackness" of film noir's morally dark characters can also be interpreted in terms of "the form of a passage out of whiteness" (546). Film noir is often about white men, in other words, who lose coherent sense of themselves as white and privileged subjects. Danny in *Moonrise* can also be seen in line with these racially challenged men in noir. In a telling scene late in the film when Danny partakes on a "coon hunt" with Mose in the swamps, the term *coon* starts to slip like *hillbilly* for Danny. Though Mose seems hardly bothered by the term, which in many instances in southern film has been used as a racial slur for African Americans, Borzage dollies in on Danny's suddenly darkened face when Mose challenges Danny and says, "Who says there's no coon at Brother's Pond?"[5] While the surface reading of this shot suggests that Danny's obvious fear here is that the dogs on the hunt might sniff out Jerry's body in the marshes (and, in fact, they will), its combination of noir's brooding black-and-white style with the social contexts of the US South also speaks to Danny's underlying racial anxiety in the film. Thus a few scenes later when Danny is chased into the brackish black waters around Blackwater Mansion by the very same "coon dogs" he used to lead with Mose, an ironic role reversal comes to the fore: in the "black" world of film noir, Danny learns, the white man can also become a runaway fugitive tearing through the dark southern woods, chased by baying hounds.

With the realization of this reversal, Danny is left in the film's final moments to seek out a last resort. Barely escaping authorities while hiding neck-deep in the swamp's dark waters, Danny is forced to turn to the one place that's loomed

large in his life: his home in the mountains. There all this time, fortunately, remains one of the last and best voices of counsel for him. This voice will come
from Danny's grandmother (briefly played by actress Ethel Barrymore), who
gravely attempts to dissuade Danny from repeating his father's violent end.
Though Danny tries to argue with her and rail against the many injustices he
suffered as the son of a murderous mountaineer, his grandmother steps in and
casts a different portrait of Danny's father. Handing Danny the newspaper cutout
that came out before his father's trial, Danny's grandmother says, "I never heard
Jeb Hawkins raise his voice except when he was happy. Then you could hear it
across mountains." Unlike Danny, who has been seen suffering throughout the
weight of his mountain past, Danny's father had no such regional guilt. Whereas
Danny has been "carrying mountains," his father's voice fanned *across* them, as if,
before his untimely death, he never felt the kind of shame that Danny after him
suffered. Proud of his heritage in Appalachia and his family, "Killer Jeb Hawkins"
hardly becomes the killer "hillbilly" Danny always thought he was.

Borzage further reinforces this last-minute recasting by including an insert
shot of the article. Complete with cowboy hat and bronzed suntan, Danny's father in the only picture ever taken of him looks more like a Hollywood hero
than a mountain heathen (fig. 5.1). By the noir 1940s, in fact, all was not darkness and doom for the Appalachian "hillbilly" in popular culture. While terms
like *white trash* and *cracker* before *hillbilly* were mostly used as derogatory stigmatypes meant to belittle poor whites for their lower class conditions, *hillbilly*
throughout the twentieth century was a much more ambiguous term. In the
1920s and 1930s, when music executives realized the serious potential in selling rural white music alongside African American blues and jazz in the form of
what's known today as "race records," they began by calling it "hillbilly music"
and selling it to a growing fan base. But by the 1940s, when the discourse around
the term "hillbilly" and other poor white slurs became more and more contentious, the classification was replaced with a much less divisive title—"country
music"—which remains today as the category's standard title. *Moonrise* in 1948,
therefore, along with the story of Danny's father, arguably stands in the midst of
these many changing cultural mores. In the same way, as scholar Anthony Harkins notes, "country hats and boots became standard uniforms for country music
performers" by the noir 1940s, and offered future depictions of poor whites "far
greater romantic possibilities than did the traditional mountaineer costume" of
old. Borzage's romantic recasting of Danny's father offers a glimmer of hope for
the othered noir "hillbilly" (95).

Thus while everything in *Moonrise* seems to point toward Danny's capitula-

Fig. 5.1. The only image of Danny's "hillbilly" father.

tion at the film's end, his noir plot of crime and detection finds itself increasingly outweighed by the other story it ultimately unveils. *Moonrise*, that is, becomes a story about a poor white's persistent hope for himself one day to peacefully assimilate in the southern society around him. Although the film will end with Danny admitting guilt in front of the ever-pursuing sheriff, the film's final moments come off as strangely uplifting. As Gilly embraces Danny at the foot of the mountain and says to him in front of the sheriff, "It's wonderful to see your face, Daniel, to really see it," we realize that Danny, in spite of all possible punishment, has finally found a moment to be acknowledged by his peers in Woodville, not as a white frightening "other," but as an accepted white subject. Such an acceptance is so important to Danny that it overrides the film's noirish conclusions. Notes noir critic Eddie Muller, "*Moonrise* is unique in that it's one of the few noirs in which the redemptive power of love holds nihilism at bay" (190). The film's surprising happy ending, however, is not without notes of the bittersweet. Before he looks toward Woodville and prepares to walk back with Gilly, Danny turns briefly one last time toward Mose, who has stood with the party this whole time at the base of the mountain with his "coon dogs" next to him. The two friends there at the base of the mountain seem to share a sad smile. In

Fig. 5.2. Danny stands between his captors, with Mose watching.

order to face his new and uncertain future in town, Danny has to turn his back on Mose, who has to continue remaining, as an African American man in the US South, as marginalized as ever at the film's end (fig. 5.2).

When *Moonrise* came out, the film was poorly received by audiences. Apart from a few subsequent analyses in relation to Frank Borzage's career as a romantic auteur, *Moonrise* might have been forgotten. But due to the recent turn in noir toward rural places and the US South, *Moonrise* has rightfully gained newfound attention as an early example of this contemporary trend. The sensitivity with which this "mountainoir" approaches the precarious position of southern poor whites like Danny Hawkins—even in the pulpy, prone-to-exploitation noir tradition—proves the worth of reexamining ways rural America and its people have intersected with the genre.

NOTES

1. My *noirish* take on Appalachia's history in regards to modernization has been broadly informed by Ronald D. Eller's two excellent studies on "progress" (emphasis on the scare quotes) in Appalachia in the twentieth century.

2. For more on the technical and financial details behind the making of *Moonrise*, see Dumont, pp. 334–42.

3. As a means to declutter my prose, the rest of the essay's mentions of *hillbilly*, unless I aim to discuss the word itself.

4. For studies that address Cain's exploitive depiction of poor southern whites in *The Butterfly*, see Castille and O'Brien.

5. See the *Oxford English Dictionary*, especially definitions I.1 and I.2c.

FILM NOIR, MATTHEW MCCONAUGHEY, & QUEER CAPITAL IN THE SOUTHERN IMAGINARY

SARAH LEVENTER

HOLLYWOOD AS INDUSTRY AND MCCONAUGHEY'S NOIR APPEAL

Film noir and the southern gothic are ironically similar ghosts in the American mythos. The decadent deviance that draws audiences to the femme fatale and southern gothic creations can create an "exciting frisson" that begets social critique (Duck, *Nation's* 93). In both genres, increasingly visible groups—war veterans, newly mobile women, social underclasses, and queer populations—voice themselves in ways that show fissures in the American dream. But noir narratives can also reify national cohesion. Two other recent southern gothic noirs[1]— *The Paperboy* and *True Detective*—tell this alternative story about the Southern imaginary, class, and the nation: not of transgression, but the selective inclusion of once deviant, even overtly queer subjects into nationalist projects. What separates the texts is how *The Paperboy* deals with race: transforming the racial ambivalence in the southern gothic noir genre from subtext into text. Comparing these media, and the performance of the texts' shared lead actor, Matthew McConaughey, reveals key contours of Hollywood's latest effort at inclusion: how prominent media players have co-opted aspects of queerness, film noir, and southernness to hegemonic ends, and precisely who is included in Hollywood's current, conditional embrace.

Decoding McConaughey's performance is crucial to understanding the effects of *The Paperboy* and *True Detective*. These roles were part of McConaughey's transformation from one-dimensional romantic comedy lead to Oscar-winning artist, a transition which took place in just two years (2012–2014). That he was able to so thoroughly change his star image in such a short time signaled Hollywood's eagerness to show itself as a progressive place during and after controversies like #OscarsSoWhite. Most of the films the actor used to reinvent himself— *Killer Joe*, *The Paperboy*, *Magic Mike*, *Dallas Buyers Club*, *True Detective*, and *Wolf of Wall Street*—are neo-noirs in which McConaughey plays southern men who are hailed as queer by others. In part because the genre of film noir allows for the picturing of experiences disavowed by polite society, McConaughey was also able to capitalize on the critical cachet that comes with playing "queer" to transform himself. By promoting McConaughey's films and honoring his southern, queer performance on an institutional level, Hollywood attempted to show its commitment to diversity.

However, McConaughey, except for his role in *The Paperboy*, rarely played gay men—that is, men interested in same-sex intimacy—so that neither he nor audiences were compelled to acknowledge LGBTQ+ populations in any direct way. His performances thus hit a representational "sweet spot": they allow audiences to bask in the warm glow of inclusion and engage the idea of deviant pleasures (i.e., sex divorced from a procreational drive in a sleazy, sexy noir setting) without being forced to confront the realities of same-sex intimacy. McConaughey's performative skill is an essential component of his films' marginalization of LGBTQ+ experience. The satisfaction viewers may feel when watching his well-acted role in *Dallas Buyers Club,* for instance, is a self-effacing cover for the erasure of the lead character's real-life bisexual identity.[2] In other words, the actor's queer-but-not-too-queer reinvention may appear a one-man-show, but its very effortlessness is by design. This actorly renaissance shows a much larger process by which Hollywood has responded to and cultivated audiences in a climate that purports to celebrate difference—this is perhaps best seen by briefly examining the most popular, ostensibly progressive film of McConaughey's recent oeuvre, *Dallas Buyers Club.*

Dallas Buyers Club came at a fortuitous time when playing "queer" brought critical cachet instead of stigma. The film exploits its moment by both directly showing representations of AIDS and queer communities affected by the disease while also, ultimately, reaffirming traditional American ideologies: tolerance, individualism, and the pursuance of capitalistic success (as allegedly embodied in protagonist Ron Woodruff's members-only drug-purchasing club). Director Jean Mark Vallée's narrative choices thus make queerness and AIDS narratives palatable for two audiences with often divergent tastes: young, liberal hipsters and mainstream audiences. As the film's AIDS-positive protagonist, McConaughey provided the star power needed to distribute the film widely. The edginess of the film's inclusions (an AIDS-positive lead and a southern, LGBTQ+ community) reciprocally heightened McConaughey's appeal as an actor who would take artistic risks. *Dallas Buyers Club* was also key to Vallée's establishment as a filmmaker capable of handling full-scale projects and weighty material. In short, *Dallas Buyers Club* demonstrated anew the dividends that playing queer could have for an actor, as well as for content creators.

Dallas Buyers Club's co-opting of queerness for capitalistic ends embodies the homonormativity that recent queer theorists like Jasbir Puar, Lisa Duggan, and Michael Warner have critiqued.[3] Puar claims that to thrive in a post-queer global market, the United States no longer rejects all deviant citizens, but rather judiciously incorporates some queer subjects whose interests align with state interests. This process heightens America's economic strength by harnessing the purchasing power of increasingly visible, white, middle-class, homonormative gay subjects. Once these subjects are acknowledged as "true" Americans worthy of the same protections afforded to heterosexual citizens (i.e., the right to marry), the nation can also leverage and regulate their political clout and, in so doing, heighten its own global political reputation as a free state. This process of selective inclusion—what Puar terms "homonationalism"—provides an alibi for the United States to lionize itself as a site of liberty, to justify foreign interventions, and to abject global subjects who are judged incongruent with our definition of basic freedom. *Dallas Buyers Club* exemplifies this precarious dynamic, providing what appears to be a progressive, profitable "queer uplift" narrative, but one that in fact leverages queer representations to certify America as an enlightened, open-minded place. The actor's showmanship in this role provides the perfect neoliberal cover for larger industrial and ideological processes.

McConaughey's speech for his Academy Award–winning role in *Dallas Buyers Club* is a kind of master shot for this larger process. An Oscar is not only institutional acknowledgement; it is also an endorsement that carries financial dividends for industry players. Actors, producers, and distributors profit from a film's post-award show press coverage and subsequent theatrical rerelease. In his speech, McConaughey perfunctorily thanked the industry without mention of the shaping hand it played in his win—to be sure, such a gesture would be considered an unseemly breach. The speech also made no mention of the man he played, Ron Woodroof, or the wider community of AIDS and gay rights activists that created the conditions in which he could win. Rather the actor quickly moved to celebrate his personal hero: himself. Like a true Texas showman, the actor expertly narrated an unlikely journey to self-respect, before collapsing that rhetoric into a neoliberal celebration of himself as the epitome of individualism, industriousness, and fearless exploration of new actorly territory. The contradictory operations at work in McConaughey's speech—a pleasurable feeling of tolerance combined with a partial or total expurgation of actual LGBTQ+ populations—drives the actor's current allure. That attraction is underlined by McConaughey's southern persona, which carries its own exotic appeal.

New Yorker writer Rachel Smye, who coined the term "the McConaissance" to describe the actor's recent phenomenal rise, illustrates America's continuing, yet submerged fascination with the star's southernness. She ruminates on the small group of actors able to pull off a second-act reinvention like McConaughey and Sandra Bullock, wondering if "maybe the magic is in Texas." McConaughey's southernness indeed constitutes his appeal (Smye). His Texas drawl and southern oddball persona—the cowboy showmanship of *Magic Mike* or the use of fried chicken as a dildo in *Killer Joe*—is part of what makes him queer to national/northern audiences and it also makes his courting of the taboo alluring and palatable for heteronormative viewers. McConaughey articulates things viewers desire but can only abide when staring over the fence into the South: a region at once part of and apart from the nation. Audiences can enjoy polymorphous perversions of the McConaissance—in effect, they can "slum"—because the border that separates the national/northern and southern imaginary ensures audiences can opt to safely return from the phantasmagoric worlds of his characters to their own national/northern spaces when his films end.

When southern gothic tales are at their most subversive, they make this kind of regional disavowal impossible by showing an uncanny likeness between the national/northern and southern imaginary; in other words, such texts reveal how "southern" fantasies of unrestrained power and pleasure travel to fuel national passions. Noirs reveal a similarly precarious national identity—the precariousness of white male identity, in particular, registers in the genre's hard-bitten, damaged heroes and in queer ancillary, often villainous, characters. As the introduction to this volume suggests, southern noir also provides opportunities to glimpse the racialized anxieties and fantasies that undergird national power structures.

Of all the films of McConaughey's rise, *The Paperboy* most suggestively carries out the transgressive political project of southern gothic film noir, self-reflexively highlighting the queer, raced construction of the southern detective as well as the Texas cowboy. Midway through the film, modern "enlightened" Jack Jansen (Zac Efron) witnesses a shockingly violent sexual encounter between his older brother, Ward Jansen (McConaughey), and a black male sex worker. As the next section will discuss in detail, when the film reveals Ward's sexual desires, it also makes plain a queerness that always inhered to cowboy identity but was rarely articulated. The way that the film portrays Jack's complicated response to his brother's assault further undermines the heterosexuality and normative whiteness that governs modern masculinity. Both of these moments encourage viewers to read the ending of the film—in which Ward dies to save Jack—self-reflexively, rather than in the cathartic style with which the "tragic queer character" is typically associated.

When Ward dies, viewers are not encouraged to feel his death was just or appropriately sacrificial—rather, they are encouraged to reflect on why certain characters (such as the more normative Jack) are typically folded into mainstream film narratives while others (such as the irrevocably queer Ward) are not. Such gestures of inclusion are a microcosm of the way in which some subjects are redeemed by mainstream culture (synonymous with the national-North) and why others must be expurgated for national power structures to cohere. While the film may not radically challenge the binaries between queer/straight or North/South, it does trouble those binaries by showing their typically invisible terms. The film also illustrates how national-northern directors play out anxieties about identity and belonging in the distant, but not too distant, gothic South. In contrast, *True Detective* tames and reincorporates its potentially transgressive queer protagonist, Rust Cohle (McConaughey), back into mainstream American life in the first season's finale. Rather than "make strange" our identification with Cohle, as *The Paperboy* does with Ward Jansen, *True Detective* finds a scapegoat to exile in his place: the redneck Errol Childress. In this gesture, the television show reifies McConaughey's "safe" star pedigree and affirms the status quo it means to deconstruct.

THE PAPERBOY

Most of McConaughey's recent films, such as *Magic Mike* and *Dallas Buyers Club,* specifically reference Texas as the birthplace of McConaughey's character. Many of these films are also set in that state, thus reuniting McConaughey with his Texas roots in the public eye. This aspect figures prominently in personal accounts of his life but was less prominent in earlier romantic comedies that placed him on the California coast (*The Wedding Planner*) or in the African desert (*Sahara*). By contrast, only Lee Daniels's *The Paperboy,* ironically set in Florida, takes an outsider perspective on the way that the longer history of the Texas cowboy has infused McConaughey's persona and its appeal.

In Daniels's film, McConaughey plays an investigative journalist with archetypal Texan–style cowboy swagger who, viewers discover late in the film, frequents black, male sex workers; this practice, shown in graphic detail, calls attention to the constitutive, yet submerged role that blackness and queerness play in the larger construction of the Texan male identity. Daniels's film is one of many where McConaughey plays some variant of a cowboy southern detective, but *The Paperboy* is the only film to fully interrogate that characterization. Coming before *Dallas Buyers Club* and *Magic Mike, The Paperboy* articulates the qualities that those mainstream films would appropriate for mass consumption. Compared to those films, however, *The Paperboy* offers a radically biting critique of McConaughey's Texas cowboy persona and with it, the southern detective archetype. To understand this critique requires briefly historicizing the Texas cowboy and film noir's relation to it.

Geographically, Texas sits on the border between the South and the West. In the national imagination, it also marks the border between the civilized, industrial world and the wilds of the frontier. In the nineteenth century the state was composed of both the mechanized labor of plantations and the wide-open spaces that figured so prominently in Manifest Destiny–era discourses. It was both a slave state and, as cultural critic Jane Tompkins suggests, a "symbol of freedom . . . . It seem[ed] to offer escape from the conditions of modern industrial society: from mechanized existence, social entanglements, unhappy personal relations, political injustice" (Tompkins 4). Texas was therefore a contradictory space that promised a psychological escape from slave society and industrial labor for white citizens even while perpetuating and benefitting from human bondage. The cowboy, as an archetype, smoothed the contradictions of frontier identity. He lived beyond civilization and so was untainted by social hypocrisies, but nonetheless lived by a moral code consonant with civil society. He was forever moving west toward liberty, so that Texas's position as a slave state could recede into the background of the cowboy-driven historical narrative. A cowboy's conflict was not with black populations, but more often with Native Americans who blocked his path. Nonetheless, the cowboy remained bound to blackness (and to people of color more generally) via his locale and animating impulse. The cowboy archetype existed as vehicle through which white men could outrun the plantation system. The qualities that defined slave life (entrapment, industry, abusive power, etc.) were precisely what the cowboy defined his free self against.

The intimate ties among conceptions of masculinity, whiteness, and blackness are rarely articulated in Westerns: these ties are equally elusive in—but also equally constitutive of—film noir. As scholar Eric Lott has noted, that genre fairly insistently "thematizes . . . spiritual and cinematic darkness by way of bodies," in effect visualizing conceptions of evil along a racial axis (542). White antiheroes who make moral compromises (for example, sleeping with clients, pursuing criminal activity to right a moral wrong, etc.) are shadowed by film noir's low-key, high-contrast lighting to read as ethically *and* racially "black" (545). Coding protagonists as liminal figures—who have white skin but nonetheless cross racial boundaries each time they move from the light into shadow—

conjoins psychology and race, creating a racial ambivalence that verges on an identity crisis. As Lott argues, noir throws "its protagonists into the predicament of abjection," a state that Julia Kristeva defines as the place where all social boundaries break down. The racialized formulations of film noir are problematic not only because they equate moral breakdown with blackness and displace that fear of the Other onto white characters, but also because nonwhite subjectivities are always, already narratively marginalized. Film noirs deal with contemporary social conditions but very rarely center on racial conflict or interracial community-building. However, the connections that noirs create between men *and* between conceptions of whiteness and blackness are intimate and strange enough to be considered queer.

The Paperboy thematizes the link between queerness and race that the earlier Westerns and film noirs only imply. Daniels's film also connects queerness, blackness, and the tradition of Southern detective fiction. The plot follows brothers Jack and Ward, along with black reporter Yardley (David Oyelowo), as they attempt to free alleged murderer Hillary Van Wetter (John Cusack). The film is a frame narrative told from the perspective of Anita Chester (Macy Gray), who works as a maid for the Jansens. As in other frame narratives, Chester's position as an inside-outsider allows her unique insights on the family at the center of the text. She is the only one to see Jack's burgeoning sexuality, and to notice the faint scars that trace Ward's body. Anita's inclusion as the film's narrator is the first way that the film challenges the genre conventions of southern gothic noir. While noir narrators are notoriously unreliable, they also occupy a central space in the plot. The white male, detective protagonist usually narrates so his perspective becomes the audience's perspective. This has the effect of creating the sense that partial, damaged, incomplete knowledge is all that one subject can possess. Southern gothic narratives, too, are dominated by white perspectives. By positioning Anita in a central role, the film expands southern gothic noir's view and undermines the whiteness of the hybrid genre. The film also separates narrator and protagonist, which is the first way that viewers are permitted to engage critically with *The Paperboy*'s white protagonists, rather than automatically suturing themselves to those characters.

Before the climax we expect—the freeing of Hillary—the film turns on itself, climaxing when Jack discovers Ward in a pool of blood, knocked unconscious during a sadomasochistic encounter with a black man. Ward's scars stand explained when we learn that he frequents black male sex workers and has come to the brink of death more than once. This revelation brings important elements of McConaughey's appeal into focus: his cowboy persona's investment in blackness

and queer intimacy, the racialized tension between Ward and Yardley, and by extension, the contemporary political implications of the intimate, queer relations
glimpsed in sidelong fashion in film noir.

The Paperboy rewrites the archetypal film noir narrative—a white man puts
himself in a position of authority only to have that power compromised—as an
explicitly raced, queer, abject tale. Ward is part of a hidden archive of white men
enmeshed in the southern imaginary whose guilt or covert investment in black
masculinity transmogrifies into sexual flagellation. Roy Grundmann analyzes
another piece from this archive, Norman Mailer's essay "The White Negro." In
Mailer's infamous parallel between listening to jazz and the "pinch, scream, despair, lust" of orgasm, Grundmann identifies an ultimately "masochistic infatuation with black culture" (Grundmann 172). After the passage on orgasm, Mailer
fantasizes about an actual, but momentary, black uprising that would lead to "the
temporary but nonetheless certain spiritual enslavement of the southern white
which . . . ought to be nourishing for both races—not to mention the moral justice of it" (as quoted in Grundmann 172). This fantasy constitutes a guilt-ridden
wish to "make up" for history through a masochistic invitation to . . . counter-
enslavement . . . Mailer's guilt over the historical importation and enslavement
of blacks produces psychosexual fantasies of the white self's subordination to
blacks. Mailer's liberation of blacks is predominantly an intrapsychic phenomenon that has little to do with black liberation as a political cause (173).

Of course, in The Paperboy Ward literalizes masochistic infatuation into actual encounter, and invokes a racialized aspect of sadomasochism (S&M) culture; two common names for the male "top" are domme (i.e., dominator) and,
more evocatively, Master. As Kelly Oliver and Benigno Trigio argue, film noir is
similarly structured by "the fear of not being able to tell the difference between
blackness and whiteness" (5). The black domme in The Paperboy breaks Ward's
body and skin, with the two men's sweat and bodily fluids intermingling so that
abjection is rendered unavoidably, irrefutably racial.

Unlike Mailer, though, Ward never mistakes sexual infatuation for political
engagement. Mailer constructs a romanticized Other, then injects himself into
the center of that racialized construction to bolster his own sense of himself as
an "enlightened" subject. Ward lacks such romanticist illusions. His masochistic
sexual practices in no way preclude racist acts in the public world. In fact, the
distance between sexual interest and possible ethical interests causes substantial tension between Ward and Yardley, who knows his race motivated Ward to
choose him as a reporting partner but does not compel Ward to treat him as an
equal. Illustrating the cracks in the facade of the southern detective and linking

those fissures to taboo, uncanny truths (in this case, the haunting presence of blackness and queerness) is of course the express purpose and domain of film noir and the southern gothic.

The film further cracks the facade of the detective archetype in the way it positions Ward relative to the film's criminal, Hillary Van Wetter. Detective novels outside of the film noir genre often end with the detective satisfyingly solving a difficult case, freeing an innocent man, and nearly as frequently, saving an innocent woman. But Van Wetter is far from innocent. He is, in some ways, a southern gothic scapegoat who embodies the worst of "white trash" stereotypes: he is violent, misogynistic, racist, non-normatively sexual, caked in unidentifiable grease, and enmeshed in an extended kin network with nebulous blood and marriage ties. When he is freed, Hillary takes his girlfriend, Charlotte (Nicole Kidman) hostage deep in the Florida swamp before killing her. This murder, in fact, precipitates the final confrontation between Van Wetter and Ward. Charlotte's death reframes the detective as a complicit participant in murder (insofar as Ward is implicated in getting Van Wetter freed knowing his violent tendencies toward Charlotte). The detective cannot save Charlotte, and the ending of the film shows the bedrock assumption that the American judicial system works to free the innocent as a counterfeit notion.

In contrast to Ward, Jack is deeply compassionate toward Yardley and Anita. When she cleans his room, for instance, the two tease each other with familiarity and warmth that suggests a deep relationship. Ulterior motives pervade *The Paperboy*, but Jack is characterized as the kind of open-minded young man who would soon become a socially conscious journalist or activist, any liberal film's moral conscience. He also demonstrates heterosexual desire by lusting after the working-class Charlotte, a desire the film initially frames as relatable puppy love. He thereby functions as an obvious audience surrogate. His character speaks as eloquently to current post-racial fantasies as it would have to liberal 1960s–1970s audiences; Jack implicitly claims to see past race and class, into the humanity of others in ways that Ward cannot. The film also acknowledges desirous gay male audiences and straight female viewers through Jack, who is often only partially clothed and objectified by the camera's gaze. Dreamy Disney teen star Zac Efron walks the line between queerness and heterosexuality as a fetish object, which heightens his appeal.

The film's explosive deconstruction shows which subjects are reclaimable by social reality—vaguely queer, post-racial men like Jack—and which are not—black men, sex workers, and those interested in sadomasochism. Ward's sexuality marks him for dying because it makes social terms, the intimate ties between white and black men, too visible. Importantly, it also corresponds with a disinterest in reproduction and moral responsibility that nullify him as a potential "good" citizen. Jack, by contrast, embodies heterosexual desire and an immutable stake in social stratification. While he may treat Anita kindly, her economic survival is predicated on his whims; he holds an excess of power as long as his family employs her. For Jack's life to continue, unaltered, the unequal power relations between him and Anita must also continue, relations that empower him and imperil her.

As the film progresses, Yardley and Anita become increasingly vocal while Jack and Ward unravel. Ward is eventually eaten alive by the abject Florida swamps and the white Walker Evans characters who dwell there (on film, at least), while Jack just barely escapes. Hillary turns on the brothers when they discover his murdered girlfriend, Charlotte, and attempts to kill them both. Ward's death allows Jack to get away and become a reporter. In the best film noir manner, however, *The Paperboy* leaves viewers with a nagging sense that Jack is forever changed by his encounter with the southern swamp, and will always embody social contradictions. As the final line of the novel on which the film was based tells us, "There are no intact men" (Dexter 307).

When *The Paperboy* narrates the decline of the prominent Jansen family, it also tells the story of the fall of white southern civilization, destroyed by the weird, subjugated, or impoverished populations it produced in its entropic drive to reproduce its compromised vision. This plot is a southern gothic staple. It describes the genre's key narrative, from literary texts like William Faulkner's *Absalom, Absalom!* to filmic texts like *True Detective,* as well as the pleasures such texts afford; they allow for social critique, nihilistic humor, and experience with grotesques like Hillary Van Wetter. While *The Paperboy*'s "deliriously tawdry" exploitation aesthetic was unpopular at the Cannes Film Festival, it mirrors the construction of the Erskine Caldwell, Flannery O'Connor, and William Faulkner texts it channels (Schulman). And, as the most biting southern gothic/film noir texts do, *The Paperboy* disrupts social reality by showing its invisible terms, and thereby opens up space to critique them.

TRUE DETECTIVE

Like Ward, *True Detective*'s Rust Cohle is an abject character, caught up in a typical southern gothic noir plot. He and his detective partner Marty Hart (Woody Harrelson) work to solve the serial murders of young women in a rural, trashy southern gothic imaginary. Along the way, the detectives discover a vast, deep network of criminality and corruption. Their journey pushes Cohle in particular to the fringes. His Texan identity, what Christopher Lirette refers to as his "autistic intelligence," make the detective strange to the Louisianan community he works within, and to viewers. These characteristics, plus the close, tense relationship Cohle shares with his professional partner, also make him potentially queer.

True Detective harkens back to *Dallas Buyers Club* insofar as the HBO series is able to queer Cohle via a kind of exceptionality or strangeness without ever inferring homosexuality. *True Detective* is part of the same southern gothic noir genre as *The Paperboy* but functions quite contrarily. In contrast to Daniels's film, *True Detective* rescues Cohle from the margins to reincorporate him (and with him, McConaughey's persona) back into society. This ultimately brings narrative closure, rather than opening up space for social critique. *True Detective* thus exploits the decadence of southern gothic noir, while dulling the genre's potential critical sting.

McConaughey's performance was crucial to the first season's success at balancing wide critical appeal with controversial content. His roles in films like *Dallas Buyers Club* and *The Paperboy* (which, taken together, show McConaughey as vaguely dangerous, yet anodyne) made the actor a perfect vehicle through which HBO could push into more illicit material to court audiences back from increasingly shocking basic cable shows like *Breaking Bad* (AMC, 2008–2013). However, Cohle's final confrontation, in which he defeats the murderous, "truly" Other Errol Childress, shows how imperative it is for HBO to keep its illicit material away from its movie-star lead to maintain its reputation as a quality content provider.

HBO works hard to tell viewers that it pushes the boundaries of cultural permissibility (McCabe and Akass, "Sex" 66) in which part of the pleasure in watching is exclusive access to such content. As Janet McCabe and Kim Akass argue, HBO solicits this content from industry-recognized artists like *The Soprano's* David Chase, enabling the channel to assert its courting of controversy (ex. images of pornographic sexuality and explicit violence) as a "distinctive feature of its cultural cachet, its quality brand label and (until recently) its leading market position" (63–67). As McCabe and Akass go on to note, however, HBO's efforts to acquire the most high-profile talent "reveals a continual struggle for institutional leadership and market leadership" (67). Basic cable channels like AMC have threatened HBO's dominance in recent years with edgy programming like *Mad Men* (2007–2015). If HBO wished to continue to promote its original programming as truly singular, the company needed a hook that basic cable could not easily replicate. *True Detective*'s anthology format provided one such hook.

A series that features a different cast of A-list actors and a new plot each year is logistically tricky and financially improbable for most networks and basic cable channels. An HBO series with a limited run would provide amenable working conditions for film actors, who could schedule the series in between other projects. These conditions were precisely what attracted Matthew McConaughey to *True Detective*. The actor's "dirty prettiness" was, in turn, the perfect complement to HBO's industrial strategy ("Ellen DeGeneres' 86th Oscars Opening"). McConaughey's Grecian good looks and star pedigree make the seedy pleasures of the Louisiana landscape even more alluring. The success of *Dallas Buyers Club* further assured *True Detective*'s creators that McConaughey brought a meta-textual respectability that ensured audiences knew they were not watching smut, even as the show featured all manner of debauchery.

The show's central homosocial pairing between Hart and Cohle enhances the show's taboo yet safe, meta-textual pleasure—this pairing also connects the show to its noir antecedents like *The Maltese Falcon,* rife with charged bonds between men. As Eve Sedgwick has argued, such bonds are fraught with anxiety, and are therefore often triangulated through a third party to avoid suspicion of homosexuality.[4] In the first season of *True Detective,* Cohle and Hart bicker incessantly, which creates constant, intimate friction. Both men also sleep with Hart's wife, Maggie, and communicate emotionally through her, so that she functions exactly as Sedgwick describes. She is the third party, or screen, through which the men interact and barely ward off homosexual anxieties. Sedgwick posits homosexual connections and homosocial bonds (like Hart and Cohle's) as mutually exclusive, but erotic *True Detective* fan fiction fascinatingly confuses the two.[5]

The relationship of Harrelson and McConaughey aids in the public's romanticizing of Hart and Cohle's relationship. McConaughey played Harrelson's brother in *EdTV* and reunited with him in *Surfer, Dude*. Both men have reputations as southern, offbeat bon vivants with shades of existentialism and no shortage of peccadillos. McConaughey seems like Harrelson's younger, more handsome, less controversial double. *True Detective* avoids insinuating any sexual attraction between the two partners, and Hart is heteronormative to a fault. But while the show may resist "fan-service" plotlines, it also benefits from the pleasurable repetition that keeps viewers coming back to the show's central couple. Their relationship carries the aura of the actors' public bond—equal parts brotherhood and spiritual soul mates—that continually flirts with incestuous attraction. This is not unlike the tense, suspicious bond between Jeff (Robert Mitchum) and Whit (Kirk Douglas) in the film noir, *Out of the Past*.

True Detective also continues noir's portrayal of maleness as crisis through Cohle. As Christopher Lirette observes of the opening credits:

> The superimposition of personal onto critical geography is evident in the title sequence as a ghosted image of McConaughey's character, Rust Cohle, fades into the photo of the refinery and canefield . . . The faces of people—mostly characters from the show—break apart, joining traces of maps and machinery, becoming hybrid people-in-places. In one particular image, Rust's head appears in outline, but only the area below his nose retains photographic density, the top-half of his head fading to nothing.

This opening roots Cohle and others firmly within the southern imaginary but sketches them as shadow "people-in-places." The show takes inspiration from southern writers like Eudora Welty and Flannery O'Connor, who often create emblems for racial anxiety in shattered images of whiteness like "scenes of partial bodies, cotton lint, flour dust, displaced snow, or facial masking" (Yaeger, *Dirt* xii). Cohle's ambiguous, semispectral presence foreshadows his psychological collapse and casts it in racialized and sexualized terms.

Throughout the show, Cohle seems perpetually on the verge of dissociating, as a direct consequence of interacting with abject Louisiana populations. The opening of the show implies that Cohle's continual unraveling might not be because poor white Louisianans are strange to him, but because they become more and more familiar. All of the characters in the opening—Cohle, murdered white women, and poor whites that cast into doubt the superiority of that racial category—are cast as equally ghostly inhabitants of a landscape that is as composed of memories as it is of refineries and canefields. As an outsider, Cohle does not have access to the regional knowledge that would help him make sense of this new world. His theories about the show's central crime, along with the monologues that once had an existential intelligence, become increasingly incoherent, as his control—on a knowable world, as a detective, as a man—dissolves. Each murdered woman reflects his own disempowered status back at him in a mean irony that threatens to undo the core of his being. By the end of the series, Cohle's queer out-of-placeness registers as male defect.

The Texas cowboy that McConaughey embodies is no longer a stable paragon of American masculinity (if it ever was) in *True Detective*. He is, rather, a noir archetype. As in many neo-noirs, *True Detective* puts its protagonists on a moral mission then undercuts their capacity to handle such missions, showing the ineffectuality of making moral decisions in an irrevocably fractured world. Cohle proves himself no match for the southern landscape, just as film noir protagonists are often left with a final incomprehension of the urban underworld they inhabit. But such heroes are rarely recuperated in that genre: their exclusion marks them as unfit for civilized society and signifies their imbrication in the underworld. Indeed, the detective's exile prompts reflection on society's purported liberalism (as in *The Paperboy*). The integration of a noir detective back into the social fold would require a spectacular Other to exclude instead, and *True Detective* provides that figure in the Childresses, whose total strangeness draws our attention away from Cohle's and dwarfs it by comparison.

The season finale situates Errol Childress in the isolated, dilapidated plantation house he shares with his sister/lover. After glimpsing *North by Northwest* on television, Errol speaks in a long monologue much like Cohle does. Just as Cohle discusses time as a "flat circle," in an earlier episode, Errol sees himself as part of "the disk and the loop." Just as Cohle feels himself nearly solving the mystery in the final episode's flashbacks, Errol remarks, "I am near the final stage. Some mornings, I can see the infernal plane" (*True Detective*). In this episode, Errol speaks in an accent mixed between classic American actor and British aristocrat. This affectation satirizes the Childress's classed, media-saturated roots: his ancestors who modeled plantation society on the British aristocracy as well as the American films on which he has modeled his faux pretension. His sister Betty appears mentally challenged, and childishly asks Errol to "make flowers" on her (*True Detective*). Errol agrees, but only if she narrates an earlier molestation at the hands of their grandfather while he pleasures her. Her request that Errol "make flowers" on her suggests their sex is primarily non-procreative, symptomatic of the entropic ecosystem they inhabit. Their environment presents a panoply of sexualized southern gothicism, so much so as to be a stereotype, an excessive performance of southernness that takes the amorphous crises that once swirled around Cohle and places them definitively onto another body, Errol Childress. The logic that Carol Clover posits about the scapegoating function of the redneck in cinema holds inexorably true for the Childresses:

> The great success of the redneck in that [scapegoating] capacity suggests that anxieties . . . have become projected onto a safe target—safe not only because it is nominally white, but because it is infinitely displaceable onto someone from the deeper South or the higher mountains or the further desert. (135)

Although *True Detective* is set in the 1990s–2000s, the series mirrors the depiction of "white trash" in 1970s horror films like *Deliverance* and serves the same basic function, to demarcate assimilable southerners, like Cohle, from true white detritus.

Cohle does not end the show as a paragon of middle-class respectability, but as he and his detective partner stand in between a hospital and an expansive night sky, Hart proclaims (in a decidedly un-noirish fashion) that "maybe the light [meaning the good in the world] is winning." The two men turn their backs on the dark, inky sky and walk toward the fluorescent hospital, symbolic of an ordered world in which anxieties and problems are diagnosed, contained, and finally resolved. The show may intend this as an ironic ending, but the manner of Cohle's survival casts this theory into doubt. In other words, the content of the rest of season 1 threatens but ultimately affirms whiteness and maleness through Cohle—an ambivalent or ironic ending would not logically flow from such an affirmation.

If *True Detective's* ending differs from noir, it faces a similar narrative problem that southern gothic texts face. By regularly informing Cohle and the audience that Louisiana is utterly unlike most viewers' everyday lives and can only be interpreted from the inside, *True Detective* operates analogously to southern gothics like Erskine Caldwell's *Tobacco Road*. As described by Leigh Anne Duck, *Tobacco Road* allows its audience to "avoid the sort of self-reflection otherwise encouraged by the grotesque, which implicates the viewer in shameful or exciting frisson . . . Readers and viewers who might otherwise feel uncomfortable about seeking out sensational entertainments could assert that they valued these representations for their social realism" (Duck, *Nation's* 93). *True Detective* shares this "realist" pull for many national/northern audiences, and is able to further cultivate artistic refinement through its media platform on pay cable. HBO has infamously separated itself from network television in its advertising and through subscription fees that often box out lower-income audiences. In effect, *True Detective's* position on HBO sanctions viewers to consume "sensational entertainments" while proclaiming discerning aesthetic tastes. McConaughey's Oscar-winning persona must be preserved for that move to work. If *The Paperboy* succeeds as a southern gothic social critique, it is because it is willing to encourage viewers to suture themselves to McConaughey and then to summarily interrogate his persona. *True Detective* does not commit to interrogation in the same way; this does not make it a less compelling text, but rather connects it back to its literary antecedents and forward to TV's latest golden era.

* * *

THE MARKET AND MCCONAUGHEY

The mainstreamed pleasures evident in *True Detective*, rather than the radical potential of southern gothic noir as epitomized in *The Paperboy*, define the rest of the McConaissance. Films like *Dallas Buyers Club* and *Magic Mike* center on vaguely queer protagonists, thereby making viewers feel as though they are tolerant (and rewarding them with exotic diversion), without confronting them with the more fundamental, radical, and long-term implications of difference. By only selectively engaging the realities of LGBTQ+ life, and treating the South as an exoticized fantasy space that still fits within the boundaries of social realism, the films of the McConaissance hold a classic double value: they provide nothing radical enough to bother mainstream audiences and nothing offensive enough to trigger critics to question the deeper meaning of McConaughey's films. As his laid-back persona promises us, there is no "deeper" there. His persona encourages a contented viewing mode just as his Texas drawl soothes all manner of women, men, children, and animals within his films.

In interviews, McConaughey reveals the work required to shape that laid-back persona, repeatedly stressing that he took on his recent roles in an effort to re-brand, or as he calls it, to "un-brand" himself. Evidence of McConaughey's desire to shape his paradoxical unbrand for public consumption further abounds in his Oscar speech, which ended with his trademark "Allright, allright, allright" and his less well known "just keep livin'." In fact, McConaughey's acceptance speech at every major award show in 2013–2014 began or ended with one of those phrases, and sometimes used both. One need only look to his self-referential Lincoln car commercials that feature an amalgam of Cohle/McConaughey to see the dividends of the actor's unbranding, for the actor and for capitalist enterprises who reap new market segments using the actor's appeal with young liberal and hipster audiences.

The every-queer-man McConaissance has left viewers with a false sense of representational security. As illustrated by *True Detective*'s conditional embrace of Rust Cohle, the privileges that come with this new era of inclusion are precarious and based on ever-narrowing parameters of whiteness, class belonging, and heteronormativity. While McConaughey's films signal the degree to which LGBTQ+ populations have become representable in the last thirty years, the moment is not the counterhegemonic victory many hope for. Rather, the ease with which McConaughey seized upon LGBTQ+ identity, southernness, and the genre of noir as tools for his personal reinvention suggests how devastatingly elastic hegemony can be.

NOTES

1. This essay examines works that combine film noir and southern gothic elements in a hybrid genre to which I will refer as "southern gothic noir."

2 The film was based on the life of Ron Woodroof, who ran Dallas's "buyers' club." Upon the film's release, multiple sources including Woodroof's ex-wife and primary care physician asserted he was bisexual or gay. See "King of Clubs" by Arnold Wayne Jones, which appeared in the November 8, 2013, print edition of the *Dallas Voice* (also accessible online at http://www.dallasvoice.com/king -clubs-10161057.html).

3. See Lisa Duggan, *Sex Wars: Sexual Dissent and Political Culture* (2006); Lisa Duggan, *The Twilight of Equality: Neoliberalism, Cultural Politics, and the Attack on Democracy* (2004); Michael Warner, *The Trouble with Normal: Sex, Politics, and the Ethics of Queer Life* (1999).

4. See Eve Kosofsky Sedgwick, *Between Men: English Literature and Male Homosocial Desire* (1985).

5. See fan fiction, including "Love Poems for Men Who Aren't in Love," which appeared on *FanFiction.net* on May 24, 2015 (https://www.fanfiction.net/tv/True-Detective/) and entries from *ArchiveofOurOwn.org*, also on May 24, 2015 (http://archiveofourown.org/tags/True%20Detective /works).

DETECTING HOLLYWOOD SOUTH

In the Electric Mist *and the Changing Relations of Louisiana Noir*

LEIGH ANNE DUCK

The sixth novel in James Lee Burke's series featuring Cajun detective Dave Robicheaux, *In the Electric Mist with Confederate Dead* (1993), proclaims, in its title, its concern with revenants from southern US history. Its representation of the local film industry, however, proves prescient. Published immediately after Louisiana began providing tax credits for film production (Louisiana Act 894), Burke's plot concerns mobsters who are laundering funds through production of a Civil War movie. Dave suspects their presence is linked to the murders of several young women, but local elites resist his investigation, accepting the Mafia leader's claim that he is now in the "entertainment business" and stands to "leave around ten million dollars in Lafayette and Iberia Parish" (28, 32).

Burke's fictional gangster thus echoes the Louisiana Motion Picture Incentive Act (1990), which held that the film "industry brings with it a much-needed infusion of capital into areas of the state which may be economically depressed." By 2009—when Bertrand Tavernier's film adaptation of *Mist* was released—the state had enacted an array of intricately structured tax credits to compete with other states, cities, and even countries (Loren C. Scott 1–2). As oversight of these programs initially proved difficult, leading to widespread fraud (Scott; Sayre), onlookers likened the industry's financial shenanigans to a "film noir thriller" or "whodunnit" (Grimm; Scott loc. 138).

Burke's foresight points to how Hollywood's "runaway" production—in which major studios seek to exploit the financial advantages offered by spaces outside California, who likewise seek to expand their economic base—aligns with prominent themes in noir narrative, a contested category that is nonetheless widely agreed to probe changing geographic relations (Sobchack 129–37; Naremore 2, 169; Dimendberg). "Classic" film noir of the 1940s and '50s subtly revealed the reorganization of urban space—the growth of white suburbs and concentration of African Americans in segregated neighborhoods with increasingly limited access to capital and social services (Rabinowitz, *Black & White* 1–5, 8; Sobchack; Murphet 25–31.) Burke's novels consider a later stage of restructuring, as the manufacturing jobs that had moved to the South after WWII—lured by extensive subsidies, tax exemptions, and nonunionized labor—began moving abroad in the 1970s and '80s (James C. Cobb). As unsettled characters wander through rural and urban space, government efforts to boost economic growth render residents and ecosystems more vulnerable to exploitation. Dave's career began in New Orleans, where he bemoaned how the city tolerated the criminal activities that lured tourists. Worried that elites in "the provincial Cajun world in which [he] had grown up" are similarly "willing to sell it down the drain," he compares film production to the trade in endangered animals or the ecological depredations of oil companies (101, 93–95).

But while the film industry certainly benefits from what Cobb refers to as "the selling of the South," its products occasionally turn a critical lens on their enterprise. Many cinematic representations of Louisiana have buttressed local efforts to commodify the state's spaces and cultures, particularly for tourism: the romanticized plantation, after all, long predominated in films of the state (Cox 86). But some films, particularly in the noir tradition, have sought out settings resistant to cinematic conventions, or have examined the impacts of such clichés. For this reason, this genre's history—including the cinematic adaptation of Burke's novel—provides a useful conduit for exploring how, during Louisiana's long quest to become "Hollywood South," film production and aesthetics have interacted with state and society. *Dans la brume électrique* (2009)—the director's cut of *In the Electric Mist*—was shot in Louisiana not for a tax credit but because of Tavernier's passion for Burke's oeuvre and his convictions regarding the importance of *mise-en-scéne*; it seeks to contend, in the director's words, with a social "reality in which Hollywood is persistently uninterested" (Tavernier 260; see Prédal). Emerging at a time when Louisiana's spaces could seem fully commodified, *Brume* works to reclaim classic noir's sense of dynamic, inhabited space and also challenges conventional cinematic images of the region's history, seeking new ways to explore the relationship between local past and present.

FROM "LOCATIVE" TO NEO(LIBERAL)-NOIR

As Kevin Fox Gotham explains, silent films were important in promoting New Orleans's "destination image," a "set of visual symbols and descriptors that provide visitors and residents with a transparent and recognizable local iconography for interpreting . . . cultural attractions" (315, 308). This pattern continued during Hollywood's soundstage era, as the idealized version of antebellum life prominent in New Orleans' tourism marketing was supported by the major studios' abundant plantation romances, even if they were shot elsewhere (Cox

95–96, 155–62). By 1950, however, audiences were better travelled and accustomed to global newsreel footage; they found artificial settings less compelling than what R. Barton Palmer calls "locative realism," images that "reference . . . particular cultural and geographic" sites in the world (51–59, 48–49). Meanwhile, studios were beginning to seek savings by shooting in countries with favorable exchange rates and tax structures, inexpensive access to infrastructure, and limited enforcement of union rules or wages (Shandley 9–19), an attribute they would soon realize applied to many states outside California. As production on location expanded, the New Orleans *Times-Picayune* expressed frustration over "Hollywood . . . masquerading as New Orleans" and urged "Hollywoodians" instead to "appreciate the extraordinarily photogenic and historical locale we have here" ("New Orleans' 'Forbidden Past'"; "Filming New Orleans Scenes").

This interest in the site of production may have been intensified by Elia Kazan's *Panic in the Streets* (1950)—the most prominent "classic" noir shot in New Orleans—which attracted extensive attention for being shot entirely on location and including local residents in the cast and crew. The *Times-Picayune* reported vigorously on the hiring of local extras: "111 policemen, taxi drivers, bond salesmen, teachers, housewives, and persons representing a general cross section of New Orleans" ("Filming"). Kazan, meanwhile, emphasized how spaces distanced from Hollywood could constitute an aesthetic resource: influenced in part by Italian neorealism, he "found it most exhilarating to go into police headquarters, a union hiring hall, a cheap cafe or an old hotel, and weave the characters and general atmosphere and architecture into the script" (Brooks; "Elia Kazan"). Kazan's "locative realism" included serious limitations: where neorealists opposed Classical Hollywood's emphasis on "spectacular" plots (Zavattini 66), *Panic*'s protagonists have only 48 hours to prevent a global pandemic. More important in relation to local politics is the film's absolute neglect of African Americans' struggle for full citizenship, which had for years centered around the police department: the New Orleans Police Department finally appointed its first African American officers in 1950 (Moore 24–35). *Panic*, in contrast, barely recognizes the city's racial diversity aside from the recurrent presence of jazz, whose performers are also occluded: only one anonymous black singer appears as the camera tracks past a night club entrance in the opening scene, continuing until it finds a community made up largely of European immigrants, who will, along with law enforcement, comprise the film's plot. But as several critics have argued, such near-erasure of African Americans is typical of classic noir: unwilling to explore racial conflict directly, these films register contested boundaries through attempting to racialize moral difference (via visual or metaphoric darkness) or conveying white characters' sense that their status is precarious (Lott; Murphet; Oliver and Trigo 1–26). *Panic* mobilizes both strategies, naming the pernicious white villain "Blackie" (Jack Palance) but also depicting anxious associations across racial and ethnic lines.

Nonetheless, in the cinematic history of a state often associated with exotic destinations—whether an historic Creole city or the idyllic Cajun countryside—*Panic*'s location shooting demonstrated how New Orleans could be depicted as participating in, rather than isolated from, broader social patterns. This theme of connection is central to the plot, which concerns plague spread by a stowaway from the port, but is also embedded in the opening title sequence, as the camera tracks down Bourbon Street at night, capturing diverse geographic and cultural references in neon lights: "Dixie Beer," "Moulin Rouge," "Oriental Laundry," "Gunga Den," and more. The film's interiors reflect concerns present throughout film noir, as public spaces exemplify not touristic escapes but circumstances of class and labor; the film contrasts, for example, the spacious cafe where government employees have coffee with the tightly crowded bar near the assembly hall where ship workers seek limited jobs. Here the famously opulent homes of the Garden District stand out less for their architecture than their incorporation in a plot concerning anxious masculinity, and *Panic* provides especially vivid images of vacant territory along the dock and railroad or surrounding warehouses and tenements—areas suggesting transition and uncertainty (Solà-Morales Rubió; Gustafson). Through such uses of mundane (yet often elegantly framed and shadowed) space, the film both captures and produces a cartography radically different from that seen in the city's sentimental marketing. Instead, as the characters and camera move through diversely developed, classed, and gendered spaces, they evoke the experience of navigating dynamic urban neighborhoods, as well as the haptic encounters—vertiginous, excited, claustrophobic, charmed, or otherwise—enabled by the city's environs and its position in global transport networks (see Bruno 27–30).

Unfortunately Kazan's locative aesthetics did not persuade other filmmakers to depart from highlighting "destination images" in representations of New Orleans, and while changing production practices would soon confirm *Panic*'s sense of local and national interpenetration, these new relations served to circulate images celebrating white supremacy and to undercut labor unions (Dawson). Expanded location shooting, particularly in plantation districts, was recognized as a boon for tourism, which would constitute Louisiana's largest industry by the end of the 1950s (Bernard 48; "Old Homes"; "Travel the River Road"). Meanwhile, the State Department of Commerce and Industry began to argue that location production could "publicize Louisiana and help business interests in the state" ("Cotton Patch"). Though plantation films became more gothic and brutal than romantic, they maintained a devotion to spectacle, which was shared by the proliferation of independent B movies shot in the region. Accordingly, by the time the neo-noir cycle emerged in the 1970s, Louisiana's landscapes were thoroughly associated with conventional images, mobilized to promote both tourism and film genres.

Neo-noirs stand out, however, for the way in which they encode this process of commodifying local space and culture. Stuart Rosenberg's *The Drowning Pool* (1975), for example, begins with California investigator Lew Harper (Paul Newman) renting a car at the New Orleans airport. The film then repeatedly situates this vehicle—and sometimes just its window—against distinctively southern landscapes, including the Lake Pontchartrain Causeway and a plantation estate. Such strategies, in Amy Lynn Corbin's model, signal a touristic approach to cinematic space, providing the spectator a "protected sensibility" in relation to cultural "otherness" (8), which is generated, in this case, by the Louisiana characters' clichéd forms of excess. In contrast, the camera in Alan Parker's horror noir *Angel Heart* (1987) is far more "nomadic" than "touristic," serving more to "disorient and displace" the spectator (Corbin 10). While private investigator Harry Angel (Mickey Rourke) also describes himself as an "outsider" in Louisiana, he is prone to repeated hallucinations and often random wanderings, signified through abrupt cuts; ultimately, he discovers he is a serial killer, an amnesiac under Satan's sway. In this way, the film seems almost to deconstruct cinematic norms for noir masculinity (Cooper) and potentially even plantation space. Angel's homicidal travels through the "cotton fields and migrant shacks and ghettoes of this nation" reflect, as James Baldwin argued of William Friedkin's *The Exorcist* (1973), historic quests for property and power. But such interpretative possibilities are occluded by the film's far more vivid and stereotypical scenes of "Black religion as savage and powerful" (Means Coleman 6), a trade in exotic images that the film attributes to black New Orleanians as well. When Angel enters "Mammy Carter's Herb Store," the proprietor insists on the establishment's authenticity: though "everybody uses the name" Carter—"like Howard Johnson"—"this is the real place."

Such winks at a thriving tourist industry reflect an entrepreneurial approach to space that was shared by state bureaucracies. By 1983, the *Times-Picayune* reported, "Every state has a film commission putting the hard sell on movie and television producers" (Arnold). This rise in so-called "runaway" production reflected two central elements in late capitalism: the greater flexibility of studios' capital, and a change in the very concept of government's purpose, now oriented toward supporting private enterprise (Harvey 121–97). Regulatory structures near Hollywood had developed to negotiate relations between this powerful industry and other aspects of public life—requiring studios to pay fees, for example, when filming in civic spaces—but most other states began to develop film commissions in the 1970s as part of their shift to "entrepreneurial" governance (Edgerton). Film commissions marketed state landscapes and infrastructures in an effort to stimulate the economy: a 1984 Louisiana report, for instance, argued that film and television producers had spent $60 million in the state on cast, crew, housing, and other support (Pope). But this courtship also involved negotiating prices and procedures with local merchants and providing free public assistance—serving the industry in ways that could cause conflict with local citizens (Edgerton 42).

In terms of cinematic space, then, the most interesting neo-noirs are those that integrate New Orleans's entanglement with entertainment industries thoroughly into plot, *mise-en-scène*, and performance, enabling them to imagine existence in a city where livelihoods depended on performing roles expected by tourists. Both Richard Tuggle's *Tightrope* (1984) and Jim McBride's *The Big Easy* (1987) focus on cops who have lived in New Orleans all or most of their lives, but the plots largely play out in the sex clubs and parades of the French Quarter, popular music clubs and restaurants, and even—in both cases—warehouses for Mardi Gras floats. Historian J. Mark Souther argues that, as New Orleans began to rely ever more heavily on tourism, it became "a place obsessed with maintaining a facade . . . in essence, a city on parade" (187), and this question of how to traverse a society suffused with projections of desire and manipulative and/or mandated performances resonates with noir's long-standing interest in gender and sexuality. Where classic noir foregrounded the instability of these norms following World War II, neo-noir often seemed, in B. Ruby Rich's terms, "determined to reinstate masculinity" (10). That project proves complex, however, in an economy demanding constant spectacle.

This focus on performance is so pronounced in Jim McBride's *The Big Easy* (1987) as to prove potentially confounding: mixing noir styles and plot points into a romantic comedy, its "depiction of 'local custom,'" as the *Times-Picayune* reviewer cheerily reported, is "more than a mite exaggerated" (Baron). But McBride began his career with the experimental *David Holzman's Diary* (1967) and went on to adapt Jean-Luc Godard's *À bout de souffle* (1960) to a US context (*Breathless*, 1983); he had long been interested in cinema's influence on human experience and behavior. Revising a narrative originally set in Chicago, he distorts the map of New Orleans: for example, the protagonist's ancestral home is set, as one reporter scoffed, in "some unspecified Cajun territory apparently a quick cab ride away from" the city center (Dodds). And yet the transformation of Louisiana's spaces into more readily consumable images—a logic common to tourism and Hollywood—constitutes the central logic of this film, as characters, too, seem always to be performing for absent spectators. When protagonist Remy McSwain (Dennis Quaid) first appears, viewers see a close-up of the back of his head as we hear the sounds of police photographing a crime scene; he suddenly turns and poses with a smile that, in this aural context, evokes a red-carpet display. Shortly thereafter, as the captain (Ned Beatty) reprimands officers Dodge and Desoto (Ebbe Roe Smith and John Goodman), he complains that they have been performing the "Dodge and Desoto follies"; dramatically threatening to shoot them, he determines that they are "too much fun at Mardi Gras," as they begin to dance.

By the film's conclusion, these performative styles will have been linked to corruption, with Remy engaging in graft and cover-ups while Dodge, Desoto, and the captain murderously seek to take over the local heroin trade. The leaders of the racially segregated drug cartels are similarly flamboyant, employing different but conventional roles: the Mafia don as an elderly gentleman and the African American "Daddy Mention," whose moniker—like his associated storefront for "spiritual products"—implies uncanny power. The citizenry is overtly powerless: in confrontations with the police, African Americans in particular seek recourse through embodying cinematic stereotypes of tough silence or ostentatious acquiescence. Fittingly, the one avid investigator into police corruption—newly arrived assistant district attorney Anne Osborne (Ellen Barkin)—cannot conform to the styles associated with her profession, wearing comically oversized clothes and intermittently breaking into giggles while insisting on the need to prioritize work. Though this insistence on her awkwardness could align with Reagan-era antifeminism, it appears appreciative in this diegetic context, as Anne, however ungainly, finds thorough satisfaction in both pursuit of corruption and enjoyment of sex. Remy, in contrast, seems unsure how to manage his body upon comprehending the depth of the system's criminality; his voice becomes hollow and his posture unsteady. In an abrupt coda—immediately after they survive an explosion—Remy and Anne appear in wedding apparel; he carries her into his apartment, and they dance all alone with the closing credits, as if they require a private space in which to perform normative heterosexuality, ostensibly free from corrupting connotations.

Such a fantasy is not available in *Tightrope*, in which the far more nuanced protagonist is nonetheless deeply affected by pervasive masquerade. For recently separated detective Wes Block (Clint Eastwood), the public entertainments of a riverboat bar and the French Quarter provide opportunities to engage with love interest Beryl Thibodeaux (Geneviève Bujold) and with his daughters, but these scenes nonetheless involve tension. He and Beryl, a feminist anti-rape activist, explicitly recognize the potential for mutual caricature in their relationship, but more acutely, the innumerable performances of the Quarter—though they fill his daughters with innocent delight—emanate danger. Here the camera, which has repeatedly turned to reveal a masked serial killer, emphasizes the impossibility of ascertaining identities amid a churning, costumed crowd. As Wes pursues and is shadowed by his antagonist—traversing brothels, strip clubs, tattoo parlors, and sex clubs—his own attraction to sexual toys and performances becomes clear, and he fears these desires align him with the murderer. In this context Eastwood's famous face also functions as a mask: while its stillness echoes, as Christine Holmlund argues, his "tough macho" roles, his expression, in repeated close-ups, suggests sexual uncertainty and insecurity (32–33). Like *The Big Easy,* *Tightrope* reverts to a heteronormative ending with outrageous suddenness (34), with the implication that Beryl will accept the pleasures and burdens of helping Wes adapt to his lost belief in patriarchal masculinity. Earlier in the film, when he admiringly notes her commitment to helping women, she corrects him: "Oh, men too!"

Each of these films quite conventionally requires a "good woman" to solve problems created by a marketplace that demands overwhelmingly or confusingly gendered performances. Further, as Helmlund argues of *Tightrope*—wherein the figures of murdered women "are displayed for our consumption" (38)—these neo-noirs maintain Hollywood's long-standing "patriarchal vision" (Mulvey). Thoroughly bourgeois, they neglect or caricature racial conflict. Still, they do seek, as Jyotsna Kapur and Keith B. Wagner argue of contemporary cinema more broadly, "an understanding of, if not identification with, the conditions that produce [late capitalist] subjectivities" (4). Submerged in networks of profit-oriented performance, these protagonists devote extensive energy to managing self and image in a manner that unsettles even the desire for social ties (McNay). Whether their efforts to achieve socially stipulated norms prove broad, polished, and brittle or restrictive, anxious, and fractured, they only become capable of meaningful interaction when on the verge of breakdown. And their inability to comprehend this discomfort parallels the encompassing film's approach to social dynamics: in a *mise-en-scène* where culture is so thoroughly packaged for touristic enjoyment, social dynamics appear timeless, inaccessible to interrogation or change. Tavernier would go on to disrupt this relentless presentness—characteristic of postmodernism's cinema of surfaces (Jameson, *Postmodernism* 17)—through crystalline narration.

JUKE TIME IN CRYSTALLINE NOIR

In contrast to neo-noirs, which foregrounded dependence on the "destination image," *Brume* returns to the mundane spaces of classic noir. Here, for example, Louisiana's wetlands—clichéd signifiers of an exotic culture—are both interrogated and tethered to everyday conversation and labor. Reasons for these differences are undoubtedly multiple, including the source novel's avowedly "sociological" approach to crime (Golsan 167), the director's longstanding appreciation for noir produced in the United States (Vanderschelden), and perhaps even the fact that, by the time this project began, "Hollywood South" had been fully incorporated into law, industrial practice, and public discussion. Any contemporary film seeking to stage an encounter between capitalism and the polity critically—a prominent, albeit ambivalent, tendency within classic noir (MacCannell)—might thus incorporate cinema's own "internalized relation with" what Gilles Deleuze calls film's "most intimate and most indispensable enemy": money. This "conspiracy" necessary for "industrial art" had, after all, become openly imbricated with the state (77).

Brume presents aspects of this relationship between cinema, capital, and polity overtly: in addition to the investors' relentlessly iterated support of the industry, the plot incorporates a director, Michael Goldman (John Sayles), who has no concern for the needs of the community, not even identification of a murderer. His art, he explains, depends on lowering costs, and thus resisting intrusions by the police, but despite his proudly auteurist stance, his film seems likely to distort local history: its title, *White Doves,* suggests Hollywood's familiar pattern of sentimentalizing the Civil War and eliding the slavery for which the Confederacy fought. *Brume* also nods to the industry's rhetoric and variable practice of supporting local communities (Mayer 13, 70–71), as Dave's wife Bootsie (Mary Steenburgen) persuades lead actor Elrod (Peter Sarsgaard) to autograph posters for the Hurricane Rural Recovery Fund to sell. But the most substantial impact of this fictional film on *Brume*'s plot is generated via the alcoholic Elrod's wanderings, which uncover not only the decades-old skeleton of a lynching victim, Dewitt Prejean, in a neighboring parish—remains of a crime Dave witnessed as a young man, when he could not persuade local government to investigate—but also a troop of Confederate soldiers existing, uncannily, on the fringes of New Iberia.

Through contraposing these histories, Tavernier sharply diverges from cli-chéd representations of the local past and implies a need for cinema to contest its own history. For Dave (Tommy Lee Jones), vision is trained to overlook fresh information, a problem he must overcome in investigating cases: "If you don't look, you never will see, [but] if you look a little less, you might see a hell of a lot more." Viewers may recognize this challenge as inherently cinematic, par-ticularly if familiar with Deleuze's philosophy, which holds that cinema's abil-ity to disrupt routine visual responses—though often impeded by its financial interests—constitutes its greatest potential: "All the powers have an interest in hiding images from us . . . in hiding something in the image. On the other hand . . . the image constantly attempts to break through the cliché" (21).

Brume unsettles the ontology of its images in multiple ways: through its film within a film, the hallucinogen that someone slips into Dave's drink at an industry party, Dave's ongoing memories and dreams, and the Confederates' untimeliness. Deleuze describes this method as "crystalline description," in which an "actual image" is presented alongside its "virtual . . . double," an imagined or mediated image diegetically distanced—but visually indistinguishable—from the film's "real" or "present" (77, 68–69). This indeterminacy casts doubt not only on the referent of the image on-screen but also its position in time, such that "the pres-ent begins to float, struck with uncertainty" (116). Examining a space in which cinema (and other aspects of culture) have predominantly sought to elevate the history of slaveholders and minimize recognition of racial oppression, these im-ages encourage viewers to reconsider the relationship between present and past.

The need for such chronological disruption, particularly for white southern-ers, is explicit from *Brume*'s overture. When Tavernier, frustrated at the conven-tionality of the screenwriters' proposed opening, wrote Burke to request an in-troduction to the protagonist's "mental universe," the novelist responded "hours later" with a monologue challenging the differences between primitive and civ-ilized, dead and living (Tavernier 28):

> In the ancient world, people placed heavy stones on the graves of their dead, so their souls would not wander and afflict the living. I always thought this was sim-ply the practice of superstitious and primitive people, but I was about to learn that the dead can hover on the edge of our vision with the density and luminosity of mist, and their claim on the earth can be as legitimate and tenacious as our own.

Both the narration and the scene's cinematic qualities—its haunting opening chords, camera movements embedding the police in deep forest and mist, and

Dave's quick, anxious sign of the cross as he observes a murdered body—suggest a timeless scene, but they also introduce a specific event that will force Dave to confront fundamental aspects of local history. Abruptly after interviewing local workers about the victim, Cherry Leblanc—whose father abandoned the family "after he was accused of molesting a black child" who lived nearby—Dave narrates his recurring nightmare of "a white wolf who lived in a skeletal black tree on an infinite white landscape" and "would drop to the ground and eat her young, one by one," connoting a society in which racial oppression has metastasized into cruelty toward youth of all races. And yet he develops a meaningful friendship with one of the revenants: General John Bell Hood (Levon Helm), who, "having served venal men in a vile enterprise," is eager to help Dave sort through his feelings about patterns of corruption and abuse in the Vietnam War (where Dave was a lieutenant) and in contemporary Louisiana. These encounters with the past elicit contrasting affects—shrinking from inexplicable cruelty and connecting to a sympathetic patriarch—that each involve cinematic icons, but crystalline narration allows new relations to develop between traditionally static images.

As Dave narrates his dream of the infanticidal wolf, the screen presents a familiar image of the Deep South—shadowed cypress rising from bright water. These lovely landscapes, far from facilitating fresh consideration of social dynamics, lead instead back into film history, a problem Tavernier had already contemplated in his documentary *Mississippi Blues* (1983). For Dave, this image is stupefying: as the scene returns to him sitting in his car, the camera circles him so quickly as to render his face a blur, and Dave wonders how much he really wants to learn regarding Cherry's killer. But these reflections are disrupted as Elrod's car careens past, and their ensuing visit to Prejean's bones yields more facets to the crystal-image of the swamp. As their boat speeds through the wetlands, the contemporary landscape is connected to mundane aspects of investigative work, and as Dave examines the skeleton, the image vacillates between present and past: white men talking on wet ground, and a chained black man falling in shallow water. While the latter image clearly connects to Dave's nightmare of vicious whiteness, that circuit alone would render the film "too nostalgic about [southern] traumas," in Patricia Yaeger's words, isolating any revelation to Dave's consciousness (*Dirt* 61). Instead, this recurring recollection joins with the film's other images of wetlands to evoke, for viewers, a space both historic and continuing, traumatic and banal.

Meanwhile, the Confederate revenants provide a means to mediate Dave's encounter with regional history in a way cinema rarely seeks—both conscious of the desire of some viewers for heroes and attuned to the war's profound ethical stakes. Dave initially attributes Elrod's vision of ghostly Confederates to the production of *White Doves*, asking, "Aren't y'all making a movie about the War between the States?" Elrod's response—"You know that's not what it is"—ambiguously confronts Dave's skepticism that the dead can manifest to the living and/or his euphemism for the Civil War, which occludes the South's insurrection against the union of which it was part. Either interpretation suggests Dave's unwillingness to take his own perceptions seriously: though viewers might be unaware, ghostly figures regularly appear in Burke's Robicheaux series (Gaitely), and we soon learn that Dave has preserved a Confederate pistol found by his father. But the production of *White Doves* leads Dave to contemplate a perception he might otherwise have dismissed: neither viewers nor Dave can be certain whether the uniformed figure he sees in the distance when speaking with Goldman constitutes an actor preparing for a shot or an uncanny figure from the past. Dave next encounters this revenant after being dosed with LSD, but the image suggests a more cinematic intervention: as Dave walks among scenes of wounded soldiers illuminated dimly by torchlight and surrounded by deep shadow and mist, differences in lighting fracture the screen as if distinct eras are being conjoined through special effects. Though Hood will later appear to Dave in his own milieu, this opening shot suggests that their meetings depend on a specifically cinematic form of time, where past and present can interrogate each other.

As Dave confronts his ambivalence toward regional history through these multifaceted encounters with the past, he becomes so unsettled that he seems to observe his body from outside: after attacking some mobsters as they are eating brunch, he tells Bootsie, "It was like a drunk dream." The film suggests that the images destabilizing him were not so much repressed as detached from his daily life; as these distinct "sheets of past," in Deleuze's formulation, begin to mingle with experiences in the present (99), Dave can consider their connections. The need for such inquiry is underscored by the plot, as Dave almost overlooks one of the perpetrators in Prejean's and Cherry's murders because he is seeking a singular category of person for each crime. Instead, Murphy Doucet (Bernard Hocke)—working as a parish cop, a state trooper, and private security (including for the mob)—has proceeded from lynching to serial murder across the state. A petite white man unassuming in appearance—attributes Tavernier sought for "dramatic and moral" purposes (83)—Doucet comprises both the perfectly itinerant neoliberal subject and an embodiment of long-standing racism and misogyny, an object lesson in the need to think across periods and forms of hate crimes.

Such investigation, however, exceeds individual thought: for Dave to understand the circumstances of Prejean's murder, he needs knowledge contained in the African American community. And while *Brume* posits cinema as a medium that can illuminate circuits connecting past and present, imagination and actuality, its approach to race is instead to highlight recalcitrant boundaries. To do so, it repurposes a spatial logic from classic noir, in which, as Sobchack argues, the "bars, hotel rooms, and roadside cafes" constitute zones of alienation, where transient characters struggle to hide their "shady" pasts and to imagine a future (159, 131–32, 139, 159–67). In contrast, for the middle-class protagonists in New Orleans neo-noirs, clubs are spaces for leisure and performative entertainments: these qualities represent the city's material realities in an indirect way—observing but not analyzing a tourist economy. *Brume*'s juke joints evoke social relations more directly: though Dave is happily married with a child and home, these spaces constitute concrete reminders of his former alcoholism and sites in which to interview bartenders, cleaning staff, musicians, and prostitutes. They also encode—along with their distinct regional name—a history of race relations: political separation and hierarchy, economic exploitation, and occasional ambivalent cultural exchange. Thus, where the viewers of classic noir see how its lounge patrons struggle with intimacy due to their transient relationships to time and space, the social boundaries of the juke are racially grounded. Questioning a cleaning woman (played by Adella Gautier) at a club where Cherry worked, Dave maintains physical distance as if to emphasize his lack of ill intent, but when he probes too assertively, she reminds him, from across the grill she is scrubbing, that the young white girl was not likely "to give the name of a rich white man to an old black woman."

These divisions are articulated most richly in Dave's interactions with Sam "Hogman" Patin (bluesman Buddy Guy), whose talent takes him to a range of performance scenes but whose past includes seventeen years at the notorious Angola state penitentiary, where he was regularly tortured. Dave provides this information through narration—noting, "I liked Hogman"—but Hogman's first words announce that the parameters of their conversation are shaped by this history: "I don't like to have nothing to do with white folks' business." While he is willing to talk about Cherry, whom he mourns, he speaks of Prejean only elliptically, first using metaphors and then insisting, "The past is past." This dynamic continues through multiple scenes, but Dave is also culpable: in one instance, Dave's voice-over—complaining about Hogman's "evasive[ness]," even as he is still visibly speaking—precludes the possibility of learning from him. Late in the film, after one of Dave's colleagues has been murdered, Hogman calls him out of compassion to offer advice, but when Dave asks for a name, Hogman reminds him, "This is still the state of Louisiana." While they share the quality Sobchack finds in protagonists of classic noir, who cannot "imagine being at home in history" (166), they experience it differently. Dave's relation to the past is cushioned by his socioeconomic status and even his friendship, however constituted, with a local historic hero, while Hogman remains poor and vulnerable to racist violence.

Lest viewers forget that, Dave himself is seen brutally beating a black man who lures young white women into prostitution in a New Orleans bus depot—a stark shift in tone for a protagonist who, through much of the film, seems conventionally sympathetic. Attacking Adonis Brown (Tony Molina, Jr.) from behind, flinging his body from wall to wall, and never identifying himself, Dave showcases his dominion as a white cop, proudly proclaiming that he will kill Adonis if he doesn't "find an honest line of work." But in this shot/reverse shot sequence, the camera lingers on the palpably pained and frightened Adonis, who asks helplessly, "Why you doing this to me, man?" This scene echoes Tavernier's first extensive engagement with US southern literature, *Coup de torchon* (*Clean Slate*, 1981), particularly a moment in which the protagonist mournfully lectures a black man on morality while forcing him to dig his own grave. This momentary convergence merits attention because the styles of these two films diverge sharply, a distinction that arises in part from the source texts. The earlier film revises Jim Thompson's novel *Pop. 1280* (1964), a blend of biting social critique with bawdy farce, leaving readers, as Tavernier explained, "no easy way to cope with the situation" (Hay 95). Relocating Thompson's plot to colonial West Africa in 1938, Tavernier seeks to capture Thompson's style through jarring disjunctures in score and editing and moving the Steadicam in a way "that kept shifting . . . the physical equivalent of earth that isn't solid" (Yakir and Tavernier 21). More than twenty-five years later, *Brume* is far more subtly disruptive, exploring a web of relations between iconic tropes and everyday images, past and present, thoughtfulness and occasionally explosive and even racist violence within a single complex protagonist—revising the noir genre to allow for consideration of both social and cinematic history (Vanderschelden 117–23).

And yet this relative delicacy was deemed too extreme for US audiences, as the producer's cut, *In the Electric Mist*—released straight to DVD and streaming platforms for this country alone—differs in many of these respects. It reduces *Brume*'s crystalline perspectives on the landscape to make more time for destination images—more shots of Dave driving along the bayou, and far more footage of Goldman's party, an occasion perfectly suited to *The Big Easy*. It simplifies the character of Hogman, who spends more of his screen time performing. Most disturbingly, it insinuates justification for Dave's brutality toward Adonis: in *Mist,* the latter's name comes up specifically at the moment Dave and an informant are discussing serial murder, after which the film cuts immediately to the bus depot, suggesting Adonis might be the killer. In *Brume,* in contrast, Dave hears Adonis's name solely in relation to prostitution from a different informant, whose language is unabashedly racist—a dubious source in a meandering investigation. Given that Louisiana has repeatedly proved a flashpoint in the nation's ongoing struggles with police brutality against African Americans—in New Orleans after Hurricane Katrina (2005), in Baton Rouge through the shooting of Alton Sterling (2016), and allegedly in Iberia Parish for many years (Mustian; Rich)—*Mist*'s alternate editing stands out all the more sharply as an ethical failure. Testifying simultaneously to a need for transformation in cinematic views of the state and to the direct resistance capital poses to such change, it encapsulates the history of Louisiana noir, films torn between dueling fascinations with money—to understand it and to reap it.

ACE ATKINS, *TRUE DETECTIVE,* & THE MYSTERY OF THE "NO-ORLEANS"

JAMES A. CRANK

O n the back cover of my hardbound copy of the Ace Atkins detective novel *Dirty South,* Kinky Friedman declares, "If Raymond Chandler came from the South, his name would be Ace Atkins"—a dubious bit of praise, it seems to me, partly because of Friedman's implication that Chandler's aesthetic is so rooted in his urban West Coast milieu that it is profoundly untranslatable to southerners, but also because Atkins novels seem to me to write against the tradition of Chandler and his cults of masculinity and hierarchies of sexual value. Perhaps a more fitting bit of praise for Atkins would be that his writing is so original that he inhabits his own space in American detective fiction. Because what Friedman really suggests with his back-cover blurb is that *Dirty South* is a novel hard-boiled enough that the most jaded detective reader can enjoy it, even if it is set *down there.*

Down there: The South has long proved an intuitive setting for all sorts of genres of literary play—magical realism, fantasy, horror.[1] But detective fiction, with its emphasis on sprawling urban landscapes, sophisticated heroes, and gritty transactional violence, feels slightly inauthentic when placed in a southern setting. And yet while the South is routinely read by popular culture as a terrifying frontier of backwardness—the last, vast, unexplored rural nowhere—the truth is that the region's urban centers, Dallas, Atlanta, Memphis, Birmingham, Charlotte, and New Orleans, are just as complicated and multidimensional as many of the cities that Chandler, Leonard, and Hammett, made famous: noir spaces like Detroit, Los Angeles, San Francisco, and Chicago.

As one of the South's most complicated urban spaces, New Orleans' setting in detective fiction works just as compellingly as Chandler's Los Angeles, both cities murky and mysterious, clogged with violence and intrigue. The city is routinely named one of America's most dangerous places to live:[2] its crime and murder rate per capita attracts television arcs for crime dramas like *NCIS: New Orleans* and movies like *Bad Lieutenant: Port of Call New Orleans.* In short, for detective/ crime writers like Atkins, New Orleans is the South's Los Angeles, only dirtier, more dangerous, fraught with anxieties over class and race, and easily exploited by a global imagination that manufactures an authentic version of Louisiana citizens as a weird collection of archetypes. Thinking through articulations of New Orleans in both detective fiction and film/television offers some pretty useful insights about representations of region, race, and waste in the twenty-first century American imagination.

I want to look at two different imaginings of New Orleans as a site of crime-fiction/drama and examine the ways in which both (ref)use the urban setting of the city as a space of static inauthenticity. Further, I want to look beyond the city itself and explore how both these works offer a version of "southern authenticity" in the margins, the shadows of, the Big Sleazy. I also want to suggest some questions about this crossing from the "Noir Orleans" to "No-Orleans": What does it mean when we move into, through, and beyond New Orleans in works that focus so specifically on crime, criminality, and law? Who gets left out, exploited, and misrepresented when these authors and directors imagine "Noir Orleans" as a fantasy of justice or a space of ethical atonement? What histories do we compete with, deny, contest, or ignore in our spectatorship of these works, and what are the real consequences of our investment in New Orleans and its margins as a site of play and imagination?[3]

TRAVERSING THE DIRTY, BLACK "NOIR ORLEANS"

> As cultures clash, the story winds its way through the infamous Calliope
> housing projects, the newly built mansions of New Orleans' lakefront,
> and ultimately to the brackish muck of Bayou Savage.
> —inside dust jacket cover of *Dirty South*

Writing about representations of the city in detective fiction, Vaughan B. Baker investigates what makes New Orleans so appealing to readers who come to think through mystery, crime, and the darkness of the city's spaces:

> Popular mystery fiction set in the Crescent City outnumbers all other Louisiana
> locales, and most other American ones . . . What cultural preconceptions attract
> these readers?
> . . . Views of New Orleans as a city where crime is rife and sin is safe and
> Louisiana as a state where people vote for crooks whether it is important or not
> have captured the national imagination.

Noting that "Mystery fiction far outsells historical monographs," Baker nonetheless locates what makes New Orleans such an attractive setting to noir writers: it is a city haunted by the worst excesses of human indulgence—crime, murder, sex, drugs, alcohol. It is a world uniquely situated for the kind of detective-protagonist that noir fiction celebrates. One could easily make a case for New Orleans as the *ultimate* noir setting because of the very space it occupies in the American imaginary, the world of a "Noir Orleans" detective already saturated with blood, filth, stale beer, and corpses. "New Orleans fictional detectives typically tend to be a troubled lot," Baker concludes, not the least because "the folks they encounter [are] even less adapted to mainstream American behavioral mores."

Ace Atkins's novel *Dirty South,* first released in 2004 by Harper Collins, is the third book in the series involving noir protagonist Nick Travers. True to his name, the private eye travels throughout the nation, but he is rooted in the culture of the South, where he solves crimes and untangles mysteries most of which are connected in some way with music (especially the blues). In many ways, Nick Travers is an amalgamation of many Louisiana icons mashed into a single entity—he is an ex-football player with the New Orleans Saints, a professor of music history at Tulane, a part-time harmonica player at a local club, and of course, a detective for hire. Because he has such a facility with local customs, Travers makes an ideal go-between in the worlds he has to explore as an ad hoc private eye. He is equally as comfortable with the tourists on Bourbon Street as he is in the suburbs of Metairie, the Calliope projects, and, of course, in the rural outlands of Mississippi and Louisiana, where he begins his journey in *Dirty South:* on Highway 61.

At the opening of the novel, the detective sets out to collect stories from an old buddy of Sonny Boy Williamson, but before he can do so, he must first enlist the help of his old friend JoJo who, with his wife Loretta, used to own a New Orleans nightclub before they retreated to their ancestral farmland in Mississippi. The couple are important characters for Travers; they are responsible for instilling values in the detective, as well as teaching him the history of the blues. Setting up a familiar theme in *Dirty South,* Travers uses JoJo's race to help him gain entry into the man's house ("This man doesn't like white people," JoJo offers to Nick as they head out on the dusty roads of Mississippi; "You think bringin' along a black man will help." [Atkins 1]) From the prologue, it's clear that Travers is obsessed with authenticity. He wants the "real" story from the "actual" people who were present at the time of Sonny Boy's recordings. Nick Travers believes in the power of music to articulate a "real" identity, and authentic music becomes one of the crucial themes to the novel. Throughout *Dirty South,* Atkins plays with two different expressions of African American music: blues and hip-hop. The author's epigraphs are lyrics, one from 1930s blues musician Little Walter, the other from 1990s Louisiana hip-hop icon Lil Wayne. Both the quotations connect violent rhetoric with authenticity: appearing first in the language of blues ("Tole you packin' .45") and in hip-hop ("gun right in my grip"). The connection is important because Travers will have to come into close contact with the culture and hierarchies of the New Orleans hip-hop community, a world that he doesn't understand or appreciate, and his interactions with that world come largely through violent exchanges involving disputes over intellectual (and economic) ownership.

But Nick Travers's quest to understand New Orleans bounce hip-hop makes *Dirty South* a different kind of detective novel: though the private eye is tasked initially with investigating the inner workings of complicated criminal actions, the real mystery Travers explores involves unlocking the key to New Orleans's (and, I would argue, southern) authenticity. By piecing together the language, aesthetics, hierarchies, and values of hip-hop artists in the city, Nick Travers is really attempting to solve the complicated, racialized realities of what it means to live in a changing New Orleans.

The nominal "mystery" of the novel is a missing $700,000 that Travers's best friend—former Saints teammate Teddy Paris, now turned hip-hop producer— reports stolen from one of his musicians, a fifteen-year-old rapper, ALIAS, who appears in the novel not just as a subject to be wondered at but in actual voice. Atkins interjects Travers's first-person narrative with sections in italics in the second-person voice of ALIAS, where he articulates his intellectual journey. Travers's friend needs the money to pay off a bounty that has been put out on Teddy's head by Cash, the leader of a rival record label. Teddy appeals to Travers to help find the stolen money and to safeguard the kid-rap-prodigy despite the fact that Travers is actively antagonistic towards both the lifestyle and the message behind the music Teddy produces. At the beginning of the novel, the detective cannot understand how dirty south hip-hop articulates anything authentic about the world of *his* New Orleans. Travers's lack of imagination is clearest when Teddy approaches the detective for help. Travers jokes, "I can't rap," after doing an embarrassing pastiche of hip-hop dancing. Travers scoffs inwardly at the inauthentic world of dirty south hip-hop and its obsession with gaudy commodities:

"What? You want me to 'Shake That Ass'?" I asked, naming one of his New Orleans competitors' top-ten hits. Asses, champagne, and platinum usually dominated his preferred style of music. Dirty South rap. I shook my butt a little while continuing to work under the hood of the truck before turning back around. (Atkins 13–14)

Unlike the blues, with its call and repetition, simple riffs and lyrics, and emphasis on articulating hurt and pain, dirty south hip-hop seems to Travers like a vehicle simply to promote artifice and waste. Similarly, Teddy cannot understand the importance of blues music. They bicker over the value of both musical genres; their back-and-forth dialogue over issues of authenticity, value, aesthetics, and art becomes one of the central conflicts of the novel. Atkins seems to tease the idea that, as much as the mystery of the novel becomes who's stealing from whom, he's also just as interested in determining what expression of music most authentically captures the essence of New Orleans.

At heart Teddy and Travers argue over different conceptions of value in the music they profess to be authentic. For each man, the other's taste in music is trashy, and Atkins seems to work through visions and fantasies of disposability throughout *Dirty South,* including disposable bodies, women, disposable income, material culture, and disrespect based on regions (East Coast versus West Coast, or neighborhood rivalries within New Orleans). Late in the novel, Travers and Teddy argue about hip-hop and its aesthetic of "waste." Travers reads Teddy's lavish lifestyle as an investment in trash, but Teddy disagrees: "See you still don't get it . . . The culture of our world, right. That's what my people want to see. They want to see you livin' large and steppin' out with the Gucci and Vuitton and all them suits from Armani." Teddy and Travers argue over what constitutes value, and the detective's anxiety over dirty south aesthetics suggests his problems stems chiefly from Teddy's "disposable" income. Here, as in other key places in *Dirty South,* Travers's racial politics are naive; the detective's reading of value oozes with privilege. The cars and cash mean something different to Teddy because of his skin color. "When I walk into Canal Place, man, people waitin' for me at the door. They don't see black no more; they see green. You understand" (Atkins 162)? Travers doesn't answer, but it's clear from his behavior in the novel that he lacks the ability to comprehend Teddy's experience as a black man in New Orleans. When Travers offers that Teddy can be a different role model for the youth of Calliope, Teddy shoots back: "You ever been black" (Atkins 161)? Travers lack of racial imagination cripples him throughout *Dirty South.*

If parsing the connection between race and authenticity is a key part of Atkins's "Noir Orleans" aesthetic, so, too, is the very idea of value and ownership. Teddy positions his rival Cash in essentialist terms: "This ape raised in Calliope like my man ALIAS," he explains to Travers. "But he don't have no heart like the kid. He's an animal . . . Stole everythin' he have. Even his beats . . . Now Cash eatin' steaks and lobster, screwin' *Penthouse* pets" (Atkins 18). In a novel deeply anxious over identifying an authentic New Orleans culture, it's difficult to work through the nativism and racial complications that attend characters' articulations of value (especially by a white author like Atkins). If ALIAS is authentic because he lives in the Calliope, the "infamous neighborhood" referenced on the dust jacket of the book, how is Cash inauthentic? After all, he is also Calliope-raised. The two characters of Cash and ALIAS exist as dark doubles throughout the novel, Cash the robber-baron gangster, and ALIAS, the sincere, tough kid with his music as salvation. It's hard to make an argument for which character is more essentially a product of the New Orleans projects—the heartless Cash, or the sensitive artist ALIAS? Both characters connect in crucial ways: While Cash gets his money from stealing, ALIAS gains economic mobility from his music. Though we never hear Cash's thoughts or motivations in the first person, Atkins lets us "see" ALIAS's "heart" through his voice: "Y'all know Calliope—its own little galaxy in New Orleans. Findin' your people on the other side is like shooting over the moon," he tells us in his first section of the novel (7). And yet, even by the end of his first chapter, ALIAS confesses to the reader that his whole label started because he robbed a "white girl . . . with a knife . . . made from an oak tree splinter" (Atkins 9); in a sense, the young rapper begins his upward economic mobility through armed robbery, just like his dark double, Cash. Just a few pages into *Dirty South*, it's clear that Calliope is a site where value is related to economic means; when ALIAS gets his advance stolen, for example, "they say you $500,000 less a man" (10).

The white Nick Travers is forced to cross into ALIAS's neighborhood of Calliope, a world of blackness, a space where value, ownership, and power have different meanings than they do in the Mississippi Delta. The move into Calliope marks the beginning of the "mystery" Travers is tasked with solving, but it also signals an entrance into the true heart of "Noir Orleans," a space of literal and metaphorical blackness. Together, Teddy and Nick cross over into the new "galaxy" of Calliope in a scene laden with anxieties over class, race, and value. Even though Teddy compliments Travers that he is "the blackest white man I know" (13), the private eye feels a sense of unease as the unfamiliar neighborhood "swallow[s]" them: "endless rows of four-story colorless brick buildings seeming to sag with exhaustion. Fire escapes lined each building in V patterns; some hung loose like broken limbs. In a commons that reminded me of a prison yard, Dumpsters spilled trash onto the wide dirt ground. Along the walls of project houses, signs read NO DOG FIGHTING" (20). Travers immediately recognizes that he doesn't belong in ALIAS's world, and rather than safeguarding the boy in his house, the detective convinces the young man to come back to his neighborhood. Travers cannot offer ALIAS any kind of economic mobility, but he can offer a physical mobility: by becoming the boy's guardian, Travers shares with his young charge his eponymous ability to travel, to cross, to escape, just as ALIAS offers Travers the opportunity to explore a different part of his identity.

Atkins's portrayal of Calliope and its inhabitants dialogues continuously with the world of blackness, not just racially, but in the darkness that lurks on the corners, behind the curtains of the projects, and in the shadows that fall over relationships. Calliope is a space of shadows and dirt, a world of darkness; the "Noir Orleans" world of the Calliope feels like the perfect setting for exploring crime and mystery: it is a space of exoticism but also transaction. Each relationship in the neighborhood has social as well as economic value, and Travers has to piece together the meanings if he wants to help ALIAS, and, by extension, Teddy. But Travers's understanding of the economic and cultural realities of the neighborhood make him unsuited for such a role: "If you don't help," I said, "your boy Cash is gonna mess Teddy up bad."

"What the fuck do you know about Cash?" ALIAS asked. "He ain't my boy" (22). In the dim, dirty, shadowy world of "Noir Orleans," Travers's usual detective work becomes increasingly unfamiliar to him; he doesn't have a good read on how the world of Calliope or the hip-hop moguls value their people or products. "At least with the greaseballs," one of his informants Curtis bemoans, "you knew where the shit was flyin'" (37). With no context for the world of Cash or ALIAS (or rappers like Dio—who becomes a central character late in the novel), Travers can only collect information. When he meets Coach Lorenzo Woods, an old acquaintance of Cash's, he gets an education in both music and the world of the street artist (41):

> "I grew up in Calliope," he said. "Proud of that. Most of my [football players] come from there or Magnolia. I got out by workin' block parties. Hustlin' for any money I could make. I invented bounce, man. You know bounce?"
>   "It's the Dirty South sound." "Damn right," he said. "That's me." "Cash took it."
>   "Took my beats, put his lame-ass raps over it, and threatened all the record stores in Uptown. Made 'em sell his record or he'd fuck their ass up."

In the crucial exchange with Coach Woods, Travers learns both the aesthetic of bounce, the origin of ALIAS's dirty south compositions, but also how creative and artistic endeavors become values to be commodified in Calliope. Like money, beats and rhymes can be a key for mobility and escape, but they can also be stolen and resold. Cash's style isn't that of the con man, but of the bald-faced thief: "He'll lie, steal, and cheat. But he'll do it face-to-face," Coach Woods explains to Travers (42).

Cash becomes one of the competing poles of authentic blackness with which Travers has to shepherd ALIAS; the other is JoJo, Travers's mentor. The two black men offer different fantasies of economic viability that rework the traditional associations with "noir" fiction into something that dovetails rather explicitly with the root of the word itself. Because it becomes clearer as *Dirty South* works towards its conclusion that the authentic world of "Noir Orleans" exists between the two fonts of darkness that Travers sees in Cash and JoJo. When a young ALIAS goes to meet Cash at his mansion uptown, the man explains his philosophy on reclamation and ownership:

> I like that history shit. You know what the Civil War is . . . You know some peckerwood white folks used to keep us like hogs, right, and there was a big war 'cause of it . . . Reason why is 'cause the man who was the peckerwood president of the Confederacy or some shit died in my house. My house, nigga. Ain't that a trip? Wonder what that boy would think with the Red Hat crew all up in it? (45)

Cash's philosophy on power comes solely from a revenge fantasy focused entirely on possession—once you are stolen from, you have the authority to take from anyone. His is an economic vision of ownership that essentially offers ALIAS the ability to take the best of what he finds and brand it. Cash's "Noir Orleans" is a space of infinite value all free for the taking.

Travers believes that ALIAS must escape from Calliope and the "Noir Orleans" because it is a city and neighborhood in which Cash's vision of reclamation, replacement, and flimsy thievery is being used against its citizens. The detective notes:

> About ten years ago [1994], New Orleans East was a suburb of corporate apartments and yuppie condos along with the usual strip malls and chain restaurants. But since the Hope VI federal housing initiative took off . . . it was Sheetrock and flimsy plywood—no apartment manager having to answer for shit while the slumlords grew rich and wrote off millions on their taxes. (66)

It's crucial to note that the "authentic" world of "Noir Orleans'" racial crossing and blackness is set against a world of (white) tourism and fantasies of exoticism. Even in that French Quarter space, though, whiteness shines: Robert E. Lee peers down "tall on his pillar at Lee Circle" (26), and a city where a racist police detective "divided the blacks of New Orleans into different tribes, and according to him . . . most blacks were the same as they'd been in Africa" (49). "Noir Orleans" is a fitting title for a space in which all crime shifts into fantasies of binaries, a black and white imaginary of transgression and justice: "Work this job for two days and tell me what you see out there," Detective Hines tells Travers. "Tell me what it's all about from inside of your office at Tulane" (51).

Travers encourages ALIAS to reject Cash's way of thinking, and the foil the detective offers is JoJo (and, to a lesser extent, JoJo's wife Loretta), who takes ALIAS in and teaches the boy self-respect through an emphasis on what we might term country (or rural) values. Initially reticent to deal with ALIAS ("I don't mess with those project folks in New Orleans," JoJo tells Travers), the couple warm to the kid. They force ALIAS to do chores, work around their farm, and go to church, but more importantly, they teach the boy to read. ALIAS's competing educations couldn't be starker in contrast: on the one hand, Cash's violent competitiveness and thievery in the "Noir Orleans," and JoJo and Loretta's sincerity and hard work in Mississippi. At first, ALIAS chafes at the country life of JoJo and Loretta. Working hard reminds him of Cash's reading of history: "I ain't no slave," he confidently tells JoJo when asked to help paint the barn (133). ALIAS learns from JoJo and Loretta an alternate system of values, but the lessons they teach him have personal reverberations for Travers, who also learned to appreciate the blues through the couple.

Though rural Mississippi is not liminal as a site of pseudo-urbanity, JoJo and Loretta's presence as former residents of New Orleans (JoJo once owned a blues bar where Nick played) renders JoJo and Loretta's home as a kind of go-between, a rural site inhabited by urban and urbane city dwellers. JoJo and Loretta speak to ALIAS as members of the Mississippi community, but also as "authentic" former residents of the city. And it is there in Clarksdale, Mississippi—the "home of the blues"—that Travers delivers ALIAS a chance to glimpse a "truer" vision of himself (117):

> "I'm gonna do whatever ALIAS want to do."
> "That have anything to do with Tavarius Stovall . . . You know that your name comes from a plantation where we're headed . . . "
> "My people come from Mississippi?"
> "Where did you think they came from?"

"All I know is Calliope."

"Maybe we can stop by," I said. "Always good for the soul to know your roots."

This escape from "Noir Orleans" to another shadowy and hybrid space suggests a number of troubling ideas for *Dirty South:* Atkins (a white author) seems to suggest that a truer form of "blackness" is rooted in understanding the complicated history of ownership (of things, people, ideas, art, and music). ALIAS is delivered to JoJo and Loretta to protect the boy from the criminals who want to prey on him in "Noir Orleans," but ALIAS is brought to Mississippi also on a spiritual quest that will, ultimately, help the young artist understand who he was meant to be.

It's especially significant that, in order for Travers to save ALIAS's life— physically and spiritually—he must get him out of Calliope and away from "Noir Orleans," away from the French Quarter and Calliope and into a new space, one where the boy's soul and body can finally grow and flourish. ALIAS recognizes his neighborhood in Clarksdale—"The stores have sheets of wood in the windows, just like the places round Calliope, and boys work the corners with their rock just the same" (171)—but Clarksdale has a rhythm completely different than Calliope. With JoJo and Loretta as guides, Clarksdale becomes a salvation for ALIAS, a city where the rural blackness that surrounds him offers space to breathe and understand himself.

A DARK CROSSING: RETREATING TO THE "NO-ORLEANS"

> Take a ride to the other side of New Orleans, away from the neon gloss
> of Bourbon Street, to see what the *Dirty South* is all about.
> —back jacket flap of *Dirty South*

> Touch *Darkness* and *Darkness* Touches You Back
> —slogan on poster for HBO series *True Detective,* season 1
> (*emphasis mine*)

Late in *Dirty South,* Travers remembers fondly how his mentor, Willie T. Dean, wouldn't take "no" for an answer from his informants. Willie and Travers travel all over Mississippi collecting information, working out of a car, learning how to use their skills at interpersonal connections and conversation to put people at ease. "But New Orleans wasn't the Delta," he concludes (167). "New Orleans wasn't the Delta" could very easily be the tagline that describes much of the action in the climactic second half of *Dirty South*. Atkins clearly distinguishes the world of "Noir Orleans" (city of intrigue and racial anxiety) from that of the Mississippi Delta (a fantasy space of open interpersonal exchange between those of different classes and races). If Travers's racial politics are naive, it is likely because he seeks to explore the city of New Orleans and the projects of Calliope, in the same way he operates the rural nowhere roads of Highway 61 and Mississippi. Unlike "Noir Orleans," value in the world of the Delta is not economic but rather, symbolic, related to the power of one's word and the morals to which one adheres. When ALIAS gets caught stealing from JoJo, Travers cautions that his money can't buy the boy back dignity: "That old man only deals in respect" (188).

While Clarksdale and the rural Mississippi Delta offer ALIAS a space for self-reflection and growth, Atkins moves away from both rural Mississippi and urban New Orleans for the crucial climaxes of *Dirty South;* those take place not in the white glare of the French Quarter, or even in the easily identifiable neighborhoods like Calliope, but in the middle of nowhere—not the city, not the urban space, not even the suburbs, but in what I want to call the "No-Orleans": " . . . the dead zone. Nothing but warehouses and vacant shotguns. Rusted cars and spare parts from the World's Fair in 1984" (Atkins 82). The "No-Orleans" is a world of trash, waste, refuse, of what's left over after the city world has used it of its value. It's liminal space—not quite urban, not quite rural, not country, not city—and the setting works as a kind of new noir aesthetic in which authenticity is not a subject to be wondered at but is present to be gazed upon. In the dark world of trash, the truth shines like light on metal. As subjects, the "fringes" of New Orleans become more than just another setting of *Dirty South*, they become the site through which all the mysteries of the novel are solved. The climax of *Dirty South* unravels in the very margins of the city: first in Metairie and then in the middle of Lake Pontchartrain, where Travers finally learns that his longtime friend Teddy has been deceiving him for years. As Travers tries to get his old friend to remember their relationship together, the detective realizes, "We were on the edge of Orleans Parish, the edge of the Bayou Sauvage. I could smell the foulness of the bayou rot as we moved away from the lake and deeper into the high grass" (279). It is not coincidental that the entire plot of *Dirty South* gets sewn up not in the city proper but on the margins of its borders: not on land or even the lake itself but on both water and land, on sinking mud, in the brackish and shadowy waters of its borders. *Dirty South* ends in dirt. There Christian (the true villain of the novel) and Teddy get stuck in the mud, and are forced to confront Cash, ALIAS, and JoJo, who arrive just in time to save the day.

ALIAS's trajectory is complete. The novel ends with the boy as a moral hero, raised on the streets of "Noir Orleans" but living the code of the "No-Orleans." Though ALIAS leaves the city to make a name for himself, the boy's final section makes clear that he will always come "home" to his "roots." Crucially, his appreciation for the blues, the music of Clarksdale, also becomes important to his artistry. "The music is old," he notes, "You don't like it. But you can't help move your feet. 'Cause you been to where it come from and some way you knowin' more about yourself" (287). Travers, too, has come to understand that place is tied to his identity. "I still travel the Delta when I find myself lost," he says in the Epilogue (289).

The journey from "Noir Orleans" to "No-Orleans" is crucial to understanding *Dirty South*'s implications for racial crossing, ownership, economic empowerment, and the critical unraveling that must take place in order to solve the mystery of identity (in its symbolic detective narrative). It is only in the backwater nowhere, bathed in the dim lights of New Orleans, that Nick Travers and ALIAS can come to solve the mysteries dogging them—both the complicated criminal exchanges between Teddy and Cash, and also the mystery of what it means to be "true" to themselves. Because Atkins is pulling at so many strands of truth, the symbolic quest of the novel sometimes confuses the literal double-dealings of the characters and plot. But what Atkins does through his move from "Noir" to "No-Orleans" is suggest that a search for a truly authentic identity—in this case, the contested identity of New Orleans culture—can really only be found outside the city itself. That quest for true authenticity is also central to the HBO show *True Detective*, and like *Dirty South*, the crime drama insists that, in order to understand the dark workings of criminality, one must first understand one's true identity. And both truths are only available in the margins of the city: the "No-Orleans."

The first season of the 2014 HBO drama *True Detective* follows Louisiana homicide detectives Rustin "Rust" Cohle and Martin "Marty" Hart as they investigate the murder of a woman, Dora Lange, and uncover a much larger, secret criminal enterprise responsible for the disappearance, molestation, and murder of numerous women and children over almost fifteen years. The show is set in Vermillion Parish and south Louisiana. And yet the specter of New Orleans haunts the show. Much of the filming took place in the very spaces Atkins sets his novel, the brackish gulf waters, flanked by chemical plants and honky-tonks. Like *Dirty South*, *True Detective* explores a doubly noir world in both setting and tone: the hard-boiled detective Cohle spouts existentialist philosophy while investigating ritual murders of children in the deep nowhere of rural south Louisiana ("We are things that labor under the illusion of having a self, this accretion of sensory experience and feeling, programmed with total assurance that we are each somebody when, in fact, everybody's nobody," he tells policemen who ask him simple questions about a crime investigation ["The Long Bright Dark"].) It is a dark show with dark characters who seem obsessed with investigating the darkness inherent in criminals; not only does the show's creator, Nic Pizzolatto, set his sights on an exploration of the soul of a child predator, but he also makes exploring the demons of his detectives the central revelation of the first season of his television show.

Pizzolatto also grew up on the margins of a city; *Vanity Fair* writer Rich Cohen describes his hometown "on the outskirts of Lake Charles, Louisiana, a mean little oil city between New Orleans and Houston. Squeezed by the banks of the lake and the banks of the interstate, this chemical landscape has served as the backdrop for his best work. The I-10 corridor, ramshackle towns, Pentecostal churches, fishing camps trapped in an eddy of the uneven flow of time" (Cohen). Pizzolatto seems to suggest that it is the not quite rural, not quite urban spaces, between two urban centers, that is somehow the most authentic version of Louisiana. He uses the adjective "True"[4] in his very title, and the detectives he presents to the audience are obsessed with finding the truth, both to the mystery of the murderer and to the meanings of their existence that continually seem to elude them. It's clear that the first season of *True Detective* is far more anxious about rendering the authenticity of its setting than it is its characters or any kind of true crime. "I tend to be influenced by places as much as anything," Pizzolatto tells Cohen. "You look around and notice details and it starts to form a world and then you find characters to inhabit this world" (Cohen).

Pizzolatto's show obviously tapped into a fantasy shared by many; the first season of *True Detective* was a huge success. The strong acting of both Matthew McConaughey and Woody Harrelson were key in its appeal, but more importantly, the setting became the soul of the series. The "No-Orleans" backdrop seemed to be the real star of the show; Cohen describes Pizzolatto's achievement largely in his ability to render his setting—a show "as much about place as people"—so effectively:

> *True Detective* was a hit from the start. This can be credited to a number of factors. There was the look of the show, for one thing: the weird landscapes and streets, the first season having been filmed around New Orleans, on the bayou, in abandoned churches and inlets, the strangest part of America, everything south of New Orleans having been built by sediment carried down the Mississippi. Not

land, but fill, the innards of the continent vomited into the Gulf of Mexico. From the air, the islands look like green suds. (Cohen)

Cohen's description here should give us pause: his emphasis on the bodily/ bestial "vomit" of the "No-Orleans" ecology and also his terming of the land as "The Strangest Part of America." What do we mean when we speak in such code about the rural outskirts of New Orleans or the marshland on the margins of its banks? Because what Cohle and Hart find in the finale of *True Detective*—deep in the heart of the "No-Orleans"—is nothing short of a monster, a deformed, scarred, incestuous, murdering cannibal hillbilly straight from the hixploitation movies of the 1970s and 1980s. What does it say about that space that, when Pizzolatto wants us to believe in the world of Cajun monsters and savage religion, it's not the urban landscape of New Orleans that we see, not the bright, vibrant music culture that a show like *Treme* celebrates, it's the margins of the city, the rural spaces in the shadow of the Big, Dirty Easy? What is it about New Orleans that designated its margins as the site of the authentic version of southern identity, and what does it mean that these visions of "real" Souths are themed decidedly noir?

For Pizzolatto's part, he finds his setting to be the true character of the work. Talking about *True Detective* in relation to his novel *Gavelston*, he tells Cohen, "These stories take place in areas where the revelation has already happened. The apocalypse has come and gone, and no one's quite woken up to that fact." The "No-Orleans" is literally a burned-out shell, a site crossed with urban decay and reclaimed by the natural world, liminal, haunting.

Both *True Detective* and Atkins's *Dirty South* highlight crossings into and out of the "Noir Orleans" and what it means for both works to find their truth in the margins, as though southern noir must, of necessity, escape beyond the city and into the dark world of its shadow—a world that feels decidedly reflective of the interior world of the characters themselves. "No-Orleans" southern noir is a genre that, ostensibly, attempts to uncover a truth, solve a mystery, and complicate seemingly simple causations by suggesting counternarratives, multiple alibis, and a myriad of potential victims and criminals. But, at some point, the crossing becomes unimaginative. Instead of working through truth, it offers a gothic fantasy that seems to overwrite any authenticity to which both *Dirty South* and *True Detective* appeal.

What Pizzolatto does with his southern detectives in the shadow of the "Noir Orleans" is create a kind of cultural interrogator of the South's true ontology. Through their engagement with issues of rural/urban spaces, problems of representations of women and race, and southern monoliths, Cohle and Hart become arbiters of southern authenticity in a century that feels more and more trending away from the Post South and into something more like the Theme South. It makes sense that such an artificial world would be shadowy and dark: Noir. Heavy. Unresolved and unsolvable. But in *True Detective*, the detectives work on the outskirts of "Noir Orleans," tasked with not just finding a killer or an embezzler but locating the very font of southern authenticity. Crucially, they uncover a version of southern authenticity, not in the urban space of New Orleans, not in the suburbs of the city, and not even in the rural expanse of dark nothing, but instead in the desolate, black swamps of the rural-urban margins of the city. The "No-Orleans" is not a world of bright truth; it is a dark, retreaded fantasy of the gothic South. McConaughey tells Cohen of the south Louisiana blackness, it's not its borders that make it visible, but its lack of cohesion: "I don't find it scary, I find it mysterious. It lurks. Mother Nature is the four-dimensional queen—she encroaches from every direction. Where many civilized cities and states use a vacuum cleaner to define their structure, Louisiana used a broom or merely a rake. Everything merges there. If you wear your morals on your sleeve you're liable to get your arm burned." Outside the "civilized" city of New Orleans, one can encounter the shadowy authenticity that exists inside all of us—or so Pizzolatto would want us to believe; the show's slogan is: "Touch Darkness and Darkness Touches You Back."

It should be noted that *True Detective* failed spectacularly in its second season, when it moved from Louisiana to Los Angeles. After negative reviews and a host of reports about the showrunner's meddling in direction and casting, HBO has remained skittish on announcing a third season of the television show. And Ace Atkins has acknowledged that his early work on the Nick Travers series might have some problems with stereotype; in one interview, the writer begs his interviewer not to read *Dirty South*:

> *Dirty South* I guess I wrote when I was in my early thirties . . . I really learned what not to do . . . There was a stylistic element, something that read like fiction, and that's what I try totally not to do now. I try to quit writing fiction and bullshit. (Pendarvis)

Dirty South offers possible redemption through a third symbolic region of Clarksdale (and, to a larger extent, the entire region of the Mississippi Delta), and however troubling that obsession with southern authenticity might be on the surface, it's really the southern gothic "No-Orleans" that feels like a species of bullshit in *True Detective.* Working through Pizzolatto's television show as a kind of noir fantasy, it's as though the genre he invests in so heavily works only to further obscure real issues of crime, racial violence, and the lived lives of southerners into fantasies, national imaginaries that only entrench the binaries that have long dogged the region. But knowing how noir, with its emphasis on turnabout and shocking revelations and discoveries, ends, one could almost imagine that Pizzolatto is purposefully twisting the knife—making his audience unknowing victims, in order that he might take off his mask at the end, and show himself the faceless executioner of the banality of their imagined investments.

Even so, imagining *True Detective* in concert with "No-South Noir" and the gothic world of vampires, zombies, werewolves, and sprites, it's clear *that* Pizzolatto is just playing around in the swamp.

NOTES

1. See especially *American Cinema and the Southern Imaginary,* edited by Deborah Barker and Kathryn McKee (2011) and *Undead Souths: The Gothic and Beyond in Southern Literature and Culture,* edited by Eric Gary Anderson, Taylor Hagood, and Daniel Cross Turner (2015).

2. The *Times Picayune* reports, "Louisiana had the highest murder rate per capita among all states in the country last year [2015], a streak the state has maintained every year since 1989, according to new data released by the Federal Bureau of Investigation on Monday (Sept. 26). The state's high murder rate figured as one of several metrics in data that showed murders throughout the United States jumped by 10.8 percent from 2014 to 2015—the largest percentage increase since 1971 . . . With the number of murders in New Orleans rising from 150 in 2014 to 164 in 2015, the city claimed the nation's fourth-highest murder rate among major metropolitan areas. New Orleans logged 41.7 murders per 100,000 people, sandwiched between Detroit and Milwaukee" (Beau Evans).

3. I also want to make clear that I am looking at two works that land on different sides of the line dividing the pre/post New Orleans world of Hurricane Katrina. The American anxiety over the South as an outland is articulated clearest through film and television, such as Court 13's *Beasts of the Southern Wild* (2012), or the HBO series *True Detective* (2014), whose first season explores disturbing criminal conduct in south Louisiana.

4. One of HBO's other hit shows explores vampires and werewolves living on the swamps of north Louisiana. Its title suggests a similar obsession with outlandish articulations of an authentic south as Pizzolatto's: *True Blood.*

THE SUBURBAN NOIR HEADS SOUTH

From Desperate Housewives *to* Gone Girl

SUZANNE LEONARD

In a 2014 *Telegraph* article, novelist Erin Kelly characterizes the suburban noir genre as populated by "disappearing partners, toxic marriages, dark secrets, and the lies we tell ourselves as well as each other." This cultural phenomenon is likewise often referred to as "chick noir" and credited to Gillian Flynn's 2012 bestselling novel *Gone Girl,* and its filmic adaptation, an international sensation that spawned a cottage industry of novels, films, and television offerings. While critics frequently name *Gone Girl* as the ur-text of this new genre, this article instead nominates *Desperate Housewives* (2004–2012) as a precursor to *Gone Girl* and identifies both as suburban noirs that centralize the domestic dissatisfactions of wives. If "noir plotlines frequently evoke an underworld of crime, passion, and perversion that lurks beneath and alongside the world of respectable daily life," as Eric Dussere claims, this article posits that in the suburban noir specifically, the spaces of domesticity play host to lurking perils and do so under the guise of reassuring accommodation (34–35).

The comparison between *Desperate Housewives* and *Gone Girl* forces contemplation of the regional, economic, and classed realities that undergird the sociocultural milieu of twenty-first century America, and highlights two primary points with respect to the operation and ideological impact of the suburban noir. First, the comparison signals the increasing visibility and potency of female revenge in postfeminist media culture, and the way that performances of traditional femininity can obfuscate the fact that female anger finds outlet in surprisingly nefarious ways. In *Desperate Housewives* and *Gone Girl,* anodyne locations like supermarkets and malls double as sinister cauldrons where female rage simmers before boiling over into bloody crime. "The subject of female vengeance is increasingly central to postmillennial noir," notes Samantha Lindop (16). Secondly, and crucially for this volume, the comparison lays bare *Gone Girl's* regional specificity, wherein the South reads as a location host to an inexorable struggle between self-preservation and self-immolation, a thematic plotline signaled by Amy Dunne, the femme fatale and female mastermind, as well as the rural poor, whose desperation and capacity for cutthroat maneuvering rival and perhaps even outdo hers.

Gone Girl dialogues obviously and with great precision with the circumstances of the Great Recession and southern poverty, and can in this respect be considered a southern noir. After the diabolical Amy frames her unfaithful husband for her implied murder, her flight takes her from the economically depressed region of North Carthage, Missouri, to a more recognizable version of the South in the Ozarks. The financial exigencies of Amy's plight become increasingly dire the farther south she gets, particularly after petty thieves steal her stash of survival money and also symbolically rob her of the postfeminist privilege that she has enjoyed her whole life. Her downward trajectory—both literally and figuratively—illustrates that southern motifs can be used to undercut and destabilize power and status, and throws into relief Amy's lack of acumen when matched against adversaries for whom crime is a matter of opportunity and access rather than, as it is for her, an operatic act of elegantly orchestrated revenge.

Despite the sizable distinctions between these two texts, I will argue that *Gone Girl* anchors a very similar set of narratives, affects, and actions as does *Desperate Housewives*. Both focalize on the idea that female domestic disillusion may instigate violent retribution, yet only *Gone Girl* places these realities in a regionalized and classed context. In so doing, *Gone Girl* offers a compelling primer on the southern imaginary, figuring it as a space that dispels postfeminist pretensions—particularly those born from Amy's elitist East Coast upbringing—undoing them with a swift dose of economic urgency.

HISTORIES OF THE SUBURBAN & CHICK NOIR

> These tales of secrets and betrayals reveal the murderous heart
> of darkness—marriage.
>   —Paula Rabinowitz, "Tupperware and Terror"

As alluded to earlier, the terms *suburban noir* and *chick noir* gained particular purchase in 2014, a year that coincided with the cinematic adaptation of *Gone Girl*. While the two terms are related, they do have a slightly different valence. *Gone Girl* is the quintessential chick noir, a term that refers to a psychological thriller and trades on the suggestion that romantic partners are both unknowable and dangerous, a sensation that fuels passion and fear. Chick noirs "deal in the dark side of relationships, intimate danger, the idea that you can never really know your husband or partner or that your home and relationship is threatened," according to novelist Lucie Whitehouse. Chick noirs are in this sense very much marriage thrillers, with titles such as *The Silent Wife, The Husband's Secret, Before We Met, Before I Go to Sleep*, and *How To Be a Good Wife* betraying the lurking unease that haunts the genre. At the same time, these titles illustrate the genre's investment in interrogating the heterosexual marriage contract.

Gone Girl both invokes and exploits the assumption that danger lurks in the supposedly safe sanctity of the home. A wife's disappearance seems to point squarely in the direction of her evasive and adulterous husband, until it is revealed that she staged the violent scene herself. The trope of the unreliable narrator—another hallmark of the genre—dislocates the audience's perception of the reliability of the tale and their own interpretations. Specifically, Amy's posture of wholesomeness and naiveté, a persona referred to in the novel as "Diary Amy," turns out to be a fabrication designed explicitly to cast doubt on her husband. Dangerous sexuality is likewise not visited on Amy but rather perpetrated by her. Though she claims victimhood both at the hands of her husband and a devoted ex-boyfriend, she sets up the ex-boyfriend and claims that he kidnapped and raped her. In a move recalling the *vagina dentata* myth, she slits his throat mid-coitus, a scene that the film version depicts particularly graphically.

The chick noir elevates romantic insecurity and domestic dissatisfaction to an art form, featuring a disjuncture between who people are and who they claim to be. The chick noir is in turn elliptically related to the suburban noir, and both *Desperate Housewives* and *Gone Girl* present a hybridization of the two forms. More capacious and multivaried than the chick noir, the suburban noir has less of a prescriptive plot formula. Perhaps most strikingly, the suburban noir's somber storylines do not match its aesthetics, and may even be overtly and ironically contrasted with them. Whereas shadowy urban spaces define the noir, suburban noirs typically feature sunny track houses whose crisp contours of desperation are bathed in glorious hues. David Lynch's disturbing and iconic film *Blue Velvet* (1986) symptomatizes the American suburban noir, featuring shots of the fictionalized town of Lumberton, North Carolina, where images of colorful flowers, red fire trucks, school children, and white picket fences are interrupted by a man's sudden collapse while he waters a lawn. This setup gives way to a grotesque sequence where the camera tracks through the grass of a suburban lawn to reveal a mass of beetles eating each other. Lynch's televised series *Twin Peaks* (1990–1991) traded on the same eerie blend, wherein terrifying acts such as incest and murder give the lie to the town's appearance of safety and down-home folksiness. (Lynch's 2017 reboot of the original television series served as yet another testament to this narrative's longevity and continued appeal.)

The trope of using a seemingly benign milieu in order to hint at the hidden ugliness that lies within also animates cinematic offerings as diverse as *The Step-ford Wives* (1975), *The Incredible Shrinking Woman* (1981), *Edward Scissorhands* (1990), *Serial Mom* (1994), *Grosse Point Blank* (1997), *Pleasantville* (1998), *The Truman Show* (1998), *Happiness* (1998), *American Beauty* (1999), *Donnie Darko* (2001), *Unfaithful* (2002), *Brick* (2005), and *Little Children* (2006). Yet in many of these suburban noirs, the space of the suburb is explicitly connected to the Northeast (Connecticut is a favored locale) or the Midwest. While the locations are acknowledged, they tend to lack local particularity and serve instead as a syn-ecdoche for American culture writ large. There is therefore a need to appraise the noir in geographically specific ways, a void this article begins to attempt to fill.

Suburban noirs have also tended to focus on malaise felt primarily by men. While a few of the films on the aforementioned list do narrativize the struggles of suburban women, the affective center of the portrayals tends to be middle-aged men in the grip of the realization that their youthful dreams have become casualties of the exigencies of economic and reproductive imperatives. These men have been betrayed by "heteronormative time/space constructs," to use the formulation advanced by Jack Halberstam in *In a Queer Time and Place*, formu-lations that demand markers of progress connected to reproductive futurity, namely stable jobs, permanent homes, monogamous partnerships, and multiple offspring (10). Even *The Stepford Wives*, a film that centralizes women, depicts a plot driven by power-hungry men. While its dystopian critique calls out con-ventional gender normativity as an ideology undergirded by monstrous and even murderous logics (men kill their real wives to turn them into pliant, ultrafemi-nine automatons), the realities of male competition and corruption organize the film's action.

The time has come to situate women and their dissatisfactions in a more predominant location vis-à-vis the suburban noir, and perhaps even to claim narratives for this designation that do not immediately register as noirs. This article employs this strategy with *Desperate Housewives*, arguing that products about women and geared primarily to female audiences may also employ and deploy noir convention, and put it in service of the sort of biting cultural critique that has earned noir its status as a critical darling. While the suburban noir has long been the genre du jour to extemporize on the lot of unhappy husbands, it has the same potential to expose the resentments, discontents, and general pique of wives. This reframing allows for an assertion of the utility of the noir genre to unearth the grim undercurrents of domestic unease, a structure of feeling as acutely visited on women as it is on men. Surely, of course, the noir's femme fatale has long been a reminder and caution against trivializing or discounting bored females, lest their ambitions run amok. Yet the femme fatale rarely presents herself as the source of audience identification, and her interests and inclinations generally do not register as emotional touchstones. In the two texts I survey here, women occupy precisely this space of narrative dominance.

DESPERATE HOUSEWIVES & DOMESTIC DISCONTENT

In an early anthology devoted to a study of *Desperate Housewives*, editors Janet McCabe and Kim Akass attempt to pin down the tone of the series, noting the "retro-cool, Lynchian overtones, bleakly comedic, anti-, pre-, or post-feminist feel to it" (McCabe and Akass, *Reading* 1). That these authors would reference David Lynch is both telling and prescient since Lynch favorite Kyle MacLachlan—star of both *Blue Velvet* and *Twin Peaks*—was cast in *Desperate Housewives* during the end of the show's second season. Appearing as the enigmatic Orson Hodges, a man suspected of abusing his first wife and causing her disappearance, as well as possibly murdering his next girlfriend, Orson's marriage to Bree (Marcia Cross) contains all the hallmarks of chick noir. As the genre demands, Bree struggles for months to discern the true character of the man living in her house and sharing her bed. Orson's former wife, along with his mother, also plot to kill Bree, hence the wife's murder exists as a lurking peril. *Desperate Housewives*'s status as a suburban noir rests in part with its macabre roots.

Series creator Marc Cherry ties its origins to a conversation that Cherry had with his mother after depressed mother Andrea Yates drowned her five children in the family bathtub, a news story that shocked the nation and brought needed attention to the reality of postpartum psychosis. In the discussion, Cherry's mother admitted having at times felt similarly hopeless and alone (Stransky 33). In addition to drawing inspiration from a series of grisly child murders, *Desperate Housewives* deliberately references other suburban dystopias. Its disembodied, from-the-grave voiceover invokes *American Beauty,* and shares with this film a fascination with middle-aged rebellion. Cherry has likewise acknowledged a debt to *Edward Scissorhands,* citing the series penchant for depicting the "nasty things" that lie under the veneer of suburban perfection (35). Fittingly, the conceit that begins *Desperate Housewives* and provides its resounding drumbeat is when a supposedly ordinary housewife shoots herself in her house after she realizes that she will soon be fingered for the murder of her son's biological mother.

Multiple murders in *Desperate Housewives* are in fact domestic in nature and specifically connected to sex and sexual betrayal. The last season of the series, for example, staged a very *Twin Peaks*-esque subplot, revolving around the return of Gabrielle's (Eva Longoria) stepfather, who repeated sexually abused her as a child and who attempts to rape her again before he is killed by her husband. Subsequent to the homicide the housewives engage in an elaborate cover-up, literally burying the body in nearby woods. Given that a long-ago matricide and a fresh suicide ground season one, and pedophilia drives the action in season eight, it seems fair to claim that *Desperate Housewives* is literally bookended by gothic elements. Likewise, the show uses the prominence of domesticity to twisted effect: rather than serving as safe havens, domestic locales provide a backdrop to killings or exist as weapons in and of themselves. Causes of death in the series include: being impaled on a flying fence post, being crushed by a house during a tornado, being smothered by a wardrobe, and having a wrist slit by an angry wife.

Desperate Housewives argues that suburbia is actually a dystopia threatening to women's lives, which is yet another way that *Desperate Housewives* connects to the genealogy of the noir. The pilot, for example, features a scene that mimics a touchstone sequence in the original *The Stepford Wives*. That film closes after the murder of housewife Joanna Eberhart (Katharine Ross), who has been killed thanks to her husband's desire to turn her into a patriarchy-loving robot. In the final scene, the camera pans across a grocery store, where placid, hyper-feminized automatons float effortlessly through the aisles, greeting each other in soft tones. *Desperate Housewives* reimagines that moment with a visual homage: the same shot begins the sequence, panning through the aisles, and settles on an exasperated Lynette (Felicity Huffman) flanked by rambunctious children, demanding a return phone call from her absent husband. Lynette's wild and poorly behaved children, as well as her persistent sadness, suggest that she inhabits a sort of spiritual death.

Desperate Housewives's fondness for utilizing what Dussere has called a "supermarket epiphany" (28) was also evident in a season three sequence where wronged wife Carolyn Bigsby (Laurie Metcalf) shoots at her cheating husband and then takes a series of shoppers hostage, eventually killing one of them. The episode offers a chilling reminder of the potential for violence to pierce the everyday, and twists the supermarket, which typically serves as a synecdoche for consumer culture, housewifery, and suburban homogeneity, into a site of raw and unfettered violence. In the course of the hostage situation Carolyn shoots and kills the woman with whom Lynette's husband conceived a child, and who is now trying to come between Lynette and her husband. In response, Carolyn says to her, "You know you wanted her dead," an accusation that is hard to deny. Similarly, watching the events unfold, and while waged in a bitter, nasty divorce proceeding, Gabrielle says to her estranged husband Carlos (Ricardo Antonio Chavira), "I understand her. I could be her. The rage I've felt these last six months . . . I don't know what I'm capable of anymore . . . this divorce has turned me into a bitter, angry person, and I don't like her." *Desperate Housewives* reinterprets the sites of domesticity, repurposing them as both cause and symptom for anger. At the same time, it suggests women's capacities for brutality.

GONE GIRL, FEMALE RAGE, & ECONOMIC INSECURITY

Commenting in a blog post on her website that men "have a vocabulary for sex and violence that women just don't," Gillian Flynn adds, "we still don't discuss our own violence. We devour the news about Susan Smith or Andrea Yates—women who drowned their children—but we demand these stories be rendered palatable. We want somber asides on postpartum depression or a story about the Man Who Made Her Do It." Flynn's determination to provide a vocabulary for female brutality, and to delve into female culpability rather than offer rationalizations for their anger, recalls both the origin story of *Desperate Housewives* and the nascent understandings of female violence advanced on that series. *Gone Girl* nevertheless doubles down on that premise, reinventing and regionalizing the suburban noir. Specifically, the novel uses the genre to give voice to the economic and psychological devastation wrought by the Great Recession, and employs the backdrop of the South to stymie Amy's enjoyment of the sort of racial and class privilege to which the femme fatale is typically entitled.

On the East Coast, where she grew up, Amy Dunne is a golden girl blessed with good looks, sharp intellect, and a sizable bank account. She is also the inspiration and titular star of a children's book series penned by her parents, the appropriately named *Amazing Amy*. Financial hardship, however, demands her demotion from cheery children's book icon to vengeful wife. When the bank forecloses on the Brooklyn brownstone that Amy's parents helped the couple to buy, her parents suffer bankruptcy from their own bad investments, and the eroding publishing industry renders both her and her husband unemployed, she and Nick move from New York to her husband's hometown in Missouri. A spiteful Amy reads the situation primarily as a betrayal of her. Her relocation to Carthage is therefore but the first in a series where Amy's transition southward highlights her increased loss of control, both of her image and of her ability to author her own life.

Importantly, Amy symbolically conflates the move to Nick's hometown with their marital breakdown because, while there, he begins an affair with a student from the junior college where he finds part-time employment. Bitterly recalling the turn of events, Amy fears not so much the loss of a partner, but rather the obliteration of a self-image founded on her exceptionalism: "I could hear the tale and everyone would love telling it: how Amazing Amy, the girl who never did wrong, let herself be dragged, penniless, to the middle of the country, where her husband threw her over for a younger woman. How predictable, how perfectly average, how amusing. And her husband? He ended up happier than ever. No. I couldn't allow that. No. Never. Never. He doesn't get to do this to me and still fucking win" (234). Amy's determination not to abide this symbolic demotion into ordinariness—what she calls her descent into "Average Dumb Woman Married to Average Shitty Man"—propels a twisted revenge plot whereby she frames her husband for her murder (234). The couple's stressed financial circumstances lead her to be dragged "penniless" (her words) to Missouri, crippling her self-actualization and heightening a sense of powerlessness. She likewise accuses her parents of letting Nick "bundle me off to Missouri like I was some piece of chattel, some mail-order bride, some property exchange" (238). While she does not invoke the term directly, Amy's disordered thinking elliptically invokes the slave trade, oddly and somewhat pathologically aligning herself with enslaved groups.

This sense of personal victimization (however misplaced) confirms that Amy's revenge plan initially takes inspiration less from the noir than from the gothic, with its tales of vulnerable women abused by potent forces outside their control. To fuel the suspicions of the authorities, she pens a fake diary in which Amy is puzzled by her husband's behavior, but generally trusting and well-meaning. Diary Amy consistently ponders her husband's thoughts and motivations and endures his violent and mysterious moods. As the real Amy admits, "I wrote her very carefully, Diary Amy . . . They have to read this diary like it's some sort of Gothic tragedy. A wonderful, good-hearted woman—*whole life ahead of her, everything going for her,* whatever else they say about women who die—chooses the wrong mate and *pays the ultimate price*" (234). While Diary Amy is a feigned persona who exists only in the pages of a fictionalized memoir, the real Amy accuses her husband of a different sort of murder—that of her spirit. "He took away chunks of me with blasé swipes: my independence, my pride, my esteem. I gave, and he took and took . . . That whore, he picked that little whore over me. He killed my soul, which should be a crime. Actually, it is a crime. According to me, at least" (238).

While the gothic patterns provide Amy a convenient template to tell a story that unfairly implicates her husband, Amy does actually appear to believe that her husband has drained the life from her. In this way, her tale elevates the idea of the spiritual death, a narrative trope common to the gothic, and suggests that it deserves the sort of retribution generally reserved for actual murders. Importantly, she also plans to literalize this threat, eventually killing herself for real after she sees Nick convicted of her murder. Nick's sexual betrayal admittedly spurs a great deal of Amy's wrath; graphic and spiteful passages describe the sex she assumes him to be having with his younger girlfriend. At the same time, Amy's anger connects to their own reduced economic circumstances, which are grafted in the novel to the brutalizing effects of the Great Recession. As Nick explains of his hometown, the closing of the Riverway Mall ravaged the town economy: ". . . the downfall of the mall basically bankrupted Carthage," leaving in its wake "two million square feet of echo" (72). In a move that recalls the horror film *Dawn of the Dead* (1978), after her disappearance the authorities discover that Amy attempted to buy a gun at the mall, now inhabited by zombie-like homeless men. (Again, she has carefully manufactured this detail to add credence to Diary Amy's claim that she fears Nick.)

Gone Girl conflates the reality of a crumbling marriage with a crashing economy, pointing out the imbrication of economic circumstances and spousal self-images. In Missouri, Amy and Nick live in a subdivision peppered with foreclosed houses. "Driving into our development occasionally made me shiver," Nick confesses, "the sheer number of gaping dark houses—homes that have never known inhabitants, or homes that have known owners and seen them ejected, the house standing triumphantly voided, humanless" (22). This is a noir vision of marriage and home ownership, to be sure, an inverted copy of the sparkling subdivisions one finds in *Desperate Housewives*'s 1950s-inspired Wisteria Lane. This gloomy setting also imperils Amy's self-image, evacuating a vision of herself as an agentic, independent subject with a charmed life. Prior to the recession, Amy was the quintessential neoliberal subject, and a master of what Emily Johansen calls "postfeminist performance" (45). In New York Amy prided herself on her chameleon-like versatility: "The way some women change fashion regularly, I change personalities. What persona feels good, what's coveted, what's au courant?" (222). Crippled by the couple's financial drift away from the comforts of easy security, Amy laments the loss of the promise of reinvention that accompanied her former status as a consummate marketer of self. Amy's sense that she has lost control of her own narrative—being turned against her will from "Amazing Amy" into "Average Amy"—gives lie to the postfeminist promise that self-direction, autonomy, and self-confidence ensure economic and interpersonal success.

This plotline highlights the hypocrisy at the heart of neoliberal postfeminism, which seems to promise agency if the subject simply wills it strongly enough. Faced with economic and sexual circumstances in which she is no longer favored, Amy loses power and marketability in both the sexual and monetary economies. Amy's unwelcome ordinariness confirms her invisibility, a reality underscored by the fact that Amy discovers her husband's infidelity because she literally sees him with his lover while she cowers in the shadows of the parking lot outside the bar he co-owns. In the wake of what she perceives as obsolescence, Amy attempts to harness the noir script, asserting herself as a femme fatale/criminal mastermind. Crafting and executing her fake death in order to ruin her husband's life represents an attempt to will a new persona, specifically by abandoning the gothic victim persona in favor of the agentic femme fatale. This transition is disrupted, however, by her increasing journey southward, which ratchets up the desperation of her plight and works in opposition to her attempts to claim agency.

As mentioned, Amy's initial transition from New York to Missouri is the first stage of her decline. Images of the Mississippi River in *Gone Girl* echo this metaphor of increasing abjection, and a move down the Mississippi reads as a step towards death, perhaps in homage to the ugly American legacy of slavery. The town of Carthage sits directly on the river, and the couple's house backs up onto it, a fact that fuels Amy's imagination and plays an instrumental role in her plot to frame her husband. In a statement that foreshadows his wife's fascination with the river, Nick returns home on the morning of her disappearance and is surprised to see the couple's cat outside: "Amy knew she'd never see the cat again if he ever got out. The cat would waddle straight into the Mississippi River—deedle-de-dum—and float all the way to the Gulf of Mexico into the maw of a hungry bull shark" (23). Amy's obsession with murder on the Mississippi, and specifically the idea that a journey down the Mississippi represents a descent into death, is likewise an integral component of her plot to frame her husband. Amy deliberately uses Nick's computer to do an internet search of the phrase "Body Float Mississippi River," a search she is confident the authorities will uncover.

This image of her floating dead body similarly provides Amy imaginative fodder while on the run after her implied murder. Amy vividly pictures her body decomposing in the river, "my slim, naked, pale body, floating just beneath the current, a colony of snails attached to one bare leg, my hair trailing like seaweed until I reach the ocean and drift down down down to the bottom" (246). This image also informs her suicide plan: she expects to throw herself into the river and travel south, where "I will meet up with my body, my pretend floating Other Amy body in the Gulf of Mexico" (247). Both in symbolic creation, and in actual fact, the descent southward signals an ominous tract with a nihilistic conclusion.

The grim implications that attend the process of traveling southward only intensify when Amy executes her plot and goes on the run. When Amy begins her stint as "Ozark Amy" (244) she gains weight, darkens her hair, and tans her skin. (In the film version, she claims to be from New Orleans while tanning poolside, and effects an appropriately southern accent to match her invented backstory.) In addition to the obvious racial implications of her transition, Amy begins to live for the first time with a sense that money is not an infinitely replicating substance, which is in itself a realization for someone who has never had to worry about personal finances. As Amy admits, "I never had to think about day-to-day stuff, coupon clipping and buying generic and knowing how much milk costs off the top of my head. My parents never bothered teaching me this" (281). In the south, Amy's economic ignorance allows others to take advantage of her, such as the shopkeeper who charges her more for incidentals like milk because she has no idea what a reasonable price would be.

As "Ozark Amy" she takes an almost perversely touristic pleasure in "slumming it," taking up a residence in a long-term cabin community inhabited by other transients. There she eats hot dogs ("cylinders of phosphates with relish so green it looks toxic"), potato chips, and beer, the sort of cheap and fatty foods old Amy would never permit herself (282). Yet the raw economic necessity of maintaining a life on the run, and doing so while remaining incognito, renders her vulnerable in unexpected ways. After deciding that she actually does not want to kill herself, Amy divulges to the cottage colony owner that she needs money and is seeking odd jobs. She is also known to pay cash for everything, hence revealing that she is not interested in leaving traces of her presence. After a harrowing expedition with her neighbor Jeff, a petty thief, where he agrees to pay her to help him steal fish, Amy becomes increasingly suspicious that he knows who she is. Shortly thereafter Amy is robbed by Jeff and his girlfriend Greta, a woman who passed as Amy's friend, and the couple express conviction that Amy will not go to the police because they know she does not want to be found. In short, her poverty renders her visible, and it is precisely the wrong sort of a visibility.

This situation again highlights the way that race, class, and regional privilege work to assure women like "Amazing Amy" exactly the sort of legibility they desire. In Amy's former life, her decision to be seen or noticed was a matter of choice and preference, and only when she feels this status has been wrenched from her by her husband's lover does she plan retaliation. In the southern setting of the Ozarks, Amy abdicates her nice clothes and good looks, and her poverty lowers her cultural capital and her symbolic value. Likewise, she lacks the requisite skill sets to manipulate others, and her perception that she can control what they see proves to be a dramatic miscalculation. Part of what renders Amy at the mercy of Jeff and Greta is that she neglects to cast them as self-agentic characters in their own right, or to notice that their drive for self-preservation is as strong as hers. As she realizes, "To have assumed I could control them, when they are feral creatures, people used to finding the angle, exploiting the weakness, always needing, whereas I am new to this. Needing" (284). Amy's hubris blinds her to the fact that Jeff and Greta can sniff out her desperation. The trip southward therefore signals an almost atavistic journey whereby the farther south Amy gets, the clearer it becomes that she lacks basic survival skills. In noir terms, she loses the cunning craftiness that ensures one can remain a femme fatale—she is the "mark" rather than the other way around. Similarly, it suggests that once the gaze of the other (in this case, the other being the economically disenfranchised) has been trained on her, she exists as prey rather than predator.

Amy's move to the Ozarks underscores that southern poverty—and the sort of aptitudes it demands—exist in contradistinction to the postfeminist promise that was inculcated in her "Amazing Amy" role. Not only does her move southwards bespeak her declining stature, but it also confirms that her expertise as a postfeminist subject originated in her upbringing as an affluent, white, attractive, East Coaster. When such identities are dismantled, even the mechanics of manipulation take different forms. The couple who rob her size her up accurately, whereas she fails to notice their desperation or their cunning. In stealing from her, they disrupt Amy's cherished illusion that her privilege is somehow inherent to her birthright, and give the lie to the notion that she is capable and superior even while stripped of her beauty and money. In fact, darker hair and skin, bad clothes, an overweight body, and money problems render Amy not merely average, but disadvantaged, a position with which she has scant familiarity. Amy claims, "I am penniless and on the run. How fucking noir" (319). In fact, Amy is robbed of her ability to function as a femme fatale, and neither her East Coast roots nor her prized postmodern ability to shape-shift lend her the survival skills she needs.

It is therefore particularly fitting that in order to regain a position as a femme fatale, Amy must travel northward. After Amy realizes that her sole possession is a beater car and a tank of gas, she maps out her remaining options in cartographical terms. As she muses, "I can drive only about an hour in any direction, so I must choose the direction carefully. South is Arkansas, north is Iowa, west is back to the Ozarks. Or I could go east, cross into Illinois. Suddenly I know what I must do" (319). Importantly, what she does is to drive "north to the meeting spot, a river Casino called Horseshoe Alley" (323) where she meets up with her ex-boyfriend Desi, whom she calls "another man along the Mississippi" (324). There, she convinces him to hide her in his family's posh lake house, which he and his mother have proudly modeled after a Swiss chalet. This journey northward is a transition toward life, one that represents Amy's rediscovered access to wealth and, by implication, her reclamation of the sort of aptitudes and acumen that allow her to manipulate others.

Changing herself back into a version of "Amazing Amy," she swindles an unsuspecting Desi with tales of her abusive husband (a classic noir move) and cons him into thinking that she has fallen in love with him. To be sure, Desi is a controlling and somewhat scary presence in his own right, and here *Gone Girl* does not entirely abandon its gothic overtones. Desi locks Amy in his house, doles out her food, monitors her appearance, and curates multiple rooms that seem to have been designed to lure her (particularly a tulip room, which was her favorite flower when they were dating). Yet, while she is there, Amy loses weight, regains her appearance, and reclaims her sense of invincibility. She is once again feted, celebrated, and thought to be a perfect specimen of femininity. Though she is momentarily captive, she simultaneously reinvigorates her status as a femme fatale, and it is in this milieu that she hatches the plot to kill Desi and frame him for her kidnapping.

Recapturing her power proves to be the turning point in Amy's entire saga— subsequent to murdering Desi, she returns home to Carthage to great public fanfare and to a cowed husband who knows the atrocities of which she is capable. To further trap Nick, Amy secretly impregnates herself with his sperm, blackmails him into staying married to her, pens a memoir about her ordeal simply called *Amazing*, and contents herself with a facsimile of domestic perfection that she reads as a victory.

* * *

CONCLUSION

Gone Girl not only intensifies themes that were latent in *Desperate Housewives*—female fury and anger, a disillusion with heterosexual marriage, and the recognition that images of domesticity are flawed, unstable, and can be manipulated—but also uses the southern lower-class setting and the tropes associated with it to render those themes grotesque. Women avenge their betrayals, often doing so ruthlessly and with very little compunction. If, as Becca Rothfeld claims in a review of *Gone Girl*, women in the real world are often "powerless to hold men accountable" and "female emotion is valued as a fundamentally worthless currency," suburban noirs insist that such emotions matter and render them incendiary. That said, these are admittedly dark and cynical portrayals, where women's victories tend to come in the form of revenge and retribution that may severely outweigh the crimes committed against them. Similarly, reconciliation (if achieved at all) is compromised and founded on highly shaky ground. Such offerings coldly emphasize lack of earnest or true connection possible in a situation where power is the ultimate arbiter of success. Deftly repurposing hallmarks of the noir genre such as murder, manipulation, and revenge, this new breed of suburban noirs put violent acts in service of avenging a heterosexual order where male sexual betrayal typically remains unchecked.

The deadly woman of the neo-noir "has always been an active, calculating character, but since the emergence of postfeminism has become, in many instances, overwhelmingly powerful, autonomous and self-determining," Lindop asserts (14). If the neoliberal actor is an agent of the self, wronged women feel themselves both called and compelled to recognize, name, and retaliate in the face of their (perceived) mistreatment. Though recent suburban noirs betray a profound cultural unease about what happens when women aim to punish their oppressors, and hand-wringing about who might additionally get wronged in the process, they forcefully insist on female presence, action, and voice, but only if they remain in the middle-class, middle-American suburbs. Amy's brush with powerlessness in the Ozarks nevertheless reminds us that the suburban noir script only works when the femme fatale can deploy the advantages of economics and education. Stripped of these luxuries, Amy is neither amazing, nor even average—instead, she can perhaps best be labeled "Inadequate Amy."

PART II

PRIVATELY DETECTING THE SOUTH

ELNORA MAY HARDIN

Creating Space for a Complex Black Woman in Southern Noir

DOMINIQUA DICKEY

E lnora May Hardin revealed herself to me after years of reading detective novels, viewing old noir films, and listening to stories about the amazing women in my family. I see her as wholly original and unique, but also a composite of numerous influences. Similar to most noir heroes, she is flawed and offers no apology for her lack of perfection. With Humphrey Bogart's Sam Spade and the Spenser and Easy Rawlins series strong in my imagination and memory, the necessity of an unapologetic Elnora became impossible to ignore. Of course, there are other women in classic noir, such as Barbara Stanwyck's unforgettable Phyllis Dietrichson from *Double Indemnity,* Joan Crawford's unwavering *Mildred Pierce,* and Teresa Wright's Charlie from *Shadow of a Doubt,* to name a few, with each representing a specific archetype while facing unimaginable situations, but none of them encounter the challenges of a black woman in the Jim Crow South.

I can think of no region in the United States that possesses the level of preconceived definition more than the Deep South, in particular, Mississippi. Whenever I introduce myself and acknowledge that I grew up in the state, my new acquaintance's eyes will widen, and in a hushed tone, I am asked, "What's it like? Is it [racism] really that bad?" After over a decade of creating a succinct polite response—"It's like anywhere, and racism is racism"—the questions should no longer surprise me. Racism is not location specific and definitely not centralized to one area. Elnora's ability to navigate across color lines reflects the Mississippi that I know and the stories that older family members have shared. Her story of a black woman confronting miscegenation, a missing child, and complicated relationships, both familial and romantic, may appear pure plot-driven fiction, but is actually inspired by family history.

My maternal great-great aunt Elnora who resided in the very real Grenada, Mississippi, with the help of her older sister, raised my grandmother Hattie subsequent to her mother's death due to complications from childbirth. Like the fictitious Hattie, my grandmother's white father would often remove her from the home she shared with her mother's family until her aunts traveled, sometimes out of state, to reclaim the fair-skinned, blue-eyed child. Eventually my great-grandfather ceased making these excursions to Grenada to claim his daughter, and she would later marry three black men and have six children, including my mother.

The paternal side of my family provides excellent inspiration for storytelling as well, with my grandfather having a similar background as my Grandma Hattie. Born in Pike County near the beginning of the 20th century to a black mother and a white father, my Grandpa Britt grew up fully aware of the lineage of his siblings and himself, who were publicly claimed by his father's side of the family. The idea that race-mixing, interracial relations, or the more formal term, miscegenation, was a strongly held secret in Mississippi small towns could not be more false. Whether the relations were consensual remains known only to the participants, the results of the pairings were acknowledged and never hidden in the vault of family secrets.

The combination of my maternal grandmother's early life with my paternal grandfather's came naturally as background for "God's Gonna Trouble the Water." I have often warned new writers against using "real" people as characters and their lives as plot lines, because attachments can be hard to release, especially in a workshop setting; however, I offer no defense for my hypocrisy here. I will admit to adjustments to create a work that is more fictitious than biographical. The parts that reflect my family are sprinkled into the narrative like seasoning in a pot of stew, just enough to give flavor, but not too much to overpower the main course.

Noir brings to mind dark, gritty, urban settings. Chicago and New York have historic skyscrapers and distinct vibes. Los Angeles comes with landmarks and the infinite promise of fantasy, with Hollywood looming like an expensive backdrop. A small southern town bordered by cotton fields and former plantation houses may not be considered the first choice for the die-hard noir connoisseur. But dark alleys are everywhere in 1930s Grenada and many continue to exist today. The invisible color line that once separated the neighborhoods is evident in the older section of town with the larger homes and manicured lawns on one side of the main strip and the smaller, cramped shotgun houses on the other side. Often overlooked details such as sidewalks and landscaping also reveal the attention as to which areas were thought to deserve those conveniences and which did not. Of course Grenada, as most small southern towns, maintains its dignity with a town square and the obligatory stone Confederate soldier standing guard. Elnora Hardin's sins and absolution could not achieve effective resolution anywhere but in Grenada, in a time when societal norms restricted her by gender and race.

Social media plays a significant impact in our lives. We have Facebook, Twitter, Instagram, Snapchat, texting, and more. Our smartphones keep us connected whether we want to be or not. Instant access to the latest news is only a click or thumb push away.

Amber alerts are issued for missing children and if we are in the vicinity, our phones will inform us with the details. Newsbreaks interrupt our scheduled programs to give us the latest information. However, for Elnora, her greatest ally in her search for little Hattie is not social or news media, but word of mouth: in short, plain ole gossip, the sustenance of most small towns.

When I think of Grenada, I am reminded of the bar in the late 1980s sitcom, *Cheers*, where upon entry every character is acknowledged by name. Often, strangers would approach me who either knew my parents or my siblings. Some attempted to pronounce my name while others referred to a nickname that only my family and very close friends used. Random information about my family usually followed the strangers' awkward, gregarious greetings. The Grenada where I came of age is no different from Elnora's 1930s fictitious version. The citizens—such as Juju, Sal, and Octavia—know everyone and are well informed. Juju and Sal's excuses are due to their occupations as cab driver and grocer, respectively, but Octavia has no defense aside from a healthy curiosity.

My familiarity with Grenada is equal to that of my family's history. On July 4, 1836, two warring towns married the daughter and the son of its prominent families to create one city, Grenada. Line Street exists to this day to mark the former separate municipalities. A century later, the division remains evident in Elnora's world except this conflict reveals itself in terms of race. Pragmatic and cognizant of laws and limitations, Elnora cannot envision an inclusive Grenada. Baby Hattie serves as evidence of a promising future for her white father, Graham Lee, but he is the only person who holds that vision.

The dream of a racially utopian Grenada in 1936 is unimaginable to the characters because of the focus on outward appearances. They are unable to recognize the many associations that already bind them despite the rules of what Jim Crow has determined as allowable. Sal Romano's brotherly protection of Elnora is just as intense as Rayford Drew's blatant desire and need to provide for her. Of the three men, Graham Lee is the only one whose honest intentions prevail. He, like Elnora, is not a perfect fit for the space and time.

Elnora's approach to life, love, conflicts, and joy fascinate me. Like most noir heroes, she has a code, but hers does not pertain to the use of violence. She abhors gossip and commands respect by maintaining her composure and strong sense of dignity. When she makes a promise, she stands by it. As I type these sentences, I am aware that the possibility of perfection is creeping into this character, but she is nowhere near that label. Elnora's need for control in an era that demands she have none has rendered her a bit brusque with her emotions. She fears vulnerability and losing herself completely to anyone, be that her child or her man. She is described as a character who can fix things, but in actuality, she is in need of "fixing" more than anything or anyone else. This black woman with a plethora of secrets in a small southern town yearns to maintain her sense of autonomy, but when her grandchild is missing, she has no choice but to go against her instincts and rely on the assistance of others. This terrifies her.

A terrified heroine? In noir? How can this be? Stanwyck's Phyllis is seductive and detached while plotting her husband's murder in *Double Indemnity*. Wright is the perfect combination of innocence and righteousness as her Charlie uncovers the truth about her namesake in *Shadow of a Doubt*. Crawford's *Mildred Pierce* wavers a bit during her confession to murder, but lying to protect her daughter strengthens her resolve more than fear of prosecution. Femmes fatales assume roles to achieve their desired goals, but they are rarely beset by inner fears. Instead, they are tigresses, collecting prey with style and sass. Elnora contradicts most parameters that I learned as a young avid film buff.

I push against my strongest truth as a fiction writer if I say that I developed Elnora and created her to be this contradiction intentionally. The birth of my characters is in collaboration between them and me. Every writer has a process, and I acknowledge that mine is a mutual effort. Elnora's sense of self and purpose comes through not entirely because I was driven to create a character so opposite the traditional noir heroine, not just by race but also temperament and actions. Elnora, while inspired by certain family members, is not a true reflection of anyone, living or dead.

My introduction to the story began with Cissy and Elnora's voices and a brief conversation between the two, which follows:

> "You good at fixin' things."
> "Ain't nothin' I'm good at fixin' but hair and a mess of greens."

The plot of Cissy's missing child and Elnora's becoming an investigator arrived of its own accord. My great-grandfather's desire to be a father to his mixed race daughter wove itself into the narrative, but Graham Lee Donner is not a composite of my great-grandfathers. His true love for Cissy and Hattie came as gravel tones when he first whispered his lines to me. While Cissy was direct and somewhat manipulative, Graham Lee pleaded. His uncle spoke with authority. A distinctive southern drawl gave Rayford Drew's voice a seductive quality, which did not in any way compromise his power. Ed Jenkins vibrated with the passion of youth, justice, and his love for his woman. Finally, Elnora hinted that she had little patience for fools or games and welcomed sincerity.

Regrets dogged her, but she pressed on by building a life that made her proud.

I cannot say that Elnora's trust in my willingness to tell her story her way came easily, but it came. I learned with previous stories not to instill too much of my will into the narrative as this only causes the flow to cease and the characters to stop talking. As I stated before, every writer has a process. This one works for me. I freely acknowledge that at times I am their typist and I am fortunate to be allowed to relay their lives. Of course, that situation is known as the first draft. Subsequent drafts and revisions fall on me and what I have learned from the experience of getting to know each character and the goals and motivations that define him or her.

Elnora May Hardin chose Grenada in 1936 because the time and space beckoned. In a genre consumed by strong, capable men, the emergence of a black southern woman fills a void. Elnora's ability to adapt to the environment and her understanding of the social classes and culture within a small town afford her the courage and strength to move into spaces that usually exclude women. She is not the female version of Easy Rawlins. Nor can she be classified as the typical femme fatale. Elnora embodies the spirit of a perfectly flawed individual in pursuit of the American Dream without being disturbed or bothered by petty gossipers or nonachievers.

DOWN THESE MEAN STREETS
(WHOSE NAMES NO ONE CAN PRONOUNCE)

GREG HERREN

> Don't you just love those long rainy afternoons in New Orleans when an
> hour isn't just an hour—but a little piece of eternity dropped into your
> hands—and who knows what to do with it?
>
> —Tennessee Williams, *A Streetcar Named Desire*

New Orleans is a city very much aware of its history. Converted buildings
that used to be slave quarters still have holes in the brick walls where the
manacles used to hang. Maspero's Café now sits where the slave auctions used to
be held. The Napoleon House, now a restaurant famed for its Pimms Cups, was
named that because a resident offered the house as a residence for the French
Emperor after his second abdication.

General Jackson, hero of the Battle of New Orleans, doffs his hat to tourists
on his rearing horse in the center of the square named for him. Felicity Street is
still cobblestone. Everywhere you look, it seems, no matter what street or neighborhood you are in, you can see historic markers and plaques mounted outside
gates or on the homes themselves. The tomb of Marie Laveau is one of the most
visited sites in St. Louis Cemetery Number One. Madame LaLaurie's house of
horrors, where she tortured and maimed her slaves, still stands on its corner.

New Orleans treasures its past, and both resents and resists change. But
change comes to the city inexorably, just as the river continues to sweep by on
its way to the gulf, carrying the detritus and garbage from almost two-thirds of
the continent along with it. A modern-day Blanche duBois can no longer take
a streetcar named Desire. The Desire streetcar no longer runs, clickety-clack,
through the French Quarter, and hasn't since the city ripped up most of the
streetcar tracks (or paved over them) back in the late 1950s. The Desire line still
exists; only now it's a bus, belching black smoke and diesel fumes, with the name
82 DESIRE.

Needless to say, telling someone to take a bus named Desire doesn't sound
nearly so poetic or romantic. Regardless, the directions Blanche received upon
her arrival in New Orleans—to "take a streetcar named Desire, then switch to

one called Cemeteries and get off at Elysian Fields"—were not correct, anyway. The Desire streetcar didn't originate at the bus/train station; the start of the line was at the corner of Canal and Royal Streets, and once aboard, the Desire street-car would have taken her to Elysian Fields without any need to change lines.

But the wrong directions are necessary so that great quote can exist, and also sub-textually tell People Not From Here (always capitalized that way) that direc-tions, like so many other things here, are *different*. The normal, standard points of a compass have no meaning in New Orleans: asking a local which way is north will simply get you a confused look, a shake of the head, and finally, a knowing smile: "You're not from here, are you?" In New Orleans, everything has to do with water, the reason the city exists and yet still, the eternal enemy; water is both a blessing and a curse. Our compass points are lakeside, riverside, uptown (up the river) and downtown (down the river). The Mississippi River has always defined and shaped New Orleans, curling and twisting and bending its way to the delta, the city nestled inside two of those bends so that the river, which in theory flows south to the Gulf from its starting point up in Minnesota, actually flows west to east through the city; so the "West Bank" is actually south, despite actually being the west side of the river. The streets themselves are confusing—the French Quarter's streets don't match up to the ones on the other side of Ca-nal Street, nor do they have the same name. Once they cross Esplanade Avenue into the Marigny District, they also take a ninety degree turn southward, to fol-low the path of the river. In the Central Business District, there are three one-way streets in a row that all run the same direction. A two-way street will sud-denly become a one-way at an intersection without warning. Camp Street and Camp Place run parallel to each other, with only a neutral ground (what would be called a median in another city; why they are called 'neutral grounds' is yet another one of those things that makes New Orleans so different—originally the French Quarter was separated from the American settlement by the 'neu-tral ground' of Canal Street) separating them, but they are not the same street. Some streets only exist for a block or two; some streets run parallel in one part of the city only to bisect in another. The newcomer will also be confused by the way the streets are pronounced: *Chartres* is *charters*; *Calliope* is *call-ee-ope*; and the emphasis is on the second syllable, rather than the first, in *Burgundy*. And if someone directs you to "chop-a-toolis," good luck translating that into what the street sign reads: TCHOUPITOULAS.

> New Orleans . . . a courtesan whose hold is strong upon the mature,
> to whose charm the young respond. And all who leave her, seeking the

virgin's unbrown, ungold hair and her blanched and icy breast where no
lover has died, return to her when she smiles across her languid fan . . .
  —William Faulkner, *New Orleans Sketches*

New Orleans is a city that hates change and holds fast to its history; but despite
that dislike of change, things change all the time. K&B Drugstores are gone,
replaced by CVS and Rite-Aid; Schwegmann's Grocery Stores are now Rouse's;
the big Maison Blanche department store on Canal Street is now a Ritz-Carlton
Hotel; and if Ignatius Reilly were going to wait for his mother underneath the
big clock on Canal Street, he would be in front of a Hyatt Regency instead of
the D. H. Holmes Department Store.

That history, though, is part of what gives the city its charm; combined with a
strong, distinct local culture, New Orleans continues to seduce and beguile writers. New Orleans chose me on a sultry hot August night in 1994. I was an airline
employee in my early thirties with aspirations of being a writer, come to the city
for a birthday weekend with friends. When I got out of the cab, stepping out onto
a bent and broken sidewalk, and breathed in the thick air redolent with grease
and magnolia and jasmine and honeysuckle over urine and vomit and stale alcohol, I knew I was home. I knew that New Orleans wanted me to live there,
become a part of the polyglot fabric that made up the city, and she also, above
all else, wanted me to write about her. To date, I have written countless short
stories and fourteen crimes novels set in New Orleans; I have barely scratched
the surface, and she gives me more to write about every day.

I came out in the French Quarter years before I came out in the
Garden District.
  —Tennessee Williams, *Suddenly Last Summer*

I started writing my first crime novel shortly after finally moving to New Orleans
in 1996. I had created an outsider to tell the story; like me, Chanse MacLeod
was not a local with family ties going back generations, who knew what the
difference between going to De La Salle or Jesuit or Newman meant. Like me,
Chanse was in love with the city and felt like he belonged there. An ex-cop and
a graduate of Louisiana State University, Chanse was from East Texas and went
to college on a football scholarship.

His first case was actually based on something that happened here: someone
blew into town spending a lot of money and founded a nonprofit whose purpose
was ostensibly to work for LGBTQ+ rights. After throwing some great parties

and raising a lot of money, he disappeared in the middle of the night, leaving behind a pile on unpaid bills, some angry donors, and a lot of questions.

There hadn't been a lot of gay fiction written or published about New Orleans at that time; as a voracious reader one of the things that annoyed me the most about LGBTQ+ fiction was its focus and emphasis on New York, San Francisco, and (to a lesser degree) Los Angeles. The absence of New Orleans from the LGBTQ+ fiction shelves was criminal to me. The longest operating gay bar in the country is in New Orleans, and there is a long history of drag and being, if not accepting, then at least tolerant of the LGBTQ+ community. There are gay Mardi Gras krewes and balls, scores of gay bars, and at one time the city had two LGBTQ+ newspapers. One of the oldest operating gay bookstores was in the Marigny District. The city inspired Tennessee Williams, who called it his spiritual home. Truman Capote was born here. Every independent bookstore in the city's "local authors" section was crammed full of books—everything from vampire romances to literary fiction to comedy to crime.

So where was the LGBTQ+ fiction? Poppy Z. Brite was writing fantastic horror novels with gay and bisexual characters, and J. M. Redmann' fantastic Micky Knight series covered New Orleans beautifully from the point of view of a cynical, world-weary, hard-drinking lesbian private eye. But no one was writing the kinds of books about gay New Orleans that were being written about gay New York or gay San Francisco.

When I was a deeply closeted gay teen in Kansas, coming across gay characters in fiction was rare. I have always been a voracious reader, and as a child I tore through the Hardy Boys and Nancy Drew and every other mystery series for kids that I could find. I moved on to Agatha Christie, Ellery Queen, and Erle Stanley Gardner in junior high school, and encountered my first obviously gay character in Ellery Queen's *The Last Woman in His Life*. That gay character was closeted and madly in love with his eventual victim; it was only when he realized that the object of his obsession was disgusted and repulsed by him that he became a murderer. Periodically, I would come across characters in Christie that were coded—any number of "confirmed bachelors"—but the first definitely queer characters I found in Christie were two spinster women who lived together in *A Murder Is Announced*. One was more masculine and wore pants and brooked no nonsense from anyone; the other was feminine and ladylike and a bit empty-headed. Misses Murgatroyd and Hinchliffe were the first lesbian couple I came across in crime fiction, and I often, as a boy, thought about writing crime stories with a gay main character.

I also thought it would never be possible.

I discovered the works of Gordon Merrick and Patricia Nell Warren on the racks at the News Depot on Commercial Street in Emporia, Kansas; I was stunned to see that books were being published that were about gay characters and depicted gay sex so frankly and explicitly. Merrick's books were Jackie Collins/Harold Robbins/Sidney Sheldon style books about very wealthy gay men, or men on the fringes of high society; Patricia Nell Warren's *The Front Runner* was about an Olympic level distance runner and was very in-your-face about the gay rights struggle. The main character in Harold Robbins's *Dreams Die First* was bisexual; there were some fairly steamy male-on-male sex scenes in that book. Usually though, on the rare occasions when I would come across a gay character, they were effeminate, and a figure of contempt or scorn, or a victim of some sort. I wasn't aware that there was an entire genre of gay and lesbian fiction with subcategories; that came when I moved to Tampa and discovered the gay bookstore, Tomes and Treasures. My first time in the store, I asked the guy working there to recommend some books to me, and I walked out of the store with *Dancer from the Dance* by Andrew Holleran, *Faggots* by Larry Kramer, and *Tales of the City* by Armistead Maupin. I continued to visit the store from time to time, and soon discovered that what I dreamed of as a teenager—crime fiction with gay men as the main character—now existed. I read Michael Nava, Richard Stevenson, Mark Richard Zubro, John Morgan Wilson, and R. D. Zimmerman. But even then, only Stevenson was writing about a private eye who was gay.

There were also a lot of New Orleans crime novels. Julie Smith, Tony Dunbar, Chris Wiltz, Caroline Mooney, James Sallis, and Ace Atkins, among others, were writing exceptional crime series set in New Orleans and covering almost every aspect of it, from a Garden District maid to a music professor at Tulane to a NOPD detective to a slightly crooked lawyer. Barbara Hambly was writing a brilliant series set in pre–Civil War New Orleans from the point of view of a "free man of color."

But while gay men might pop up in one of those books from time to time, they were never the center of the story—and they were never even the case driving the story. I wanted to change that. I thought it was time for someone to write about crime and New Orleans from a gay male perspective. My motivation wasn't to document history or create great art; I simply thought it was something that needed to be done and since no one else was doing it, I ought to give it a shot. I wanted to explore gay themes, characters, and stories with a New Orleans setting, and I also wanted to show the city from that perspective.

So I created Chanse MacLeod, an emotionally closed-off gay man from a deeply religious upbringing in a small, claustrophobic Texas town (similar to the one from Larry McMurtry's *The Last Picture Show*) who has moved to New Orleans in order to feel free enough to live as an openly gay man. He was at the start of his first real relationship. He was six feet, four inches tall, 220 pounds of solid muscle from being a scholarship football player at LSU; football was his ticket out of his stifling small east Texas town and poverty. He had been sexually promiscuous, but also wasn't comfortable with the bar scene—it was a means to the end of getting sexual satisfaction. He still had some residual self-loathing about his sexuality: "I'm gay, but I'm not one of *those* gays." The purpose of the series was to show him growing and learning to accept himself, and finally being able to have a successful and happy relationship; each case was to show him learning something about himself.

Having scenes where Chanse was evaluating other gay men based on how attractive they were to him was only different from established hard-boiled crime fiction in that it was a man looking at other men; the Travis McGee books and many other hard-boiled/noir crime novels with straight men as the main characters had scene after scene after scene of the straight male gaze evaluating the women they came into contact with based on, to be crude, their fuckability; I made it into the gay male gaze instead.

And despite Elmore Leonard's admonition to writers to never begin with the weather, I opened my first book just that way:

Never come to New Orleans in the summer. It's hot. It's humid. It's sticky. It's damp. It's hot. Air conditioners blow on high. Ceiling fans rotate. Nothing helps. The air is thick as syrup. Sweat becomes a given. No antiperspirant works. Aerosol sticks, powders, and creams all fail. The thick air just hangs there, brooding. The sun shows no mercy. The vegetation grows out of control. Everything's wet. The buildings perspire.

Even a simple task becomes a chore. Taking the garbage out becomes an ordeal. The heat makes the garbage rot faster. The city starts to smell sour. The locals try to mask the smell of sweat with more perfume. Hair spray sales go up. Women turn their hair into lacquered helmets that start to sag after an hour or so.

Even the flies get lazy.

It wasn't until after Hurricane Katrina irrevocably altered the face of New Orleans, and the image it presented to the world, that I realized I had documented a world that no longer exists. It became even more apparent when I reread my first book several years ago to prepare it for an ebook edition. So much of what I'd written about was gone: Kaldi's Coffee Shop and Museum on Decatur Street, the K&B Drugstore on Magazine Street, the battered, graffiti-decorated public telephones. Some of the gay bars I wrote about didn't reopen afterwards.

Pre-Katrina New Orleans hated and resisted change with grit and determination. Before Hurricane Katrina, there were well-documented battles over whether a Wal-Mart should be allowed in the lower Garden District. Despite its tolerance for the LGBTQ+ community, there were protestors at Southern Decadence (called 'gay Mardi Gras' by some, it takes place every year over Labor Day weekend) and moves from evangelical Christians to have it cancelled (in one of those "only in New Orleans" moments, the preacher leading the anti-gay charge, Grant Storms, was later convicted of public indecency for masturbating in his car by a playground). The desire of Starbucks to move into the New Orleans market was viewed in about the same light as the Union Army was viewed during the Civil War. But Katrina, and the flooding that resulted from the levee failure after the storm passed, brought inevitable change in its wake. New Orleans would never be the same afterward; the flood waters washed away what was and left in its wake the possibility of something new, something better, but that something had to still be rooted in the city's past and reverence for its way of life.

I write fiction, but the fiction is based in the reality of New Orleans.

My first novel after the flood, *Murder in the Rue Chartres*, was a book I never wanted to write, but one that I felt I had no choice but to write. Chanse returned to his devastated city on the same day I returned after the evacuation, feeling enormous guilt about abandoning the city to its destruction but determined to be a part of the rebuilding process. I opened the book with the following sentence, which I felt summed up not only how *I* felt, but how we all did:

It was six weeks before I returned to my broken city.

Everything Chanse sees in that book is what I saw when I returned; from the uprooted live oak trees to the military vehicles with machine guns mounted on the hoods. I also saw an opportunity to link the tragedy of Hurricane Katrina to another specifically gay tragedy that occurred in New Orleans: the fire at the Upstairs Lounge. The Upstairs Lounge fire was, until the 2106 shootings at the Pulse Nightclub in Orlando, the largest mass murder of citizens in American history; a horrific arson fire in which almost thirty were killed, burned to death, some of the bodies so badly burned they weren't recognizable. I had always wanted to write about the Upstairs Fire after hearing about it, and being able to link the two tragedies in the pages of a crime novel helped me, in some ways, to heal my own wounds after the Katrina flooding disaster.

The New Orleans of today is vastly different from the New Orleans I originally fell in love with and started writing about twenty years ago, but New Orleans will never stop inspiring me. Riding the St. Charles streetcar, visiting a cemetery, walking to the park in my neighborhood, or just walking through the French Quarter on my way to the bank, I am always awed, amazed, and inspired by the city. Riding the streetcar home from a lunch date inspired my short story, "A Streetcar Named Death." A visit to the ruined neighborhoods of the lower Ninth Ward in the fall of 2005 inspired my short stories "Annunciation Shotgun" and "Survivor's Guilt." The closing of Our Lady of Good Counsel by the Archdiocese of New Orleans, and the angry protests by the parishioners, provided me with the framework for *Murder in the Irish Channel.*

I once joked, when asked why I write about New Orleans, that it was impossible to love her and not write about her: "How can you not be inspired by a city where every day is Anything Can Happen Day?"

New Orleans chose me, and I will always be eternally grateful.

EVOLVING SECRETS

Eudora Welty and the Mystery Genre

HARRIET POLLACK

A rguably Eudora Welty's signature version of modernism is a spare, whittled story-puzzle. She asks readers to don their detective caps and search for clues in fictions that defy readers' expectations. A strategy of secrets is clear across her career. Welty characteristically adapts mystery conventions without bringing easy resolution, thickening rather than solving mystery. And so it is not shocking that Welty literally defines the released secret as the source of pleasure in fiction. It is the hallmark of her story form. In her signature technique, the discovery of a secret happens not only in plot, but also when readers are surprised by her displacement of narrative conventions. When readers' expectations fail, surprise and discovery direct them. It is consistent that Welty calls surprised expectation "the source of the deepest pleasure we receive from a writer" ("Reading" 49). Welty—perhaps wryly impersonating the self-serious language of criticism—called this the pleasure of a writer's "quondam obstruction" (49), or more simply, obstruction that once was. She comments that "deliberate obscurity" is "a fault in the teller," but that "mysterious is something else" (Prenshaw 190). In Welty's puzzle-texts, it is exactly Welty's innovative play with a reader's competencies with conventions, producing surprised expectations, that makes her a paramount modernist, a woman writer with a most cunning swerve, a short story writer of the first rank, and a remarkable literary innovator.

Beginning with *A Curtain of Green* (1941), Welty's first story collection, it is quite clear that her fiction is mysterious: her stories are built circling secrets. Something needs clarification, explanation, interpretation, a puzzle needs to be defined. In "The Hitchhikers" (a noir fiction, first published in 1939), thirty-year old travelling salesman Tom Harris is on the road to Memphis when he stops for two hitchhikers. Before the night is over, one hiker kills the other in Harris's car. The action is known, but there are discoveries to be made by the reader, hinted at in a fiction that invites curiosity and speculation in readers. At the story's end, Tom Harris's driving on does not restore order, offer resolution, or create peace. Rather we sense, as we often do in Welty's fictions, what remains unknowable and yet asks to be understood. Her puzzles are not resistant to careful scrutiny, but beyond first solutions there's another level of mystery, a fissure between what we know of characters and what we don't. It is most helpful to say—as Suzanne Marrs has—that her fictions "reveal, rather than resolve, mystery" (200). Similarly in "Flowers for Marjorie" (first published in 1937), the secret we work on is not *who* killed Marjorie; we know her husband did it. The official police solution closing the tale resolves nothing for a reader. Rather it is the reader who locates a sense of motive in Depression-era unemployment, in an implied crisis of masculinity, and in the weight of urban anonymity.

There are rumors of murder, abuse, crime, and mystery in tales belonging to other–even comic–genres. In "Powerhouse" the riddle playfully concerns who killed Gypsy. In "A Piece of News," the puzzle concerns Ruby Fisher, who reads the newspaper report of another Ruby Fisher violently shot by her husband. It is not only a husband's violence that we discover, but rather, and more mysteriously, Ruby Fisher's imagination. In "The Key," the enigma features a red-haired stranger who drops a key picked up by a deaf man, and then, after observing or imagining the mute man's relationship with his wife, bizarrely offers the wife a second key. Readers find secrets in these puzzle-texts designed to create mysteries that, to a degree, they solve in order to and as they read the story.

Technically, Welty creates her stories' secrets by both evoking and displacing familiar conventions. Not about restoring order by solving a crime, her story-puzzles characteristically allow mystery to linger. While taking her career interest in the mystery form into account, this essay—so focused on crime fiction—explores Welty's late career unpublished drafts of "The Shadow Club" and "Alterations"—projects that tangibly reflect the influence of her close friendship with the eminent detective fiction writer Ross Macdonald, and the impact of her admiration for his work in the mystery genre.

It is not really surprising to learn that Welty was a lifetime consumer of popular crime and detective fiction, murder mysteries, and police procedurals. A visit to her house, itself one large bookcase, makes this background clear. Moreover, her early consumption of the form shows in her juvenilia, and particularly in a detective spoof, "The Great Pinnington Solves the Mystery" (1925), a parody written for a campus publication while she was a precocious 16-year-old freshman at Mississippi State College for Women (*Early* 82–89). Her early familiarity with pulp publications that followed the prototypical magazine *Black Mask* is also clear from allusions she makes in stories: *Startling G-Man Tales* pops up in "Petrified Man" and *Terror Tales and Astonishing Stories* in "Old Mr. Marblehall." Her steady consumption of mysteries is additionally evident in her correspondence and in her offers to loan those books to friends. And when she wrote book reviews, she discussed the detective in Faulkner's *Intruder In The Dust* and in Ross Macdonald's *The Underground Man,* the review that led to her meeting Ken Millar (pen name Ross Macdonald), to their remarkable friendship, and to her years of consequential correspondence with him.

Paradoxically after a lifetime interest in writing mystery, in 1970, six years after she published "The Demonstrators"—an evident murder mystery[1]—Welty fell into a most significant relationship with the celebrated mystery writer. This association further influenced the work she would attempt in the late years of her life. Because Welty and Millar physically met on only six occasions, their epistolary infatuation essentially records their relationship, with only the six gaps of their face-to-face meetings left for us to imagine (Marrs and Nolan, *Meanwhile* 6). Millar had first written Welty in 1970 to praise *Losing Battles,* and for a year they traded preliminary messages. Then in May 1971, in New York from his home in Santa Barbara, California, Millar "engaged in . . . real-life . . . stake-out" in the lobby of the Alqonquin Hotel, hoping to encounter Welty, who had recently published a *New York Times* review of his novel *The Underground Man* that bolstered his reputation—as a detective fiction writer deserving a literary, as well as popular, following. "His stakeout paid off. As Welty approached the hotel elevator, Millar/Macdonald . . . introduced himself. Abandoning whatever plans she had had, Welty was thrilled to sit and talk" (Marrs 1). Living across the country from one another, the two writers then carried on their exchange of letters until Alzheimer's disease ended Millar's part of the correspondence in 1980; Welty continued her side solo until Millar's death in 1983. These letters provided the literary intimacy that Welty had once attempted with John Robinson, a man who ultimately disappointed her as much when he did not manage the writing career that she wanted for him as when he chose another life partner.[2] Marrs and Nolan describe the Millar–Welty relationship as friendship moving towards love, complicated by Millar's marriage (Marrs and Nolan 387). Interestingly, in Millar's last novel, *The Blue Hammer,* his signature detective Lew Archer has an unexpected love interest, Betty Jo Sidon, a woman writer who has not had the disadvantage of being beautiful. Archer is attracted to her through her work. And their intimacy is more than sexual, but limited by her.

Macdonald's Lew Archer series had established him as preeminent creator of hard-boiled detective fiction, a member of its so called "holy trinity" along with Dashiell Hammett and Raymond Chandler (K. B. Smith). Macdonald had added psychological depth to its solutions and developed a compassionate detective, thus taking the crime novel in new directions. His Archer is a private eye who solves mysteries, but also tries to understand them. And Macdonald's plots repeatedly attend the hidden histories of families, sins of the past shaping the present, secret emotional scars of victims and murderers alike. These plots, Millar was ready to acknowledge, reflected his own childhood experience with an absent father and rootlessness.

In their late fiction both Welty and Macdonald turn to investigate the crimes mass-produced by American culture as much as the individual murders that drive the plots: Macdonald writes the story of American ecological transgression and its consequences, and Welty writes the story of race in America. Commenting on *Underground Man* (1971) and *Sleeping Beauty* (1973), Michael Kreyling writes that "a forest fire and an oil spill, respectively, add . . . to the formula for evil . . . [and mark] the heavy human tread on the fragile ecology of California" (*Novels* 17). Comparably, correspondingly, in "Where Is The Voice Coming From?" (1963) and in "The Demonstrators" (1966), as well as in still later fiction she drafted as part of her unrealized plan for a volume targeting "the 'troubles' in the Bad Sixties in Mississippi" Welty addressed the iniquity of racism more straightforwardly than ever.[3]

Their influence on one another's work is apparent in the record of their exchanged letters. Millar's words seep into Welty's *The Optimist's Daughter* and Welty's *The Optimist's Daughter* seeps into his *Sleeping Beauty*.[4] Is it happenstance or transformation that in both novels a central character is named Laurel, and in both, an endangered bird becomes a dramatic focus? Having read and reread Archer novels in this period, Welty begins to draft a new crime fiction in 1975, "The Shadow Club." Additionally, she is also influenced by reading and rereading mysteries from August 1973 through January 1974, after Millar asks her to help suggest writers and texts for his anthology, *Great Stories of Suspense* (1974). The letters of those months show them swapping judgments on James M. Cain, John Cheever, Agatha Christie, John Collier, Roald Dahl, Kenneth Fearing, Dick Francis, Graham Greene, Dashiell Hammett, Margaret Millar (Ken's wife), Flannery O'Connor, and Robert Louis Stevenson—all writers who made it into Macdonald's volume. But the two also mention writers who don't—Charlotte Armstrong, Arthur Conan Doyle, Algernon Blackwood, Ray Bradbury, W. R. Burnett, Raymond Chandler, Elizabeth Daly, Helen Eustis, Michael Gibson, Sheridan Le Fanu, Ngaio Marsh, Patrick O'Brien, William Samson, Julian Symons, Hillary Waugh, and Patrick White.

Following this propitious education, Welty began "The Shadow Club" and worked on its composition intermittently over the next decade of her life. In the surviving drafts of this never-published text, she perpetually revised, changing character names and reimagining structural boundaries. The tale extended into drafts for other stories, at times perhaps suggesting a story cycle along the lines of *The Golden Apples,* in this case pertaining to Observatory Street rather than Morgana, Mississippi. That place name suggests the James Observatory on Jackson's Millsaps College campus, a local landmark, but it also evokes the watchful "neighborly" monitoring of the lives shared and attentively observed there. Housed at the Mississippi Department of Archives and History, the bits and pieces of the story's manuscript exist in eleven boxes, plus fifteen more in which there are related portions within manuscripts developing other stories, especially "The Wells" and the later sequence of Henry stories: "Henry," "Affinities," and "The City of Light." The various fragments, sections, and revisions of the changing text are archived there by the informed principle that the order and disorder of the author's found papers be kept intact. Working in these many boxes, you discover that Welty wrote on anything: on the backs of deposit slips, advertisements, and envelopes, for example, as well as in and on typed drafts. The manuscript can only be known in pieces, and yet the outline, plot, concerns, risks, and strengths of "The Shadow Club" come clear in a plainclothes gumshoe investigation of its extensive higgledy-piggledy fragments.

The story's plot first germinated from a newspaper clipping about a burglary in a schoolteacher's home, which Welty sent to her friend Nash Burger:

> Did you hear about poor Miss Annie Lester's terrible experience with a burglar?
>
> She is in the hospital with a broken arm—surprised a 21-year-old negro man at 2 or 3 o'clock in the morning, and I know nothing more except that there must have been a struggle—afterwards, she drove herself (he had cut the phone wire) to her brother's house. I can't really grasp how anybody could have done that to her, with her steady blue eyes direct and her innocent mathematical nature, and now old, too.[5]

The "that" done to Annie Lester is not spelled out in this letter as it is in Welty's story, as rape—but it is apparent from the news article and letter that there is a culturally familiar and culturally problematic race-rape crime plot hinted at in the story origin cue that Welty's version will redirect. The details of her handling that plot eventually suggest an audacious homage to Richard Wright's portrait of black boys too unaware of the forces that drive them to be well prepared to cope.

In "The Shadow Club," the conventional Jim Crow plot of a black boy who is a lurking threat to a white woman is alluded to when the cast of characters, speaking callously and reductively, chat unselfconsciously with and about that racist mythology. When a group of white women, the victim's friends, discuss the history of rape in their neighborhood, their sweeping generalities expose their tendency to profile and mythologize: ". . . on Observatory Street it couldn't have happened at all. This was a faculty neighborhood . . . offenders were all black . . . or if they weren't black, they were all escapees from the penitentiary or mental institution."[6] Welty builds her plot in contrast to this dubious chatter by developing the narrative lesson she describes learning in *One Writer's Beginnings*: how one secret may reveal a worse one. In that memoir Welty recalled as a child asking her mother about the secret of sex; then the pursuit of that discovery unexpectedly provoked the revelation of a lost sibling, not "how babies could come but how they could die." There she writes, "The future story writer in the child must have taken unconscious note and stored it away: one secret is liable to be revealed in the place of another harder to tell, and the substitute secret when nakedly exposed is often the more appalling" (17).

In a plot revealing the substitute secret discovered, the current mystery leads to a forgotten crime, one committed neither by a black person nor a prison escapee. Nell Downing (also called Caroline, Cam, May, Justine, and Rachel in drafts), raped in her home and left on the floor conked, concussed, and on display, returns to consciousness surrounded by friends—white women of a certain age, both frank and evasive on the topic of rape—with no memory whatsoever of what happened to her. When interrogated by a young woman who is considered rude when she asks brusque questions about the assault but who argues that rape deterrence does not allow its victims "the right to expect privacy," Downing reflects, "If there is a 'message' in this for me, I'll get it. In my own way. . . . I believe messages come in their own time."

What comes is the unlocking of Downing's locked-up past. The violence she in time recalls is not her own rape story; that will emerge, but from the rapist's own altering point of view. Memory instead brings to Downing the repressed recollection of another supposed break-in at her house: as a child, she discovered her mother naked and shot, slowly bleeding out in her helpless daughter's presence, only feet from the bloody body of Downing's father, who had shot himself in the head after killing his wife. She suddenly recalls, after a lifetime of avoiding and repressing the secret, being tenderly and, as a child, unwittingly led by her mother's lover (a professor, neighbor, and father) to keep the secret of the murder-suicide and to instead accept and promote a cover-up story about a "robber" who allegedly entered the house—the house she still lives in—to kill her parents.[7] The memory has seemingly been shared by her friend and neighbor Ralph Ledbetter, the adulterous professor's son, a gay man, whose comfortable relationship with Downing seems temporarily thrown off-kilter by her girlfriends' stories of her exposure as a female body on display. The exhibition re-evokes an original discovery scene in which the two as children, shocked and confused, had stumbled onto their parents sexually involved.

The portrayal of violence and death in this manuscript is graphic and arresting, an indication of Welty's ongoing extension of herself as a writer. Downing unearths the memory of finding her parents in their death scene. In it, running with and trying not to spill a glass of water that her shot, naked, and perishing mother seems to want—although what the dying Hallie has begged for is water from Macready Wells, a place of family happiness—the child arrives in time to make some chilling observations:

> Her [mother's] hair looked dark and was hanging wet to her forehead and she was panting, as if she'd just been swimming in Paradise Pond.
>
> But as [she] held out the glass of water, her mother turned her head away. A dark stream poured out of her mouth. It looked like muddy water she had somehow come to swallow by mistake. [She] saw a muddy spot on the sheet where Mother's hand held it close to her breast, like a belonging.
>
> [She] bent over her mother and under the bed below her, both Father's feet were sticking straight up from the darkness on the floor. His big toes like signals.
>
> Mother rolled on the wet pillow and then she crawled across the bed to the other side and lay down on her breast, with a wanting sound. Her wanting sound was her breathing.

The graphic violence in this story, particularly in this account of Hallie's death, may have some relationship not only to Welty's interest in Macdonald's work and in noir as a genre, but also to her then most recently lived experience of crime: the 1975 murder of her close friend Frank Hains. Details of Ralph's portrait in the story also support that character's connection to Hains, suggesting that Welty's loss of her friend was one trigger for the story, mirrored throughout. That is, Kevin Sessums's memoir, *Mississippi Sissy*, which contains an account of both the slain man and his brutal murder, describes Hain's particular love of his 78-rpm record collection, and Ralph in Welty's story is closely and movingly connected to his vintage Red Seal record trove. The story is thus linked to two actual crimes that Welty had felt personally: Annie Lester's and Frank Hains's.

The discovery of Nell's exposed body by her girlfriends in "The Shadow Club" echoes and inverts the discovery of the mother's body by her daughter first and then by her clandestine lover. There is transformation and inversion at work in the story's counterpoint assaults: the violence against the grown daughter, per-petrated by a needy schoolboy and not the result of desire in any usual sense, is the inverse of her mother's more traditional crime scene where she was at-tacked by her jealous husband. The rumor of Nell's exposed and violated body echoes the attack on Annie Lester, but also Kevin Sessums's report of finding Frank Hains's naked and attacked body. That scene had riveted Jackson society in 1975 when, following his death, the community aggressively othered him, essentially blaming the victim by suggesting he had brought the murder onto himself through his gay lifestyle. This was a reaction that Welty equally assert-ively countered by writing the last installment of Hains's column "On Stage" for the *Jackson News*, and forming it as a tribute to the value of her respected friend.[8]

The raced rape story of "The Shadow Club" thus opens into the plot of adul-tery and murder. The story's title calls up the popular radio hour named for its detective crime fighter, *The Shadow*. The show, which debuted in the 1930s, ran until 1954 and was serialized in pulp magazine spin-offs; it captivated audiences with its signature refrain emphasizing the noir of its plots: "Who knows what evil lurks in the hearts of men? The Shadow knows!" In "The Shadow Club," the rumor of the black body is at first an associative marker for a noir tale ex-actly discovering the dark murkiness of whiteness, in this case darkening Down-ing's reckless, bright, and fair mother, Hallie. Her name recalls Halley's Comet that streaks the night sky with light: she is a woman associated with popularity, pleasure, country club success, and her bridesmaid girlfriends who make up the Shadow Club itself, the seemingly conventional group representing a commu-nity in which relationships that span generations are full of shadowy secrets blurring moral boundaries, some shocking, some petty, some simply tragic.

The sidestepped story of the rape in this tale is finally uncovered not by Downing's memory but in a section written from the perpetrator's (Elroy Co-rum's) point of view. More than Jim Crow's black violator rape plot, this section evokes the narratives of Richard Wright's black protagonists in his fictionalized autobiography and in his version of "crime fiction" stories, especially "The Man Who Was Almost a Man" and "The Man Who Killed a Shadow." Corum, escaping the Downing house, has gotten no farther than the ubiquitous town-dividing railroad tracks when he thinks, "if they were to find him and ask him what he'd done . . . he'd say he couldn't remember." The account that follows is not exactly a memory, but rather is filled with Elroy's surprise as he discovers his own un-raveling actions and feelings.

Elroy's narrative is the story of a boy, aimlessly and all night "walking . . . where his feet would carry him until it would be safe to go home." Wandering into a white neighborhood at the end of his sanctuary-seeking sleepless night, he sees a door "standing wide open" and enters the house. After he boxes himself fearfully into a closet, Downing, a teacher preparing for the opening morning of the school year, opens the closet door to confront her intruder; she reads him correctly for what he is, "nothing but a child." Humiliated by her estimation of him as harmless, he tells her he has come for her purse; nevertheless, she feels comfortable enough to command him instead to report with her to school. Then "before he knew it . . . he landed her a punch right on her thinker." While she is unconscious and stretched out, reminding him of a church sister receiving "the holy spirit," with a face that "seemed to be granting permission to the whole world," he opens her refrigerator and eats plates of food—pickles, bread—and drinks sweet milk. He returns to find her eyes open although she is still comatose. In one manuscript draft, "her knee at a push showed its underside to him, yawned white as a cottonmouth moccasin opening to strike." Seemingly never before having been close to a woman, "before he knew what happened, he fell, as hard as she'd fallen, on top of her and his hands fought through the fumbled clothes.

He bolted into her. She didn't know. She lay as before, her eyes turned up at the clouds."

The keyed-up boy's erratic thoughts obscure his unpremeditated and precipitate act of rape; they are bound both to a yearning for his bolstering but now-lost childhood home with an aunt who has died, and to his dysfunctional current life with his father, his father's lady friend, her children by another man, and sometimes that other man as well. Elroy's thoughts wander and then lodge on a painfully childlike, simple, surreal aspiration, frankly felt as nonetheless unattainable: an ambition to grow up to be the exterminator man, to drill houses "with plenty of what it took to smoke [termites] out," and to drive the yellow truck with its "red and green termite as big as a full-grown hound, dressed up in a hat and gloves like wedding clothes and two pairs of high-topped shoes, riding the roof of the cab." The reader has a suspenseful and anxious moment when the boy—realizing the woman is hurt, "tumbled . . . like a dove that hit itself on the glass"—disturbingly worries that she is dangerous to him: "It was dangerous to pick up hurt things, hurt and still alive. They could hurt you. Maybe fly at you and try to put your eyes out. Then he saw the little trail of blood moving on her forehead . . . yes, it moved." But Elroy resists striking out at the wounded woman; rather, he takes "back his trust, as if it had been tricked out of him" and, frightened, stumbles away with her purse. Dumping the purse, which contains "no credit cards, no money, . . . no smokes," under a bridge in bushes that hold other dumped purses, he paradoxically thinks, "one sure thing I didn't need was no library card." As a train passes in the dark, Elroy impulsively jumps into an open boxcar, and rocks and sways with it into his future.

Nowhere are the allusions to Richard Wright's works clearer than in this ending, which echoes the train hopping of "Almos' a Man." On one page of her drafts, Welty even considered the possibility of having Elroy find the hidden gun of the Downing murder-suicide, and she wrote at the top in red pen, "Elroy // He Rode Off Into The World With His Gun." This line could not more clearly call to mind the plot of Wright's Dave Saunders in "Almost a Man," just as the library card reference calls up Wright's different story in *Black Boy* when, with self-determining purpose, the character Richard works to inveigle a card in order to borrow books and imagine a liberating future. Jumping a freight car, like Dave Saunders before him, Elroy "rolled, was rolled halfway across the floor sometimes, and his head would bounce as the train ran along." Escaping but still without defense against forces that toss him, Elroy thinks that "the lady was gone, no more on the floor of his mind, glimmering no longer. Out there, stars had come out . . . they danced like popcorn on the bottom of a black skillet." Welty's image of white popcorn stars moving on a black skillet pictures whiteness as explosive, unpredictable, and yet tantalizing, a detail that helps to reveal Elroy as at the mercy of exploding emotions and hungers, overwhelmed, and wishing for self-determination.

"The Shadow Club" is also replete with details that surprisingly evoke the less well-known Wright story "The Man Who Killed a Shadow," itself a turn on the Jim Crow rape plot. While Welty might certainly have seen the frequently anthologized "Almost a Man," first published in 1940 as "Almos' A Man," in any number of locations other than Wright's collection *Eight Men* (where it emerged with its third and strategically informing new title, "The *Man* Who Was Almost A Man"), she could only have known the later story from that 1961 volume. In it, the shadow referred to in the title is explicitly glossed as the "shadow of a [young black man's] fears" (*Eight Men* 193). Like Elroy, Wright's protagonist Saul Saunders is described as a boy who inhabits a "world split in two . . . the white one being separated from the black by a million psychological miles. Saul . . . saw the shadowy outlines of a white world that was unreal to him and not his own" (193–94). This unreal world is one where "things had names but not substance," suggesting the possibility that the boy's behaviors there also seem unreal to him. (I cannot help but think that Welty also knew her close friend Ralph Ellison's 1964 essay collection, *Shadow and Act*, which also brings the idea of shadow—with the implication of living among those who see only shadows—to the story of race in America.) Like Elroy, Saul as a boy lived with and took comfort from not an aunt but a grandmother, who has "passed suddenly from his life," and as a result, "the shadowlike quality of his world became terribly manifest" (*Eight Men* 195). While Elroy aspires to be an exterminator, Saul takes a job as one: "something in his nature . . . made him like going from house to house . . . putting down poison for rats and mice and roaches. He liked seeing the concrete evidence of his work and the dead bodies of rats [that] were not shadows" (197–98). At this point the stories diverge. Fired for defending himself against a slighting remark from his boss, Saul takes a job as a janitor in a library. There, cleaning, he is more than once bewildered by a virginal librarian, a "strange little shadow" of a white woman, who approaches him unexpectedly, crudely, and insultingly to fulfill her sexual fantasy. When he slaps her, she screams, and Saul, like Bigger Thomas in Wright's *Native Son,* manages his traumatic fear of being caught in and killed for physical contact with a white woman by killing the female shadow.

While the two stories are pointedly different in their revisions of the raced rape plot, they share attention to it as well as to the notion of a black boy traumatized by and at the mercy of forces he does not fully understand and cannot manage. It is possible that the reason Welty never published this story was that she or a publisher perceived the awkwardness or the risk of a southern white woman writing the story of a black boy as Richard Wright might. As usual, Welty performs a signifying element—in this case the raced rape plot—in ways that highlight her awareness of and deviation from the generic convention she adapts.

"The Alterations" (dated by the Mississippi Department of Archives and History as circa 1987) is still another mystery story/crime fiction that Welty began; it is seemingly the last story that Welty started as her capacity, but not desire, to write gave way to dwindling health. At the story's center are two bodies, one female and abused, and the other male and dead. Its draft makes Welty's precomposition process instructively visible. Her jottings on two unlined letter tablets and one unlined notepad are eventually followed by some pages of more fixed and cleaner draft, still handwritten but labeled "to be typed" following her plentiful markings. Throughout the notes, one can see Welty return persistently to her idea, writing it again, varying the dialogue completely, seemingly looking for a best line or version to make itself apparent. In her predraft process, she repeatedly rewrites the scene, not culling but exploring the episode anew, producing assorted renderings before settling notes into draft.

"The Alterations" is fascinating in part because its topic is unanticipated—for a reader who hasn't been following Welty's history with crime plots. With alternate titles—"It's a Lost Art," "A World of Patience Is What It Takes," and (best) the French term referencing silk, literally "silk skin," frequently used in wedding gowns, "Peau de Soie," it is the tale of a dressmaker who kills her long-endured abusive husband by literally undertaking to make "alterations" to him. As the character is interviewed by the police, Welty seems to cross her Edna Earle Ponder with the mad narrator from Poe's "The Tell-Tale Heart" to create a woman ripped from the pages of the *National Enquirer*. She is as fantastic as Lorena Bobbitt (another woman who made extreme alteration to her abusive husband, not infamous until 1993), but more inventive and idiosyncratic in the bizarre logic of a battered wife's sensational personal solution. Welty seems to have drawn on a local murder committed by a wife who stabbed her husband twenty-seven times with scissors before covering his wounds with Band-Aids. Welty's protagonist, alternately named Frieda, Doris, Willy Mae, and Evelyn, but perhaps emerging as Genrose Hopper, is at work over the body of her husband when the police respond to a report of trouble from a client who, expecting to pick up her completed tailoring, has seen a body on the living room floor.

This murder mystery adapts and parodies the police procedural. Procedurals, as critic George Dove comments, are usually about "run-of-the-mill" squad procedures and teamwork that sorts out a crime, rather than a principal detective (118). And they usually focus on the cop story—a convention that Welty jettisons to spotlight her wacky woman murderer. Recalling television's *Dragnet* (and the countless descendants of that series), its prototype of gritty but droll detail, its attention to ethical dilemmas in the story of justice, and its enforcers who request but are unable to keep informants to "just the facts, ma'am," Welty's officers act as straight men to her quirky wrongdoer.

In Welty's manuscript, the patrolmen, at first bewildered by marks on the victim's skin, interrogate the dressmaker, asking if "something stung him" to make "these ugly risings." In one version, the officers note "fresh superficial needle punctures" that are not drug tracks. Gradually the seamstress identifies the neat mending she has done, after using her stork scissors to repeatedly prick, and then stick, her husband. Grotesquely, but comically, she has repaired the wounds with "invisible darning" and the contents of "a box full of Ouchless 3-inch bandages." "You were sewing on him?" they ask. "'Looks like you been vaccinating him for the smallpox." When the detectives ask if her husband had objected to her darning him to death, she earnestly explains that, drunk, he snored as she worked until, without her at first noticing, he stopped. "Sometimes he puffed out a little sound and once his lips made a little pop, like somebody that's just made a mistake. I stuck my needle back in my collar and my thought turned to Band-Aids." "He was bleeding a little faster than my fingers. It was something I hadn't thought of."

Over the pages of these unlined notepads, the couple's history emerges. Saturdays were both the husband's day off and his wife's "busiest day. . . . All her alterations were promised and there was a stream of chattering women and final fittings." The women's activity routinely infuriates Mr. Hopper (alternately named Bud, Floyd, Earl, and Mr. Hobbs). In one version the police note the wife's "black eye." In a few crossed-out lines, the wife reports having asked, "'Did I hit a tender place?' I'd say, 'Well women are tender all over, did you ever think of that?'" The officers remember a previous incident when "neighbors called us. . . . Sure. You was the one that got hit. He put a wrench to your head and a wonder you ever got up."

On this particular Saturday, sodden with liquor, naked to the waist, and behaving badly, her husband slipped or fell in his stupor. "He was weaving. Waxing. Then he just went over." The police question her role in his fall, asking if she did "more than touch him . . . just a little bit?" Genrose describes it: "I put out my finger, just to shame him, poked him one little push . . . he was ripe to fall. . . . I don't think he knew what hit him . . . it was my hard clean floor." Having left him where he rolled, she comically describes her work on him. "I completely forgot about myself. That's what a wife is good for." Contemplatively she ruminates that "some wives might have kept on once they got started—might have cut on deeper down when they got to where his heart is and cut it out. I never even thought of doing that. I swear I never. That's just when I stopped, and went back and got my soap and water, and my Band-Aids. He looks in good shape, all neat now. Except for his eyes. I'm not responsible for them." Content with her job, she credits herself with his transformation: "how peaceful . . . I'd made him an angel." The dark comedy of the murderer's self-justifying self-presentation, of her obsessive tendencies and pride in her work, and of her belief in her innocent intention are all underscored. And the possible trigger for her unexpected assault is the wedding dress worn by her dressmaker's dummy: ironically, "just on the other side of the curtain . . . in the shadows" of her parlor, it signals its symbolic outrage "through its glimmer. . . . It was there as if in the wings, as if awaiting its cue to enter on its squeaky little wheels [for its day on center stage]" (Welty's brackets).

Notwithstanding the Welty signatures of humor, surprise, and homage to literary history (here an assured wink toward the voice and situation of Poe's "The Tell-Tale Heart"), and despite her characteristic reflection of and on popular culture and her recognizable feminist concerns, it is a surprise to discover Welty drafting a comic police procedural uncovering a sensational murder. But in her plan for "The Alterations," Welty is still experimenting and evolving as a writer, even after she had, at the age of 78, perhaps contentedly, or regretfully, surrendered the disposition to finish and publish her fiction.

And yet I'd argue it is also a turn steadily foreshadowed across Welty's career—by the violent abuse explored not only as early as the stories in A Curtain of Green, but even earlier in a 1937 draft of a first novel, a largely unknown work I found in 2014 as a result of some sleuthing of my own. This 115-page copy of a manuscript, not currently housed in the Mississippi Department of Archives and History—where one would expect to find it alongside her other collected papers,—but in the New York Public Library's Russell and Volkening (R&V) historical papers, was sold to the library by Tim Seldes, Welty's R&V agent, contingent to his selling the agency in 2012.[9]

The common assumption has been that, as a young writer, Welty forcefully resisted market pressure to produce a novel rather than short stories, even though stories were generally judged as scarcely marketable unless supported by a novelist's previous reputation. But this manuscript shows that Welty had at first tried to comply with editors' advice. In Author and Agent, Michael Kreyling, telling the story of Welty's evolving relationship with her representative Diarmuid Russell, describes both the pressure publishers applied as well as Welty's opposition to it. He also writes that in 1938, Welty entered a Houghton Mifflin contest for first novels, but thought even the finalized version of her submission—The Cheated—not very good, and accordingly threw that manuscript away after the contest. My informed conjecture is that "The Night of The Little House" is a surviving draft written for that project. The Mississippi Department of Archives and History houses about thirty related draft pages titled "The Cheated," but not yet this longer manuscript. The Welty House has now found that it has the original from which the New York copy was made.

Most surprisingly, the manuscript brings together versions of characters whom we associate with the not-yet-written stories of "Why I Live at the P.O." (1941), "The Whistle" (1938), and "The Key" (1941) as well as characters from 1937's "A Piece of News" and "Lily Daw and the Three Ladies"—stories published or in final process as she drafted "The Night of The Little House." The novella is narrated by a twentysomething woman from New York, Martha Galen, who has come to Victory, Mississippi, to paint after she's left her work at a school for the deaf. As it begins, Martha looks for a key to her rental house to come to her by mail, and accordingly her first stop is the town's post office where its postmistress lords over its domain with comic authority as Sister will in "Why I Live at the P.O." Then when Martha Galen heads out to paint the landscape and is caught in a sudden storm, she seeks refuge in a nearby cabin. She's been warned that her only neighbors are Clyde Fisher, a moonshiner, and his wife Ruby (characters from "A Piece of News"); it is their house in which she takes refuge.

So this manuscript touches bits of many Welty stories, some not yet written. Eventually Welty will excise and finish nine pages from "The Night of the Little House," perhaps next whittled in the subsequent drafts of "The Cheated," but only published in final form as "The Key" in *Harper's Bazaar*, August 1941. Stripping her text down to nine enigmatic pages, she's both recognizing and claiming as her own the distinctive methods of her modernism. She's affirming the minimalist puzzle-text as her signature story form.

But to glean the full significance of this early novella for Welty's mystery patterns, you need to know that in it, Clyde and Ruby Fisher have a daughter, Avis, who is abused by her father. In a scene recognizable as one of many recurrent flashings of another woman's body reflected on by Welty's sheltered women narrators,[10] Galen—taking Avis as an artist's model—discovers Clyde's brutality from Avis's nudity:

> I told her quietly and matter-of-factly, "Take off your dress, Avis."
> Instantly she did. With no questions, [but] with a rapid, mechanical, tired motion, she pulled it off. . . .
> All across her body were the marks of a whip. . . .
> "What made those marks on your back!" I asked her finally.
> "Pa beats me . . . But he's been doing that."

Without going into detail on the novella's full cast of characters and their further activities, it suffices to say that Martha seeks to protect Avis with the help of Red Harper—the red-haired stranger she first observes in a train station encounter with a deaf couple (as in "The Key"). In keeping with the features of mixed-gender detective teams, in Martha's ensuing collaboration with Red, repartee and banter echo the screen flirtations of 1930s cinema and the teamwork of Dashiell Hammett's Nick and Nora Charles in *The Thin Man* (1934). Ultimately their shambling progress towards protecting Avis lumbers towards the novella's end in an astonishing Hollywood-style apocalypse where guns are fired and lives threatened. Martha's rented house burns to the ground, but Red—taking advantage of chaos—promises, "We will now spend the rest of the night in my room in the Hotel Constantinople . . . If Albert Morgan has hung onto the key," a line certain to amaze and amuse readers familiar with Welty's final version of the Morgans' story.

This early manuscript's concern for Avis helps me recognize abuse, a characteristic of crime fiction, in plots across Welty's career. Abuse is not only at hand in "Flowers for Marjorie," "The Hitchhikers," and "A Piece of News," but in the other early stories of *A Curtain of Green.* In "Clytie," suicide, committed by plunging head first into a rain barrel, is the result of family torment. In "A Curtain of Green," after a tree crushes Mrs. Larkin's husband, the woman, in her grief and rage at insurmountable catastrophe, experimentally aims a potentially maiming hoe at the vulnerable head of her young black garden helper, "To punish? To protest?" (*Collected* 111). In "The Whistle," class abuse is institutionalized in the agricultural system, and in "A Worn Path," institutionalized neglect is expressed in the disappointing response of a clinic nurse ("You mustn't take up our time this way, Aunt Phoenix"). The signal of abuse also applies to comic fictions in the collection. In "Lily Daw" a local girl escaping her father's violence is bullied by the town's droll ladies. In "Petrified Man" women farcically scheme to enhance their dominance of their husbands, but face their comeuppance when they contemplate the reality of a rapist. In "Why I Live at the P.O." a daughter uproariously elaborates on insult within her family. On the other side of Welty's career, the pointer is still omnipresent. Uncle Daniel tickles Bonnie Dee to death in *The Ponder Heart.* In *Losing Battles,* Lexie Renfro withholds even pencils in her caretaking marriage to the bedridden and dying teacher Julia Mortimer. Fay Chisom lays hands on her hospitalized husband in *The Optimist's Daughter,* putting his operated-on eye at risk, and then he unexpectedly dies from the trauma. And Dr. Strickland provides a sedative but no hospital care to Ruby in "The Demonstrators," relaxing her into her death. *Many* Welty fictions have a flirtation with murder about them.

What I hope to have shown on these pages is that Welty—"detecting the South"—was indeed both a practitioner and pupil of the mystery genre. Her career illustrates how she repeatedly built her varied modernist fictions through innovative transformation of genres that she loved, in this case, crime fiction.

NOTES

Passages from Eudora Welty's unpublished manuscripts and correspondence are reprinted by the courtesy and permission of the Eudora Welty Collection, Mississippi Department of Archives and History; of Russell and Volkening as agents for the author, copyright © by Eudora Welty, renewed by Eudora Welty LLC; and of Russell and Volkening records, Manuscripts and Archives Division, The New York Public Library—Astor, Lenox, and Tilden Foundations.

1. See Rebecca Mark and forthcoming, Jacob Agner, "Welty's Moonlighting Detective: Whiteness and Welty's Subversion of the American Noir Tradition in 'The Demonstrators'" in *New Essays on Eudora Welty, Class, and Race* (UPM, 2019) for their different handling of this story as detective fiction.

2. See my chapter on the topic of their relationship, "Eudora Welty in John Robinson's Closet," in Pollack, 2016.

3. Letter to Tim Seldes, Russell and Volkening Records, Manuscript and Archives Division, New York Public Library, Astor, Lenox, and Tilden Foundation. This letter is discussed and quoted with the permission of the New York Public Library and of Russell and Volkening as agents for the author. Copyright © by Eudora Welty, renewed by Eudora Welty LLC.

4. See Marrs and Nolan (76–77) on *The Optimist's Daughter.*

5. From the Nash Burger Correspondence in Select Correspondence, Welty (Eudora) Collection, Mississippi Department of Archives and History, Jackson. Quoted with permission of the Eudora Welty Collection and of Russell and Volkening as agents for the author. Copyright © by Eudora Welty, renewed by Eudora Welty LLC.

6. Welty's unpublished manuscripts "The Shadow Club" and later "The Alterations" are discussed and lines reprinted here by permission of the Eudora Welty Collection at the Mississippi Department of Archives and History and of Russell and Volkening as agents for the author. Copyright © by Eudora Welty, renewed by Eudora Welty LLC. This essay in its sections on "The Shadow Club" and "The Alterations" draws on discussions of individual unpublished fictions included in Pollack, *Eudora Welty's Fiction and Photography: The Body of The Other Woman,* 2016, while elaborating and putting them to a new purpose here.

7. If the Observatory Street project bears some resemblance to the story cycle of *The Golden Apples,* played out in a different genre, Professor Ledbetter at moments resembles the philanderer King MacLain performed in a crime novel register. At his death, there is community speculation that the professor is Downing's father and that the tenderness he has shown toward her is in recognition of that secret. Similarly in "The Wanderers," at another funeral, there is a suggestion that King is Virgie Rainey's father, a conjecture that gives their exchange there a tender nuance.

8. See McMahand and Murphy for more on this topic.

9. This manuscript in is discussed and quoted with the permission of the Manuscripts and Archives Division of the New York Public Library; Astor, Lenox, and Tilden Foundations; and of Russell and Volkening as agents for the author. Copyright © by Eudora Welty, renewed by Eudora Welty LLC.

10. See Pollack, 2016.

REFUSING A "SINGLE SONG" OF THE SOUTH

The Frustrated Detective in Donna Tartt's The Little Friend

CLAIRE COTHREN

D onna Tartt's sophomore novel, *The Little Friend* (2002), follows amateur detective Harriet Cleve-Dufresnes as she searches her Mississippi community for clues to the murder of her older brother Robin. By making sense of this cold case, twelve-year-old Harriet hopes both to uphold justice and to help her family heal, a decade after the crime occurred. But in retracing the series of events that preceded the murder, Harriet often encounters very gruesome obstacles, aspects of the text upon which the novel's early reviewers have tended to fixate. Ruth Franklin asserts that the presence of a "corpse, human or animal, in every chapter" threatens to subvert the psychological impact of the novel and complains that Tartt simply retreats into the macabre haven of the southern gothic instead of considering death seriously. David Hare, too, expresses frustration with the novel's 500-plus pages of "blood spurting" southern horror.

Such commentary suggests the novel's lukewarm reception among reviewers and scholars[1] may be attributable, in part, to its treatment of the Mississippi setting—one replete with violent meth cookers, Confederate war memorials, and extremist Evangelicals. Leigh Anne Duck notes that since the 1930s, the South has been increasingly fictionalized via dramatic tropes of excess: the "tremendous and ghastly visions" of its white supremacists, the "lunatic, disintegrating wildness" of its evangelical Protestantism, and a culture "linger[ing] in the dark backward abysm of time" (*Nation's* 18). Such depictions, in the minds of many scholars like Patricia Yaeger, tend to present southern history as an inescapable nightmare where "everyone bumps into the passive voice" and is haunted by old ideas about race and class that will not go away (*Black Men* 13). Others, such as Theresa Goddu, contend that images of a still racially violent South simply position the region as "the repository for everything the nation is not" (76)—a space in which to confine the horrors of racism, anomaly, and mindless ritual.

However, this essay will argue that rather than simply echoing regional stereotypes, Tartt strategically reworks the conventions of detective fiction to establish troubling connections between Harriet's reconstruction of the crime against her brother and the narrative processes used historically within the American South to enforce social hierarchies. Harriet often relies on the long-standing class and race stereotypes to solve the mystery of Robin's death, moving from a simple investigation of her primary suspect, Danny, into a production of his criminality. In underscoring this problematic aspect of Harriet's quest, Tartt makes clear that the true objective of her novel is not to guide readers toward the murderer's identity, as in most traditional detective texts. Instead, Tartt employs elements of "metaphysical" detective fiction that thwart the neat investigative conclusion the sleuth seeks, encouraging both protagonist and reader to look beyond regional stereotypes.

As Charles Rzepka explains in *Detective Fiction*, literary scholars often have relied on the works of social and political theorists such as Louis Althusser to explain how detective fiction, like much modern culture, functions as a "device for the perpetuation of norms of behavior that enforce the power of ruling groups extra-legally" (48). As part of "modern mass entertainment," the genre helps to "interpellate its readers" into the conformity of white and middle-class values in Western societies, thereby maintaining "hegemonic control of the populace" (21). In that readers "perform the same mental activity of inductive reasoning," they are encouraged to identify with the detective, a process that Tartt facilitates in *The Little Friend* through her portrayal of the innocence, empathy, social activism, and benevolent intentions of the child protagonist. But in fostering this close relationship between reader and detective, Tartt also deliberately muddies the ways in which her detective occasionally defends those "hegemonic norms and self-perpetuating cultural value systems" (Rzepka 22) endemic to the Jim Crow South. Readers must, therefore, be most mindful of the clues that Tartt provides to the normativity of Harriet's detective agenda and not, like Harriet, become fixated on the identity of Robin's murderer. With this approach, Tartt progressively reimagines the political functions of detective fiction, highlighting the troubling role of power in shaping historical "truths" of the American South, particularly those that attempt to justify the brutal policing of divisions in race and class.

COMMITTED TO THE COLD CASE: A CRIME DENIED MEANING

Tartt firmly links her narrative to the violent racial history of the American South through the details of the crime scene that Harriet investigates. When Harriet is only six months old, her nine-year-old brother, Robin, disappears while the family is busy preparing for a Mother's Day celebration. After conducting a brief search, they discover his corpse in the backyard, "hanging by the neck from a piece of rope, slung over a low branch of the black-tupelo tree" (14). As A. O. Scott rightly observes, the hanging of a little boy from a tree in Mississippi "cannot help evoking the grisly history of lynching" that "flourished across the South between the end of Reconstruction and the 1960s" (Friend and Glover 12). This region gained a reputation as the "lynching belt" because a significant majority of such crimes took place here—approximately 600 in Mississippi alone. Indeed, when Emmett Till was brutally murdered in 1955, his death led Langston Hughes to lament that Mississippi "must lead the world in the lynching of children" (qtd. in Ward 229). Yet crucial details distinguish Robin's murder in the early 1960s from most other victims of lynching in the state: namely, that he is affluent and white.[2] Deliberately positioning Robin's hanging just outside of historical context, Tartt calls critical attention to the ways that violent spectacles, like lynching, were used to manufacture narratives of racial "otherness." According to historian Amy Louise Wood, lynching of African Americans in the South in fact occurred much more infrequently than "other forms of terror and intimidation that blacks were subject to under Jim Crow," but—because of their public and visually sensational nature—they generated "a level of fear and horror that overwhelmed all other forms of violence" (1). In the face of white southerners' growing fears about racial equality, lynching was meant to reestablish racial hierarchy and to convey the terrible consequences of transgressing that system. The sight of a lynched black body in the Jim Crow South thus functioned not only to intimidate African American spectators but also to impart an important message to whites about their supposed supremacy. Given the longstanding significance of such brutality, it makes sense that when Harriet's family recounts the sight of Robin's hanged body, they note that his "copper-red hair, which ruffled and glinted in the breeze . . . was the only thing about him that was the right color any more" (15). In this region where lynched bodies have historically been black, Robin's hanging destabilizes the Cleve family's comfortable positions as spectators, converting whiteness itself into spectacle.

That Robin's murder creates a specifically racialized disturbance within the Cleve family is most apparent in their subsequent refusal to consider its implications. Before the hanging, the Cleves would eagerly "seize" upon bits of information about fatalities, elaborate upon those details as a chorus, and finally arrive together at a "single song" that was "memorized, and sung by the entire company" until it "came to take the place of truth" (4). Tartt's description of this narrative process echoes the work of a lynch mob that, as Wood explains, "[produces] and [disseminates] images of white power and black degradation, of white unity and black criminality" to perpetuate for white spectators "a sense of racial supremacy" (2). When Robin is killed, however, the Cleves only find solace in a sort of "willful amnesia" about the incident, shirking entirely their would-be roles as spectators. They conclude that there is "no logic to be inferred, no lesson in hindsight, [and] no moral to this story" of Robin's death in large part because he is a white child. Having bought into the notion that whiteness is not a "race" but rather what Richard Dyer describes as the "powerful position of being 'just' human" (15), the Cleves simply conclude of this racially evocative hanging that "no one," whether "rich [or] poor, black [or] white . . . could think who might have done such a thing or why" (18).

A WILLING BUT WILLFUL DETECTIVE

In various regards, Tartt's young heroine distinguishes herself from the Cleve family "chorus" in that, through her detective work, she is willing to grapple with all the disturbing aspects of her brother's murder. Initially Harriet's queries into the crime seem purely scientific, in the vein of the "greatest" of all her heroes, detective Sherlock Holmes (76). She catalogues details about Robin's classmate, Danny Ratliff, who ten years earlier bragged to a peer about his role in the murder. She also attempts to validate this information by checking it against the first-hand account of her caretaker, Ida Rhew Brownlee, a woman who, instead of being consulted for information about the crime scene, was indirectly assigned blame for the child's death because she was pouting about missing Mother's Day with her own family. When Ida reveals to Harriet the information that she personally chased Danny Ratliff "out of the yard not ten minutes before" Mrs. Dufresnes found "poor little Robin hung off that tree limb" (150), Harriet believes her deductive reasoning process to be complete. Having collected from witnesses a record of her suspect's "confession" as well as incriminating details of his whereabouts, she forms the "logical" conclusion that Danny must be responsible for her brother's murder.

But when Ida Rhew adds to her testimony that Danny was a "nasty little loudmouth" whose "white trash" family once set ablaze her predominantly black church (18), Harriet's thinking begins to skew in a notably more inductive direction, inferring conclusions instead of deriving them from indisputable premises. After Ida Rhew reveals to Harriet a "six-inch patch of seared flesh" (147) that she identifies to Harriet as the result of the Ratliffs' hate crime, Harriet begins— more than ever—to proceed through her investigation out of sympathy for and identification with those involved. In observing this injury, Harriet experiences

a double shock, not only to learn of the violent bodily imposition of racial "difference" on African Americans like her caretaker, but also to discover that the
Cleves declined to avenge this crime. As historian Kristina DuRocher argues
in her text *Raising Racists,* most white children coming of age in the Jim Crow
South were indoctrinated to uphold white supremacy, and they were not able to
see its tenets fully take shape until they encountered specific instances of white
violence toward African Americans (94). Indeed, until viewing Ida's scar Harriet
cannot "detect" the brutalities used to sustain the racial order in Mississippi. The
terror of this spectacle entirely reshapes Harriet's investigation, leading her to
develop more general conclusions about the white community's condemnable
role as "spectators" to and enablers of racial violence.

Despite mounting evidence of the Cleves' complicity in perpetuating the
brutal mistreatment of African Americans in Alexandria, Harriet resists identifying herself and her family as part of the "race problem," scapegoating instead
the members of the "white trash" community she perceives as most directly responsible. Harriet's focus on this group, Tartt emphasizes, is based partly on inductive reasoning connecting this group to her experiences as a gender-deviant
child, one who rejects the clothes, activities, and adult roles expected of girls in
her community. Tellingly, the uncooked "wiener" shape of Ida's "puckered and
pitted" scar (147) anticipates the "tainted," sweating hotdogs at the evangelical
summer camp where Harriet later burns with "shame" at pamphlets that project
"wombs and tubes and mammaries" over images of women's bodies (407). These
cause her to resent the "horrifying new indignity of being classed . . . a 'Teen
Girl': a creature without mind, wholly protuberance and excretion" (407). And
she especially rails against a group of camp counselors who lump her with the
"sweaty, menstruating, boy-crazed lot" (408) of "trashy" girls from Tupelo whose
hometown, significantly, shares its name with the tree where Robin was hanged.
Harriet's church camp experiences thus reaffirm for the young detective induc-
tions about "white trash" involvement in Robin's death given the community's
related corporeal abuses against herself and Ida.

In a literary genre that, according to Charles Rzepka, has traditionally identified adult males as the "ideal 'subject position'" from which to "[exercise] the
cultural prerogative of authoritatively reconstructing [the] history" of crime
scenes (48), Tartt upholds Harriet and her sleuthing as a possible alternative.
In Harriet's world, girl children are too often given "insulting board games" like
"*What Shall I Be?*" in which, "no matter how well you played," the only possible career options were "teacher, ballerina, mother, or nurse" (85). But Harriet
dreams of being a detective like Sherlock Holmes. And though she is not adult

or male, Tartt identifies some benefits to the ways in which youth and gender directly shape Harriet's inductive reasoning process, leading her, for example, to give credence to witnesses like Ida Rhew, who "legitimate" detectives were unwilling to validate so many years before. Thus when Tartt incorporates passages that reveal, unbeknownst to Harriet, intimate details about the Ratliff family's drug use, racial violence, abuse of minority populations, and, most damningly, their attempts to apprehend Harriet, Tartt seems—if briefly—to celebrate Harriet's potential to take up the detective career she so admires.

But while *The Little Friend* ultimately provides irrefutable support for Harriet's identification of Danny Ratliff as "murderer" when he shoots his own brother, Tartt also emphasizes the complications of such a character indictment by sharing with the reader clues to Danny's humanity that Harriet sometimes willfully misunderstands or to which she does not have access. To the extent that detective fiction invites and empowers the careful reader to "solve the problem along with the detective," many scholars, such as John Scaggs, have suggested this literary genre remains popular for its "game-like" aspects (37). In *The Little Friend*, however, the "problem" to be solved is not exposing the identity and motivation of Robin Dufresnes's murderer; rather, it is to see in Danny what Harriet cannot: that, in spite of his poverty, drug use, and lack of education, he is a sensitive person with aspirations, and a love for members of his family. The readers of Tartt's novel, then, must attempt to resist what W. H. Auden identifies as the "cathartic ritual of scapegoating" in detective fiction: the reader's desire to throw off "the restraints of civilization and release its suppressed impulses toward violence" through identification with detectives who hunt down supposed "criminals" (qtd. in Rzepka 37). They must resist the narrative that Harriet crafts to justify her discrimination against Danny.

In seeking evidence of Harriet's normativity, readers would be well served to remember that the best clues in detective fiction are often "camouflaged as ordinary" and "assume significance only in retrospect" (Rzepka 29). Indeed, when applied to the beginning stages of her investigation, this truism of detective fiction provides important new ways to understand Harriet's desire to investigate her brother's hanging. Early in the novel, for example, Tartt records Harriet's fascination with the "eloquent" and "highly decorated" (43) family stories about their former plantation, Tribulation. In this "fairy tale" space (44), Robin was alive, Harriet's aunts and grandmother still had money, and all the Cleves enjoyed secure social positions. Although her grandmother now laments that the family estate has fallen, most evidently in the plantation's conversion into "welfare apartments" for African Americans (41), Harriet vows to recreate Tribulation as a "mighty, thundering, [and] opulent" (44) palace in her mind where her brother can "[move] like a prince through the rooms" (42). However, it is in "restringing the skeleton of the extinct monstrosity which had been her family's fortune" that, Tartt hints, Harriet first displays "the narrowness of vision which enabled all the Cleves to forget what they didn't want to remember, and to exaggerate or otherwise alter what they couldn't forget" (44). As these details make clear, Harriet's attempt to come to terms with Robin's murder stems, at least in part, from a desire to resurrect a family legacy "tainted" by financial ruin and racial instability.

Many aspects of Harriet's early investigation, too, suggest a shortsightedness in the amateur sleuth related to limitations in her understanding of social equality. When, for example, Harriet interviews Ida about the day of Robin's death, she notes that her caretaker conflates details about the "white trash" Ratliffs and the "white trash" Odums, another lower-class family living nearby. But when Harriet calls attention to this mistake, Ida Rhew simply retorts "same difference" (144), a flippant comment that Harriet is quick to overlook. In her simple acceptance of Ida's assessment, Tartt likens Harriet to the "spy" of Louise Fitzhugh's famous children's book. *The Little Friend*'s early reviewers have noted already the connection between the two tomboys who take up work as amateur detectives, trailing "suspicious" members of their communities while scribbling unkind observations about them in a notebook. But Tartt's Harriet most importantly evokes Fitzhugh's Harriet Welsch in her experiences with a mentor, Ole Golly, who encourages her to appreciate that there are as "many ways to live as there are people on the earth" (32), even as she promotes sleuthing as a means of distinguishing oneself from "lesser" others. In much the same manner, Harriet Dufresnes loudly professes a desire to broaden her worldview and to correct the injustices carried out against African Americans in her Mississippi hometown; however, she does not understand that by relying on circumstantial evidence about "white trash" people, her subsequent identification of Danny as Robin's killer perpetuates the very forms of discrimination she initially aimed to combat.

Even though Harriet envisions herself as an agent of social justice, avenging her beloved caretaker and brother through her indictment of the Ratliffs, Tartt provides clues from the outset of the novel indicating Harriet has been too hasty in settling on Danny as her primary suspect. Any time that Harriet attempts to reduce the Ratliffs to social "riffraff," for example, Tartt identifies subtle but related flaws among the "aristocratic" Cleves, particularly in terms of their racism. The Ratliffs are notorious perpetrators of racial crimes in Alexandria, often terrorizing a nearby creek where black community members like to fish. Standing atop a bridge, they fire shotguns into crowds of men, women and children, laughing and shouting at victims to "get a move on" (130). On the surface, the Ratliffs' behavior stands in stark contrast to the mild-mannered Cleves; yet Tartt asserts that they are equally cruel in their subtler brand of racism, instructing lifelong employees to "get a move on" after firing them with little thought to their security or well-being. Harriet herself becomes a party to such mistreatment when a complaint to her mother about Ida's cooking leads to the woman's casual dismissal. It is only after she is gone that Harriet realizes how faintly Ida's presence remains throughout the house in which she worked for over a decade and how little information Harriet knows about Ida's identity in the larger world. That she, a "detective" who thrives on the compilation of data, has never sought Ida's personal information—not even her address or telephone number— demonstrates how fully Harriet participates, even if unwittingly, in what critic Patricia Yaeger describes as her southern community's "evisceration" of African American subjectivity (*Dirt* 143).

THE DETECTIVE'S FINDINGS IN DISARRAY

Tartt ultimately undermines the work of her detective by revealing to readers that Danny is *not* the individual responsible for Robin's death. Like most detectives, Harriet constructs what John Scaggs terms a final "array" about the crime, or a sequencing of events as she believes they originally occurred (19); in this array, she maintains that Danny is responsible for hanging Robin, then leaving the crime scene, and later bragging to his classmates about committing the murder. But in contrast to traditional detective texts, Tartt ultimately rewards those readers who remain wary of her sleuth's conclusions by providing a more comprehensive "array" of events from Harriet's primary suspect. Through Danny's perspective, readers not only learn of his innocence almost one hundred pages before Harriet does, but they also discover that he was, in fact, Robin's defender, or the "little friend" of the novel's title (516). And while information of the boys' relationship would have been impossible for even close readers to detect before Tartt reveals it outright, their careful attention to Harriet's processes of inductive reasoning should provide sufficient evidence that her conclusions about Danny could not be sound.

Writing *The Little Friend* from an authorial omniscient point of view, Tartt enables readers to drop down into the minds of poor white characters beyond the reach of Harriet's investigation, learning about their experiences in a way that Harriet remains unable to do. Those moments in which the reader gains access

to Danny's thoughts are particularly illuminating, as they help to define him outside the limited figure that Harriet paints of a white trash, meth-addicted criminal, and instead reveal a nuanced history in which he faces issues of class and
gender discrimination not altogether different from those that Harriet experiences. Tartt shares in his array, for example, that the Ratliffs had always hated the
Cleves, a "certain snooty class of whites," who they regarded as "traitors to their
race" for equating poor whites with the "common yard nigger" (515). Danny's
grandmother Gum even rejoiced when Tribulation later caught fire, since she
remembered the embarrassment of having to pick cotton in its fields as a girl
(515). But Danny's array illustrates how he and young Robin did much to bridge
the class divisions separating their families, noting that Robin made him feel like
an equal when he bypassed their families' fraught history by welcoming Danny
to his birthday party at Tribulation. In this legendary house, Danny recalls savor-
ing a lovely white piece of cake that seems an apparent proffering of the racial
"purity" his family resents being denied, but he also observes that Tribulation,
with its moth-eaten rugs, broken plaster, and cracked ceilings, was not the infal-
lible monument to white supremacy he imagined. In this manner, Danny's array
explains that, even as a boy, he had already intuited what Harriet fails to: that
notions of racial superiority are, like Tribulation itself, a construct that can only
be undone through the strengthening of human bonds.

Although Danny's attendance at Robin's party begins the process of bridging
deeply entrenched social gaps, it also indicates how Robin's death marks their
even more formidable reinstatement. As revealed in his array, Danny had already
been humiliated at school by a teacher who forced him to wear a woman's wig
for a week as punishment "for something or other" (516). Thus when he breaks
down crying at the news of the murder, Danny feels particularly vulnerable.
He doesn't want to incur the wrath of his father by shedding tears, and when
another family member snivels, "guess [Robin] was your boyfriend" (517), the
comment is enough to prompt Danny's fateful boast at school the next day that
he is responsible for the hanging. Admittedly, Harriet does not have access to
this information about Danny's past before she identifies him as her primary
suspect. But such is the point of Tartt's decision to employ a "chorus" of narrative
voices throughout *The Little Friend*: to propose that, had Harriet been willing to
investigate beyond the limits of her "single song," she would have discovered in
Danny not only his similar experiences as the victim of gender policing but also
a shared affection for Robin.

In its various subversions of genre conventions, particularly in compromising
the authenticity of the detective's array and refusing to establish narrative clo-

sure, *The Little Friend* can be read as a "metaphysical" detective novel. Patricia Merivale and Susan Sweeney outline in *Detecting Texts* that such works often avoid "neat endings" that answer all the narrative's questions and that "can therefore be forgotten" (2). Instead, the metaphysical detective's apparent inability to decipher the mystery strategically casts doubt on the reader's shared attempt to make clear sense of the text, prompting them to consider: "How, if at all, can we rely on anything besides our own constructions of reality?" (Merivale and Sweeney 4). Even if readers have not fallen under the same narrative spell that leads Harriet to suspect Danny, Tartt encourages them to consider what preconceived notions might yet shape their suspicions about Robin's killer and what it means that they, too, cannot make sense of the racially charged murder act that the Cleves refuse to address.

Metaphysical detective texts also differ distinctly from genre conventions in that they feature investigative processes which endanger the identity of the detective. In their pages, the detective is more likely to discover that she is "the victim she avenges, the criminal she seeks, or both at once" (Merivale and Sweeney 248), a conundrum that Harriet faces not only when Danny later attempts to strangle her, but also when she attempts to orchestrate Danny's death, making a spectacle of this innocent man by shooting at him and leaving him in a water tower to drown. In direct contrast to the uncanny intuitions of predecessors like Sherlock Holmes, metaphysical detectives like Harriet often find that their only answer to the "perennial question—'Whodunit?'—is 'I.' And 'Who is 'I'?' is another question entirely" (Merivale and Sweeney 248).

Ultimately Harriet fails to solve her brother's murder; but instead of "confronting the insoluble mysteries" of the crime or her own unstable identity as detective, she simply sets about fabricating a new array designed to promote the legitimacy of her telling of events. Tartt earlier demonstrates this problematic narrativizing tendency in the Cleve family's singing of the "single song," a behavior that resurfaces in Harriet's investigation of Robin's murder. For example, when her queries uncover a photo of Danny, she finds that she is unable to see him as "a boy or even a person," omitting all other details about her suspect until he comes to represent for her nothing less than "the frank embodiment of evil" (479). When she finally overhears her father identify Danny as Robin's "little friend," she remains steadfast in her refusal to accept any other reading of his character, simply concluding that "it would be easier if Danny Ratliff really had killed Robin" (620). Given her relatively stable social position as a upper middle-class white girl, the "rich possibilities" for such a story soon "open like poisonous flowers all around her" (620), enabling her to protect her sense of self by defining Danny as the criminal she desires him to be. It is little surprise, then, that when local authorities finally pull Danny out of the water tower where Harriet left him to drown, his face is "so distorted that it [looks] less like an actual face than a sculpture of melted wax" (615). Harriet's prejudices against Danny and his "white trash" family have so warped him that all who observe his "twisted," "skull-like" visage on the front page of the paper are likely to follow her lead in reading it as horrific.

Tartt's graphic depiction of this violence against Danny represents a flagrant departure from conventions of detective fiction, a form which traditionally does not display the punishment of criminals, especially not punishments carried out by the detective. John Scaggs notes, for example, that the "conspicuous absence" of legal punishment in detective fiction is "at odds with the nature of crime itself" since the "violation of a community code of conduct" demands "a response in terms of the code that has been violated" (45). However, some scholars, including Scaggs, have suggested the tendency of traditional detective fiction to ignore the legal repercussions of crime is intentional, and can be read as a part of a "repressive state apparatus" in its implication "that the law and the system of legal punishment [should be] invariably accepted as givens" (45). If this is the case, Tartt's very *un*conventional decision to feature Harriet's horrific treatment of Danny, including her attempts to shoot him point blank and then drown him in a water tower, can be interpreted as Tartt pulling back the curtain surrounding the workings of the Jim Crow South, emphasizing that dominant, oppressive narratives of racial and social hierarchy are upheld via aggression—not "natural" divisions. Fittingly, Harriet's primary role model shifts at this point in the novel from Sherlock Holmes to Harry Houdini as her mastery of the magician's "Dead Man's Float" stunt enables her to ensure both her own escape and Danny's arrest for drug possession and murder. Harriet is no longer simply in the business of uncovering criminality, as is Sherlock; rather, she is in the business of *producing* criminality through sleight of hand and illusion. It is a "business" that Tartt ties indirectly to the racially evocative murder at the novel's center. In making a murderer of Danny, Harriet becomes complicit in the same criminal mythmaking endemic to the Jim Crow South through segregation and the ritual of lynching.

THE FALLOUT OF FALSE DETECTION

In many ways, Harriet's turn from Sherlock to Houdini has the effect that she intended: the local newspaper prominently features an article about Danny as a captured "murderer," and Harriet enjoys new clout with her best friend, who celebrates her incrimination of Danny as a victory. But Tartt also strategically highlights how Harriet's narrative "victory" comes at a great personal cost, much like that facing her literary namesake. Although the extent of Harriet Dufresnes's problematic sleuthing is not made public in the same vein as Harriet Welsch's, her vengeance-based investigation does fail to produce desired results—namely, securing the return of her beloved caretaker, Ida Rhew, or a sense of closure to Robin's death. Ultimately it even subjects her to the same violence of meaning-making that she would impose on others.

Only hours after following Danny to the water tower where he will be captured and branded a criminal, Harriet falls violently ill, and a series of fainting spells lead to her admittance at the local hospital. There are, Tartt suggests, several possible ways to interpret Harriet's ailments. Throughout the novel, she experiences episodes that others classify first as heat stroke and later as an acute response to emotional distress. At other times, Harriet's grandmother expresses her concern that Harriet's fainting may be the result of the filthy, newspaper-filled surroundings in which the child lives. And the reader, in turn, wonders whether Harriet's submersion in the meth-laced waters of the tower or her summer practicing the breath-holding exercise, "Dead Man's Float," may be to blame for her most recent illness.

But despite these many possibilities, Harriet's doctor only hears her family's claim that she has had a "seizure" before he declares her "epileptic." Harriet's doctor here ignores any information that does not fit with his theories about her symptoms, labeling her with a condition that her best friend's mother whispers will forever mark her as a danger to herself and others. In this way, the doctor's hasty diagnosis makes Harriet the victim of a narrativizing process not unlike her earlier assessment of Danny. Though Harriet may not face the same horrible implications of such labeling as those citizens in Alexandria who are poverty-stricken or black, Tartt hints that Harriet will now encounter limits to her mobility that evoke the limitations of the South's built-in racial and class hierarchies. Thus the "discoloration" that Harriet's doctor later notices on her neck (580) must not be read only as a product of Danny's attempt to strangle her but rather, an indication that despite her unwillingness to recognize the damage she inflicts, she too must experience the repercussions of false "detection." With Harriet's failure, Robin's death returns to its status as "cold case" at novel's end.

Yet in recounting Harriet's desperate, futile pull to reopen the investigation, Tartt comments on the ways that the American South continues to function as a place imagined and constantly reinvented by different people and cultures. Certainly, it is geographically, historically, and culturally locatable (Roberts), but it does not exist in some single, "authentic" form, like Harriet and her family seem to believe. Tartt instead concludes that the region's history, much like the spectacle of Robin's death and the array of events that Harriet crafts in response to it, has been recurrently fabricated to local specifications with an eye to maintaining the interests of certain empowered parties. And though it references so many of the different stereotypes that have traditionally been used to describe this space, Tartt's novel forcefully moves beyond a simple reinscription of the South as an intrinsically backward location by allowing the careful reader, if not the detective herself, to uncover the violent means through which such historical narratives have been upheld, even in the interest of "progress." It is the intersectional "symphony" of voices Tartt assembles that challenges the readers, as would-be detectives, to forego a "right" way of knowing, refusing a "single song" of the South.

NOTES

1. Though the novel was later nominated for an Orange Prize, it has yet to attract the attention of literary scholars and did not go on to match the success of either Tartt's debut novel, *The Secret History* (1992), or *The Goldfinch* (2014), which won the Pulitzer Prize for Fiction.

2. Of Mississippi's lynching victims, approximately seven percent were white.

A FAILED SOUTHERN STRATEGY

Detecting Race, Gender, and Region on CBS's Yancy Derringer

PHOEBE BRONSTEIN

The Christmas episode of CBS's Reconstruction-era drama *Yancy Derringer* (1958–1959), "Old Dixie," ends on a seemingly hopeful note: the eponymous hero Yancy (Jock Mahoney) gathers his friends at Waverly, his plantation home, to celebrate the holiday. Earlier in the episode Yancy, with the aid of his African American servant Obadiah (Bill Walker), has rescued the plantation from a fallen southern belle bent on stealing treasure buried on the property. As Yancy welcomes a diverse array of guests, Obadiah stands behind him at the edge of the frame. After all the guests have arrived, Yancy moves toward the portrait of his father—followed by Obadiah—clad in a Confederate uniform that hangs over the mantle. Looking fondly up at the portrait, Yancy offers a toast to close the episode: to the "good days that are gone," he says, and then as the camera holds still Yancy looks back to the group and continues, "and the better days to come."

Yancy's toast posits no break between past and future, a sense echoed and reinforced by Obadiah's loyal and continued servitude to both Yancy and Waverly and his consistent positioning in the background. At the same time, Yancy's turn towards his guests suggests that this new group, which includes a white madam, Obadiah, a Chinese restaurant owner, and Pahoo (X Brands)—Yancy's Native American sidekick—posits a new and seemingly economic and racially diverse South. Here Obadiah's and Pahoo's happy participation in the toast erases the racial violence of the past and present plantation system. Their participation helps reimagine racial hierarchies as benign, natural, and mutually beneficial, much in line with the ethos of the plantation novel (Williams, *Playing* 101). Meanwhile the white and debonair Yancy remains unquestionably at the helm of this group. This televised vision of the South, picking up from already-available scripts about the region like *Birth of a Nation* and *Gone with the Wind*, reworks these representational histories for television, setting the stage for later depictions of the region and its political savior: the white southern moderate.

Yancy Derringer wasn't CBS's first attempt at a southern drama: a few years earlier *The Gray Ghost* (1954), which overtly championed the Confederacy, was swiftly canceled due to fear of a northern backlash. Just a year after *Yancy Der-*

ringer ended, ABC launched its own southern drama, *Bourbon Street Beat* (1959–1960): the crime-of-the-week show followed the Randolph & Calhoun detective agency as it investigated haunted plantations, disappearing jazz musicians, and, of course, murder. *Yancy Derringer*'s fleeting run garnered little popular or scholarly discourse. Yet its afterlife in syndication suggests that the drama was very much part of the national imagination ("Warner Sets Up"). In a 1961 issue of *Sponsor*, an advertisement for New Orleans local TV station WWL-TV notes that *Yancy Derringer* continued to have some of the strongest ratings in the Monday night slot. That same year *Yancy Derringer* was sold into ten local markets including New York, Chicago, and Los Angeles ("WWL-TV"). Together these programs reveal a concerted and early effort, albeit a failed one, by the networks to dramatize the South and thus engage a southern audience.

Despite the seeming failure of *Yancy Derringer*—the drama only lasted the one season—the hero at the drama's center reveals much about the foundations of televisual representations of the South.[1] Paired together with *Bourbon Street Beat* and *The Gray Ghost,* these southern dramas showcase a pattern and history of imagining white extralegal male heroes as redemptive forces for a white South amidst the civil rights movement. Not quite a typical detective figure, Yancy's construction is rooted in the mash-up of the Western (in film and on TV) and post-plantation genres. While a year later *Bourbon Street Beat* would embrace the more standard detective genre, *Yancy Derringer* showcases an early evolution of that same style of white masculinity. The new white order characterized by *Yancy Derringer* rejected those challenges posed by the civil rights movement to the racial, political, and "social structures in the America of television viewers in the 1950s and 60s," and instead reaffirmed the nostalgic fantasy of a benign white patriarchal order (Newcomb 296). Throughout the series, like in "Old Dixie," the companionship of both Pahoo and Obadiah further asserts this racist structure: both willingly and happily aid Yancy in all his endeavors to restore New Orleans to its supposed former glory. Meanwhile, the fallen white women Yancy encounters, saves, and sometimes fights suggest and reflect the dangers of this new South: *Yancy Derringer* maps the political crisis onto the bodies of its white female characters.[2] In portraying the old white order as benevolent, despite clear historical evidence to the contrary, the series implicitly asserts that the white elite, like Yancy, will guide the civil rights–era South through social and political change from within, even as the toast in "Old Dixie" asserts that perhaps change is not entirely necessary or has already come.[3]

This essay reads these oft-contradictory representational logics within the context of civil rights news coverage, the rise of the Ku Klux Klan and White Cit-

izens' Council, and the rise of television itself. The series functions as a rationalization to the older southern order's continuation—from making light of lynch
mobs to rebuilding Yancy's own plantation—despite the broader seismic social
shifts of the 1950s. Yet the racial politics of *Yancy Derringer* are complex, as the
series imagines racial discord and violence through Pahoo's experience, mobilizing the Western genre to reimagine and reroute southern racism onto both the
past and onto the only Native American character. The drama reflects the unhappy fissures in narrating and restoring the old South on primetime television.

THE PROMISE OF TELEVISION & THE SOUTHERN PROBLEM

Television rose to the status of a national medium within the fraught social and
political climate of the civil rights movement—a rise that also coincided with
the medium's expansion in the South. The hope for this new medium, as Lynn
Spigel has articulated it, was that television could serve "as a panacea for the
broken homes and hearts of wartime life" and as a means to "restore faith in family togetherness" (2–3).[4] The South as represented through news footage of the
civil rights movement, then, presented a clear and present danger to this white
middle-class fantasy replete with happy housewives, nuclear families, and white
picket fences: by 1955, Dr. Martin Luther King Jr.'s "Gandhi-inspired crusade,
which always ran the risk of bloodshed, began to draw cameramen and tape re-
corders, sometimes resulting in 2-minute items on newscasts" (Barnouw 207).
At the helm of this violent civil rights South were southern policemen, who
came to be easily categorized as unruly and irrational villains. The sheriffs featured on civil rights news broadcasts all looked like versions of the same: sweaty,
overweight, deep southern accents, and of course white.[5] This image would become an emblem of all that was bad and violent about the South, a visual rhetoric that erased systemic racism and condemned bad white men rather than a
system for the violence and injustice suffered by black citizens. This representational climate—coupled with the expansion of audiences in the South after
the end of the FCC freeze on new affiliates in 1952—created complex and often
competing conditions that shaped late 1950s representations of race and region.[6]

Scholars such Allison Graham, Carol Stabile, Sasha Torres, and Stephen Classen have shown that as news coverage of the civil rights movement gained mo-
mentum in the 1950s, so too did networks and advertisers increasingly worry
about black representation in prime-time entertainment programming. In
addition, as television's reach in the South grew, advertisers and networks increasingly courted and pandered to southern segregationist tastes with region-

ally themed programs and by halting and even reversing initial trends towards more diverse fare. For instance, in 1956, Nat King Cole's 15-minute variety show premiered on NBC, garnering high praise from critics and support from the network, yet Cole could not find a national sponsor. Madison Avenue—as Cole would reveal later in *Ebony*—blamed the South for its refusal to back the star on a national level (31). As Joe Stevenson reported in *The Chicago Defender*, sponsors avoided Cole's show "for fear that they would suffer in the sales of their product in the southern part of the United States" (10). This racist anxiety governed how entertainment programming would represent both blackness and the white South in late 1950s and early 1960s television.

Representing the South would beget a series of bizarre and often conflicting representational moves that worked both to avoid any gesture towards complex black or diverse representations and any overt critique of the region's racist politics.[7] An episode of *Yancy Derringer*, "Panic in Town," makes these competing impulses clear. The episode begins at night as a young white woman with blonde hair and wearing a white dress with black trim—the latter making her look even more white against the gray backdrop—runs through the streets of New Orleans. She is clearly terrified as she runs looking over her shoulder until she pauses, looking straight at the camera and framed in a medium close-up. She then screams as a black-gloved hand reaches out and attacks her, the attacker's body initially hidden outside the frame. The music drops deeper, becoming increasingly foreboding as the figure—cloaked in black and wearing a clown mask—appears on-screen and begins to beat her. The clown then cuts her hair and runs off just as Yancy and Pahoo arrive to rescue the young victim. Here the clown villain mobilizes familiar racist scripts of black masculinity as a threat to white femininity—the cutting of her hair symbolizing her violation, standing in for her rape—showcasing the dangers white women face in this new, unruly, and plantation-less South.

Meanwhile, a white group calling itself the Freedom League holds rallies and decries the northern administrator, Mr. Colton: "This administrator puts up with anything: wantonness, drunkenness, gambling," they suggest to a group of onlookers, and then they argue, "the men of the Freedom League will protect you." The league aims to rid New Orleans of undesirables like the clown villain, protect New Orleans's white women from harm, and secure the autonomy of the city from northern intervention. The rhetoric of the group sounds unmistakably like that of states' rights advocates, or more pointedly, the Klan. Yet the episode mocks and condemns this same rhetoric, when in a final plot twist the clown is revealed to be none other than the leader of the Freedom League. Leagues such as this are not nor should be, the episode suggests, the new face of the South. Indeed, white women in this New Orleans are only in danger from the rogues of the Freedom League. This episode thus distances its racial politics from those of the Klan and White Citizens' Council. However, even as episodes like "Panic in Town" offer a critique of white supremacist rhetoric and politics, *Yancy Derringer* defangs that critique through its color-blind treatment of New Orleans. This representational move erases the inherently racist underpinnings of the tropes of the black rapist and white female vulnerability—rhetoric at the heart of the Klan, White Citizens' Council or, by extension, the language of states' rights.

This erasure of the racist violence and the logic it supports is especially clear in the episode "Game of Chance," which invokes the image of a lynch mob. Yancy and the jailer joke about lynch mobs and then use a fake one to entrap a white murderer, a representation that would have been easily and eerily familiar to southern audiences: a dark shot filled with torches features men shouting as they approach the jail cell. Close-ups of the mob reveal their angry faces and their torches—the sound bridge that carries their screams makes the violence of the mob feel imminent. Again, all those under threat are white, despite the fact that lynching was predominantly used as a terror tactic against black men in the South—a threat inextricably connected to and justified by the supposed protection of white women. As with "Panic in Town," the episode obscures the racist violence underlying these plots and the role of white women in supporting and condoning that violence. These episodes invoke race and the rhetoric of southern racist violence specifically, yet rarely mention or discuss race itself, in line with long-circulating rhetoric about the Civil War, which omitted slavery and emancipation in favor of emphasizing national unity (Gallagher 4).[8]

The drama, then, imagines issues like states' rights—or as the Freedom League leader puts it, "southern autonomy"—as rooted not in racism but southern pride and freedom symbolized by the plantation system. *Yancy Derringer* thus obscures southern racism, reflecting what Tara McPherson refers to as the "cultural schizophrenia" that governs southern representation: the South is the site of a vast nostalgia industry rooted in celebrating the plantation, a rhetorical move that requires detaching the plantation from the horrors and violence of slavery (3). Discussions of the past omit slavery and its attendant violence, instead paying homage to plantations and past white ways of life, like the toast to Yancy's father's portrait in "Old Dixie." In "Loot from Richmond," for example, Yancy travels to a plantation to help recover a Confederate treasure. When he arrives at the plantation, a shot frames the older white building from a low angle, enhancing its majestic quality, as Yancy remarks, "Derrion Hall . . . home, proudly standing there defying the ravages of time and war." Like in "Old Dixie," the building lives on as celebrated and nostalgic monument to a revisionist and Lost Cause–styled past that the show does not overtly condemn and at times even appears to support.[9]

This erasure of racist southern politics worked to, or at least attempted to, address the "race question without offending southern sensibilities," imagined as particularly sensitive to critiques of the region's racist politics (Slotkin 377). Using its past setting and employing elements of the Western, *Yancy Derringer* could obscure contemporary concerns about civil rights or communism, for instance, by wrapping those concerns into plots about Native American–white relations. Set in the contemporary moment, plots about racism and discrimination would likely have drawn scrutiny and censorship, like Rod Serling's attempts to dramatize Emmett Till's case for television (Graham and Monteith 17). Within this frame, *Yancy Derringer* reflects the competing impulses and contradictions of representing the South on television in the late 1950s and, moreover, the ways in which dramatizing the region posed a threat to the redemptive promise of television. However, safely lodged in the past, the Western, with its requisite tale of "white-Indian conflict and peace-making" allowed television producers "to raise questions of war and peace and to entertain" diverse political possibilities in a text that appears, at least superficially, as pro-segregationist (Slotkin 367). Here, the Western-cum-plantation romance enabled the "retelling of civil rights stories" in a less politically volatile form, casting Reconstruction-era New Orleans as an historical analogue of the present-day civil rights movement (Graham 152). In this formulation, the South's new heroes needed to be visually distinguished from those white sheriffs appearing on the nightly news, while they also needed to represent a continuum between past and present, a sense that with the help of a few good white men, nothing in the South—and perhaps by extension the nation—need change.[10]

A PLANTATION COWBOY IN NEW ORLEANS: YANCY AS THE SOUTH'S WHITE SAVIOR

Distinct from emerging representations of southern police as rednecks and illiterate bullies, Yancy is part Western hero and part Rhett Butler–styled southern gentleman, rejecting southern institutions of law and order all together. Yancy is an extralegal white male hero, functioning outside the confines of the law, to protect and serve the citizens of New Orleans and assert, each week, that perhaps white supremacy was indeed benign. *Yancy Derringer*'s representational order foreshadowed later civil rights news coverage, which positioned the moderate white—and often male—southerner as the South's savior. The "new southerner," Aniko Bodroghkozy writes, was "a white Southerner who accepted that the ideology of equal opportunity provided the ultimate solution" for racial strife (53). This new iteration of the South was visually distinct from the racist southern lawman whose violent opposition to democratic processes, such as peaceful public protests, was already a common feature of civil rights news coverage. Instead of sweaty, aggressive, and overweight white men, the heroes of this new South—on the news, *Bourbon Street Beat,* and *Yancy Derringer*—were fit, handsome, benevolent, and above all, ethical white male heroes.[11]

Yancy's small-screen image (including his luck with ladies) unmistakably replicates *Gone with the Wind*'s Rhett Butler (Clark Gable), with slicked-back hair, a mustache, and white plantation hat. Craig Thompson Friend argues that "Rhett Butler became the masculine ideal for many white southern men because he represented a new form of individualized honor, one that revered drinking, hunting, swearing, cunning, physical pleasure with women, and even fighting as a powerful remedy for weakened southern masculinity" (xviii). Week after week and woman after woman, Yancy proves his strength, virility, and masculinity via his sexual prowess and charm—the mostly female party which attends Yancy's Christmas toast in "Old Dixie" is a testament to this sensibility.

Furthermore, Yancy's position as a former Confederate officer positions him in a lineage of Lost Cause masculinity nationalized by texts from *Birth of a Nation* to *Gone with the Wind.* This brand of masculinity was rooted in "extoll[ing] gallantry of Confederate soldiers," while denying the centrality of slavery in secession and the Civil War (Gallagher 4). As Rogin notes, *Birth of a Nation* represented an early and successful attempt to "nationalize the southern view of Reconstruction," mobilizing a representational politics that supported yet did not overtly endorse or condone a southern understanding of the Civil War South (154). By the end of the pilot, Yancy, himself a former Confederate captain, reclaims his family home of Waverly and restores its honor, thereby embracing his role as a part of an older southern society rooted in familial lands and their attendant racist traditions, though the drama certainly doesn't envision them as such. Yancy's nostalgia-ridden characterization inevitably mourns the loss of the Confederacy and the institution of the plantation, as the pilot or episodes like "Loot from Richmond" and "Old Dixie" reveal, and conjures nostalgia for the Old South, as if that vision is detached from the violent and virulent racism that supported the region.

Yancy's characterization also draws heavily from the tradition of the Western cowboy. Despite the lack of a clear Western aesthetic, contemporary publications and marketing for the series envisioned *Yancy Derringer* as a Western and its eponymous hero as coming from this particular American stock: a 1959 issue of the fan magazine *TV Radio Mirror* included Yancy Derringer in a photo essay as one of the "Wondermen of the Westerns" while an earlier article in the same publication referred to the drama as a "western adventure-detection story" (4, 42). A lone individual, the cowboy was unhindered by the rules and regulations of society and so he was free to roam and enact violence as he pleased in the name of justice. Cowboys, then, merely enact and help along the natural order, which is guided by essential masculine qualities such as aggression, competitiveness, and territoriality (Connell 46–47). Richard Dyer and Allison Graham take this sensibility a step further, pointing to the racist framework of the genre: in *Framing the South*, Graham writes that "most fictional frontiersmen of the 1950s and 1960s had stalked the plains on a mission of racial and ideological purification" (152). In *Yancy Derringer*, Yancy's violence is aristocratic, with duels and swordplay; it is never brute and it is always, like the cowboy's, directed at those the narrative leads us to believe deserve punishment. Like the cowboy, Yancy operates in a legally and morally ambiguous framework, but adheres to a clear dualistic logic aimed at protecting New Orleans and often its white women from harm. Further, Yancy represents, following Brinkmeyer, a seemingly southern rethinking of the cowboy figure: American writers often "celebrate a solitary hero breaking out from a restrictive society and *into* a world of uncharted freedom" whereas southern literature "tends to celebrate those who do not leave" (Brinkmeyer 4). Yancy's return to New Orleans and his rebuilding of Waverly plantation—the emblematic institution of white southern culture—suggests New Orleans as the unruly frontier, while Yancy's drive to reinstate his plantation aligns him with reestablishing past southern heroes, concerns, and values.

Yancy's characterization and costuming provide a legitimate and unthreatening face to the very southern order under threat (distinct from Harold Strider and the other faces of violent southern law enforcement). Yancy presents a benign model of older white southern masculinity, and his new South—still built around the plantation home—betrays an allegiance to older models of the region. In this context, figuring Yancy as an "an angel" for New Orleans, a man who loves the South, and a former rebel turned unpaid southern undercover agent working outside the law and bent on restoring the region, discloses an allegiance to segregationist politics ("Return to New Orleans"). His all-white costuming enhances and reveals his heroic position on the side of good and morality, even though he works outside the confines of the law, something his frequent trips to jail remind us. This combination further enhances his alignment with segregationist groups like the Klan or its legal and more respectable public face, the White Citizens' Council. The Council's strategy, as Stephen Classen writes, was "to guard powerful communication outlets and to reproduce 'respectability' for its race-based politics" (37). Medgar Evers, a prominent civil rights activist, sometimes referred to the Citizens' Council as "the Klan in suits," a description which points to the clothes of the Citizens' Council as costumes to make racism appear respectable and legitimate (qtd. in Classen 37).

In Yancy's construction the show rejects those challenges to the social order stressed by the civil rights movement and instead reaffirms the fantasy of a benign white patriarchal order. Where *The Gray Ghost*'s version of the South openly championed the plantation past—hence CBS's anxiety over airing the series—Yancy's efforts to rebuild an old southern order, grounded in restoring family homes and rooted in the code of honor, conveyed a similar, albeit covert, nostalgia for the Confederacy. Even so, episodes like "Panic in Town" help distance the series' racist politics from contemporary states' rights groups—like by overtly mocking the episode's Freedom League—and those southern sheriffs and governors appearing on the nightly news. Meanwhile, the ongoing presence of Mr. Colton, the new northern-born administrator of New Orleans, serves as a metaphor for federal intervention in the South. Yancy's work with Mr. Colton, then, envisions and oddly condones federal intervention and national unity, a position antithetical to states' rights advocates. *Yancy Derringer*, thus, draws from a representational politics similar to *Birth of a Nation*, cloaking its brand of racism in a similarly styled white nostalgia. Black characters, like Yancy's servant Obadiah, continue to labor happily in the production of white supremacy, while the drama displaces discussions of race that might disrupt this racist fantasy onto Pahoo.

INFERENTIAL RACISM & THE WHITE SOUTHERN SAVIOR

On the surface, *Yancy Derringer* suggests that racial hierarchies produce a peaceful southern climate wherein African Americans contentedly labor in the service of whites. For example, Obadiah not only remains at the Waverly plantation following the end of the Civil War, he seems happy to serve Yancy: in "Old Dixie" Obadiah attends to Yancy, brings him drinks, decorates the Christmas tree, and even puts his life at risk when a fallen southern belle arrives and tries to steal a treasure buried at Waverly. In the final sequence of the episode, Obadiah, along with a variety of Yancy's friends, participates in the toast to both past and present, while standing behind Yancy on-screen. Earlier in the scene, he also stands silently behind Yancy as guests arrive, acknowledging Yancy and not Obadaiah, whose silent presence at the edge of the frame reiterates Yancy as master of the house. This racist formulation draws heavily from those visions of the region popularized by plantation novels. As Linda Williams notes, these novels imagined plantation masters as kind white men and slaves as "faithful and happy or sometimes misguided rebels; whippings occur only rarely and for the slaves' own good; escaped slaves find unhappiness in the North and pine for the paternalistic care of their former masters" (101). These narratives, like on *Yancy Derringer,* foreground the plantation as a happy, paternalistic, and benign place for African Americans. These narratives refuse to question the racial structure of the plantation past, even as nightly broadcasts of the civil rights movement challenged this vision.

In production of this seemingly racially harmonious New Orleans, *Yancy Derringer* relies on and perpetuates stereotypes of black Americans. For example, in "V as in Voodoo," black characters figure as voodoo priests and priestesses. When Yancy and Pahoo arrive at a voodoo ceremony, black bodies fill the screen for the first time in the series. This encounter with a group of black worshippers occurs through Yancy's determining and racist gaze, portraying these characters as irrational and primal. They are unthinking and possessed as they dance and chant in a circle performing a mystical ritual.[12] This sequence is grounded in and reproduces racist "unquestioned assumptions" without overtly calling attention to that racism (Hall, "White of Their Eyes" 91). Even the voodoo ceremony denies the black characters agency: initiated by a white woman, the ceremony enables a plot to unfold in the white world. In this way, the series consistently frames black experience through white perspectives. Similarly, Pahoo never speaks and instead uses his hands to sign—signs which Yancy must translate both for the characters on-screen and the viewers at home. Within this context, characters of color function to reassure and reinstate the dominance of whiteness even as the drama disavows racial strife.

In the absence of overt black-and-white racial strife, racial conflict appears on *Yancy Derringer* via Pahoo's experiences. Even though black characters never encounter overt racism, Pahoo remains the consistent target of explicitly racist remarks and treatment. For example, on a journey from New Orleans to Washington, D.C., in "Fire on the Frontier," Yancy and Pahoo sit together on the train. When the conductor arrives, he calls Pahoo a "redskin" and then demands that Pahoo sit in the cargo car. As Pahoo sits in silence, Yancy vehemently defends Pahoo's right to sit in first class. As a result, as the next shot shows, the duo and their other white travelling companion wind up together with the chickens in the cargo car. Later in the same episode, a hotel clerk refuses Pahoo entry into the hotel, causing Yancy to punch a man. After a scuffle in the hotel, the travelers find new accommodations in a horse stable. Yancy's commitment to Pahoo juxtaposed against the racist conductor or hotel clerk assures his good and unbiased nature. The episode later extends the antiracist label to the federal government: Pahoo speaks—via Yancy—to the senate and convinces the federal government to uphold a treaty with the Pawnee people in the wake of an unprovoked attack on the group by renegades. Pahoo's triumph suggests a systemic benign white patriarchy and that racism is merely the fault of a few rogue individuals.

Even as the series narratively presents Yancy's race-blindness and a more racially progressive—if not, conflicted—politics than *Bourbon Street Beat* or *The Gray Ghost,* so too does *Yancy Derringer* rely on unsigned racism to replicate racist structures. From Yancy translating for Pahoo to Pahoo's stereotypical construction as a noble savage happily serving Yancy for the remainder of his life, the series relies on racist tropes couched in narratives about race neutrality or color blindness. Yancy becomes a mediating force between Pahoo and the racists they encounter, a narrative move that both ensures Yancy's goodness and implicates him as part of a new racially neutral South in league with the federal government. This brand of racial representation is particularly insidious as it represents an awareness of racial inequality yet uses those moments to argue for the good nature and natural dominance of a white hero like Yancy. Furthermore, this narrative relies on positioning white women, not people of color, as the ultimate victims of this new, yet old, southern order—a narrative derived from and underpinned by racist assumptions that white women must be protected from black men. The series of course obscures this historically racist narrative, like in "Panic in Town," while still employing its recognizable tropes that envision the white belle as lost without the protection of the plantation. She, perhaps, becomes the biggest argument for restoring the old white southern order.[13]

DETECTING A TELEVISUAL SOUTH AND *YANCY DERRINGER*'S LEGACY

While images of a decaying older South dominate *Yancy Derringer,* the drama's version of the South in crisis rescues the region by employing a mediating white masculinity. Yancy serves here as a redemptive force and as the head of a new southern order that looks remarkably like the old plantation one, to imagine black Americans outside the confines of white supremacy embodied by new, supposedly benign, white southern men. Within this seemingly color-blind ethos, the drama allows for an exploration of black-white racial conflict through Pahoo's construction and his encounters with overt racism. Further, this problematic formulation obscures the different and diverse experiences of Native Americans in the South. Within this frame, racial anxiety is recoded as anxiety about gender and the southern belle's construction captures most clearly the anxieties about the old racist order's potential collapse. A year later *Bourbon Street Beat* foregoes any seeming concession to the political moment, instead unabashedly mourning the loss of the plantation and the racist system it upheld. These peculiar representational maneuvers articulate the complex and contradictory impulses that organized representations of the South and race in late 1950s television. Within its diegesis, *Yancy Derringer* replicated contradictory, confused, and rupturing visions of the South, incompatible with television's promise of restoring the post-war white nation.

What *The Andy Griffith Show* would reveal when it premiered in 1960 to top ratings, was that the southern sitcom was suited to the task of representing, rehabilitating, and profiting from a region in crisis. *Andy Griffith* embraced the complete omission of difference, whitewashing a rural South helmed by a handsome and benign Western-styled sheriff. While *Yancy Derringer* remains a mostly forgotten drama, along with its southern-set counterparts, the trope of westernstyled white southern hero impacts the contemporary television landscape, which is saturated in complex southern and frontier imagery. For instance, dramas from *The Walking Dead* to *Justified* continue to celebrate plantationromance-meets-cowboy-masculinity in the construction of their central heroes, Rick Grimes (Andrew Lincoln) and Raylan Givens (Timothy Olyphant) respectively. Excavating *Yancy Derringer* and detecting the traces of this early South in contemporary television reveals our heroes as problematically indebted to these early visions of white southern masculinity. By recycling this construction, television dramas like *The Walking Dead* repetitively communicate that even contemporary television worlds run amok by zombies remain grounded in the centrality and invisibility of white supremacy.

NOTES

1. This brand of southern representation draws from filmic predecessors, perhaps most notably *Gone with the Wind* and *Birth of a Nation*. With *Birth of a Nation*, "the North was ready for a film that, though it did not endorse the traditional southern view of the Civil War, sympathized with the antebellum South and nationalized the southern view of Reconstruction" (Rogin 154). Similarly, *Yancy Derringer* and *Bourbon Street Beat* reworked this representational world within the confines of late

1950s television and culture, neither overtly endorsing nor critiquing the white backlash against civil rights progress.

2. This method of representing women as a threat to the South, patriarchy, and by extension the nation, also appears in *Birth of a Nation* (both the Dixon novel and later Griffith film). As Michael Rogin articulates it, "Traditional patriarchal forms were under siege at the end of the nineteenth century. [. . .] And women, whether out in the world or confined to the home, stood for that regressive, disorganizing power. Partly they [women] stood as a symbol and scapegoat for a more distant social and political disruption" (158).

3. *Yancy Derringer*, along with the *Real McCoys* (1957–1963) and *Andy Griffith* (1960–1968) combine and conflate the western and southern hero, employing western tropes in the service of remaking the southern white gentleman. This narrative appears in an early and televisual version of what Robert Brinkmeyer articulates in *Remapping Southern Literature:* early twenty-first-century southern fiction's interest in the West and the Western (3).

4. Amidst this crisis in southern representation, networks programmed a surge of crime dramas featuring detective-types like Perry Mason and Joe Friday; white family sitcoms like *Father Knows Best;* and a myriad of Westerns from *Have Gun, Will Travel* to *The Lone Ranger* and *Gunsmoke* (Barnouw 213). Eric Barnouw writes: "By 1958 thirty western series were in prime-time television, dominating every network" (214).

5. For example, in 1955, the "obese, tobacco-chewing" sheriff of Sumner, Mississippi, Harold Strider appeared on television during the murder trial of Emmett Till's killers (Graham and Monteith 17).

6. Television's spread in the southern United States, coupled with the rise of civil rights news coverage, created complications for television networks, as southern stations would often boycott or blackout more racially progressive fare. For more on the blackouts, see Stephen Classen's book *Watching Jim Crow.*

7. For example, Graham and Monteith discuss *Twilight Zone* creator Rod Serling's two attempts to dramatize the Emmett Till case, in 1956 and 1958. Both ventures featured heavily censored programs that removed any and all recognizable references to Till's brutal murder (Graham and Monteith 17).

8. This notion made its way into national popular culture, as Rogin also shows with *Birth of a Nation,* including films like *Gone With the Wind,* monuments like Stone Mountain in Georgia, and the writings of Jubal Early (Gallagher 4–5).

9. Gallagher provides a more comprehensive description of Lost Cause politics: "Lost Cause advocates consciously sought to establish a retrospectively favorable account of the Confederate people and their short-lived nation. Among other points, these ex-Confederates denied the importance of slavery in triggering secession, blamed section tensions on abolitionists, celebrated antebellum southern slaveholding society, portrayed Confederates as united in waging their war for independence, extolled the gallantry of Confederate soldiers, and attributed Union victory to sheer weight of numbers and resources" (4).

10. Robert Brinkmeyer notes that this resistance to the future is a distinct part of southern literature, citing examples in the works of Eudora Welty, Carl Degler, and Lucinda McKethan (15).

11. For more on *Bourbon Street Beat*'s construction of masculinity in the southern detective drama, see Bronstein, "Failed Souths: Race, Gender, and Region in *Bourbon Street Beat*" in *Quarterly Review of Film and Television.*

12. It is worth noting here that *Bourbon Street Beat* has a similar episode about voodoo, and the sequence wherein Rex watches a voodoo ceremony is virtually identical to the one in *Yancy Derringer:* "Knock on Any Tombstone" (Bronstein 355).

13. This script of white femininity draws heavily from those cinematically cemented by films like *Birth of a Nation*: "White supremacists invented the black rapist to keep white women" and, I would add, black men, "in their place. [. . .] Griffith wanted what one viewer called the 'contrast between black villainy and blond innocence" (Rogin 164)."

ECOLOGICAL ANARCHY & PHILOSOPHICAL ANARCHISM IN THE FLORIDA CRIME FICTION OF JOHN D. MACDONALD

KRISTOPHER MECHOLSKY

Two predominant visions of humanity's relationship to nature are typified by the two Genesis stories of humanity's creation. One depicts humankind's dominion over an established nature, and the second depicts its expulsion from a paradise created for it. These competing visions fashion a tension in how nature is represented in Western culture, particularly in literature of the American South—and perhaps nowhere more overtly than in fiction about the last frontier there: Florida.

Florida seemed to inspire a vision of paradise in practically everyone who visited it. As one of the last two southern states admitted to the Union, Florida's beautiful, undeveloped wilderness was to its settlers either a frontier paradise to be molded or a natural paradise that would be spoiled. Insofar as "the *idea* of nature is an important tool in the construction of the idea of the South," as Christopher Rieger argues in *Clear-Cutting Eden* (1), the urbanization of the South in the 1930s and 1940s prompted several of the major literary authors of the South to write in a "pastoral literary mode as a way of reconceiving South-erners' relationship with the natural world" (2). In fact, two of the four authors Rieger examines in detail hail from the Sunshine State, indicating the degree to which Florida modeled for the South possible economic, political, and cultural responses to the post-Reconstruction industrialization of the region, whether the region chose to notice or not.

But the pastoral mode was not the only way the South's relationship to the natural world was reconceived, despite that mode's popular predominance. In fact, we need to revisit works like those of John D. MacDonald to explore more fully Florida's place in the national and southern postbellum imaginary, particu-larly insofar as the state reveals an intensely focused conflict between the natu-ral environment and the postindustrial capitalist expansion of Western society. Though his predictions of their solutions evolved, from his first novels to his last, MacDonald characterized the basic problems facing Florida in the same way: widespread political and business collusion and corruption—driven by ig-norant, rapacious greed and spurred on by attempts to commodify and capitalize on Florida's image as a frontier paradise—are degrading the state's coastline and interior ecosystems. Ironically, of course, that natural environment was crucial to the image of paradise that Florida had represented in the colonial and national conception of the American South. In selling a commodified image of its nat-ural beauty—primarily by housing people right on top of carelessly engineered versions of it—Florida began replacing much of its paradise with views to try to gaze at it. In novels like his first, *The Brass Cupcake* (1950), MacDonald suggests that a disgraced but principled hero might fashion a return to restore political and ecological justice; by the end of his career, though, MacDonald instead im-plies that nature will simply come to reclaim Florida from humanity. Any vic-tories the MacDonald hero can muster will be localized in effect, temporary in duration.

Much of MacDonald's crime fiction then is indicative of a kind of ecolog-ical, political southern fiction of Florida that depicts the state as the site of a doomed, disastrous collision between two mighty, natural, and complex systems—humanity and its natural environment—in the Anthropocene. The "Anthropocene" is a controversial environmental and geologic term proposed to define the epoch of a strongly human-impacted environment, but here it ap-pears in lowercase to define narrowly the period of "Great Acceleration" of hu-man activity (beginning at the end of the Industrial Revolution but really tak-ing off in 1950) marked by increases in population and urban concentration, water use, energy use, greenhouse gas emissions, surface temperature, and so on. MacDonald's crime fiction ultimately advocates an absurdist, philosoph-ical anarchist response to this anthropocenic collision of systems through its very characterization of postindustrial capitalist humans. Particularly through his Travis McGee series, MacDonald depicts Florida in the Anthropocene as a bellwether of the coastal South, where the worst excesses of business and pol-itics intersect the best individual rebellions against them, where the inevitable ecological devastation at best might be slowed (but not stopped) by humanity. In fact, Florida's ecological transformation parallels the state's relationship to its evolving southern identity in the postbellum South, and MacDonald's novels evoke this parallel: McGee's peculiar philosophical anarchism encounters and responds to the southern and ecological turbulences of the twentieth century, ultimately suggesting that regardless of man's actions for good or ill, nature alone will prevail.

THE SOUTH IN FLORIDA, FLORIDA IN THE SOUTH

The point of inscribing MacDonald particularly as a southern writer stems from an overarching goal to more fully explain the South through Florida (and Florida through the South), as well as to highlight MacDonald's work as constitutive in that mission. Not as widely read or remembered today to the degree many of his contemporaries are, MacDonald was a prolific writer of popular fiction, primarily publishing various types of crime thrillers. He also dabbled in science fiction and fantasy—and in novels of "manners and morals," as Lewis D. Moore called them (2), which tended to examine the sexual mores of the white American middle class. Born in Sharon, Pennsylvania, in 1916, MacDonald studied business and settled into insurance in upstate New York with a wife and child by 1940, when he was asked to join the military (Hirshberg 7–8). He turned to writing full-time after the war, moving around the country and spending winters in warmer climes. On his way to New Mexico in the fall of 1949, his family decided to sojourn in Florida. He fell in love with the state and the then-small town of Sarasota, and they ended up residing there permanently (19).

MacDonald's exclusion from southern letters stems from a long-standing cultural struggle to identify the "authentic" South and southerner. His place has in fact been actively obscured by critics who have fixated on questions of authenticity. One need only turn to J. K. Van Dover and John F. Jebb's *Isn't Justice Always Unfair?: The Detective in Southern Literature* for a particularly uneasy essentialist reading of writers like MacDonald who were not born in Florida and who write about its cities. Scott Romine has critiqued approaches like these in *The Real South*. In fact, his broader point—that "the South is a noun that [often] behaves like [an imperative] verb" and that "the 'real South' often turns out to be the one I desire . . . either relationally . . . or coercively" (14)—is also a governing idea in historical ideas of Florida in the South (and the South in Florida). No other state in the contested region has been so twisted up with individual and collective desire, with authenticity and falsity, with ideas of both the essentialist identity of the South and of the non-South (from self-identified northerners and southerners alike).

Struggles over Florida's southern identity have been borne out in Florida fiction before MacDonald, too. While Florida has long had a great diversity of populations (e.g., Native Americans, Spanish, French, Africans, Menorcans, Greeks, Cubans, and Bahamians), novels about whites, by whites, dominated the literary market (Mason 7). Of lower-class whites, the "Crackers" and "Conchs" particularly, only the Cracker received significant literary treatment, most notably in the writings of Marjorie Kinnan Rawlings, whose popular, award-winning works brought rural Florida life to national attention. Rawlings's career is important here for two reasons. First, her works' popularity and her general critical identity as a southern writer reflect the biases that govern how and when Florida is seen as southern and not southern—and how and when its chroniclers are seen as southern and not southern. Second, we can thus understand MacDonald as Rawlings's mirrored doppelgänger: a transplant who critiqued the burgeoning urban Florida through *direct* depiction in *popular* fiction instead of by *romanticizing* the disappearing rural Florida in *literary* fiction. The fact that one transplant who depicts life in Florida is considered a southern writer while another is not succinctly exposes how *popular* notions of southern identity and southern writing continue to shape Florida's own relationship to southern identity and writing—and it indicates how integral nature is to both.

As it turns out, Florida has almost always been identified with a future South, more than anything. Anne E. Rowe illustrates repeatedly in *The Idea of Florida in the American Literary Imagination* that throughout its recorded history and up until the early twentieth century, Florida was "an untapped natural resource, an untapped imaginative source, waiting for economic and spiritual (or imaginative) exploitation" (9). Florida, she writes, has been for the American imagination not merely a geographical region but

> an image, a garden, Eden-like, where the striving and seeking, the rigorous pioneering and getting ahead that characterize the Land of Opportunity has been tempered and diverted by the languors of a tropical climate washed by the Gulf Stream and the balm of an always warm sun. (4)

But MacDonald actually uses some of these very words to describe Florida from the mouths of his characters. In the 1953 *Dead Low Tide*, for instance, the northern transplant hero (Andrew McClintock) implies, when casually and briefly recounting his life, that his entire motivation for his move to Florida was that he "came down here to the Land of Opportunity. The New Frontier" (7). In these respects, Florida in the early twentieth century resembled what the North tended to love most about the South while it dissembled those aspects the North tended to find distasteful or objectionable.

By the time Rawlings's historical novel *The Yearling* won the Pulitzer Prize in 1939, the crackers' way of life, like other rural economies in the state, was about to give way almost completely to tourist land development, and at a much faster pace than in the rest of the South. Arguably, Rawlings's popularity was more an indication of romanticized nostalgia on the part of the country than it was of interest in contemporary verisimilitude, as Christopher Rieger also argues ("Don't" 199). Rawlings's rural South was written and received with more affection than that of Erskine Caldwell or William Faulkner. Rawlings provided an acceptable literary escape in her yearning for an agrarian past in the face of urban development. Certainly without intent, pastoral depictions like Rawlings's might have even encouraged Florida's over-development in America's urbanization by propping up notions that Florida was still an Old South frontier ready to be civilized.

Florida was thus primed for drastic and continuing economic and geographic change, much more so than the rest of the South. By the turn of the century, politicians and northern land developers like Henry Flagler and Henry Plant had begun transforming even the southern tip of the state—a veritable frontier in the antebellum period—into a habitable, visitable, and desirable location that the automobile and railroad helped rush to fill (Rowe 78). Both coasts from the top to the bottom of the state exploded with tourists and attractions. A thriving land speculation and tourism economy swelled the state in every way. As the state's population grew 280 percent between 1900 and 1930, concentrated mostly in cities, the state's resources were severely strained. In the 1920s, while the urban population increased 114.9 percent, rural areas did so by only 15.2 percent (Dodd and Dodd 34–36). Indeed, Mark Derr points out—in his masterful history of the ecological relationship between humans and the land in Florida—that many parts of rural Florida in the 1930s and 1940s even resembled the old frontier mining towns, replete with "cowmen engaged in pitched battle with sheriff's deputies and mine operators over a phosphate company's fencing of ten thousand acres in Polk County" (123).

Thus the patchwork land transformation continued to inspire and encourage great influxes of new denizens, decade after decade. Residents and the newly transplanted further encouraged the swarming of the state since the millions who arrived needed land, resorts, and entertainment. The feedback loops accelerated growth, and economic upheaval came hand in hand with great ecological upheaval. The transformation of natural ecosystems to farms, tree plantations, and cities effected the transformation of the natural rural land first to the Old South and then to the New in Florida. But over the course of the twentieth century, Florida's lead in the economic recovery period of the Sunbelt South (Cobb 180), along with its eccentric tourism and space industries, seems to have forever marked Florida as an interstitial, red-headed step-state—unmoored from the past and too successful at being the future; too overrun with snowbirds but too provincial and undeveloped; too geographically constrained but still ethnically eclectic.

Before the Civil War, it was the least populous southern state, and after it was the most populous. Florida always seems neither southern nor northern, neither western nor eastern.

SHABBY KNIGHT ERRANT IN A PAVED SOUTHERN PARADISE

It was into this mid-twentieth-century Florida milieu that MacDonald moved and began writing fiction professionally. Given the relative lack of socioeconomic diversity in popular literary depictions of the state before him, MacDonald's fiction signaled a new literary concern with the variety of experiences in Florida life beyond many rural southern stereotypes, featuring detailed depiction of Floridians from many socioeconomic strata—such as developers, surveyors, construction workers, mechanics, bankers, farmers, secretaries, police officers, lawyers, prostitutes, photographers, dancers, academics, factory workers, store owners, maids, doctors, artists, and so on—caught in the advancing grind of the Anthropocene. While MacDonald broadened the scope of Florida literature by focusing on the many echelons of white classes responsible for and complicit in the anthropocenic transformation of the state, he does not grapple significantly with the lasting legacies of racial terror that Florida was founded on—slavery, American Indian removal, massacres, wars, Jim Crow. His very few meanders into racial issues are well-intentioned but clumsy. Nevertheless, MacDonald was uniquely suited to sketch the strata of white middle-class Florida—the sector driving the state's ecological and economic transformation—given his residence in Sarasota. Derr recounts that

> resettlement followed an identifiable geographic pattern, with northerners and midwesterners predominating in the St. Johns region and Central Highlands and ex-Confederates clustering in the old plantation country of the Panhandle and along the Gulf coast. The two groups mixed, in places like Fort Myers and Sarasota, where a smattering of wealthy northerners admired the climate, fishing, and isolation. (64)

MacDonald's Florida spanned the older southerners as well as the new arrivals. It was in the most popular set of books he wrote that MacDonald formed his model frame for understanding Florida beyond stereotypical trappings of the Old South. The Travis McGee novels were the adventures of a private detective–like figure who calls himself a "salvage consultant" because he "advises people about how to go about salvaging something . . . on a contingency basis, [for] a percentage of recovery" (*Cinnamon* 170), recovering things as various as lost fortunes, stamp collections, honor, sanity, and more. McGee is a free spirit, a self-described beach bum who lives his life in semiretirement, "taking it in chunks as I go along," "whenever I can afford it . . . [since] retirement comes when you are too old to enjoy it completely" (*Deep Blue* 4; *Dreadful Lemon* 8–9). More than that, though, he's a loner, "wary of the whole dreary deadening structured mess we have built into such a glittering top-heavy structure that there is nothing left to see but the glitter, and the brute routines of maintaining it" (*Deep Blue* 16). And so instead of helping to maintain the State, McGee makes himself a kind of ironically self-conscious Don Quixote, a "shabby knight errant" (*Empty Copper* 50) bent on protecting vulnerable individuals from the various mechanisms of industry and government and nature that threaten and bear down on them. But he is no ascetic Galahad or scowling Jeremiah. In his wanderings outside civilization, McGee also often seeks to maximize his own existential pleasure with food, drink, sex, love, conversation, friendship. But he usually only does so in thoughtfully moral ways. He takes pains to be ethically hedonistic. He describes his near-perfect happiness thusly: "a fine long hot lazy summer, a drifting time of good fish, old friends, new girls, of talk and laughter. Cold beer, good music and a place to go" (*Pale Gray* 7).

The character was a culmination for MacDonald since similar protagonists pepper his earlier fiction. Moore points out that when MacDonald starting writing his McGee series,

> he had a fund of narrative experience . . . [of characters who explore] the familiar aspects of the hard-boiled character who can both endure punishment and fight back while reaching an accurate conclusion about whatever mystery the novel contains . . . [who] share many attributes with McGee and foreshadow the types of difficulties he will undergo . . . [including Cliff] Bartells [*Brass Cupcake*] . . . Bill Danton (*Damned*), Lloyd Westcott (*Empty Trap*), Sam Bowden (*Executioners*), Leo Harrison (*Beach Girls*), Sydney Shanley (*On the Run*), and Paul Stanial (*Drowner*). (8)

David Geherin similarly finds substantive aspects of many pre-McGee protagonists to be his precursors (19–35), as does Edgar W. Hirshberg (42). With McGee's appearance in 1964, MacDonald also solidified the character as a kind of mouthpiece for many of MacDonald's own sociological and ecological views, as MacDonald acknowledged often (Merrill 2). Most important, McGee was a partial embodiment of and wandering gaze on the radically shifting upper-, middle-, and lower-class people of mid-century Florida—a national image of a New South, a twentieth-century frontier for modern farming, city living, and beachside luxury.

McGee's grasp and embodied partial representation of Florida's strata is driven almost entirely by his "shabby knight errant" ethos. McGee is a self-exiled fatalist wandering at the fringes of a civilization he loves to hate, lifting its veil from the outside while he alleviates its doomed victims. Ultimately, he regards his society from a distance, anthropologically, as a collective of human animals, and this critical distance grounds his political, social, ethical, and moral compass.

"YOU CAN'T HARDLY WIN"

What becomes apparent first in a glance over MacDonald's southern fiction is how intricately entangled the economic and ecological development of the New South is with its government. While MacDonald is remarkably attuned to McGee's evolution over the course of the series, writing four books at a time to keep his transformation consistent and believable (Schmidt),[1] certain noticeable plot patterns do emerge. They can be subdivided in a number of ways—which Geherin, Hirshberg, and Moore have done distinctly—but as Moore points out, "almost every novel in the series presents a criminal threat to the freedom of innocent citizens" (115), and in those books primarily set in Florida (a little under two-thirds of them), the threat is almost always integrally tied to abuse of Florida's land: through its "development," its tourist economy, or smuggling because of the state's unique geographic position. In MacDonald's fiction, businesses and local governments are always corrupt, deeply entangled in blackmail and otherwise profiting off of the individuals they are supposed to be serving or protecting—which mirrors the state's actual history, as Derr has chronicled. In fact, he notes that "during the nearly 170 years of American possession of Florida, state officials have been most noteworthy for their eagerness to give away or sell for a pittance the natural endowments of the peninsula whose stewardship they claimed as their duty" (15).

Corruption plot points are not unique to the McGee series, either. Actually, in MacDonald's earlier fiction, the small-town corruption and corporate and private greed that pepper the landscape of much mid-twentieth century noir—and especially characterize Florida's social and economic development at the time—are actually overcome effectively. Further along in MacDonald's career, though, and especially later in the McGee series, the triumph of legal justice is uncertain, and sometimes doomed. The 1968 McGee novel *Pale Gray for Guilt* is a particularly good example of this. Travis runs into an old football friend, Tush Bannon, whose business has been squeezed at a minimum by local construction and pollution from a nearby factory. Bannon later learns and reveals to McGee that a local real estate figure, Preston LaFrance, is behind the legal attempts to kill off his business to obtain Bannon's land for Gary Santo, a large developer. This legal squeezing first ends in a foreclosure threat and then culminates in Bannon's murder, staged as a suicide. To help Bannon's widow, McGee plans financial revenge on all of the land developers, and in the course of his machinations, he also discovers that the full extent of corruption extends, as usual, to the police department. McGee executes the financial revenge for Bannon and his widow, and the disgraced cop responsible for Bannon's death is killed in a struggle with McGee after fleeing authorities. But any victories in this novel (like several others in the series) are relatively minor compared with the personal losses of McGee's friends. While the real estate man is ruined financially, it's clear that the developer was only mildly frustrated by his setback. He will continue to prey on people like the Bannons, legally squeezing them of their land and livelihood in the name of land development. Thus only the replaceable cogs in the wheel of progress—Bannon, LaFrance, Hazzard—have been removed, development will continue, and McGee can only slow down and mitigate the plight of those closest to him.

The plot points themselves tend simply to uncover the deep-seated business and political corruption more than the ecological havoc wrecked by it, which is evaluated and analyzed with respect to the southern natural environment in McGee's thoughts through MacDonald's first-person narration. For instance, in *Bright Orange for the Shroud* (1965), a legal swindle, with extralegal physical coercion, extorts hundreds of thousands from an old acquaintance of McGee's on the promise of profiting from a land investment syndicate, quite similar to the driving criminal scheme in *A Tan and Sandy Silence*. When the con's target, Arthur Wilkinson, comes to McGee for help, he traces the violent, "extralegal" member of the con artists to a small Florida town, upon which McGee contemplates:

> Marco Village saddened me. The bulldozers and draglines had gotten to it since my last visit. The ratty picturesque old dock was gone, as was the ancient general store and a lot of old weatherbeaten two-story houses which had looked as though they had been moved down from Indiana farmland. They had endured a half century of hurricanes, but little marks on a developer's plat had erased them so completely there was not even a trace of the old foundations. (*Bright Orange* 60)

This aside is related to the plot only insofar as Marco's devastation from development reflects the kind of investment Arthur had tried to participate in. This is just any town in Florida. In *The Girl in the Plain Brown Wrapper* (1968), a controlling, sadistic businessman, Tom Pike, leads an intricate land-investment syndicate in the small Florida town of Fort Courtney, driven by the blackmail control he obtains through a corrupt special investigator with the sheriff's department. The syndicate Pike runs is tellingly called Development Unlimited and is described in vague terms throughout the novel, with one common motif: building and land. As ne'er-do-well attorney Rick Holton observes, Pike has a "land lease in one syndicate, construction loans and building leases in another," and his schemes are summed up thusly: "He's got bankers tied into the deals, savings and loan, contractors, accountants, realtors. Hell, if he ever screwed up, the whole city would come tumbling down" (*Girl* 202). And in *The Dreadful Lemon Sky*, a corrupt attorney and local political actor, Fred Van Horn, heads a drug-smuggling operation in Florida, funneling marijuana from the Caribbean, Mexico, and South America.[2] To describe the town at the center of much of the action, McGee casually glances at it, but he already knows it by heart:

> It was easy to see the shape and history of Bayside, Florida. There had been a little town on the bay shore, a few hundred people, a sleepy downtown with live oaks and Spanish moss. Then International Amalgamated Development had moved in, bought a couple of thousand acres, and put in shopping centers, town houses, condominiums, and rental apartments, just south of town. Next had arrived Consolidated Construction Enterprises and done the same thing north of town. Smaller operators had done the same thing on a smaller scale west of town. When downtown decayed, the town fathers widened the streets and cut down the shade trees in an attempt to look just like a shopping center. It didn't work. It never does. This was instant Florida, tacky and stifling and full of ugly and spurious energies. They had every chain's food-service outfit known to man, interspersed with used-car lots and furniture stores. (49)

Again, the development of the town is only incidental to the plot insofar as this is the playground of people like Van Horn, who will be state senators "up there [in Tallahassee] riding point on what they want around here. Deepwater port for the phosphate down in the south country. Refinery. And all the goodies that go along with it that only a few fellows get a piece of" (199).

Given this unrelenting collusion between business and government, patterns of anarchist motifs are unmistakable in MacDonald's fiction and in the McGee series especially. MacDonald's characterization of McGee's Florida focuses on how flawed individuals are faring in the grand procession into the Anthropocene: how they are ground up and how they are trying to resist, but also how in seeking to escape the anthropocentric mechanisms of progress some try to dominate them instead. Throughout, McGee's interior monologues scrutinize the individuals he encounters, especially in terms of their overall relation to each other, their society, and their natural environment. Even more so than MacDonald's plots, McGee's interior monologues reveal the full extent of the philosophical anarchism that undergirds MacDonald's work, and they align that social perspective with a stance toward humanity's unceasing ecological devastation that exposes a calamitous, transhistorical ecological anarchy.

Anarchism is a controversial and contested term, of course, and it has been defined several ways since its conscious development in the nineteenth century. As used in this article, anarchist terms reflect the thinking of both Paul Goodman and Robert Paul Wolff. Goodman eloquently defines the practice of anarchism as "the extension of spheres of free action until they make up most of social life" (34), but Wolff gets to the heart of the matter with regard to political reality when he argues that "anarchism is the only political doctrine consistent with the virtue of autonomy" (18). Indeed, Wolff continues, "only one form of political community . . . offers any hope of resolving the conflict between authority and autonomy, and that is democracy," because humans "cannot be free so long as they are subject to the will of others" (18). However, as Herbert Read notes, "a people cannot be continuously assembled to govern itself; it must delegate authority as a mere matter of convenience, and once you have delegated authority, you no longer have democracy" (18). But "if autonomy and authority are genuinely incompatible," Wolff finally reasons that

> only two courses are open to us. Either we must embrace philosophical anarchism and treat *all* governments as nonlegitimate bodies whose commands must be judged and evaluated in each instance before they are obeyed; or else, we must give up as quixotic the pursuit of autonomy in the political realm and submit ourselves (by an implicit promise) to whatever form of government appears most just and beneficent at the moment. (71)

This is apparently McGee's conclusion as well: he evaluates his relationship to legal structures situationally and holds himself to a rigid moral standard and others to a looser ethical one, preferring to live according to individually established contracts and locally established social norms.

Other scholars have also noted the threads of individuality and rebellion in MacDonald's writing that anarchism signals. Moore points out that although MacDonald does not frequently characterize very specific dominating groups, he does indicate repeatedly that "the individual's dilemma in American culture is how to achieve personal freedom amid multiple social and economic influences without clear standards" (115). In his essay criticizing McGee's rebellious attitude—the only piece I can find that does so in an extended way—Mark Leier argues from a Marxist perspective that although McGee "rages against the false god progress . . . [in protests that are] always passionate, often eloquent, always contrasting the good and the human against the impersonal, the plastic, the monolithic" (91), he nevertheless is no "critic of the system, only its effects . . . has no sympathy for victims of the system . . . [and] is unable to conceive of any alternative to the status quo" (92). Leier's essay is quite excellent, though I do not come to his same conclusions, and it deserves a longer and more cogently argued rejoinder than I can provide in this space. In essence, Leier's Marxist critique finally claims that McGee's rebellious stance is a lower-middle-class illusion that insidiously replicates the capitalist culture. Leier suggests that McGee is largely an image of allowed, contained protest in a capitalist system, that his politics "support the very system and its evils that he hates. . . . [And because he] mystifies cause and effect, because he refuses to think systematically, because he offers no way out . . . [he] fulfills the task of mythology and props up the existing order" (100).

Leier's frustration arises out of McGee's apparent inability to see how the effects of capitalism that he detests stem irrevocably from its causes, and further from his refusal to provide a resistance and replacement program to capitalist America. However, I am not convinced that McGee does not understand that the progress he decries "is created and defined by humans with political and economic power who operate in accordance with the rules of the system" (92), as Leier argues. Nor do I think McGee "blames the victims" of capitalism instead of those responsible just because he tends to rail against practically everyone for complicitly participating in the society as they do (92). In fact, nearly everyone in the state *has* been complicit in the disastrous ecological transformation that inversely transformed the economy. But the unceasing corruption in MacDonald's fiction challenges Leier's contention that "McGee is unable to move beyond a criticism of individuals to a criticism of society" (95). It would be more fitting for Leier to accuse McGee of blaming everyone—which is not untrue and not unwarranted. Finally, McGee's refusal to provide an organized resistance and programmatic future is a hallmark of his fatalistic, philosophical anarchist tendencies.

Leier rightly points out that McGee tends to harshly criticize people in the abstract, but to substitute those moments of rhetorical excess in place of the genuine sympathy, empathy, and generosity McGee actually shows for wounded and disenfranchised individuals throughout the series is misleading. He thrives on helping others "buck the power structure" since "this is a complex culture, dear. The more intricate our society gets, the more semi-legal ways to steal" (*Deep Blue* 4). Throughout the series, McGee happens upon a number of lost souls (in Florida particularly) who comprise a strange mix of hedonists, sadists, loners, philosopher bums, artists, hobby enthusiasts, (religious) crackpots—in short, outsiders—who collide with one another. Not fully true of any other region in the United States, the state's natural beauty, temperate climate, abundant and untapped resources, and its undeveloped, frontier potential have made it a magnet for the marginal of the nation: those looking to escape the past; those looking for a new future; those looking to create new societies; those looking to escape society; those looking to relax and live in moral and ethical hedonism; and those who are "so caught up in the pursuit of self-gratification that they fail to establish any significant meaning in their lives" (Geherin 28). One of Mac-Donald's dominating motifs in all of his fiction is skewering particularly those who live in elitist ostentation and at the expense of the vulnerable. They are all spiritual descendants of the kind Derr recognizes as characteristic of Florida's postbellum occupation: "Even more so than during the war years, Florida collected an assortment of refugees" (304). While several were "the roughest lot [John Muir] had seen" in his travels, Derr also observes that many "craved nothing more than escape from foul winter weather or, more profoundly, from a ruined life" (304). McGee, himself trying to escape general society and live a life of ethical pleasure and leisure, spends his many adventures among all of these sorts of Floridians, often protecting one type from another.

SLAPSTICK ANIMALS IN A MAKE-BELIEVE GARDEN

In these waves of oddballs, McGee most frequently acts as a kind of errant knight-anthropologist, happening upon psychologically damaged people, analyzing them, and trying to help them out in the manner that best fits their peculiar social environment. MacDonald's later main characters tend to be naturally wild people (in "good" and "bad" ways) barely contained by the trappings of society and civilization, but often also quite adept at manipulating the inner logic of civilization to their benefit. This pattern is part of a broader theme in MacDonald's fiction that R. Gordon Kelly demonstrates in his excellent essay, "The Precarious

World of John D. MacDonald," namely that "a central element in MacDonald's fiction is a vivid sense of the precariousness and vulnerability underlying life in American society . . . [wherein] civilization is at best a fragile, isolated structure contrived in a universe of chance" (149, 156). Kelly argues that MacDonald suggests that "civilization tends to soften the very instincts which may be needed to defend it" (155), and he criticizes MacDonald for using what he sees as "certain tenets of late 19th century naturalism . . . which have generally been discarded by intellectuals in this century" (154). The "tenets" are found within his recurring characterization of most antagonists as "without conscience or even the possibility of conscience" (154). Moore similarly identifies this aspect of MacDonald's work, pointing out amoral characters who are described, quite simply, as naturally evil. The most memorable example of this kind of character is Max Cady from *The Executioners* (1957), memorably performed by Robert Mitchum and Robert De Niro in the *Cape Fear* film adaptations (1962, 1991). Both Moore and Kelly indicate that many of these characters have no apparent environmental causes at the root of their villainy. These characterizations, Kelly argues, are at odds with the more "highly regarded mystery writers . . . [like] Raymond Chandler or . . . Ross Macdonald . . . [who] accord much more readily with the environmentalism . . . at the heart of the liberal reform tradition that has dominated social thought in this century" (154).

That MacDonald is out of step with other mid-century mystery writers is certainly true, but he has not abandoned psychological environmentalism completely, nor is his approach inherently outdated or backward. First, as mentioned earlier, McGee takes a certain satisfaction in analyzing what social forces have conspired to warp and twist the outcasts he meets, using it as an opportunity to lift the veil on civilization to demonstrate its shaky hold on humanity, compared with the natural elements it must contend with: climate change, predatory behavior by humans who slyly use the system to steal and exploit in "semi-legal ways," out-and-out violence, disease, pollution, and more. Second, earlier in MacDonald's career, a greater number of the antagonists were carefully depicted as shaped by environmental factors. A memorable example is the fierce, fundamentalist Christian secretary (Angie Powell) in *The Drowner* (1963), whose deep repression of her own sexuality, at her mother's behest, has been sublimated to a murder spree through which she experiences sadistic sexual release. And yet Angie also points in the direction MacDonald took the bulk of his antagonists for the McGee series. While environmental forces certainly shaped Angie—her mother severely damaged her sense of sexuality through her punitive religious instruction—it is also clear that Angie has an overpowering, natural urge toward sadism and violence. Her obsession with sexual purity and Christianity are merely tools of civilization that she uses to try to legitimate her own natural urges. MacDonald is not suggesting that social factors have no role in personal development—he is suggesting that many natural urges cannot be forcefully removed by society, only masked by social propriety. McGee sees humanity as an animal in nature, naturally and anarchically evolving despite self-imposed social constraints. McGee has thus developed a deep distrust of large-scale human communities since they rely on fictions and ideology to bind them together, a unique quality in the animal kingdom, as Michael Tomasello argues in *A Natural History of Human Morality* and Yuval Noah Harari argues in *Sapiens*. And yet, as Harari observes, any "dramatic increase in the collective power and ostensible success of our species went hand in hand with much individual suffering" (97). Groups will first seek to maintain their own integrity, at the expense of any individual members, and that is something the shabby knight errant McGee simply cannot morally abide by.

But even beyond his distrust of groups, McGee's conception of humans as animals first and foremost has left the deepest impression on him, and arguably grounds his political, social, ethical, and moral compasses fundamentally. Read's defense of anarchism to Marxist critiques in fact comes from a similar conception. "Man is an animal," he states. "You cannot be dialectic in thought or anything else unless you posit a realm of essence over against the realm of matter" (151), which echoes McGee's own frequent admonitions against idealistic fanaticism of any sort. Read's conclusion regarding the difference between Marxism and anarchism responds succinctly to Leier's criticisms and expresses why McGee is better characterized as an anarchist than a failed Marxist: "Marxism is based on economics; anarchism on biology" (154).

McGee has no time for economics, for politics, for organized resistance. As much as he helps the various transients of Florida escape the crushing wheels of progress, his mind remains on the lasting effects of those wheels, regardless of his actions. While the plot points of the McGee series indicate in very precise terms *how* various businesses get away with thoughtlessly razing Florida's natural ecosystem to make way for more resorts and tourist support, McGee's interior monologues reveal the momentous impulses behind his self-exile. Herein, too, lies Florida's modern southern identity embodied: the state's natural beauty and wilderness attract people from all strata, for whom disastrous development makes way, and they split into those who continue the land's devolution and those left to bemoan it.

McGee's dark ruminations occur repeatedly, almost overwhelmingly. And it is not simply McGee fantasizing; it's his prediction. In *Bright Orange for the Shroud* (1965), McGee overhears a southern bigot complaining about "the decay of the nashal moral fiber, mob rule in the streets" (64), and he drifts off into his own thoughts, considering how people en masse are like grasshoppers that physically transform into locusts when they swarm: "Forty million more Americans than we had in 1950 . . . And density alone affects the frequency with which mobs form. . . . There is no decline in the moral fiber of the grasshopper. There is just a mass pressure canceling out all individual decisions" (64). Humans, on the whole, are locusts to McGee at this point, and on the whole not deserving of their natural home, which he does not expect they will keep for long. In an even deeper contemplation in *Bright Orange,* McGee considers the Everglades, "dark strange country, one of the few places left which man has not been able to mess up" (57), and in lyrically flowing language, considers the epoch of human activity there—from the Calusa Indians through European colonization and the Seminoles' time and the American Indian removal wars—detailing specifically how successive waves of humans have started to overwhelm their environment, coming to terms with it finally in his recognition of the awesome, lasting, anarchic power of the natural world that is beyond the control or final destruction by any outside force:

> Now, of course, having failed in every attempt to subdue the Glades by frontal attack, we are slowly killing it off by tapping the River of Grass. In the questionable name of progress, the state in its vast wisdom lets every two-bit developer divert the flow into the draglined canals that give him 'waterfront' lots to sell. . . . As the Glades dry, the big fires come with increasing frequency. The ecology is changing with egret colonies dwindling, mullet getting scarce, mangrove dying of new diseases born of dryness.
>
> But it will take a long time to kill it. And years from now foolish men will still be able to kill themselves off within miles of help, hopelessly lost among islands which all look exactly alike. It is a black land, and like every wilderness in the world, it punishes quickly when a mistake is made, quickly and with a casual, savage indifference. (58)

Persistently, McGee ponders humanity in the course of its whole existence and likens humans to insect-like animals—in evolutionary equality with other bugs who may in fact evolve to a point of superiority—who have reached a new, calamitous evolutionary stage. They have overwhelmed Earth's resources to sustain them in their concentrations and have done so with stunning ignorance and rapidity. Additionally, they have blinded themselves through their actions, making a grotesque carnival of their development and willfully walling themselves off from the ecological consequences of that development. But as McGee's reflections continually show, the natural world is relatively indifferent on geologic scales to humanity. It will survive; humankind may not.

Ultimately, MacDonald's work suggests that humankind and the natural world, while distinct systems, are still fundamentally integrated as part of the larger natural world in a matrix of capitalist encroachment and ecological resistance. Indeed, he identifies the rural south and Florida in particular as ground zero for this confrontation. McGee acknowledges the pattern repeatedly: humankind, crammed together, have polluted their food and home and neighbors in pursuit of a placating fantasy world that disguises the lasting effects of their carelessness. These patterns reveal how MacDonald's fiction depicts Florida as a bellwether of the coastal South, a paradise being paved and replaced with plastic, permanent tourist versions of it that will distract its residents until the paradise reclaims itself.

Ironically, MacDonald has concluded that capitalist industrialization of the New South is actually accelerating the visible *re*-integration of humanity and the natural world. Rather than separating us from it further, as has been traditionally accepted and feared, our destructive acts in the Anthropocene are prompting more intense responses from the natural environment, confirming how entrenched we have always been in it. Despite MacDonald's gloomy vision of humanity's future, McGee has embraced vitality in the present. In *Dress Her in Indigo* (1969), he complains of those who take life too seriously: "We are all comical, touching, slapstick animals, walking on our hind legs, trying to make it a noble journey from womb to tomb, and the people who can't see it all that way bore hell out of me." And for as little as he thinks of the human world, more often than not he prefers to leave those relative innocents he meets and helps in better shape (or at least not much worse off) than he finds them: "at least have the grace to try to put the make-believe garden back in order" (*Long Lavender* 102). MacDonald's McGee is a philosophical anarchist-absurdist hero. He dodges oppressive systems of authority, creating what existential happiness he can in the face of an indifferent natural world, one that humanity is carelessly spoiling to such a degree that nature's restorative forces are starting to displace humanity.

* * *

NOTES

1. Apparently republished from *The Sarasota Times* (Pete Schmidt, "When John D. Met the Movies and McGee," November 12, 1989) posted on Steve Scott's blog, *The Trap of Solid Gold*, though I have not been able to confirm its initial publication.

2. That corrupt lawyer dies in one of the most Floridian ways possible: fire ants.

PART III

DETECTING SOUTHERN COPS

SHERIFF ANDY TAYLOR & THE NON-PROCEDURAL IN MAYBERRY

THERESA STARKEY

O n October 3rd, 1960, *The Andy Griffith* show aired on CBS for the first time. Though named for its star, and by extension for the character he played, Sheriff Andy Taylor, the show's scope and ambition were communal, introducing American audiences to the fictional Mayberry, a town where even the businesses (like Weaver's Department Store, Floyd's Barbershop, Walker's Pharmacy, and Foley's Grocery) bore the names of friends and neighbors. The pace of the town was depicted as slow and easy. Men passed the time at the barbershop and talked about community affairs or their most recent catch at the lake, and local women in nice print dresses gossiped in front of Foley's or lunched together at the counter at Fred's, organizing church socials and dances.

Like its humorous characters, the show had its flaws. The lunch counter at Fred's remained untroubled, idyllic, and entirely white. Much has been written about how the series projected a South at odds with its own historical moment, averting the reality of racial tensions, discrimination, and segregation. What to make of this benign and smiling sheriff, whose image contrasted so starkly with that of Bull Connor and the other violent lawmen documented by journalists covering the civil rights movement during the show's eight-season run? Connor and Taylor shared the same TV screen but different realities.

However, for critic Matt Zoller Seitz and others, Mayberry "felt like a real place" (Sepinwall and Seitz 173). Seitz singles out *The Andy Griffith Show* for its writing ("believable, sometimes believably uneventful") and its filmmaking ("thoughtful and expressive, tracking the characters' movements through intricately detailed interiors, making time and space for quiet conversations and wordless moments of interaction"). Above all he praises "the show's aura of quiet dignity (173)," which keeps it popular and perpetually available. Although some choose to engage with only the surface details of the qualities described by Seitz, turning *The Andy Griffith Show* into a fetishistic totem to a Southern pastoral dream world that never existed, the actual content of the show is more complex and questioning, even within its whitewashed perimeters.

Andy's good-natured policing does not extend to everyone. The irredeemable Other, in the form of the hobo, is still kept outside the boundaries of Mayberry. The forest functioned as a repository for the nation's id, a place where racial, class, and gender issues intersected, and were projected onto the body of the vagabond.

The town and its periphery, and especially its people, all fell under the jurisdiction of Sheriff Taylor. Much of what he policed was the mundane, the personal, the embarrassing, and the screwball, handling each case with good humor and tact. Lawman, rube, domestic paragon, public servant, middle-class community member, both mother and father (as single parent to his child), guardian and delineator of civilization, flawed individual, hero, and friend, Sheriff Andy Taylor is endowed with a hybridity that sets him apart from others of his kind in the cultural imagination. His jurisdiction is the human heart, which he defines, patrols, and embodies for his community. His police procedures are informed not by the latest forensic science or profiling techniques, but rather by a humanistic and empathic approach to policing. A typical show in the "police procedural" genre focuses on

> how the police and the courts apply their problem-solving skills and technical routines to the case at hand. But police routines, like the routines of the everyday person, are not static, fixed, and unmoving. Times change and with changing times come the development of new procedures as old ones are allowed to fade away into obsolescence. (Ruble 15)

Andy Taylor's manhood and unconventional police techniques can be viewed through the lens of "hard-boiled sentimentality," a concept coined by Leonard Cassuto, who argues that

> hard-boiled fiction and sentimentalism require both domestic ideology to draw on, and a market-based public world to explore and criticize. Both position the home as a center of value against the public market economy, and at the same time acknowledge that the two realms aren't really separate—thus making an unarticulated contradiction of the pervasive public ideology of separate male and female spheres. (11)

Taylor's positionality is informed by the entwining of these two forms, and is visible in aspects of his personal code and behavior. In more than just his interactions with his son Opie, the sheriff displays both maternal and paternal qualities. This blurring produces a hybrid performativity, as when he tells the "town drunk" Otis bedtime stories in his cell or comforts him during a rainstorm, or constantly reassures Aunt Bee that she is appreciated (a plot trotted out more than once), or tries to teach manners to uncivilized mountain men like Darling Briscoe and Ernest T. Bass, or has to reset the town's moral compass after one of its many close calls with a fall from grace at the hands of a honey-tongued outsider.

One of the most pivotal and acclaimed episodes in the series is entirely domestic in nature and involves the crime of murder. The offense takes place in Sheriff Taylor's home with Opie as the perpetrator. In "Opie the Birdman," the sheriff's son takes the life of a mother bird with his slingshot, after repeated warnings from his father to be careful with it. With his carelessness, Opie has destroyed a family. From his bedroom window Opie hears the baby birds cry. His father tells him that the birds cry for their mother, but they don't know she is not coming back. In Seitz's view, this is the moment when "the episode literally darkens. The father seems to loom over the son like a specter whose outrage is held in check by grief" (Sepinwall 175).

The sheriff tells his son that he must raise the birds—in short, be a mother to them. The act provides Opie with the opportunity to reform himself, as it merges his own boyhood identity with a strain of maternalism not unlike his father's. On a deeper level, it resonates with the absence of Opie's own mother. As Seitz puts it, "Opie's killing of the bird has awakened the trauma of a primal loss" (175). In the end, Opie learns he must eventually surrender the birds and let them literally leave the nest. Like his father, he perpetuates the natural order of a community. Outsiders are often more problematic as they arrive bringing prejudgment and condescension, a trope established as far back as the pilot, which aired as an episode of *The Danny Thomas Show* and introduced the character of Andy Taylor to the public. Numerous examples would follow. A rich kid, spoiled by his absentee father, gets arrested for causing a wreck and tries to buy his way out of the situation. A big city publisher fails to pay a citation and thinks he can grease the sheriff's palm. Virtually no one passing through views the small-town sheriff as an equal, and all underestimate his intelligence and his clear sense of justice. This extends even to outsiders who share his profession.

The narrative arc about the judgmental lawman come to town—revisited again and again throughout the course of the show—was established early, in the second episode of the series. Captain Barker from the state police ignores the sheriff's advice on how to conduct an efficient manhunt in the area, which he knows so well. Instead of listening to the sheriff, Barker suggests that he and his deputy busy themselves with local affairs: "chicken thieves and such" ("The Manhunt"). Of course, it is just such homespun knowledge that allows Andy to think critically about what the escapee might do, were he to cut through the woods toward the lake and pass by the home of Emma, the sweet old lady with the habit of putting fresh pies out on her windowsill to cool. With the help of Deputy Barney Fife, the sheriff sets a trap and leaves his old leaky fishing boat unattended as bait. The ploy works, but not before the state police arrive and look on in dismay as the convict feverishly paddles away from the dock.

Barker calls Andy a "fool" for letting the man get the boat, shaming him in front of fellow law enforcement officials and, ungallantly, the sheriff's own son: "I don't know how you got to be a sheriff in this state, but when this is over I am going to see that you are thrown out. There is no place for such incompetence in a peace officer." But Opie shares in his father's folk wisdom, excitedly exclaiming, "That's our boat ain't it, paw? You let him take it on purpose didn't you?" The big-city captain gets bested by the sheriff with the thick southern accent and aw-shucks demeanor, the classic figure of the wily rube. In the final scene, Barker tells the sheriff that he intends to see that a citation gets sent to him for a job well done. The sheriff good naturedly shrugs off the honor and instead asks that "one of them [state] maps with the sticky buttons" instead. His reluctance to receive accolades, to showboat, or to lose his cool reflect his natural modesty and his values as a lawman.

In "The Cow Thief," the local mayor thinks he will serve (and impress) his constituents best by bringing in a special investigator from Raleigh to solve a string of local cattle rustlings. In the opening scene the mayor tells a disgruntled farmer that he will call "the capitol and have them send down a real professional. . . . I am going to see to it personally that you get results. . . . I will have a man here . . . who really knows something about solving crimes." The scene establishes the hierarchical political/power structure of the town and also emphasizes the rift that exists between the municipality of Mayberry and the surrounding rural area.

The mayor who believes that his sheriff cannot handle the situation, combined with the farmer suspicious of townsfolk and elected officials, present the sheriff with a twofold problem: to demonstrate public trust through action both "upwards" (for the mayor) and "downwards" (toward the rural farmer), not through argument over methods, either with the mayor, the farmer, or the special investigator from the outside.

Parolee Luke Jensen, or "the bad penny," as Deputy Barney Fife calls him, appears in the second scene. Jensen's arrival in Mayberry provides the sheriff with an explanation for the thefts. Jensen's questionable or dirty nature is emphasized by his rooting through a trashcan alongside his dog as Barney and Andy watch through cracked office blinds. From the sheriff's vantage point the dog and parolee are interchangeable. Both present the image of the scavenger and neither understands the boundaries of the of law. The two represent something to be watched and disciplined, which the sheriff makes clear when he tells Barney that "with a fella like Luke it's a good thing to let him rest his eyes on a sheriff's badge now and then." The sheriff lets Luke know he's being watched when he warns the man that there is "no harm in looking" at the bin of goods he has been rummaging through, but that he better not "take that 'Serve Yourself' sign too seriously."

Luke Jensen isn't the only character depicted as shiftless and untrustworthy. The figure also surfaces in episodes such as "Opie's Hobo Friend" and "Opie and His Merry Men." As can be surmised from the titles, the shadowy drifter is seen as a potential corrupter of children, and thus a disruptive influence on the root of society. The latter episode presents as a domestic mystery for Andy to solve when pies, poultry, and pantry items go missing from people's homes. It turns out that Opie and his friends took them, not a fox come down from the hills. The goodhearted Mayberry boys believe they are taking from the rich to give to the poor, represented by a homeless man camped out in the forest. The sheriff demonstrates to his son that the man in the woods is unworthy of the children's charity. He is exposed as a low individual who lacks self-reliance and a good work ethic. Here is the harsher face of Andy's embodiment of the stable community.

The repeated story line reinforces a conservative ideology, implying that if individuals fail in life that it is due to a lack of virtue, not structural forces inherent in the larger society. An antecedent can be found in the Ragged Dick tales of Horatio Alger Jr. As Heather Tapley observes in her study of late nineteenth-century representations, the hobo was presented as either a "parasite, certain to deprive the United States of the fruits of its productive, profitable endeavors, [or an] embodiment of anti-capitalism, an antithetical and highly romantic stereotype. Regardless of this range of representations, however, the American hobo was always cast as a form of masculinity" (26). Whatever the form, the incarnation signified "a failed version of working-class and bourgeois masculinities" that Andy Taylor exemplified (Tapley 27).

Sheriff Taylor doesn't send men like the hobo to jail or make them serve "thirty days" or go through the grinding "machine of Justice" like the vagabond men found in Jack London's nonfiction piece "Pinched" (32). He just makes sure they leave town and that a lesson has been learned.

Patrolling the boundaries of the county and its forests protected the community and its impressionable youth against such figures, who were viewed as idle, lazy, immoral, and beyond the civilizing effects of community, law, or the family unit. As the sheriff tells his son "an able-bodied man," if he's down on his luck or confronted with hard times and is above all honest, "don't want charity," but instead "wants a chance to work, make a living" ("Opie and His Merry Men"). His statement reinforces hegemonic notions of a perceived white middle-class manhood, where performativity, labor, and productivity are directly linked to the prosperity of the nation-state.

If the hobo functioned as representation of failed masculinity and as a suspect body in need of surveillance and social control, so did the black male body in the cultural imagination. The free and enfranchised African American man was often depicted as a threat and, like the hobo, pathologized through a medical discourse which depicted him as sexually aggressive and in "a state of arrested development" (Tapley 33). Each contrived articulation of flawed masculinity privileges white bourgeois manhood against an oppositional "other." *The Andy Griffith Show* episodes that centered on hoboes, and to a lesser extent the ones about hill people and farmers, may be seen as a sublimated exploration of the racial issues that producers refused to deal with directly. As Tapley observes:

> Medical discourse produced the (white) hobo/tramp as lazy (labour) and, therefore, licentious (sexuality). Unemployment functions, here, as the root cause of the tramp's inability to restrain his reason and, by extension, his sexual conduct. Inherent in this construction of masculinity—will, reason, and the pursuit of profit—was the production of its opposite, the feminine. Like women, the African-American male and the tramp were produced as lacking reason and, therefore, in need of control. (35)

One has only to look at D. W. Griffith's *Birth of a Nation* to see this stereotype unleashed on the cultural imagination in the famous and infamous scene in which Lillian Gish, as the frightened southern belle, has her virtue threatened by an unruly black militia man (played by a white actor in blackface). The problematic scene unfolds in the forest, which is literally the southern pastoral penetrated by a dark force. Southern vigilantism is presented as swift justice and a solution to the danger as the Ku Klux Klan arrives on horseback.

The outskirts of Mayberry were flanked by an agrarian community that consisted of local farmers, thick forests, and the North Carolina mountains, where giddy, rock-throwing Ernest T. Bass roamed, an anarchic threat to small-town civilization whenever he ventured into Mayberry. Bass's fellow hill people, the unruly Darling family, were only slightly less dangerous to the status quo, rejecting traditional law and order in favor of their own mountain code. The idea of an isolated backwoods people who make their own justice has persisted, featured prominently, for example, in the film *Winter's Bone* (2010) and TV shows like *Justified*, which debuted the same year.

In a similar fashion to the unpredictable rover, "hillbillies" like the Darling family and Ernest T. Bass required surveillance and supervision. Yet unlike the hobo, who was regarded as beyond the reach of community, the hillbilly was depicted as relatable, if immune to assimilation, a piquant reminder of the chaos that lay on the outward fringes of a community bound by law. Perhaps they were a reminder, almost nostalgic in nature, of the darkness from which that community emerged.

Well before he became Sheriff Taylor, Andy Griffith made a name for himself by playing bumpkins not far removed from the hill dwellers of *The Andy Griffith Show*. He gained recognition in 1953 for comedic monologues such as "What It Was, Was Football," in which he took on the persona of a backwoods country preacher come to town, swept up in a crowd making its way towards a college football game. The sheltered preacher has never heard of the sport and for the first time sees:

> . . . this whole raft a people a-settin' on these two banks and a-lookin' at one another acrost this purty little green cow pasture! Well, they was! And somebody had took and drawed white lines all over it and drove posts in it and I don't know what all! And I looked down there and I seen five or six convicts a-runnin' up and down and a-blowin'whistles! (Griffith)

From there Griffith made his way to Broadway where he played the near saintly yokel Will Stockdale in the hit *No Time for Sergeants*. His star continued to rise and he appeared in well-received movies like *A Face in the Crowd* (1957), directed by Elia Kazan. Griffith's character, Lonesome Rhodes, is a sinister subversion of the naive, good-humored Stockdale. Rhodes is a drifter who plays guitar, tells stories, and sings his way into the heart of American audiences.

Not realizing that the microphones are still on, he reveals his true nature to TV viewers at the end of his variety show when he mockingly says "those morons out there . . . I can make them eat dog food and they'll think it is steak . . . You know what the public's like? A cage full of guinea pigs . . . Good night, you stupid idiots, good night, you miserable slobs. They're a lot of trained seals. I toss them a dead fish and they'll flap their flippers" (*A Face in the Crowd*).

Sixty years later Kazan's film seems like a prophetic omen. He presents audiences with a symbol of the ultimate TV reality star and huckster, always ready to play upon the sentimentalities of an eager public yearning for proof that America's populist spirit lives on in good country folk.

The Darlings and Ernest T. Bass are sources of comedic dysfunction whenever they appear. Unlike the rootless hobo, the hillbilly was shown as belonging to a mountain community and as someone with family ties, a connection to the land and to the region. Briscoe Darling, for example, shared a bond with the sheriff: a love for music. Their spontaneous hootenannies worked to temporarily destabilize class and cultural tensions. These musical moments functioned as temporal interruptions that blurred the boundaries between mountain and town, high culture and low. In Anthony Harkins's view, the popular Ernest T. Bass and Darling episodes:

> . . . were not randomly selected storylines, but were shaped by and reflected their historical context. The Darlings and Ernest T. Bass appeared in eight episodes between March 1963 and December 1964, but only in one additional show thereafter, and no mountaineer characters appeared on the show after October 1966. (184)

Harkins links these appearances to the incredible popularity of *The Beverly Hillbillies*, which first aired on TV in September of 1962, as "part of the explanation for [the] brief surge in mountaineer portrayals" on *The Andy Griffith Show* (184).

He also sees the "mountaineer" representations as "a response to the sudden reemergence of the southern mountain region and people in the national consciousness and the conception of Appalachia as a distinct 'problem region'" (184). According to Harkins, the problem of deep poverty in the region proved troubling to middle-class sensibilities and a nation that perceived itself as a "classless society" with "an ever-improving quality of life" available to all (184). But it is important to emphasize that *The Beverly Hillbillies* provided audiences with a very different image of the hillbilly, one that was more satirical and grotesque, linking the traditional figures to new money for laughs and turning a mansion into a carnivalesque funhouse space in which poor hill people ran amuck. This image contrasts with the way mountain people were portrayed in *The Andy Griffith Show*. Singing folk songs with the sheriff reinforced the value of a cultural, musical tradition. Performance was presented as a joyous and revered act, a sentiment reinforced by ethnomusicologist Alan Lomax, who worked to record and collect this important part of America's musical legacy. The American folk music revival hit its peak during the run of *The Andy Griffith Show*.

If music humanized him for Andy Taylor and Mayberry, it was unchecked sexual desire and deviant impulses that destabilized the hillbilly's ability to maintain moral or legal control: another threat to Taylor's quiet, civilizing influence. Fears of a perceived hillbilly hoard appeared in the 1958 *Harper's* article, "The Hillbillies Invade Chicago," by Albert N. Votaw. Harkins uses Votaw's piece to highlight how writers of his ilk perpetrated "fear mongering" against poor white southern migrants and how racial stereotypes like poor, white, and black were interchangeable when it came to constructing an "other" based on class/regional/gender differences. Votaw described the rural newcomers as:

> ". . . clannish, proud, disorderly, [and] untamed to urban ways." They have "fecund wives and numerous children," their "housekeeping is easy to the point of disorder, . . . their habits—with respect to such matters as incest and statutory rape—are clearly at variance with urban legal requirements." (qtd. in Harkins 176–177)

Libido caused both Ernest T. Bass and Briscoe Darling to cross paths with the sheriff on more than one occasion. Part of his role was to police their behavior, especially when it came to encounters with the opposite sex. Offenders crossed gender boundaries: Briscoe's daughter was as forward as his sons were tight-lipped. (From the big city, that other pole of excess, came the recurring characters "The Fun Girls," a pair of blond barflies—one with an exceptionally deep and raspy voice, almost masculine—whose sexual openness and aggression visibly discomfited both Andy and Barney and threatened their sedate domesticity.) Farmers, while physically and economically closer to the heart of Mayberry, remained on the periphery, and weren't exempt from this type of surveillance—more than necessary in the case of Big Jeff Pruitt, who enjoyed picking up women like rag dolls and squeezing them as a sign of affection, a less lethal version of Lenny in *Of Mice and Men*.

The search for a woman often took Briscoe, Bass, and Big Jeff Pruitt into Mayberry, and more specifically into the middle-class home where their manhood and manners stood in stark contrast to the sheriff's notions of middle-class virtue. In "Briscoe Declares for Aunt Bee," Darling's attempts to romance Aunt Bee fail. Disgruntled with his role as suitor, Briscoe opts to kidnap her and whisks her away to his mountain cabin. There he imagines that she will be not only his wife, but mother to his grown children, too.

Ernest T. Bass is notorious for destroying property. He throws rocks through windows in a sublimated attempt to pitch woo. It is also his way of acting out when he feels slighted by someone, such as in the episode "My Fair Ernest T. Bass," when the spry trickster comes down from the mountains in search of love and crashes a high society social hosted by Mrs. Wiley. He is run off and reported to the sheriff.

Displaying more empathy than he has with various hoboes, and working outside of his narrowly established role, the sheriff takes on Ernest T. Bass as a social reform project and becomes his etiquette teacher, advising him on what to wear, how to make polite conversation, eat, and behave as a respectable member of the community. The etiquette lessons take place in the sheriff's home, blurring the boundaries between masculinity and the "feminine" domain of domesticity.

While Andy Taylor, over the course of the series, does actively investigate cases of disturbing the peace, loitering, domestic violence, theft, and other acts punishable under law, this definition of crime proves to be too narrow. As we have seen, Sheriff Taylor's bailiwick is both larger and more intimate. His role is to enforce not only the law, but the golden rule, too, as he patrols and defines the boundaries of his community and home.

In the episode "The Clubmen," for example, the sheriff turns down an invitation to join the prestigious Esquire Club because its members snub his friend, coworker (and, as revealed in early episodes, cousin) Barney Fife. Unlike his superior, the junior lawman longs for inclusion. But at the invitation-only dinner for potential new members, he tries too hard to gain acceptance and respect. His social awkwardness reveals his naiveté. Barney is incapable of successfully navigating the boundaries between rural and urban, working-class and elite. Significantly, Andy Taylor is a force for cohesion and homogeneity because he moves freely between categories, seemingly comfortable in his own skin. He keeps his town together the way he keeps himself together, while Barney Fife is all fragments, a barely contained bundle of neuroses, a counterpoint and even threat to the cool, composed sense of societal order represented by Andy Taylor.

It is no narrative accident that the club is located in the neighboring big city of Raleigh. The show makes clear that Barney Fife's admiration for the cultural and political importance of the state capitol is misplaced. As its representatives from the Esquire Club demonstrate, Raleigh lacks substance and a moral center, the very qualities that make Mayberry (and Andy) seem whole. The Esquire men commit a transgression against Barney with their snobbery. At the episode's conclusion the deputy mistakenly believes that Andy is the one who was not accepted. The sheriff never reveals the true facts. His easygoing indifference to the mechanizations of social climbing is depicted as noble. Like his antecedents—the sheriff from Western dime novels or the detective found in hard-boiled fiction—Sheriff Taylor abides by a personal code of conduct.

The belief in cultural and moral difference between urban and rural regions has a long history in American mythmaking, centered around the figure of the "rube." Harkins traces the national incarnation of this "nearly universal cultural character . . . to the earliest years of New England colonization." He often outsmarts his supposed betters. Harkins notes the "deliberate ambiguity of these characters," who are "simultaneously objects of ridicule . . . and deriders of the pretensions and values of their social superiors" (Harkins 14). Andy and Barney, A and B, represent a splitting of the icon into its yin and yang, its sage and ridiculous components.

One has only to follow current events to glean how this figure and its accompanying narrative resonate in our nation's political discourse and continue to provide journalists and academics alike with ample fodder for analysis and debate. The briefest search of recent headlines calls up (to cite just a few): "The power of groupthink: Taking out the white trash: America's urban-rural divides" (*The Economist*, 1 July 2017); "The great American fallout: how small towns came to resent cities" (*The Guardian*, 19 June 2017); "Rural divide" (*The Washington Post*, 17 June 2017); "Cities vs. Trump: Red state, blue state? The urban-rural divide is more significant" (*New York Magazine*, 18 April 2017); "The Rural-Urban Divide in America" (*The New York Times*, 16 January 2017); and "'Duck Dynasty' vs. 'Modern Family': 50 Maps of the U.S. Cultural Divide" (*The New York Times*, 27 December 2016).

In fact, Andy Griffith's hometown of Mount Airy, North Carolina, turned up as a "Social Issues" feature in *The Washington Post* on January 5, 2017. In an article entitled "How nostalgia for white Christian America drove so many Americans to vote for Trump," writer Sarah Pulliam Bailey explores why members of the small mountain community pulled the lever for Trump. The town's economic past is mapped out as she chronicles the decline of the textile factories, as well as the furniture-making and tobacco industries that once put people to work. She observes that the large granite quarry is all that remains active from the town's past economic zenith. Interviews with the mayor reveal how he and his chamber of commerce continually try to think of innovative ways to draw businesses to their region, often resorting to tourist attractions (foreshadowed by episodes like "Crime-Free Mayberry") playing up Mount Airy's de facto celebrity status as the supposed inspiration for *The Andy Griffith Show.*

The Mount Airy depicted in the *Post* is caught in a twilight moment where some residents still "try to live the good old days" and "yet even as this city of about 10,000 nestled in the Blue Ridge Mountains fills its coffers by selling nostalgia, many of its residents would agree with the now-popular saying [in the community] 'We're not in Mayberry anymore'" (Bailey). Bailey illuminates that slippage between fantasy and truth when she highlights how:

> In a 1998 television interview, Griffith said the idea of Mayberry came from the producers. "I've argued about this too long. I don't care," he said of people in Mount Airy. "Let them think what they want to think." Andy Griffith never returned to live in his home town either, dying in 2012 at his coastal home in Dare County. (Bailey)

As previously noted, the series itself addressed such fantasies and their impact on the community in "Crime-Free Mayberry" and "Mayberry Goes Hollywood." In the episode "Crime-Free Mayberry," the townspeople get suckered by two con men. The men seem genuinely interested in the community because of its reputation for having the lowest crime rate in the state. One of the men poses as a reporter and tells folks that he's writing a feature, while the other passes himself off as an FBI agent. People in the community get carried away by their attention and by the thought that Mayberry will become a tourist destination.

Floyd the barber, for example, moonlights as a tour guide and charges people two bits apiece to see the Mayberry jail with its two cells. He locates marks for his tour at the local bus station. Barney writes a folk ballad to glorify himself and Andy. The town establishes the Greater Mayberry Historical Society and Tourist Bureau to be headed by Taylor's own Aunt Bee. The mayor envisions large sums of revenue. It turns out the real goal of the two men is to case the town and rob the local bank.

The con creates disorder in the heart of the community. Are the residents behaving like something other than their true selves, or are they revealing their secret worst nature at the first available opportunity? With each revelation, the sheriff faces member after member of his community with a sense of disbelief, much like Hawthorne's poor Young Goodman Brown. Can it really be so easy for the charmingly befuddled Floyd to lose his way as a virtuous, harmless businessman and make a deal with the devil?

In "Mayberry Goes Hollywood," a location scout comes to town and is charmed by the people he meets. He admires the attractive storefronts and main street, and is taken in by the majesty of the oldest oak tree in town, shown off to him by the sheriff. The tree is a cherished landmark, one that Andy has loved since boyhood. Once more the town loses its sense of self with the thought of receiving such prestige and attention.

In anticipation of the film crew's arrival, Mayberrians shed what they see as their parochial appearance. Local businesses transform their storefront windows, men and women change their style of dress, and civic leaders organize a welcoming committee, with pageantry including a performance by the local band, a song sung by the mayor's daughter, and a group of women at attention, ready to present their homemade pies.

The ultimate gesture of celebration and gratitude is their ironic willingness to cut down the town's oldest tree, which they suddenly view as an eyesore and impediment to filming. Sheriff Taylor watches his community but refuses to take part, or to change, on the mayor's orders, into a regal uniform which looks like something pulled from a theatrical wardrobe trunk. Andy's disobedience is preservative rather than destructive. He practices both inner and outer discipline, but no one listens as he cautions against excess.

It is easy to read the episode as a comical reflection of how the naive small town reveals its self-conscious identity to the outside world, especially when the Hollywood scout returns and is shocked to find the place and the people so transformed. Surprisingly, it is he, not Andy, who prevents the populace from cutting down the old tree. He shames them by telling them that what won him over was their unspoiled honesty and naturalness. It is supposed to be a note of restoration, but haven't the townspeople revealed that the small-town ideal is pure wish fulfillment, a figment of Hollywood's imagination, not unlike *The Andy Griffith Show*? Mayberry is vain and dishonest, not naive, in its attempt to present a facade to the outside world.

Fingerprint powder, plaster casts, and the latest criminal profile technique help law enforcement agencies like the state police solve crimes and maintain order, but their procedurals are flawed, because they are informed by an act of disavowal. *Feeling* is framed as unprofessional and unscientific; disconnected authority figures advocate for a specialized knowledge unrelated to the maternal and the domestic, favoring a cold process deserving of the workmanlike name "procedural." His embrace of warm, empathetic, and humanistic procedures allows Andy to exercise a more compassionate control over his jurisdiction. Stripping away superficial readings of *The Andy Griffith Show* reveals a sheriff unafraid of exposing the flawed side of his community, and perhaps even his country, which, like the psyche of its rawer avatar Barney Fife, is in danger of fracturing and splintering without Andy's guidance and seemingly innate sense of order.

ARRESTING VISIONS

Film Noir, Visual Detection, and the Invisible Corpse in Ron Rash's
One Foot in Eden

RANDALL WILHELM

The dead don't hear and they don't speak. What do they do, Sheriff?
They just disappear.
—Ron Rash, *One Foot in Eden*, 6

Far from the mean streets of urban noir, a farmhouse stands alone in an isolated valley, silhouetted against looming mountains, a small patch of drought-ridden crops burning in the summer sun. Blackened tops of tobacco plants sag in a puzzled maze punctured only by a thin ribbon of water curling in the near distance. Like the classic film noir starring Humphrey Bogart and Gloria Grahame, we are "in a lonely place." Homestead of newlyweds Billy and Amy Holcombe, the first-generation landowners in Jocassee Valley in the South Carolina mountains struggle to keep their crops and marriage alive in an area known as "The Dark Corner," a moniker earned through the region's history of violence, lawlessness, poverty, and isolation from the rest of the state. The Holcombe farm is also the site of a murder and cover-up that renders the crime effectively invisible from the eyes of law enforcement. A crime and investigation told through five first-person narrative sections. Rash holds the gap-ridden narrative together through a skillful deployment of vision and visual tropes inherent to the detective, film noir, and metaphysical thriller genres. As David Lehman and others have pointed out, the detective genre often relies on the primacy of vision to see beyond surfaces to find the "smoking gun," the elusive "eye" in eyewitness, or the overlooked clue as a key to solving the "perfect murder." But as Rash's Sheriff Will Alexander tells the soon-to-be murder victim Holland Winchester in an opening scene, visual detection struggles to solve crimes where the dead "just disappear" (6).

But despite the absence of a body or a legal conviction, Ron Rash's *One Foot in Eden* is a study in visual detection and visionary states that lend philosophical and spiritual heft to a work the *Los Angeles Times* called "equal parts vintage crime novel and Southern Gothic" (10). Although Rash seeds the text with elements from the crime novel and gothic traditions, *One Foot in Eden* is more complex in its use of genre codes, visual strategies, and interrogation of "the conflicting collection of images" in what Deborah Barker and Kathryn McKee have called the southern imaginary (2). In fact, Rash challenges genre categories and codes by merging a panoply of elements culled from the detective novel, the police procedural, hard-boiled crime fiction, film noir, and the metaphysical thriller.

Rash has spoken about his fascination with film noir's characters, speech, and visual effects (Rash, personal interview); obviously *One Foot in Eden* is in many ways a reflection of that interest. Although Rash uses a sheriff figure in the novel, Alexander is imbued with many of the traits Rash found most interesting in the private eyes of noir films. Denis Porter has argued that the "private eye/I(nvestigator) . . . suggests among other things; a solitary eye, and the (forbidden) pleasures associated with Freud's scopic drive; a non-organisation man's eye . . . an eye that trusts no other; an eye that's licensed to look; and even, by extrapolation, and eye for hire" (95). In addition to Sheriff Alexander's "investigative eye," Rash employs other types of vision, or scopic regimes, that work to shape a narrative tangled with sight lines and blocked views, glances and gazes, stare downs and look-sees, a strategy that propels a crossfire of visions in a type of ocular mapping that runs throughout the novel. Characters look often and intensely in *One Foot in Eden*. They look after; look back; look down on; look forward to; look within; look out; look sharp; look daggers at; look for trouble; and look the other way. Freud's eroticized pleasure of looking as an end in itself is met with other scopic regimes as Rash weaves the carceral, prurient, objectified, and undead gazes with visual modalities such as hallucinations, dreams, premonitions, mental projections, displacements, and second sights.

To complicate matters further, Rash melds these complex visualities with the doubling motif common in crime fiction and film noir. As Mark Osteen has discussed, doubling and "[m]irroring devices pervade the noir canon" (13) and find expression in many ways, ranging "from self-divided protagonists such as *Out of the Past*'s Jeff Markham/Bailey . . . [to] look-alikes such as *Hollow Triumph*'s gangster John Muller and the psychiatrist Bartok . . . to Walter Neff's impersonation of his murder victim in *Double Indemnity*" (13). But in *One Foot in Eden*, Rash doubles down on the doppelganger motif by creating trebled, even quadrupled characters, a strategy that not only intensifies the motif but also evokes the tangled web of relations, sympathies, antipathies, and ambivalences that plague the novel's characters. Rash's use of doubling often includes a tertiary character, a structural ploy that delimits one-to-one comparisons and functions like a triangular web with strands flowing into, through, and wrapping around characters in circuits of tangled compression. While these filaments and tendrils spool out over the course of the novel ensnaring nearly everyone in one web or another, the most important connectives[1] are linked to each character's scopic regime, which represent their ocular, intellectual, and emotional responses to the world in which they see.

> I guess we been looking down when we should of been looking up
> (Rash 31)

The Appalachian landscape of *One Foot in Eden* is a southern space viewers of John Boorman's neo-noir adaptation of James Dickey's *Deliverance* would know well. In many ways, *One Foot in Eden* is Rash's rewrite of the film's negative stereotyping, reclaiming hallowed ground after three decades of demeaning mass media images. Unlike Dickey's cameo appearance as sheriff at the conclusion of the film that says with a steely eye, "Don't ever do anything like this again. Don't come back up here" (*Deliverance*), Rash's sheriff Will Alexander is more personally connected to a murder involving his Appalachian neighbors. Although he strictly performs protocol and procedure in this homicide investigation, Alexander, despite his intentions, struggles with a moral ambivalence often associated with noir detectives such as Philip Marlowe, whose "shadowiness" is a defining feature of the figure's position outside the institutional structures of law and order. But even though Alexander is "the High Sheriff" accompanied by law enforcement apparatuses such as deputies, patrol cars, fingerprinting, and dive teams, he is ultimately as ineffective as Dickey's hapless sheriff in solving the crime of Winchester's murder.

The story begins routinely enough. A call in the night from one of his deputies, and Sheriff Alexander sets out to settle a bar fight in a place aptly named "The Borderline." When he arrives, the brawl is over but a scene of carnage spreads out before his eyes: "[c]asualties were propped up in chairs, though a few still lay amidst shattered beer bottles, cigarette butts, blood, and teeth. It was as close to war as I'd seen since the Pacific" (4). In the back was Holland Winchester, who "sprawled in a chair like a boxer resting between rounds . . . [His] nose swerved toward his cheek, and a slit in the middle of his forehead opened like a third eye. His clenched fists lay on the table, bruised and puffy" (4). Like any good cop, Sheriff Alexander surveys the scene with a trained eye, scouring the wreckage for "telling" details. Winchester is wearing his army uniform instead of work clothes, and the Sheriff thinks "if you hadn't known [Winchester] was sitting in a South Carolina honky-tonk, hadn't seen the Falstaff and Carling Black Labels signs glowing on the walls, your next guess would have been he was still in Korea, waiting at a dressing station to be stitched and bandaged" (3–4).

Rash sets up the doubling motif that connects Alexander to Winchester—veterans of WWII and Korea respectively—through shared military experience, physical size and shape, and by a visible object; in this case, the sheriff's badge and Winchester's gold star (more of which later). Doubling implies looking; it begs for comparison; it screams difference. While they resemble each other physically, the sheriff returns with a pierced lung from World War II, while Winchester brings back the ears of North Korean soldiers. Both are scarred from their pasts but Alexander has lived longer and has borne more woes than the younger Winchester.[2] Perhaps it is the combination of these life wounds that accounts for Alexander's empathy for the sufferings of others, even for Winchester, whom the sheriff asks to pay damages in a cautious exchange: "'Next time you'll go to jail,' I said. I smiled but I leveled my eyes on his to let him know I was serious'" (5). Holland meets the carceral gaze with verbal and visual defiance: "'We'll see about that,' Holland said. He smiled too but his dark-brown eyes had gone flat and cold as mine" (5). Rash strengthens the doubling motif through their locked gazes but complicates the roles of detective, ruthless killer, and victim through the shared hardness of Alexander's and Winchester's eyes, a description usually reserved only for the killer.

Two weeks later Alexander returns to Jocassee to investigate Winchester's reported disappearance. The classical detective narrative, as Laura Marcus reminds us, is "represented as a 'closed structure,' in which every aspect of the narration leads to the exposure of the means by which the crime was committed, the discovery of the criminal, and the re-establishing of order" (248). However, in Rash's version the victim's mother has already solved the mystery, and order is never reestablished in any legal or judicial sense. When the sheriff arrives he finds Mrs. Winchester on her front porch. Visually gifted, years of investigating have deepened Alexander's visual powers. As she speaks, Alexander watches her "deep brown eyes, deep brown like her son's . . . that didn't blink when she spoke . . . [in a face] so rigid it could have been on a daguerreotype" (12). Although he pictures Mrs. Winchester as a type of nineteenth-century photograph, Alexander sees but cannot know at this point what will become the novel's "smoking gun," the deep brown eyes that will ultimately connect (dead) father and (living) son. While the sheriff may be looking more than listening in this scene, he cannot help but hear Mrs. Winchester's declarations uttered like a series of shotgun blasts: "He's dead . . . My boy is dead"; "I heard the shot"; "Billy Holcombe's done killed my boy" (12).

From here, Sheriff Alexander begins friendly police procedure, walking along the drought-trickled riverbed and into Billy Holcombe's field where he surprises the farmer at work—and is surprised by Billy's lack of surprise in seeing him: "'How you doing, Sheriff?' he said, meeting my eyes . . . as if we'd just bumped into each other in downtown Seneca, not in the middle of his tobacco field" (16). Alexander's friendly approach is seen by Billy for what it is—a relaxed pose with eyes peeled looking for clues: "You seen him?" (16). Despite Billy's calm denial, Alexander spots the visual clue he had been seeking: "When Billy said no he glanced at his clenched right hand. I knew what that meant because I'd seen many another man do the same thing in such a situation" (16). Alexander thinks he's seen the light, believing "The eyes can lie, but eventually they'll tell you the truth. . . . That right hand of Billy's had helped lift rocks from his field big as watermelons. It had helped fell oak trees you couldn't get your arms around. And maybe . . . that hand had helped hold a shotgun steady enough to kill a man" (16).

While the sheriff's vision and intuition are spot on, a clenched hand is not much evidence, and that is exactly what Alexander needs for a conviction and what he never finds: visible evidence of the crime. Initially though, after further procedural investigating such as interviewing the suspects, dynamiting the river, and scouring the area with bloodhounds, Alexander sees what he thinks is the clenching visual clue:

> Then I saw them, drifting down slow as black ashes over the trees across the river. To tell the truth I was disappointed in Billy. He hadn't kept his head about him after all. It was almost funny the way he stood in the field facing me, doing his best to look innocent while right behind him the buzzards in the sky marked a giant X where Holland's body was. (31)

The sheriff's surety, even smugness, in his detecting skills builds over the following pages, as he confronts Billy about the buzzards, gathers his men for a search, and follows his suspect across the river. Alexander congratulates himself on his visual acumen, thinking, "All you had to do was look with a careful eye. That and know where to look" (47). Boring his eyes into Billy's back, Alexander is certain "I knew now what [Billy had] done with Holland's body. . . . *Yes, Billy, the eyes can lie, but eventually they'll tell the truth. If I could see your eyes they would tell me, Billy.* But I'll know soon enough" (47).

Not quite, for in this novel of visual interrogations, Alexander's carceral gaze is conditioned by the graphic X-marks-the-spot mentality learned from police procedures and historically associated with the buried treasures of pirate lore. Such looking implies an earthbound optics that metaphorically suggests the limitations of human vision and thought beyond the purely physical. Although the sheriff's eye is "licensed to look," the body he finds across the river and under the X is the one Billy wants him to see, the carcass of his plow horse, Sam, whom Billy had used to carry Holland's corpse to this spot before putting a bullet in Sam's brain. Although the sheriff has been directed here by the visual clues of the circling buzzards, he is so focused on finding the body that he forgets to follow the clues that led him here. Although Alexander comments on the heavy stench of "dead horse" and that "the buzzards had flown up in the trees to roost for the night" (48, 47), he does not even glance upward but keeps his eyes on the horse's bloated body and the ground beneath it.

Although Alexander has guessed correctly about Billy's use of Sam to carry Holland's body across the river, his metaphorical blindness is made weirdly physical when later Billy informs us that when he discovered Sam's carcass it was covered with buzzards "like a quilt" (148). And so is Holland's body, strapped to a limb high in the full leafed white oak (more of which later). The sheriff's "not seeing" of the buzzards that Billy's section clearly visualizes offers yet another clue that conventional vision fails to see clearly in this novel, and not only because it is literally blocked and obscured from discovering Holland's "invisible" corpse. Two competing visions raise questions about the validity of optical vision to detect or understand anything. In having Alexander fail at solving the case due to a lack of visual evidence largely because of his metaphorical and physical blindness, Rash hints at the limits of legal systems and agents of law to see truly in dispensing justice, a staple of noir's antiauthoritarian world view. But the sheriff's strange myopia is also a sign that this murder must be looked at from different angles and different eyes, visions that may look with "knowing eyes" or ones that see through this physical world from beyond.

> His brown eyes stared into my eyes, puzzled-like.
>   (Rash 85)

In the following sections Rash takes readers into what he has called "a primal space" that reconfigures the novel's temporal and spatial dimensions through the "disembodied voices" of "The Wife" and "The Husband" (Rash, personal interview). Amy's and Billy's sections sends us back in time, not just to the beginning of the story but also into a space that reverses the crime story's linearity of plot and resolution. Even though the sheriff quits the investigation, Holland's in/visible corpse remains the absent center around which other characters revolve. Holland's body may be "dead to the world" in the traditional physical sense but his corpse, a rather potent one, emits undead energies throughout the novel that continue to affect characters in critical ways. Alive, Holland's brown eyes are as much a driving force as his hammering of nails into the fence bordering his land and the Holcombes'; dead, they will haunt Amy and provide the novel's signature visual clue for discovering the identity of the murderers.

Just as Holland's live body performs in a highly visible and masculine role, Amy's body exudes feminine sexuality, functioning as "a sight to behold," a site of visual transgression, and a body of evidence. Blonde, buxom, and blue-eyed, Amy is drawn from the pervasive Daisy Mae stereotype of the pure but sexualized Appalachian mountain girl. But Amy is no Daisy Mae, despite their shared physical appearance. Amy is not demure, coy, self-sacrificing, or patiently waiting on her man: She knows exactly what she wants—a baby—and will do "any or everything" (77) to get one. If the originators of this noir tragedy are, as many have suggested, Billy's impotence (a side effect of his battle with polio as a child and a sign of his "bad luck") and Amy's obsession with becoming a mother so she can be "a woman" in the eyes of other Jocassee women, then the community must take some of the blame.

In her study *In Lonely Places: Film Noir Beyond the City,* Imogen Sarah Smith discusses how noir can creep into nearly any setting, urban or rural, by examining other noir geographies such as the desert, the west, the open road, the domestic, and the small town. Robert Mitchum's famous line from *When Strangers Marry* drives Smith's thesis home: "Places are all alike; you can't run away from yourself" (qtd. in Smith 1). Even though the urban jungle remains noir's most elaborate visual metaphor, Smith details how "even the home can be converted . . . from nurturing refuge to stifling cage. In small towns"—or in mountain valleys, I would add—"the neighborliness and persistence of tradition that should be virtues are twisted into corruption, repressive conformity and hostility towards outsiders" (3). The import of Mitchum's epiphany is his emphasis on the interior spaces of the self. If, as Smith claims, "the force driving noir stories is the need to escape: from the past, from the law, from the ordinary, from poverty, from constricting relationships, from the limitations of the self," then the "ultimate noir landscape . . . is the mind, the darkest city of all" (2–3).

Spatial isolation and constriction can drive vision inward where it can become paradoxically myopic and piercingly insightful. Amy's and Billy's sections are not merely occasions for giving "The Wife's" and "The Husband's" sides of the story; they marshal in scopic regimes from the traditions of the metaphysical detective novel and psychological thriller that challenge, blur, and aggravate the supposedly objective view of the private/I(nvestigator) and the police procedural. In its subversion of traditional detective-story conventions, Merivale and Sweeney argue that the metaphysical detective story raises profound questions "about narrative, interpretation, subjectivity, the nature of reality, and the limits of knowledge . . . which transcend the mere machinations of the mystery plot" (*Detecting* 1–2). In these sections we see the "inside" story of Amy's seduction of and Billy's showdown with Holland, who resents Amy tricking him into performing as "a stud bull you can use then take back to another farm" (126). In this primal space, Rash focuses on the effects of the crime on the perpetrators, the pressure and claustrophobic insularity of fear and regret that threaten to destroy them emotionally and psychologically.

These fears and anxieties become visible in scenes of self-reflection, "thought pictures," second sights, photographs, and fever dreams. Rash's inclusion of these scopic regimes, most of which run contrary to the detecting gaze, further challenges the crime story's conventions of how to see the world. In fact, even in "The High Sheriff's" detecting section, Rash slips in supernatural elements that question the ability of human vision—"licensed to look" or not—to see or know anything. For instance, Widow Glendower, the novel's most strident Appalachian signifier as "granny woman" and/or as "witch," is gifted with second sight as she tells Amy: "I've saw things that come to pass, things that someday will. I've saw a time when the dead will raise from their graves, a time the river will drown this whole valley" (72). And it will, for adding to the sense of claustrophobic doom is Carolina Power's purchase of Jocassee with plans to flood the valley for hydroelectric power and shareholder profit, an action that will effectively erase and render invisible the mountain residents, their homes, churches, burial grounds, and cultural history under a lake of corporate-controlled water.

But Amy's focus is on the here and now, her desire for a baby so strong she agrees to Glendower's suggestion to lay with Holland, a man who *can* give her a child. But just as Amy is no Daisy Mae, and despite her "using" of Holland, she is no femme fatale either. Rash virulently breaks from both stereotypes, particularly the "dumb hillbilly" whose inner life is not shown in films such as *Deliverance*. Both Amy and Billy feel immensely, and many times Rash draws out their thoughts and emotions through visual tropes congruent with each character's scopic regime as criminals and moral transgressors and as begrudging adultress and cuckolded husband. Andrew Pepper, in discussing how "literary noir defies straightforward categorization," argues that film noir differs from the traditional detective genre "in the shift of perspective from investigator to criminal and from the 'social' to the 'psychological'" (59). While the traditional focus is on detecting (and solving) crimes, noir, or "criminal adventures," "detectiveless crime novels" and/or "psycho-thrillers," emphasize criminal psychology and "the psychic traumas of its protagonists" (59).

This is surely the case with both Amy and Billy. Several times in her section Amy looks into a mirror, a noir trope Osteen has discussed in conjunction with the double motif. Literature is rife with scenes of women looking in mirrors, and Amy's self-reflection functions in many of the same ways as a sign of vanity, masking, introspection, identity, and emotional discord. After Amy decides to betray Billy and seduce Holland, she sits "in front of the looking glass. It was like as if I hadn't looked at myself for a long time, was looking at someone who'd grown to be almost a stranger. There was something different about the face that stared back at me" (81). While she cannot speak the truth about this difference, she knows full well what is happening to her and the moral and spiritual boundaries she is transgressing. In fact, Amy is all eyes in her chapter, her vision performing as a scrupulous mapping of the landscape she traverses in visits to Widow Glendower, as lookout and spotter of her "stud bull" hammering down the fence line, and as sexual object for Holland's prurient gaze.

But Amy is not a passive sexual object; rather, she is a performer of her own visibility that lures *her* sexual object, Holland. Amy makes herself visible to him by planting a white oak on the borderline of Holcombe-Winchester lands. As Billy does in his section, Amy surveys and shapes the visual field: "While I worked I'd glance up the ridge ever so often and see Holland, close enough now to see his big shoulders, the black hair thick on his head. He came steady closer and soon I saw the muscles in his arms and hair on his chest. I knew he saw me by now too. I made myself a natural sight around the yard and there was moments I felt his eyes full upon me" (80–81). The seduction scene is also a visual event: "I stood up, faced myself toward Holland and stepped out of the tub. His dark-brown eyes laid full upon me, moving up and down my nakedness like as if it was something he was afraid he'd forget if he didn't study on it careful" (84). These scenes are also episodes of visual detection, not like the investigative eye but because both characters detect, or sense, something alluring, dangerous, and mysterious in their encounter. This mystery is increased throughout their lovemaking, both for Amy, who develops feelings for Holland, and for Holland who

never knows what to think about Amy's adulterous actions. After their first encounter, for instance, Amy tells him, "You best get back to your fence-making,"
and Holland responds visually as he does in much of the novel, alive or dead:
"His brown eyes stared in my eyes, puzzled-like" (85).

Even though Sheriff Alexander's comment, "The eyes can lie, but eventually
they'll tell you the truth," doesn't pan out in his investigative context, the adage
vibrates with undead energies when applied to the piercing stare of Holland's
dark-brown eyes. Like his gold star, his eyes supply a crucial visual clue that
affects Amy's emotional and psychological state of mind, especially when Mrs.
Winchester gives Amy a photograph of Holland as a gift after Amy gives birth to
Isaac. In what amounts to an episode of the return of the repressed, Amy again
faces the face she had seduced and caused to die: "I opened the box and there
was Holland's face staring at me. He was seventeen, maybe eighteen, and dressed
in a dark suit, a suit a man might wear to his wedding or be buried in" (98). Amy
"pondered this picture longer than I ought have," thinking how easy it would be
"to squirrel it away somewhere Billy would have no leave to look" (98). Instead,
she knows she must destroy any visual evidence so she "kills" Holland again by
laying "the picture in the fire and watch[ing] it curl up and turn black" (98).[3]

"IT WAS JUSTIFIED"

In the pilot episode for FX's *Justified*, Federal Marshall Raylan Givens guns down
a Miami mobster in a swanky outdoor restaurant in what is obviously a forced
showdown, Old West style. Or at least that is what Givens's chief tells him in ex-
asperation: "We don't do that anymore. I'm pretty sure we haven't in say, what,
about a hundred and fifty years" ("Fire"). Givens's response gives the show its
title: "He pulled first. I shot him. *It was justified*" ("Fire"). But Billy Holcombe
is no Rayland Givens. Not tall, athletic, or handsome; nor cool, calm, or confident; and certainly no Stetson. However, while *Justified* is a twenty-first-century
Appalachian noir, when Billy finds himself in a similar showdown with Holland
he does not shy away. Despite their differences in stature and status, Billy and
Raylan share one fundamental Appalachian trait: a code of honor that demands
violence in return for violence.[4]

Billy's section is also a study in visual detection, not in Alexander's legal sense
or in Amy's self-reflective, objectifying sense, but as a man who suspects his wife
of having an affair with Holland, their strapping, "hell raiser" neighbor. Billy's
section begins when he confronts Amy about her baby bump, the visible sign of
her betrayal and adultery, even though he has already seen the truth. One day

working down by the river, he sees "Holland Winchester saunter[ing] past the big white oak that marked the property line between his family's and mine," and when Billy comes in for "noon-dinner" and finds that his "beans and bread wasn't ready" he sees that "Holland had left his mark on Amy, a spot on her neck purpled like a fox grape" (116).

The murder scene appears twice, once in Amy's section and again in Billy's but we get more visual details from the husband's point of view. Unlike Dixon Steele in *In a Lonely Place*, Billy does not have an anger problem; in fact, despite previous events all he wants from Holland is for him to leave them alone. But Holland is a force that demands a response, telling Billy "What's swelling in her belly is mine, not yours" (125). Billy is clearly confused about such a show-down—"I met his eyes, eyes dark as molasses" (125)—but is even more per-plexed when Holland grabs the shotgun barrel and points it at his own chest. He challenges Billy: "Settle it one way or another, Holcombe . . . because this here is the only way to keep me from claiming what's mine" (126). And these become the last words Holland speaks as Billy's shotgun "slammed against his shoulder" and he watches the life run out of Holland's brown eyes, which "stared right at me but he was seeing something else. Maybe it was himself as a child, or in a fox-hole in Korea, or tangled in one flesh with Amy. Maybe he saw all those things, one after another flashing in front of him like he was looking at calendars filled with pictures instead of months and years" (126).

Holland's brown eyes close in death but they continue to affect Billy and spawn intense metaphysical visions. Two scenes are particularly indicative of the psychological effects of Holland's undead corpse on the man who killed him: Billy's tortured vision in hiding Holland's corpse and Holland's shadowy appearances in Billy's fever dreams. Both of these visions are indebted to Rash's fascination with Dostoyevsky's *Crime and Punishment*,[5] where the idealistic stu-dent Raskolnikov has a ghastly nightmare of a dray horse whipped and beaten to death (54–59) before he commits a double murder the next day. Although Billy's first vision is based on physical observation, he looks through the lens of the guilty and blends what he sees with a vision of punishment and doom, common in both noir and southern religious narratives:

> Holland's body circling slow as it raised into the sky . . . The rope spread Hol-land's arms out. They was stiff as fire-pokers and as he raised higher his arms looked like wings. I remembered Preacher Robertson reading from Revelation how on Judgment Day the dead would raise from the earth and sea and fly to heaven and what a glorious sight that would be. But as I patted Sam's flank and

Holland lifted another few yards toward the sky, his face gouged by barbed wire, the hole in his chest boiling with bluebottle flies and yellow jackets, I reckoned a man might witness no more terrible sight than the dead resurrected. (136)

Months later, Billy suffers a mysterious illness, a fever that lays him flat out and unable to get out of bed similar to the one Raskolnikov has after his disastrous murder of the pawn woman and her sister. Whether the fever is a metaphor of guilt that suggests "burning in hell" for one's crimes or a manifestation of undead energies by the invisible corpse, Billy continues, like Amy, to see Holland after his murder, deterioration, and reburial. In what amounts to his own Raskolnikovian vision of guilt and self-destruction, Billy's "world [gets] all blurry and dim and I hardly knew it for day or night. All I knew for certain was someone else was in that back room with me. He leaned out of the corner shadows with his dark eyes watching me with never a blink" (157).

Billy's efforts to secure Holland to the white oak with the barbed wire results in a bizarre crucifixion image where Billy sees himself as a Judas, a betrayer of God who killed His only son: "A strand of barbed wire tore into his brow. The blood from the barbs ran down his face like tears. 'What do you want of me?' I shouted at him, but he didn't answer. When Amy came in to lay a fresh poultice on my brow"—even more doubling—"I'd point to him in the corner. Soon as I did he melted into the shadows like black ice" (157). When Billy heals after three days of drinking the widow's root tea, he thinks Holland is finally gone. But Billy soon realizes that as "father" of Holland's and Amy's child, he "hadn't got away with nothing" (159) for he will be looking into the same brown eyes of the man he killed as he raises "the son," Isaac.

> Look at it good. Even if you won't hear the truth you'll see it.
>   (Rash 1)

Isaac's section begins with his realization that he is a body under observation: "I was four years old when I first knew [Mrs. Winchester] was watching me" (163). Sarah Winchester is not merely the mother of the victim; she is also a keeper of images, an eye of justice, and medium for the undead. She communicates mainly through her use of images and, like her son, a penetrating vision that locks those under observation in a haptic struggle between watcher and watched. The young Isaac, though, is no match for Sarah Winchester's gaze. One Sunday in church, Isaac looks around until he sees her sitting in another pew and "[t]heir eyes met. At that moment I realized those dark-brown eyes had watched me a long time—not just seconds or minutes, but months, maybe years, and not just here in church but from across the barbed wire fence that separated her farm from ours" (163). Under such visual pressure, Isaac feels both passive and somehow violated, trapped in Mrs. Winchester's gaze but realizing the eyes have something important to say: "Her eyes locked on mine . . . I couldn't have looked away if I'd have wanted to. Those eyes held me as firm as any arms could. They were hungry eyes" (163).

Sarah Winchester sees Isaac as a medium for discovering the location of Holland's body so he can receive a proper burial. She recruits Isaac by offering him peppermints in what seemed "like a game of hide-and-seek, played not with other children but with adults," a game of visuality in which "[t]here was hardly a word between us, like we were spies trading secrets" (164). Soon Isaac begins to visit Mrs. Winchester, often sitting by the fire with her drinking cups of hot chocolate. But resting above them on the mantel is Holland's framed photograph, "hung like a painting," from which his brown eyes stare unceasingly (165). "Who is he?" Isaac asks, to which Mrs. Winchester replies "That's my youngest boy . . . You favor him, especially in the eyes" (165). Isaac examines the photograph and meets the eyes of the man who sired him: "I looked up at the man in the uniform. I studied his eyes and saw they were dark like mine, like hers" (165).

In this scene and throughout the final section, Sarah Winchester continuously attempts to make visible what has been rendered invisible. She effectively transforms her passive role as mother of the victim into a performance as a detective hell bent on punishing the murderers. For instance, after Mrs. Winchester gives Amy the gift of Holland's photograph and his gold star, Amy burns the image and then hides the gold star in a rot-hole in a stump, rendering it temporarily invisible. After Isaac's birth, however, Amy retrieves the gold star and uses it as payment to Widow Glendower for Amy's broken promise of letting Glendower midwife Isaac. Then in what amounts to an invisible scene in the narrative, Glendower gives the gold star back to Mrs. Winchester, who then gives it to Isaac as a symbol of his murdered father Holland. At this point, though, Isaac does not know his paternity, and "buries" the gold star in a cubbyhole in his bedroom. He may succeed temporarily in rendering the gold star/ Holland invisible but the sign will rise again after eighteen years of smoldering undeadness.

Even with Mrs. Winchester's visual evidence, Isaac doesn't solve the crime but renders it visible through a series of gestural strategies. While Carolina Power engineers herd the mountain residents from their homes, law enforcement is called for the more obstinate cases such as Sarah Winchester, who refuses to leave until she sees Isaac one last time. When Isaac returns to the Winchester homestead "the front room [was] dark as a movie theater" (171). Isaac brings the gold star as a gift to Mrs. Winchester who finally tells Isaac the truth: "That there belongs to you, not me . . . He wanted you to have it . . . Because you're his son" (172–73). Significantly, words fail in this scene as Isaac rejects language, especially when Mrs. Winchester tells him that Amy and Billy were Holland's killers. And in this gap where words lose their meaning, the visual rears up in the image of the gold star, a visible sign of Holland that can prove the truth or falsity of Mrs. Winchester's claims with a single look. "Don't believe me," she tells Isaac. "Believe your own eyes . . . [or] believe your momma. Show her that gold star. Ask what she and that man of hers done to your real daddy" (174–75).

When Isaac returns to the farmhouse, he opens his palm and shows Amy the Gold Star, thinking, "I'd done the right thing because her face told me more than any words" (189). Confronted with the sight Amy recoils "against the refrigerator, almost like I held a spider or snake in my hand . . . 'Oh, God,' Momma said before she sagged like I'd punched her in the stomach. She put her hands over her face like she was trying to hide what part of her she could" (189). The visual sign elicits a look of guilt from Amy that Isaac did not want to see, but he is even more startled to discover Billy standing "in the doorway, bare-chested, shaving cream covering his face like a fake beard," who verbally confesses, "Your Momma didn't kill him. I did" (189). From here, Isaac demands Billy and Amy take him across the river to the burial spot so he can retrieve Holland's remains.

In a journey beset with a welter of looks, gazes, glances, stares, grimaces and double-takes, the three—accompanied by Sheriff Alexander—cross the river into the land of the dead. When Billy unearths Holland's remains—"a medal with the silk still attached, a couple of boot eyelets and some bone chips" (196)— he brings the invisible corpse (or what is left of it) into sight, showing visible proof of his long hidden crime. But this evidence, unseen for eighteen years, has a short visible shelf life. After the unearthing, Isaac puts the fragments in a sack but in the fast pouring rain and the river's quick rising Sheriff Alexander, channeling Marlowe's moral ambiguity regarding the strict letter of the Law, has other ideas. Nodding at the sack in Isaac's hand, Alexander says, "You could leave that too. You could save us all a lot of trouble if you did. My deputy's on his way up here. Once he sees what's in that sack this is a murder case" (197–98).

Age has deepened the Sheriff's sense of the limitations of the legal system for he has adopted a more capacious view of crime and punishment: "Let's get out of here . . . Whatever's been done has been done. We're too old to change it now. Let the water cover it up" (193). Sheriff Alexander, whose I(nvestigative) eye had scoured the area and Billy's body for clues to discover Holland's corpse, now advocates removing the remains from the visual world. Isaac understands the wisdom of the Sheriff's suggestion and raises "the sack in my right hand and held it between us for a moment before I let it slip through my fingers. The current toted the sack a few feet downstream before it sunk," becoming invisible to human eyes (198). "Let the dead bury the dead," Sheriff Alexander says (198) but the retiring lawman does not realize the prescience of his biblical reference. In this novel of the seen and the unseen two more bodies—Billy and Amy—must vanish, and they do when caught in the rising floodwaters that claim their lives in what seems like an act of divine, if not legal, justice.

But as with Holland's in/visible corpse, the return of the visibly repressed is raised from the dead in the novel's last section, underscoring the mysterious and powerful role of the supernatural in Appalachian noir. Unlike hard-boiled crime novels where both criminal and detective are often wrapped in shadowy deceptions and moral ambiguities that leave readers questioning if anyone can be trusted, Appalachian noir tends to ground its stories with hints of moral consciousness and powerful presences beyond the physical apparatuses of legal or social structures. For instance, after the controlled flood has reburied the murder scene, the Holcombe and Winchester farms, churches, lodges, stores, and cemeteries, Appalachian supernaturalism breaks through the detective narrative as Widow Glendower's coffin bobs on the water's surface, its cedar wood winking in the sunlight like a signal from the underworld.

But in *One Foot in Eden,* bodies that resist burial and blur lines between the living and the dead must be visually policed in one way or another, especially if they invoke the supernatural. Hauled in by Carolina Power and awaiting reburial in a church graveyard, Alexander's deputy, Bobby Murphree, abducts Glendower's coffin and drives a johnboat to the heart of the lake where he opens the cedar box and sees Glendower as a memento mori, her "old hollow-eyed skull grinning at me" (212). Murphree's moral failure in disinterring her remains results from his communally inspired belief in the powers of the supernatural, claiming, "You'll not rest in no graveyard with my kin, witch . . . Sink straight to hell" (212–13). In a scene that mimics Billy's raising of Holland's dead body up the white oak, Murphree dumps Glendower's remains into four hundred feet of water, seeing her disappear into the depths below: "I watched those bones drift down, the skull-face nodding back and forth, the arms unfolding off her ribs and spreading out like wings, getting smaller and smaller, the lake so clear it was like she fell through air, not water" (212). Although Murphree tells himself he has done right by scattering Glendower's bones under a body of water, he has willfully committed a crime. He is also paradoxically haunted by thoughts of Amy and Billy—whose bodies are never found and remain rife with undead energies—and who Murphree thinks may not "even know they was dead and buried under a lake" (214)—or is it the "hell" to which he has consigned Glendower's bones?

These types of contradictions between the living and dead, between supernatural agents and human mortality, between police procedural and community superstition, fuel the moral dimensions of the novel's characters in a betrayal-redemption narrative that unreels the complexity of noir vision of *One Foot in Eden*.

NOTES

1. Among the most important "webs" are Sheriff Alexander/Holland Winchester/Billy Holcombe; Billy/Holland/Amy Holcombe; Widow Glendower/Amy/Mrs. Winchester; Holland/Mrs. Winchester/Isaac Holcombe; and the doubled-double of Alexander/Billy/Holland/Isaac.

2. Chief among Alexander's personal woes are his failing marriage with his rather snobbishly detached wife, Janice; the loss of their only child to stillbirth; his alienation from his father and brother who still live in Jocassee; and his physical injuries that have worsened over time: a damaged knee from playing college football and a pierced lung while storming a beach in the Pacific during World War II.

3. For more on Rash's "pictures of the dead," see Wilhelm.

4. For a detailed reading of masculinity and the honor code in Rash's work, see Spill.

5. See Graves and Wilhelm, 82–98.

MARCOS MCPEEK VILLATORO'S *HOME KILLINGS*

Sleuthing Central American Identity and History in the New Latino South

YAJAIRA M. PADILLA

In the prologue to *Home Killings* (2001), the first installment of the Romilia Chacón mystery series by Marcos McPeek Villatoro, lead detective and protagonist, Romilia, offers readers a snapshot view of her complex subjectivity. Opening with the line, "I'm twenty-eight, Latina, and a southerner," Romilia lays claim to her pan-ethnic and gendered identity as a Latina while also distinguishing her connection to a specific geographic area within the United States, the South (McPeek Villatoro vii). Further delineating this self-identification is the fact that Romilia is of Central American descent, specifically Salvadoran, as well as a single mother. Within the broader context of detective fiction and even that of multiethnic mystery novels, this multifaceted characterization of Romilia by McPeek Villatoro offers a pioneering example of a Salvadoran American female sleuth. However, read against the backdrop of an upsurge in Latino immigration to the US South in the last few decades,[1] Romilia's portrayal and crime solving are also suggestive of the ways in which Latinos are being integrated into and are transforming this region.

McPeek Villatoro's Romilia Chacón series—*Home Killings* (2001), *Minos* (2003), *A Venom Beneath the Skin* (2005), and *Blood Daughters* (2011)—provides a novel look at this process of racial and ethnic transformation in the US South while also evincing the uniqueness of the Salvadoran, and by extension, Central American experience. Combining aspects of a traditional female sleuth with that of the hard-boiled detective, Romilia is an aggressive no-nonsense cop who enjoys southern bourbon, is haunted by the murder of her sister, and prone to violence.[2] As a single mother, she also constantly feels guilty for not dedicating enough time to her son. Caught at the crossroads of multiple subject positions, Romilia must continuously renegotiate her identity both on the basis of gender as she struggles to be a "good cop" and a "good mother" as well as on the basis of her ethnicity. As the series progresses, she must also contend with her identity as she moves from Atlanta to Nashville and, by the third book, to Los Angeles, California.[3]

Romilia's Salvadoran American background is a key indicator of a Central American presence in these narratives. While identifying with the pan-ethnic label of "Latina," Romilia's representation in these texts is also defined by her Salvadoranness, conveyed through references to Salvadoran oral traditions, cultural symbols, and *pupusas*—a staple of Salvadoran cuisine made up of a thick corn tortilla filled with cheese and/or other ingredients such as pork. Romilia's relationship with her *bête noire*, Rafael Murillo, a Guatemalan American with ties to Guatemala's military and the drug trade, adds to this depiction, since it prompts her to investigate Central America's history of civil war during the 1970s and 1980s. Admittedly, these two characters and their interactions do not speak for all the diverse cultures, peoples, and histories that form the US-based Central American population. However, as part of this group, and its two largest segments—Salvadorans and Guatemalans—Romilia and Murillo still transmit a certain understanding of Central Americans. Hence McPeek Villatoro's emphasis on Central American representation and history by way of these characters calls for deeper inquiry into how this detective fiction addresses the multidimensional Central American immigrant experience in the United States.

According to Arturo Arias, within the multicultural context of the United States, the Central American population remains largely invisible, meaning it has yet to achieve the same level of recognition, in terms of assimilation and integration, as that of other Latino/ethnic groups. Arias ascribes the purposefully pleonastic label of "Central American-American" to this population and maintains that this identity is one that cannot be fully subsumed either within the label of "US Latino" or "Latin American" given that "[t]he Guatemalan, Salvadoran, or even Central American experience as a whole is independent and irreducible to large unities that seek to discipline its singularity" (171).[4] In fact, for Arias the redundancy of "Central American-American" serves precisely to underscore how this identity resides "outside of th[e]se two signifiers from the very start" (171). Arias similarly acknowledges that the broader regional emphasis in the term "Central American-American" as opposed to individual national origins such as Salvadoran American or Guatemalan American is problematic, given its potential to obscure the historical and cultural particularities that characterize individual Central American countries and their peoples. He insists, nevertheless, that this regional categorization is a necessary one "because the Latino identity is often constructed in areas of the United States like Los Angeles through the abjection and erasure of the Central American-American [. . .]," and because it also serves as a means "[f]or opening the possibility" of recognition for this segment of the US population (172). In *Latining America: Black-Brown Passages and the Coloring of Latino/a Studies*, Milian builds upon Arias's conceptualization of "Central American-American" so as to suggest that this paradigm can also be understood as a site of knowledge-making concerning the multiple "souths" encompassed within the Global South, the discursive and ethnoracial limits of normative terms such as *Latinoness, Latinaness,* and *Latin American,* and, more generally, *Americaness.*

McPeek Villatoro's Romilia Chacón series constitutes a cogent cultural site to air and rethink the claims made by Arias regarding Central American "invisibility" in the United States. Being "Latina" and a "southerner," does not necessarily occlude Romilia's Salvadoran American identity, nor, by extension, her Central American-American identity. To the contrary, McPeek Villatoro's manifold construction of Romilia works against this erasure, while begging the question: "What does it mean to be a Latina, specifically Salvadoran American, in a New Latino South?" Hence, I argue that McPeek Villatoro's mystery series "makes visible" Central American-Americans by showcasing the complexities of Romilia's identity formation, a process that not only involves her performance of Salvadoranness and the "detection" of a hidden past of violence, but that is likewise informed by discourses of gender and geography. McPeek Villatoro's recognition of Central Americans via a "Latina southerner's" investigation into the past complicates and expands Arias's conceptualization of Central American-American marginality and identity politics in the United States. Although my analysis focuses on *Home Killings* (2001) given the text's emphasis on Nashville, Tennessee, one of the fastest growing sites of Latino population, including Central Americans (Winders "New Americans," "Placing Latino/as"), and the centrality of Central American political history to the plot, I also draw on examples from *Minos* (2003). Also partially set in Tennessee, this second installment provides further insight concerning the Latino southernness brought to bear in *Home Killings* (2001).

ROMILIA CHACÓN: A SALVADORAN LATINA DETECTIVE IN THE SOUTH?

Because *Home Killings* (2001) is a work of detective fiction, it is pivotal to recognize the literary implications and key interplay between McPeek Villatoro's use of this genre and the production of Central American visibility. Popular forms such as the detective genre have been scrutinized precisely because "such texts are not 'individualized' after the fashion of 'High Culture' literature" (Walton 258). Scholarship on detective fiction, especially that focused on feminist and multiethnic works, has attempted to counter this limited understanding by stressing the ways this genre can also be used by authors to consciously underscore issues related to gender, ethnicity, and race.[5] In his analysis of Chicana/o detective novels, Ralph Rodriguez affirms that while "detective novels can be entertaining and delightful reads . . . they also answer questions about writers who produce them and the cultures that consume them" (2). Rodriguez further suggests that "[t]hese detective novels demonstrate the emergence of new discourses of identity, politics, and cultural citizenship" (2). It is following this same premise, that I approach my analysis of *Home Killings* (2001) as a literary space in which a new discourse of Central American identity is being produced and debated.[6]

Set in the late 1990s, the novel follows Romilia's first assignment, an investigation into the murder of Diego Sáenz, a Latino journalist responsible for the bilingual supplement in the local newspaper and an important source of information for the Spanish-speaking community in the Nashville area. Sáenz is believed to be the victim of the Pyramid Killer, whose trademark is leaving a jade pyramid on the body of his victims. One of Romilia's lead suspects in the case is Rafael Murillo, an entrepreneurial businessman who secretly runs an international drug trafficking operation and about whom Sáenz was writing a story. Murillo's street name, Tekún Umán, a reference to a Guatemalan Indian who died fighting the conquistador of Central America, Pedro de Alvarado, links him to the Mayan populations of the region and their use of jade. More importantly, as Romilia discovers, Murillo is an ex-member of the *kaibiles*, a notorious death squad and military unit operating in Guatemala during its civil war.

Stuart Hall's theories of cultural identity are useful for exploring Romilia's complex subjectivity and depiction in this and in subsequent texts. Drawing from a notion of identity as a "'production' that is never complete, always in process, and always constituted within, not outside representation" (222), Hall suggests that cultural identities should be understood as "the points of identification, the unstable points of identification or suture, which are made, within the discourses of history and culture. Not an essence but a *positioning*" (226). Among the more salient points raised by Hall's conceptualization is his emphasis on cultural identity as a "positioning" that is not only contingent upon varying historical and cultural discourses, but is also an ongoing process encompassed within the act of representation. Romilia's multifaceted cultural identity is continuously evolving, privy to changes given the incorporation of or contact with new discourses and experiences. An example of this process is Romilia's ceaseless renegotiation of her identity in light of the "latinization" of the US South, which conditions her own sense of what it means to be Latina/o and her performance of Salvadoranness.[7] In essence, with Romilia, McPeek Villatoro is showcasing a Salvadoran American cultural identity "in process" that also speaks to the formation of Central American-American cultural identity and visibility.

Looking at this process of cultural identity formation requires, first, addressing what it means to be a Latina southerner as Romilia claims; and second, working within the parameters of this pan-ethnic label in order to tease out the particularities of Romilia's Salvadoranness. As Romilia discloses, she was hired by the Nashville police force because the "small retinue of southern dicks had found their deductive reasoning and acumen stunted by their inability to speak Spanish" (McPeek Villatoro 16). Romilia's hire is but one indicator of the growing Latino community in the area and the ways Latin American immigration has changed the region. While following a lead, Romilia visits a *taquería* in a poverty stricken sector of Nashville. Blending restaurant with *bodega*, the *taquería* is host to a "cornucopia of Latin foods" and Latino popular culture, including Gloria Estefan and Selena CDs as well as posters of our Lady of Guadalupe (32). The Mexican owner, Doña Marina, can hardly keep up with the demand from her Latino clientele, as she informs Romilia, and has even begun to sell her products to "*gringos* and *negros*" (35). Like Romilia's hire, Doña Marina's *taquería* and its location in a predominantly Latino neighborhood highlights the burgeoning cultural interchange among Latinos, *gringos*, and *negros*.

This "latinization" of the US South, however, is also marked by deeper economic and political tensions that are revealed in the immigration backlash spurred by Romilia's investigation. The socioeconomic incorporation of Latinos has influenced the racial dynamic in the region, which has been historically divided along black and white lines.[8] Dining at a barbecue grill, Romilia overhears one of the locals who, while commenting on "all them wetbacks coming into the area," is quick to associate immigrant workers with criminal activity, stating: "You're bound to have some nutcase in one of those trucks, saying he wants to pick tomatoes but what he really wants to do is to slit a few throats. That immigration needs to come in here and clean up" (182). This is a sentiment shared by both the white customer expressing it and the black man sitting next to him. A division is thus drawn between white and black southerners and the newer Latino settlers. To a certain extent, the segregation between whites and blacks that has traditionally defined the US South is reconfigured in light of global economic and political developments to produce yet another binary also based on ethnic and racial differences as well as citizenship (Lacy and Odem; Marrow). Underlying this dynamic of "white and black against brown," as Romilia contends, is a discriminatory fear rooted in the influx of immigrant populations and their potential threat on "American" jobs and livelihoods, paralleling the economic and demographic changes the US South began to undergo in the 1980s and '90s. This problematic dynamic emphasizes the notion of "Americans" against Latino others, and re-inscribes a false understanding of all Latinos as foreign and homogenous.

For Romilia, these conflicts among Latinos, whites, and blacks are not easily navigated given her status as a police officer. Despite her sense of the racism and sexism that permeates her unit, Romilia's critical stance is often undermined by her need to succumb to the exigencies of the institution. After discovering that one of Murillo's henchmen, Francisco Colibrí or *Pajarito,* is extorting money from undocumented immigrants in exchange for fake documents, Romilia and her partner, Jerry Wilson, a white Tennessean, decide to use the informants they captured to detain *Pajarito* and reel in Murillo. The informants, both undocumented, agree to wear wires in exchange for being cleared from any possible connections to Murillo's drug trafficking. While preparing for the sting operation, Jerry tells Romilia that they will have to turn the men over to US immigration, to which Romilia responds, "Look, I can't be bothered with their life stories, Jerry" (McPeek Villatoro 195). This calculated response is delivered within the context of a self-conscious power play between her and Jerry: "In his eyes, I suppose I was also cold-blooded, along with being sly. Perhaps my being Latina meant I had to think a certain way, specifically regarding undocumented foreigners. Right now all I wanted to think about was nailing Pajarito, and ultimately his boss" (195). Romilia's words reveal her need to prove herself to Jerry, solidifying her position as a cop over that of any possible ethnic allegiances, a preference that is also made clear by her ambivalence in critically addressing her ethnic-based hire.

Being a law enforcement agent may limit Romilia's behavior to a certain extent when it comes to her coworkers; however, it does not keep her from reflecting on her Latina identity. In fact, Romilia's continuous negotiation between being a Latina police officer and working with a Latino population is a catalyst for this type of self-exploration. After capturing *Pajarito,* Romilia is unsettled by what she perceives as "every single eye [. . .] watching me, someone of familiar skin, doing something so very foreign to one of our own" (198). Although she is performing her duty by arresting *Pajarito,* Romilia is conscious of how this act could also be read as a betrayal of the Latino community with which she identifies. Even more egregious than a white cop is a Latina cop who betrays her own people. Romilia's contradictory feelings raise important questions about how her identity is constructed in reference to and as part of a broader and heterogeneous minority group. Romilia considers herself Latina even while differentiating herself from Mexican immigrants and Mexican Americans through her Salvadoranness. Thus when she contemplates her sense of "loyalty" it is in reference to a diverse and wide-ranging Latino community.

According to Portes and Rumbaut's work on second-generation immigrant children, the complex process of ethnic identification "begins with the application of a label to oneself in a cognitive process of self-categorization, involving not only a claim to membership in a group or category but also a contrast of one's group or category with other groups and categories" (151). Romilia's use of the pan-ethnic label "Latina" exemplifies this process; her self-identification not only stresses her need to be understood as a part of a larger Latino group, but also her intention to highlight the distinction of this group from that of others, particularly in the southern region in which she situates herself. This is notable in Romilia's incessant and at times contradictory subject positioning as a Latina southerner in a predominantly biracial US South, still marked by its Anglocentrism. Yet there is also another dimension to this process of ethnic individuation, and thus identity formation, given that Romilia's subjectivity is equally developed in contrast to the dominant Latino groups in the area: immigrants and Mexican Americans. It is in these "points of identification" but also differentiation that Romilia's Salvadoran heritage takes on new meaning and, relatedly, that Central American-Americans become visible.

Language is a salient way in which McPeek Villatoro posits the distinctions among the Latino groups in the area. This is evident when Romilia attempts to access Diego Sáenz's computer files in the hope of finding a clue to help solve his murder. At her partner's suggestion that the password may be in Spanish, Romilia tries the words "*mole, chilango,* and *momia*" because Sáenz was of "Mexican descent" (108). Implicit in Romilia's categorization of this Spanish as "Mexican" are the notions that other forms of Spanish exist such as "Salvadoran" Spanish, and that not all Latinos are the same, contrary to the common perception by non-Latino groups in the area.

As a linguistic practice associated with the intimacy of the home, "Salvadoran" Spanish, characterized by the form of the *voseo,* draws attention to the familial bonds shared by Romilia, her mother Eva, and son Sergio.[9] Upon hearing Romilia say "dirty words" during one of their conversations, her mother is quick to admonish her, "*Cuidáte vos*" (66). While the use of the *voseo* in this instance denotes the Chacón family's Central American background, the added inclusion of words used in El Salvador such as *cipote* for boy, and the allusion to *el zipitillo,* a popular figure of Salvadoran lore, likewise render this Spanish explicitly

"Salvadoran." This use of language as a cultural marker, upheld by McPeek Villatoro's acknowledgement to his editor for "his allowance of Salvadoran Spanish throughout the text) [. . .]" (248), is the principle means through which Romilia marks and performs her Salvadoranness.

Following Karen Christian's analysis of ethnic performances in Latina/o fiction, Romilia's display of Salvadorannes problematizes "the concept of cultural essence" (17). That Romilia's "Salvadoran" Spanish, and Salvadoran American identity, is set in contrast to that of "Mexican" Spanish and Mexican American identity, reveals her Salvadorannes to be a product "in process," not an *a priori* essence devoid of historical, cultural, or political influences. In making this process of identity formation "visible," Romilia's performance of Salvadoranness also stresses the eclipsing of a Central American presence in the area due to the predominance of Mexican Americans and a general classification of all Latinos as Mexicans. By debunking this dominant stereotype of Latino homogeneity, Romilia's performance brings to the fore Central American–American identities, all the while accentuating the heterogeneity and the "very complexities of *Latinidad*" that, according to Arrizón, "may be the crucial distinguishing mark of Latino culture and identity in the Americas" (3).

Complicating this exploration of Central American visibility and identity politics is Romilia's relationship with her *bête noire*, Rafael Murillo. Unlike Romilia's, Murillo's ties to the US South are not the result of the international migration prompted by the civil wars in Central America. His Guatemalan father belonged to the coffee oligarchy and his mother, a white woman from Chattanooga, Tennessee, came from a well-established southern family. They met while attending Vanderbilt University. As Murillo boasts to Romilia the first time they meet, he is a "true Latino southerner," a product of privileged classes in Guatemala and the US South (55). Murillo identifies strongly with his Guatemalan origins, as exemplified by his street name "Tekún Umán," and his service in the Guatemalan national army. However, it is clear from Murillo's self-categorization as a "true" Latino southerner that his embracement of a pan-ethnic label is meant to mark him as "American" as well. To a certain extent, Romilia and Murillo share a similar understanding of a southern *latinness* that also encompasses a Central American heritage, and that sets them apart from immigrants and Mexican Americans. Yet Murillo is also half-white, which aligns him with an Anglo and empowered population in the US South.

This affiliation is duly stressed in *Minos* (2003), in which Romilia pursues the serial killer who murdered her older sister, Catalina. Having escaped to Guatemala at the end of *Home Killings* (2001), Murillo keeps an eye on Romilia from afar, sending her classified information on "Minos." Hoping to locate Murrillo, Romilia visits his ailing mother and aunt, Ruth Anne James and Kimberly, at their home in Chattanooga. The James's dwelling is a three-story plantation-style estate with manicured lawns that "spoke of money that had passed through centuries" and labor forces that "had changed from African American to low income white to Latino" (33). This depiction of Murillo's childhood home weds him and his family to a southern history of slavery and white privilege. The racist underpinnings of this history and the presumed racial superiority of Murillo's southern kin are underscored in the initial conversation between Romilia and his aunt. Kimberly describes the Guatemalan department, Petén, where her sister and brother-in-law resided for a time, as a "savage plac[e]" that still existed in a "primitive state" (35). Kimberly likewise implies that what made her Guatemalan brother-in-law a suitable match for her sister was that he was a "good man" and that he came from "good stock" (38). Although Romilia later doubts herself, it is hard to dismiss her initial sense that Kimberly's comments are racist. It is similarly difficult to ignore this aspect of Murillo's bicultural identity, especially given his failure to directly question such attitudes and the privilege granted to him as a "southerner" by his birthright.

This failure coupled with the fact that Murillo and Romilia interact with predominantly white and Latino southerners suggest a notion of a Central American Latino identity that is constructed, almost exclusively, in relation to the white-Anglo population. Indeed, aside from the aforementioned example regarding the issue of immigration, African Americans are mostly absent from *Home Killings* (2001), a trend that continues in subsequent Romilia mysteries. One exception is Darla, a Memphis-based police officer who appears briefly in *Minos* (2003). Darla helps Romilia track down a man named Blevins, who Romilia suspects of having sold Minos an attack dog used in one of his murders. Sizing up the two women, Blevins states: "Black and brown. The damn Rainbow Coalition" (106). Meant as a racist insult, Blevins's remarks nevertheless underscore the potential and need for such a minority coalition in the US South. Such a possibility, however, is quickly negated within the text by Romilia's subsequent actions. Ignoring protocol and Darla's calls to cease, Romilia employs excessive force with Blevins to make him talk. As a consequence, Darla breaks all ties with Romilia, professional or otherwise. The only other mention of Darla in the novel occurs as a minor reference to a newspaper article in which Darla is critical of Romilia.

Although the general lack of an African American presence in *Home Killings* (2001) can be attributed to McPeek Villatoro's engagement with the social reality of a racially segregated region and the racism that permeates it, this absence remains problematic. Rather than significantly contest and push back against racial asymmetries premised on white superiority, McPeek Villatoro's representation of a Central American–American identity formation by way of Murillo and Romilia seems to affirm them. Moreover, and as the fleeting and tenuous nature of Romilia and Darla's relationship in *Minos* (2003) suggests, little or no space is afforded within these novels for the possibility of coalition-building among African Americans and Latinos.

DETECTING THE UNSEEN: CENTRAL AMERICAN HISTORY AT THE MARGINS

Along with the ethnic and racial politics of the US South, Romilia's subject position as a Salvadoran American is also rooted in and contextualized by McPeek Villatoro's engagement with Central American history. Her inquiry into the past subsequently turns into an inquiry into her Salvadoran identity and background, thus underlining how a particular historical discourse informs and forces her to redefine her Latina identity. Moreover, given their differing Central American backgrounds and histories, Romilia and Murillo's charged antagonism also functions as an allegorical representation of the past. This multilayered focus on El Salvador's and Guatemala's hidden pasts of violence and struggle gives insight into the Central American immigrant experience, enacting a vital "unveiling" that is inherently tied to the assertion of a Central American social and cultural presence in the United States and an identity politics. This historical investigation, along with Romilia's performance of Salvadoranness, foments Central American visibility.

As with Latin American models that stress history as a central theme, in McPeek Villatoro's mysteries, Central America's legacy of civil war also becomes a subject of the investigation undertaken by Romilia, one that leads her deeper into her family's past and lacks a clear resolution (A. Simpson). Upon discovering that Murillo is a former Guatemalan *kaibil* (death squad operative), Romilia begins to suspect that Murillo may be responsible for Diego Sáenz's murder. She develops a working theory of a possible death squad operating in the Nashville area and sets out to learn all she can about the *kaibiles*. One unlikely source of information is her mother, Eva. Hearing Romilia question one of Murillo's henchmen regarding the word *kaibiles* triggers Eva to remember the murder of Romilia's grandparents, " . . . It was the weekend of the *Kaibil/Atlacatl* 'graduation' or whatever they call it . . . That's when it all happened . . ." (133).

Eva's account is punctuated by silences and ellipses, invoking her trauma and inability to voice the horrific acts perpetrated against civilians by the *kaibiles* and the *atlacatlas,* the Salvadoran equivalent of the Guatemalan military unit. Given her mother's "muttered scenes," Romilia must use her imagination to piece the rest together: "As I had never met my grandparents, I could only imagine an old couple whom I had seen in pictures, now dead underneath rubble and fire and the pile of other bodies strewn over a once active town" (133). Though incomplete, Eva's revelation nevertheless affords Romilia a broader understanding about her ancestors, and thereby her own identity as a Salvadoran American.

Following a leak to a local newspaper, Romilia's working theory of a death squad operating in Nashville becomes public knowledge. The article begins: "'Death squads' is not a term we Nashvillians are accustomed to using," and emphasizes the existence of death squads in "countries like El Salvador or Colombia, where drug cartels and oligarchies use such terrorist groups to keep the population in check" (178). Such an emphasis underscores the problematic manner in which Central America's history of war and violence has been and continues to be represented by the US media. Jean Franco's reflection on the "ethical vacuum in metropolitan societies" and the "tendency" of the metropolis "to regard the repressive regimes in Latin America [. . .] as purely local aberrations" is an apt description of how the newspaper account ideologically positions Nashville (and the United States) in contrast to El Salvador or Colombia (22); and by extension, Nashvillians in reference to Central American (and Latina/o) others. Although death squads and revolutionary struggle are not new occurrences for immigrants like Romilia's mother, they are for the majority of the Nashville public reading these accounts. Moreover, any reference to the role of the United States in helping to finance the Salvadoran and Guatemalan regimes that used death squads is noticeably absent from this report.[10] Only when the death squads threaten Nashvillians does this Central American social reality become credible. And even when it does, the "average citizen" can only conceive of it in a way that continues to privilege US experience over that of the so-called Third World and that affirms negative cultural stereotypes.

Implicit in this myopic portrayal of Central American history are the social and political mechanisms that have contributed to the systematic silencing of Central American immigrants. Romilia's immediate concern following the publication of the article is the possible backlash against Central Americans, "Shit, I thought. No Nashvillian was going to come out of this thinking highly of Central America or its people" (179). For Central American immigrants, this dynamic is linked to the political context that marked the first waves of mass emigration, mostly from El Salvador and Guatemala, to the United States during the 1980s. Because US foreign policy deemed El Salvador's and Guatemala's military regimes allies in the fight against communism, Salvadoran and Guatemalan immigrants fleeing persecution and war were systematically denied asylum (García 90). Being undocumented and stigmatized as "subversives" led many Salvadorans and Guatemalans to hide their personal histories of trauma, including from their children (Hamilton and Chinchilla 203). In the process, these personal experiences were also "erased" from public view. The testimonial of Romilia's mother unsettles the dominant version of Central American history constructed by the metropolis and projected in the newspaper article.

By "detecting" this history of Central American immigration, which adds to Romilia's knowledge of her family's legacy, Romilia gives voice and precedence to the experiences of civil conflict and flight that have been silenced in Central America and the United States. McPeek Villatoro's novel, then, works in tandem with Arias's claim surrounding the denial of self experienced by immigrants due to the violent oppression carried out by Central American military regimes against their own peoples and the institutionalization of discriminatory immigration policies in the United States. Romilia's recuperation of the past, however, also postulates an active response to these theories, as the barring of this past emphasizes and foments a more informed understanding of her Central American–American identity.

Ultimately, Romilia discovers that Diego Sáenz, and the other two victims of the so-called Pyramid Killer, were murdered by her partner Jerry. An addict, Jerry had been involved with Murillo's drug trafficking operation and had tried to frame Murillo by planting jade pyramids at all the crime scenes and encouraging Romilia's theory of the death squads. Following a violent confrontation with Jerry—during which Romilia saves Murillo's life and both she and Murillo are injured—Jerry kills himself. Murillo escapes, but leaves Romilia a parting gift: a love letter and engagement ring. This turn of events—as Romilia and Murillo's relationship also gives way to sexual attraction—sets the stage for future books and encounters between these two characters. If we posit Romilia and Murillo's relationship as an allegorical reiteration of the civil wars that ravaged El Salvador and Guatemala, however, this open ending acquires yet another meaning.

As her mother reveals, Romilia's family is a part of the civilian populations in Central America that were subjected to economic exploitation, violent repression, and familial disintegration at the hands of oligarchic governments and military forces. Murillo's class ties to the Guatemalan oligarchy and his militancy as a *kaibil* signal him as an active agent of those same oppressive government and military institutions. Romilia and Murillo thus evoke the "two sides" of Central American civil war history: the popular and armed struggle of the people vs. the oppression of the oligarchic State. And, while there is no reference to a "guerrilla" element, in many ways, Romilia acts as a similar countering force. Within the context of the United States, however, and unlike Romilia's family in El Salvador, Romilia is not completely powerless. Nor is Murillo above the law. As such, Romilia's continued pursuit and attempts to bring Murillo to justice for the "home killings" committed in the United States can also be seen as a means of ascertaining some form of symbolic justice for the "home killings" he, and individuals like him, committed in Central America. Moreover, it implies that this literal and symbolic quest for justice does not reside exclusively in the hands of Central American immigrants, but also with future US-born generations, as is the case with Romilia and Murillo. Consequently, not only does this interface between history and the detective genre facilitate the visibility of Central Americans, it also furthers the understanding of this process of ethnic individuation by expanding its parameters.

SLEUTHING BEYOND THE US SOUTH

Working by way of the detective genre, McPeek Villatoro's *Home Killings* (2001) not only speaks to the growing influence and presence of Latinos in the US South, but also engages in a specific process of Central American–American Latino identity formation. One of its more salient attributes is precisely this intersection of historical, ethnic, geographic, and with Romilia, gendered discourses. Through her performance of Salvadoranness and her inquest into Central American history, bringing her closer to Murillo, Romilia enacts a discernible process of Central American–American identity formation. As I have contended throughout this analysis, this particular rendering of Romilia as a Salvadoran American opens the possibility for a Central American–American politics of identity that, to recall Arias one last time, has not been feasible.

How these politics are being negotiated and shaped is still "in process," as Romilia's own trajectory suggests. As she moves outside of Nashville and undertakes new cases, cases that lead her to California, Romilia's Salvadoranness becomes infused by the presence of a significantly larger Central American population and border identity discourses. Her relationship with Murillo also deepens, giving way to the possibility of conciliatory ties between Central Americans, both victims of oppression and victimizers, as well as Murillo's redemption. Perhaps here is a claim to the necessary healing that must also play a part in this process of Central American–American identity formation. As in *Home Killings* (2001), Romilia's sleuthing in the US South and beyond reveals more than just clues. It complicates, but also initiates, new ways of thinking about Central American–American visibility, identity, and representation. Thus Central American immigrants living in the US South struggle to adapt to "American" culture; yet in the process they also forge and influence hybrid cultural formations and expressions, all giving way to a reconceptualization of this regional space as a "New Latino South" or a "New Nuevo South" (Mohl).

NOTES

This essay first appeared as "Sleuthing Central American Identity and History in the New Latino South: Marcos McPeek Villatoro's *Home Killings*" in *Latino Studies* 6:4 (December 2008): 376–397. Reprinted here with permission of Springer.

1. See Table 43 in the data set "Facts on U.S. Latinos, 2015: Statistical Portrait of Hispanics in the United States" (Flores et al.).

2. As Irons explains, this "new woman detective" alters the tough-guy formula and provides "a viable alternative to the cynical loner of another age" (xv). She seeks and finds support by way of a community and is capable of shedding light on gendered relations of power through her detecting (Irons xv). For further reading on the intersections of feminism and the hard-boiled genre, see Kathleen Gregory Klein's *The Woman Detective: Gender and Genre*, 2nd edition and *Sisters in Crime: Feminism and the Crime Novel* by Maureen T. Reddy.

3. In *A Venom Beneath the Skin* (2005), Romilia is recruited by the FBI and relocates with her family to California.

4. US Central American scholars have also begun to critically work through the alternate term "US Central American," a term that highlights, among other things, the diasporic and transnational dimensions of Central American communities in the United States and their embracing of a regional identification, one that unsettles nationalistic and US-based hyphenated identities (Alvarado, et.al.).

5. See, for example, *Multicultural Detective Fiction: Murder from the "Other" Side*, edited by Andrea Johnson Gosselin; *Sleuthing Ethnicity: The Detective in Multiethnic Crime Fiction*, edited by Dorthea Fischer-Hornung and Monika Mueller; and Stephen Knight's *Crime Fiction 1800–2000: Detection, Death, Diversity.*

6. Rodriguez provides a brief discussion of McPeek Villatoro's Romilia Chacón series, highlighting the ways in which his own discussion of Chicana/o detective fiction is applicable to other Latina/o narratives working within the same genre. Baker Sotelo makes a similar point, choosing also to include McPeek Villatoro's work and a brief historical synopsis of Central American Immigration in her selected list for further reading.

7. For a complementary, yet somewhat different view of "latinization" within the context of the US South, see Gustavo Pérez-Firmat's seminal work on Cuban Americans in Miami, *Life on the Hyphen: The Cuban-American Way.*

8. Stephanie Cole and Alison M. Parker's collection of essays, *Beyond Black and White: Race, Ethnicity, and Gender in the U.S. South and Southwest,* provides a vital intervention with regard to the defining characteristic of the US South as biracial, drawing attention to the historical presence of Latino communities such as that of Cubans and Mexicans.

9. According to Butt and Benjamin (130), *voseo* is generally considered an informal form in which the use of *vos* is akin to that of *tú* (you familiar). In addition to most of Central America, it is also used in parts of South America such as Uruguay, Paraguay, Colombia, Chile, Ecuador, and Venezuela, as well as in the southernmost regions of Mexico.

10. On this topic, see *The Battle for Guatemala: Rebels, Death Squads and U.S. Power,* by Susanne Jonas.

TAKING THE SOUTHERN BAIT

Law & Order: Special Victims Unit *and the Televisual South*

GINA CAISON

Detective Amanda Rollins (Kelli Giddish) joined the popular television series *Law & Order: Special Victims Unit* (1999–) during its thirteenth season as a character transferred from the Atlanta, Georgia, Police Department (APD) to the New York–based squad. Though the series had previously featured episodes that may have involved the US South during the course of an investigation, the appearance of Detective Rollins in the squad room marked the first time that the series staged a prolonged engagement with the region. Perhaps owing to Giddish's own background having grown up just outside Atlanta, the incorporation of Amanda Rollins's southern home comes across as more nuanced than previous attempts of the series to "go South." In this case, Rollins's southern accent is refreshingly subtle and believable, leaving the US South to function in ways beyond stereotypically forced drawls, lawless backwoods hicks, and country-mouse-goes-city rubes that typically populate many prime-time police procedurals. Despite this, Detective Rollins still brings southern baggage to her new home in New York. Over the course of her character arc we learn about her gambling addiction, troubled (and seemingly impoverished) family background, and history with sexual assault. However, the most striking recurring trope associated with Detective Rollins during the last five seasons is the police unit's strategic use of her as "bait" to catch spree criminals. This baiting of the southern character serves as a metaphor for the ways in which the US South functions in the televisual landscape, and it queries how viewers detect the southern inflections of the police procedural series, recognizing that the invocation of the US South lures them into narrative associations only to entrap their assumptions of the regionalized character. In this invocation of regional inflection *SVU* offers a "twinned" logic of regional representation, revealing not so much the differences in fictional "norths" and "souths" but the shared histories undergirding both spaces.

As a physically attractive, petite blonde woman, the use of Detective Rollins as bait calls upon historical narratives of southern white womanhood as an irresistible catalyst for the sexual desires of men. Furthermore, this narrative device has deeply racial inflections as the figure of the vulnerable white woman served historically as the manufactured reasoning to police the movements and actions of black men. While few to none of the criminals that Rollins attempts to lure with her physical body are African American, the narrative logic of such a device evokes questions of racial and regional policing. Yet time and again, Detective Rollins and *SVU* flip this logic on its head, luring criminals and viewers alike into assumptions of southern narrative markers only to place those same southern logics as deeply embedded within the northern city, all the while destabilizing Rollins's performance of distressed damsel or easy prey. In this way, the televisual South serves simultaneously as departure and homing device, evoking a myth of feminine vulnerability while undoing neatly bound conceptions of the region's racial and sexual politics.

Across the now five seasons that include Detective Rollins, audiences have come to recognize her as more than a southern belle in the northern city or even a hardened streetwise detective. Her character sits somewhat uneasily between these more familiar archetypes as she works through personal issues that follow her north. In terms of her background, we know that Rollins and her sister Kim grew up "troubled," raised by a gambling father and an alcoholic mother. While Rollins fulfills the role of the child who attempts to exert complete control as a reaction to a childhood of disarray, her sister has chosen the opposite path. Kim's appearance in Amanda's New York life causes chaos at different points in the series as Kim manages to steal *all* of her sister's possessions, snorts cocaine with strangers in Amanda's apartment, attempts to seduce her sister's fellow SVU squad member Nick Amaro (Danny Pino), orchestrates Amanda's shooting of Kim's abusive fiancé, and subsequently frames Amanda for premeditated murder of said fiancé to commit insurance fraud ("Friending Emily" & "Deadly Ambition"). If Amanda Rollins is the hardscrabble but progressive southern woman who can handle the big city on her own terms, then her sister Kim represents the underbelly of that image: a heavily drawled portrayal of down-and-out whiteness ready to lie, cheat, and steal to get what she wants via the performance of the distressed southern belle, playing blonde coquette to her sister's blonde ambition.

In addition to the havoc that her sister manages to wreak, Detective Rollins has her own problems due to her gambling addiction. While we learn by her own admission that she gambled on sports before moving to the city, she tells Captain Cragen (Dan Florek) early on in her NYPD tenure that the move to New York has exacerbated the problem because outside of work, she spends a lot of time alone ("Home Invasions"). This loneliness, while typical of many television detectives, reads differently when mapped onto a woman. As Maureen Reddy explains, "Unlike the male detectives, the solitariness of the female detectives is not presented as a badge of honour but as a condition dictated by prevailing gender conventions" ("Women Detectives" 198). This rings true for Rollins's character as her solitude appears to beget most of her problems. Even before her confession to the Captain, the audience sees hints of her gambling problem as Rollins appears especially attuned to any fact involving professional or collegiate athletes. Her SVU partner, Odafin Tutula (Ice-T), better known as Fin, offers a subtle recognition that Rollins seems to know *a lot* about sports, raising an eyebrow that suggests his surprise that a woman might be so familiar with so much athletic trivia ("Personal Fouls"). As Rollins's gambling debts mount and she is beat up by a bookie, she eventually reveals her problem first to Fin and later to the Captain. Despite her participation in Gamblers Anonymous, her addiction to sports betting remains an Achilles heel and coping mechanism across several seasons.

The other recurring background plot associated with Rollins—and one that repeatedly forces her to return to her gambling addiction—is the circumstance surrounding her desire to transfer from the APD to the NYPD. As revealed slowly over several episodes across her first few seasons, Rollins is the victim of sexual assault. When her APD colleagues visit New York for a conference about untested rape kits (directly resulting from a case that Amanda Rollins solves in the city), we learn that Rollins's attacker was her former Deputy Chief at APD. After Atlanta Deputy Chief Patton (Harry Hamlin) assaults another blonde APD detective who happens to be on the trip with him, viewers learn that Rollins left Atlanta after her reputation was ruined in Atlanta as the APD rumor mill rendered her rape by the Deputy Captain as a consensual affair in which Rollins attempted to "sleep her way to the top." After finally confronting her attacker and exposing the "good ol' boys" network that attempted to ruin her career in Atlanta, Rollins begins to reconstruct her life in earnest ("Forgiving Rollins"). The series, then, attempts to give dimension to Rollins as more than either a victim or detective of sexual assault; nonetheless, it leaves her character on an uneasy perch between distressed southern belle and hardened detective.

However, the recurring problems of her family and her gambling addiction continue to crop up as she faces different challenges. As a character, audiences recognize that she is somewhat unreliable, often attempting to go rogue to catch the "bad guys." On the whole, however, she remains as feminist as the other woman leads on the show: challenging misogynistic and masculine attitudes towards women; refusing to rhetorically revictimize women in her investigations; insisting on the recognition of women's agency within the police system; and even choosing to raise her daughter alone after an unplanned pregnancy with the recurring character Detective Declan Murphey (Donal Logue), whose continual undercover assignments with the FBI keep him away for long stints of time ("Community Policing"). Detective Rollins is flawed, but she remains steadfast in her feminist views. In a generous reading, we might consider her as a relatively progressive portrayal of a white southern woman in the larger network televisual universe despite her occasional statements to the rest of the squad that they live "in a bubble" when they criticize the rhetoric of a thinly veiled Ann Coulter–style character who is assaulted at a conservative rally, reminding them that a lot of people in the country may actually agree with the political pundit's disturbing rhetoric ("Info Wars").

However, Rollins's role as southerner is complicated by not only the somewhat-predictable backstories that follow her from Atlanta but also the ways in which her presence in a New York City–based procedural calls upon television audiences' associations with the US South. These associations remain informed by what Deborah E. Barker and Kathryn McKee term the "southern imaginary," which "is constitutive of American cinema and of the ways in which the makers of movies [. . .] have imagined the 'South' both to construct and unsettle national narratives" (1). This constructing and unsettling speaks to how Rollins's presence challenges popular notions of the region while undergirding the claims on reality of those same notions.

While one might challenge the idea that the US South intervenes at all in the New York SVU squad room, for Barker and McKee, "[t]he southern imaginary (and the cultural work it performs) is not contained by the boundaries of geography and genre" (2). It is not simply that the producers, directors, or even Giddish herself overtly perform or construct an oppositional southernness via the character of Detective Amanda Rollins, but that the very presence of the alternate regional backdrop in the otherwise homogeneously urban New York City landscape demonstrates how the southern imaginary is "an amorphous and sometimes conflicting collection of images, ideas, attitudes, practices, linguistic accents, histories, and fantasies about a shifting geographic region and time" (2).

Within this NYC landscape of the southern imaginary, SVU depicts the strong-willed southern woman detective playing victim to bait her target, and in these contradictory moments, we see the narrative friction of a televisual South. This friction permeates the television landscape of the US South. As my previous work with Lisa Hinrichsen and Stephanie Rountree argues:

Even as the content or the characters change, the televisual South remains recognizable through certain 'authenticity' markers. The representations of individual identity may seem more diverse, but certain myths of the region remain. Pastoral fantasies of rural life, family, and hospitality bump up against the equally constructed myths of hot-headedness, abjection, and cronyism. While the televisual South can accommodate changes in the region's racial, ethnic, and gender diversity, the region remains coded through the stories that television tells. It is this familiar otherness of the region that allows for its continued welcome presence in many peoples' homes. (9)

As a character, Rollins figuratively and literally challenges the preconceived notions of good ol' boy cronysim and "white trash" abjection. She fights these forces both in her subtle maneuvers (rolling her eyes as her partner Fin makes a joke about backward southerners) and in larger narrative gestures: refusing the sexual advances of her old Atlanta partner and eventually sending her former Deputy Chief to prison for rape and her scheming sister to prison for fraud and manslaughter. Repeatedly, Rollins fights the good fight for southern respectability on what many viewers might recognize as progressive, even liberal, terms. She refuses to be pulled under by the seemingly dark forces that follow her from the South. Despite her success in banishing her southern demons, however, the fact remains that Rollins's demons remain distinctly *southern* ones. Just when the narrative order of the *SVU* universe seems to present audiences with a progressive southern character, it establishes her legitimacy as a tough woman detective not because she's able to defeat the criminals of the urban North, which she repeatedly does with ease, but because she's able to win the battles against the southern narratives and stereotypical characters that prop up her backstory. Such a tension is indicative of how "the televisual can potentially resist the nostalgic and conservative impetus behind much southern tale-telling in presenting its version of the South," and simultaneously "[traffic] in fantasies of elsewheres that while seemingly eschewing southern authenticity markers reify the region through familiar tropes" (Hinrichsen, et. al. 17). Simply put, as a southern character, Detective Rollins baits audiences' desires for a progressive US South, using the very retrograde narratives such a desire hopes to escape.

Detective Rollins's presence in New York also reveals the ways in which the southern imaginary and the televisual South can illuminate the deep connections between what some might otherwise conceive of as discrete urban and regional spaces. As Barker and McKee argue, recent work in southern studies demonstrates "a critical recognition of the US South as fully implicated in the process of national self-creation" (3). Furthermore, when zooming in on the specifically small-screen iterations of this phenomenon, Hinrichsen, Rountree, and I offer that "southern studies illuminate the deeply invested narratives of place that both regional and national viewers bring to their televisual engagement" (6). What's perhaps most striking about *Law & Order: SVU,* as well as many other television franchises set in New York City, is how the quite exceptionally urban landscape frequently seems to stand in for the entire nation. While the *Law & Order* franchise has long offered a "ripped from the headlines" approach, amalgamating real cases (such as *Florida v. Casey Anthony* into the season 10 episode, "Selfish") from across the United States, these stories are always rendered as exceptionally New York, with subway scenes, taxicab intrigue, immigrant neighborhoods, limo drivers, fancy restaurants, hot dog carts, and bustling sidewalks—to name but a few. Indeed, most Americans live in cities, but New York City is hardly "Anywhere, U.S.A." Despite this landscape of urban ubiquity, rarely does the space of the city intrude as regionally codified space, and indeed, the franchise's regional iterations (*Law & Order: LA* and *Law & Order: Miami*) did not meet with much success.

Instead, the universe of *SVU*'s New York stands as near-neutral backdrop. This fact changes notably when "outsiders" such as Rollins intervene into the narrative universe of the show. In many cases, whether with a reality-television religious family from upstate New York (modeled on the Dugger Family) or with Detective Amaro's Cuban father from Miami, the dynamics of the New York universe shift only when regional "others" appear in the city ("Patrimonial Burden" & "Padre Sandunguero"). Rollins's prolonged presence as a regular cast member calls regional difference into view in a more sustained way, challenging audiences to think about the connections between the southern and northern urban landscapes. Her presence renders visible the connections between the region and the nation. No longer left to represent "everywhere," with the appearance of Rollins the New York City of *SVU* becomes regionally inflected.

This insertion of the regional is complicated by the way that Rollins's physical body also intervenes on the series' narrative. The use of the regionally inflected character Rollins as bait calls up the numerous narratives of the southern rape complex in which the imagined threat of sexual violence to southern white women by black men undergirds racist Jim Crow legal restrictions and mob violence against black citizens. First coined by W. J. Cash in his 1941 *The Mind of South,* the rape complex he describes is buttressed by the cult of southern womanhood. It not only assumes the fragility of white southern womanhood in the face of danger, but it also imagines a consummate danger to the US South itself as personified by the southern belle.

However, as Barker explains in *Reconstructing Violence: The Southern Rape Complex in Film and Literature* (2015):

> Cash's description of the southern rape complex, though not historically accurate, has played a vital role in defining and perpetuating what historian Diane Miller Sommerville refers to as the "invented tradition" of racial and gender violence imaginatively localized in the South, which still impacts American culture (*Rape and Race* 4). (7)

Cash's analysis is indeed reductive, but as Barker argues, the assumptions inherent in his descriptions continue to work in the narrative logic of film and television. This narrative work creates a set of media objects that imagine the southern woman as such a likely victim of sexual violence that the repeated use of her body as "bait" seems logical enough to use over and over in a single procedural series. Significantly, *SVU* moves this logic to the urban North, demonstrating how the US South as locality is not so much exceptional as indicative of the nation's investment in the myth of blonde white women as being especially desirable and therefore extraordinarily vulnerable to unwanted sexual contact.

Across the last five seasons featuring her character, Rollins uses herself as bait on so many occasions, that it is almost comical to count. In varying instances, she jogs in the park to attract serial rapists, pretends to be a party-girl willing to sell out her niece (another undercover detective) to a child pornographer, and plants herself as a drunken, celebrity-obsessed groupie to catch an actor who takes advantage of fans ("Educated Guess," "Collateral Damages," and "Star-Struck Victims"). These are among only some of the ways that Rollins puts her own body on the line to catch criminals. During a sting to arrest johns soliciting underage prostitutes, Fin and Rollins watch from a surveillance van as an undercover officer poses as a sex worker in a hotel room as solicitors arrive. When Fin asks Rollins how the young officer is holding up, Rollins confirms that she is doing a great job and offers as an aside that working as bait "was how she got her badge" ("Spiraling Down"). In other words, despite the fact that she has a degree in forensic science and that she is the most technologically savvy of all the SVU squad members, Rollins's physical body has long been used in Atlanta and in New York as the most desirable feature for her own advancement. As Reddy explains regarding women detectives in fiction:

> Perhaps most important is the social demand that women, to be interesting, must be desirable to men, hence young, beautiful, and marriageable. With men the presumed audience of most detective fiction, and with detective fiction, like other forms of popular culture, likely to encode the prejudices and fantasies of its target audience, the female detectives' youth, beauty, and interest in men (signaled by their desire to marry) all make complete sense. ("Women Detectives" 194)

I extend this assertion from Reddy to understand how, more than simply an appeal to men through generic "beauty," Rollins's regionally inflected womanhood might contribute to how audiences are led to understand her character.[1] Therefore, when considering Rollins as a detective, it remains important to consider her regional background as well as her physical presence as a blonde, white southern woman in the landscape of the urban North where her success in catching criminals results from her certain physical irresistibility to rapists.

Notably however, Rollins is rarely—if ever—used as bait to catch an African American suspect. Black masculinity poses no threat to her body in these situations.[2] Indeed, in some episodes of the show, there are sexual criminals who are black and in at least one story arc, there is a young black man who the audience knows rapes a young white woman. However, these moments are somewhat exceptional in the procedural world of the series, and when interracial sexual violence does occur, racial stereotypes and assumptions tend to serve as the theme of the episode. Although it does so in almost uniformly reductive terms, *SVU* attempts to nuance myths of sexual violence along the lines of race, gender, age, and class. Frequently, however, the series bumps up against its own ideological ceiling. As a network procedural, with now famously franchise-specific "twists," the show debunks some popular stereotypes while letting stand an otherwise pervasive belief in "solvable" crimes investigated by a flawed but predominantly dignified, thorough, and ethical law enforcement. It seems likely that the show avoids the optics of threatening black men and vulnerable white women because it recognizes such constructions as offensive and clichéd. In some cases, *SVU* sends up the myth of the black rapist by having white women initially accuse nameless "black men" or specific black individuals of crimes and then depicts how the squad recognizes the racism in these instances and subsequently proves how the victim is lying to protect some other secret ("Valentine's Day" and "Great Expectations"). The series, then, eschews and even critiques the myth of the black rapist while keeping the myth of the desired and vulnerable southern white woman intact.

In one sense we might read this as an example of Tara McPherson's lenticular logic, where racial representations work within an optical illusion that keeps interconnected racial histories separate by representing them as narratively and visually removed from one another.[3] While McPherson correctly identifies this schema of representation across many media objects, it fails to account for the overall universe of *SVU*. The show seems aware of its racial representations. Without a doubt, there are many, many problems with the reductive way that crime procedurals including *SVU* depict the racial logics of criminal activity and law enforcement. However, over the last eighteen years, the franchise has seemingly become more and more progressive in its depiction of race and ethnicity. Fewer criminals seem to be minorities, and one of the key twists usually involves the fact that the presumed criminal who is racially profiled is not guilty and that the true perpetuator is a white man. Again, however, this is where the show hits what I refer to earlier as its ideological ceiling. Such twists only work if the audience already understands and accepts, even if tacitly, the logic of racial profiling. The show doesn't so much participate in a lenticular logic as it uses the audience's expectations of lenticular representations to achieve its own narrative fantasies where law enforcement undoes racism via "good" police work. The satisfaction inherent in this narrative resolution comes when viewers, however briefly, see the lenticular break down and a complete image snap into place. In many cases, these moments come in fleetingly near the close of the episode, which heightens the narrative satisfaction of catching a quick glimpse of the "entire" or "both sides" of the picture.

More complicated, however, than the way that the show evokes and challenges narratives of black and white identity, is the way that it creates tensions between concepts of the US North and South. Buttressed by the narrative assumptions surrounding Rollins as a southern white woman, the series evokes a South that not only intercedes on the North but also serves in some ways as its narrative twin. In other words, it's not just that Rollins's character earned her detective's badge in Atlanta working to entrap rapists, but that her body functions in the exact same way once she is in New York. Geography fails to undo narrative, and the regions are coded not so much different as relational parts of how audiences might understand each space. For example, in the fourth episode of the thirteenth season, which is the first that features Rollins as the central detective, the relationship between Atlanta and New York emerges as a key narrative impetus. Significantly, this is the first episode of the series in which Rollins is used as bait. The episode titled "Double Strands" opens with a young blonde white ballerina practicing while an unknown person snaps photos of her from a distance. After leaving post-rehearsal drinks with friends, she is followed by a man down a dark street. He attempts to gain her attention by saying in a slight southern accent, "Excuse me! Oh life is not that bad, give her a smile. You look so much purttier when you smile, Danielle." Then he attacks her with a knife and during the assault, he commands her, "Look at me. Look at my face." This opening sequence is somewhat odd for the *Law & Order* franchise because viewers see the person commit the crime, establishing the audience's visual recognition of the criminal before the detectives do. Whereas audiences normally learn a case's details with the investigating officers, in this instance they seemingly know more than the detectives, undoing the characteristic "twists" of the series and mitigating the potential for a surprise ending. This opening sequence gives viewers the point-of-view of the assailant, the victim, and an omniscient camera, creating a narrative dynamic where the audience seems privy to all parts of the story ahead of the opening credits. Notably, one of the things that the audience knows is that this attacker has a distinct southern accent, which marks him as an outsider to his New York landscape.

After Detectives Olivia Benson (Mariska Hargitay) and Rollins respond to the crime, the woman tells them that the attacker had a "tai-chi thing" tattoo, "half white, half black," and that he also commanded that she say, "tell me you love me, Mommy." This revelation piques Rollins's interest, and she begins questioning the victim alongside Benson. Detective Benson then pulls Rollins aside and says, "I don't know how you do things down South but here in New York we think it's best that one person does the intake so as to not overwhelm the victim." Rollins then informs her that the MO of this attacker matches a serial rapist that she had been tracking in Atlanta: a man with a yin-yang tattoo who used the same language while assaulting his victims. While Detective Benson remains skeptical, audiences are inclined to believe Rollins because they have heard this assailant's voice; they know he is from the US South. Benson remains incredulous, as does the rest of the squad back at the station when Rollins details the similarities between the "Atlantic Coast rapist" and this unknown suspect until Fin asks them, "You wanna hear her out, fellows?" But as Detective Munch (Richard Belzer) points out, "This guy has never been north of Charm City. He jumps the Mason-Dixon?" Captain Cragen asks if Rollins thinks the perpetrator has followed her, specifically, to New York, to which Rollins explains that goes against the pattern, implying that his move is a coincidence ("Double Strands"). The suspect's geography accounts for the squad's initial doubt, and this detail might strike some as odd. Given that the squad frequently engages with serial criminals who appear in New York or apprehends any number of non–New

Yorkers who commit a crime while in the city, their dismissal of a suspect from below the Mason-Dixon Line appears almost comical. It seems that they believe that the Mason-Dixon serves as a veritable wall, insulating their northern world from its southern counterpart.

After releasing a sketch of the rapist, the detectives field phone calls from a tip line, and eventually they locate a man who looks exactly like the sketch down to the tattoo. Moreover, he looks exactly like the man the audience recognizes from the opening sequence, and he has a subtle southern accent. Because law enforcement previously had his DNA from the first four rapes, they are able to quickly link this suspect named Gabrielle Thomas (T. R. Knight) to the crimes. It seems like an open-and-shut case, but Detective Amaro has reservations about Thomas because his "affect" is all wrong and because he willingly offers so much information. Notably there is an "unresolved fingerprint" from a screwdriver used in one of the early attacks. Thomas attempts suicide in his cell due to his complete confusion and dismay that his DNA has linked him to these crimes. Following this, Thomas is hospitalized and Amaro and Benson learn from his wife that she and Thomas were out of town when at least one of the rapes was committed. This incredibly timely reveal of information leads them to review their investigation, allowing them to discover that unbeknownst to him, Thomas has a twin brother who might very well be the culprit of the crimes.

Over Rollins's irritation at having her squad members undermine her first successful investigation, Amaro and Benson follow the lead of the possible twin attacker. They find out that Thomas and his twin brother were adopted into different families. While Thomas grew up in a good family with supportive parents, the adoption agency placed his twin brother Brian Smith (also played by T. R. Knight) in an abusive household. While both brothers have somewhat regionally inflected accents, Thomas's is less pronounced, perhaps indicating his "respectable" middle-class background over Smith's emotionally impoverished environment, offering up a clear lesson in "nurture over nature." The detectives also discover that Smith's adoptive mother killed his adoptive father in front of him. Furthermore, Smith had sought out his biological mother, who expressed to him her complete disinterest in reconnecting with her children though she does say that she told Smith about his twin brother. Thomas, however, tells the detectives that as far as he knew, he was an only child. Smith shares a yin-yang tattoo with his brother, and his crime spree geography perfectly matches his brother's career moves as a pharmaceutical salesperson. Tellingly, though, several victims also report that the attacker had noticeably chipped teeth and a long abdominal scar, which Thomas does not have. Despite the detectives' certainty that Brian Smith is indeed the rapist, and that he has followed his brother for years, committing assaults and leaving DNA behind because he knew he could frame his unknowing twin brother, District Attorney Casey Novak (Diane Neal) reminds them that having two suspects with such similar circumstantial evidence (not to mention the same DNA) is "the definition of reasonable doubt." It seems certain, then, that Brian Smith has completed the perfect revenge against his privileged brother. The SVU squad, though, will not be outdone so easily. In discussing the twin conundrum with the D.A., Rollins proposes, "We set a trap. He does like blondes." Together, the squad and the D.A. devise a plan to announce the release of Thomas although they will continue to hold him in their unit. Notably, they do not inform Thomas or his wife about his twin brother or the unusual circumstances of his "non-release." Meanwhile, Rollins plans to run through the park where they know Smith works as a trash collector. After four days of staged running with the squad monitoring Rollins and Smith, he finally attempts to attack Rollins, and the detectives catch their real rapist ("Double Strands").

Significantly, the idea to use herself as bait seems to be Rollins's idea. She's willing to put her own body on the line to catch the evil twin, recognizing her desirability as a blonde as a certain lure for this criminal. In a way, we might say that Rollins catches her bad guy twice. The first apprehension, which relied on DNA and forensic science, proved unsuccessful given that the suspect was not the criminal. The second time, however, Rollins uses her physical body to ensnare the real culprit, and this arrest solves the case. Within this narrative, it seems that science proves impotent compared to more embodied policing. DNA cannot distinguish the twins; only a detective can render the truth about good and evil. Furthermore, it is important to note that this baiting occurs almost exclusively with the show's women detectives. In virtually no cases (with an interesting exception of Fin and Amaro pretending in one episode to be a couple to stake out a gay bar) are men detectives asked or expected to use their physical bodies to lure sexual assaulters. And even beyond this, Rollins, the blonde southern woman, is used as bait far more frequently than the long-term franchise hero Olivia Benson, a brunette New Yorker. But it remains crucial to recognize that as in many subsequent cases, it's Rollins's suggestion or decision to use her own physical body. I do not emphasize this fact to suggest that such a move represents her agency, far from it. Rather, I argue that this bodily self-sacrifice of Rollins abides by the terms in which audiences—and perhaps even the character—understand southern white womanhood as sacred symbol, sacrificial lamb, and certain seduction. The character, then, must use her "best" asset—not her degrees, brains, toughness, or savvy, but her body—to cement her place at her New York City job.

The fact that this first occurrence with baiting comes in an episode called "Double Strands" that features the main narrative point of good and evil twins calls up the ways in which the US North and South serve as twinned landscapes of racial and gender oppression, class divides, and violence.[4] This model challenges the ways the US South has been more commonly represented as a site of quarantined national issues. As Leigh Anne Duck explains, "[W]hen national discourse has acknowledged the conflict between southern conservatism and national democracy, it has typically been done so in ways that localize this conflict—a 'backward South' and a modern or 'enlightened nation'" (*Nation's* 3). This model of representation has played out repeatedly in television productions that feature the US South. For example, Matt Dischinger argues regarding *The Walking Dead* that the small-screen South works by "offering a space in which national anxieties about southern exceptionalism can be quarantined without the risk of national infection" (260–61). While in some ways it's tempting to see the series as quarantining a particular type of cronyism and abjection to the US South, the reality is that the these same types of violences and networks often appear in the New York of the series. They are, for lack of a better term, double strands of the nation's DNA, each participating in racial and gender violence that cannot be confined either to the North or the South, the rural or the urban. The SVU squad's initial incredulity of the southern rapist coming north underscores the sense of national quarantine where some violence exists within geographical limits. The corresponding metaphor of the twin brothers heightens the stakes of the detectives' faulty logic. There are no borders to national violence, and yet the imagined southern rape complex, which depends upon the myth of white womanhood, works all the same in the North.

Even in the center of New York City, Rollins's southern body works to catch rapists who might find her irresistible. Once they catch the evil twin Rollins pleads with her captain to allow her to conduct the interrogation. While both the captain and district attorney object, the suspect Brian Smith claims that he will only speak to Rollins. After she enters the interrogation room, she enhances her southern accent, and tells him, "You know, I've actually been wanting to talk to you for a long time. I'm a southern girl. I worked sex crimes in Atlanta. I'm actually the one who named you. I always thought I was your type," to which he responds in his drawl, "Down to a tee." Her rendering of herself as a "southern girl," rather than the tough and sophisticated detective that she is, suggests her strategy of diminishing herself to appeal to Smith, who seems flattered by the attention. Rollins's use of strategic essentialism to gain his trust, and therefore a confession, reveals the ways in which the use of her body as bait has been about southern femininity all along. Even in the interrogation phase as she recounts Smith's deeds as the "Atlantic Coast rapist," Rollins is still a body, an accent, and a myth of white southern womanhood.

Whereas audiences will come to know Rollins's own southern demons, this first episode featuring her character as the central detective initializes a complicated relationship between *SVU*'s first prolonged consideration of the US North and South. The yin-yang tattoo that the twins share (presumably acquired by the evil twin to help frame his brother) offers a thinly cloaked symbol representing opposed forces, dark and light, and the necessary balance of life. To be clear, the good twin Thomas has also lived much of his life in the US South. He is not simply a northern creation, but his respectability and class allows for his easier fit into his new city landscape. Whereas his brother represents a white southern abjection, Thomas's education and upbringing allow him to move through the world, from North to South and back again, without any trouble. The conclusions that the audience should draw from this twinned symbolism, however, are murky. On the one hand, the evil twin fantasy suggests that there really is a dark, and presumably southern, underbelly to liberal ideas of the North. The evil is real and identifiable, and the good twin can continue to live in freedom now that the dark twin has been caught and imprisoned—all of which indicates that the nation *can* quarantine and excise its worst violence to the South. On the other hand, this plot suggests that the liberal fantasy of good is just that—a fantasy, revealing that the good is not so much exceptional but of the same genetic material as the whole. In this case, good and bad are conditional and cannot be separated, paired from inception and joined for life. The central and lingering question of the episode is how one should understand the two parts of the whole: are they indeed separate or does their shared DNA make them a balanced, inseparable whole?

In either case, there are assumptions necessary on behalf of the audience. The New York city appearance of the southern "Atlantic Coast rapist," who is both linked and not linked to Rollins, pulls the audience into a narrative where they accept two premises: one, that Rollins's physical body is a convincing lure for would-be villains, and two, that there is a good, which must have a corresponding evil. Ultimately, both of these premises rest on the assumptions inherent in detective shows that the smart detective can parse the world's good and evil forces and excise the bad with precision. As John Scaggs explains, "the procedural is as much a part of the ideological state apparatus of control as the thin blue line of the police force is" (86). When *SVU* joins the thin-blue and Mason-Dixon line assumptions, the audience—even if subtly so—must accept some narrative baggage that the two ideas call upon. In other words, they must both see the idea of evil as previously quarantined to the US South, and they must acknowledge that this evil can permeate the borders of the US North. In the specific case of Rollins, the audience must see her southernness as both liability and asset. She has escaped the backward South, proving herself exceptional, only to put her own body on the line to eradicate the darkness that has presumably followed her from home. Simply put, she must reengage the southern narrative of white womanhood as vulnerable to sexual violence in order to save the rest of the country from that same logic.

When considering the number of narrative tropes that the audience must accept regarding southernness, it may be that *SVU* baits not so much its criminal as its audience. The premise and pleasure of the series often emerge from the foundational myths of southern white womanhood and its ever-so-sly critique of these tropes. Of course, the series sends up all of these stereotypes, and it also takes them down, but in the end we could easily say that Rollins reifies what national audiences already know about the South. Simply put, the show has all the flaws of almost all representational moments of southern characters on television. This is the point in the chapter when I could easily reach the narrative volte and attempt to argue that Rollins *is* slyly subversive, that her character *actually* upends these tropes, makes better use of them, challenges audiences on their ideas of the southern woman and the southern detective. Instead, however, I'd like to do away with both of these rhetorical moves. I imagine everyone reading this chapter knows very well that the popular representations of the US South, particularly on network television, often fall somewhere on the spectrum of ridiculous to offensive. And we all know the academic move of saying something is *actually something else*—that our object of analysis forwards a progressive vision in a "sly" way. Surely there's a next step to pointing out the faulty televisual representations, and it isn't necessarily the one that leads to recovering the meaning of everything as something that challenges, reforms, or subverts stereotypes. How might work in television studies help us to think beyond the good/ bad dichotomy of representational practices? How do we, as television audiences and critics, stop taking the southern bait? Moreover, how do we, as southern studies scholars, do the same?

Rather than simply rehearsing the academic moves of pointing out the enforcement or subversion of stereotypes, archetypes, myths, and tropes (which at its base is a fancy way of saying either "I like this object" or "I do not like this object"), I propose that we interrogate our own enjoyment of both formulations. I also argue that we interrogate how these formulas do work for the national imagination in their truest forms and in their attempts at subversion because both insist that we accept the foundational myths in the first place. In other words, they are twinned arguments that may reveal little way forward for television or southern studies. They bait critics and audiences into structuralist arguments that frequently leave assumptions about racial and gender violence intact. This is what Hinrichsen, Rountree, and I argue about the small-screen South, and such an argument can just as easily apply across television studies. The US South of the televisual landscape can appear in almost any assemblage of races, genders, classes, or sexualities. Likewise, Nickianne Moody asserts of televisual crime shows:

> The depiction of crime in film and on television [. . .] has also registered cultural mood and changing values associated particularly with class, race, and gender. In order to accommodate these ideas and interests screen crime has needed to be extremely flexible, moving swiftly between mystery or adventure archetypes and the moral or intellectual concerns of genre outside the strictly detective formula. (242)

I am, however, unsure that when considering the intersection of the US South and crime fiction that the televisual form has proven so flexible. Without a doubt the content markers offer a remarkable fluidity, accounting for difference with increasingly astonishing ease. However, just when that content pushes against the container of its form, the image snaps back into place, limited by its containment in the old-fashioned box or newfangled flat screen. Perhaps this is because at its base, television always sells something. In terms of the US South, television does not sell the region's content, television sells its form—its place as the site of national quarantine. The same might be said for the detective story. When critics think that each reveals a window through which something is revealed, they might just as easily be looking into a mirror. As Reddy explains regarding crime fiction in general:

> The situation is one in which white bonding, accomplished between text and reader, continues to be an important albeit generally unacknowledged pleasure of reading genre fiction, perhaps especially crime fiction. That pleasure needs to be disrupted, with disruption a fundamental responsibility of antiracist critics. (*Traces* 190)

In addition to understanding this pleasure, I argue that more self-reflection (without the attendant navel-gazing) on the part of critics might push us past or own clichéd criticism or endorsement of subversion narratives.

Notably, in the last image from "Double Strands," the squad reveals to Gabrielle Thomas his evil twin brother Brian Smith. They release Thomas from his holding cell and take him to the two-way mirror looking into the interrogation room where his brother is held. He looks into the room mystified, and asks, "Who is that?" to which Detective Benson responds, "That's your twin brother." Thomas stutters, "I didn't know that," to which Detective Amaro responds, "He did." Thomas stares as Smith gets up from his chair and wanders aimlessly over to the opposite side of the mirror. The two brothers then become a single image, framed side-by-side with Thomas staring at his twin while Smith seemingly gazes back at himself. The scene closes the episode with a visual paradox of sorts. The good and bad have reconciled, revealed as of the same origin, and yet the evil is quarantined while the good takes on the scopic pleasure of looking in and examining his twin from behind the safety of the glass. The good and evil are one and yet the intervention of Rollins's physical body has allowed for their separation. As the bad twin, Smith has long known his relationship to his supposedly good counterpart while Thomas has lived his life in ignorance of the evil stalking him and committing violence in his image and genetics.

In the case of Rollins, one has to wonder about how and why the investment of vulnerable white womanhood remains such a powerful trope even in the figure of the strong woman detective. In either case, the structural myth of security remains. Rollins's body creates the need for policing even while she is literally the police. She needs and provides security: physically and metaphorically. This formulation ultimately provides narrative security for the audience. The sexually vulnerable white woman is such a powerful trope that it finds traction even when stripped of its attendant regional, historical, or racial assumptions. It works within the North and within the channels of national broadcasting because, ultimately, this is not simply a southern story. The myths of white womanhood, though long associated with iconoclastic, if apocryphal, images of the Confederate South, buttress the mythos of the entire nation. While SVU can attempt to nuance its content around race, class, age, sexuality, and region, it depends upon the forms that produced these troubling narrative tropes in the first place. When these narratives are written in order to float free from—or even revise—their historical associations, it is easy to miss the structures that they do maintain and the assumptions they bait audiences into making. Furthermore, Rollins's success in the North using these old southern strategies demonstrates that these narratives are in fact bound to no geographical home. Though the fingerprints they leave behind may differ, northern and southern narratives of race, gender, and the police reveal the perpetually doubled strands of the nation's own DNA.

NOTES

1. Additionally, though reliable gender breakdowns of viewer demographics can be difficult to obtain, there is a larger cultural sense that women constitute the primary audience for *SVU*, suggesting that something is at work aside from simply an appeal to men who vie for Rollins's physical attractiveness. See, for example, Sadie Gennis, "7 Reasons Why Women Love *Law & Order: SVU* So Much," and Alex Hughes, "'Law & Order: SVU' Is an Alternative Reality Where Assault Survivors Are Taken Seriously."

2. It bears mentioning that the character of Rollins has a complex, yet under-discussed, relationship with black masculinity as represented in the character Fin played by Ice-T. Fin is frequently seen as Rollins's closest ally, yet their relationship rarely—if ever—has sexual overtones, despite the fact that Rollins has sexual relationships with her other coworkers including Amaro and Dominick Carisi Jr. The relationship between Fin and Rollins and the racial politics it suggests in the *SVU* universe deserves its own extended analysis.

3. See Tara McPherson's *Reconstructing Dixie: Race, Gender, and Nostalgia in the Imagined South*.

4. Interestingly, although perhaps coincidently, this entire "twin" plot combined with the prodigiously appearing fingerprint that solves the case is incredibly reminiscent of Mark Twain's plot and theme from his conjoined novels *The Tragedy of Puddn'head Wilson and Those Extraordinary Twins*. In particular, *Puddn'head Wilson* features a detective story and an extended courtroom scene.

PART IV

JOURNALISTS DETECTING THE SOUTH

THE TRUTH SLEUTH

The Detective Journalism of William Bradford Huie and Thulani Davis's Everybody's Ruby

RICHÉ RICHARDSON

> For my activity in the Ruby McCollum case I have been convicted of
> "criminal contempt" of the courts of the state of Florida, and, as I write
> this, an effort is being made to force me back into the Suwannee County
> jail. In such a position no author can be sure of the extent of his legal
> risk. Moreover, Ruby McCollum must yet stand trial for her life; and
> subsidiary issues may not be settled for years.
> —William Bradford Huie, from *Ruby McCollum: Woman in
> the Suwannee Jail*

Born in Hartselle, Alabama, in 1910, prolific Alabama novelist William Bradford Huie started his career as a journalist and became known for his cou-
rageous and provocative engagement of civil rights cases. Huie's work as a journalist, best-selling author of several novels adapted into films, and controversial
investigative work as a civil rights activist made him one of the most persistent
and tireless cultural workers of the twentieth century. In a sense, in his practice
as a journalist, Huie very much operated and investigated as a de facto detective. Huie often described himself as a man who was "in the truth business." He
stopped at nothing to get at the truth. He first gained prominence after he paid
the assailants of fourteen-year-old Emmett Till—Roy Bryant and J. W. Milam—
$4,000 for their confession to the horrific murder and published it in *Look* Mag-
azine in 1956, in keeping with his strategy of "checkbook journalism." Huie's
1968 book *Three Lives for Mississippi* examined the tragic losses of Michael
Schwerner, James Cheney, and Andrew Goodman who, an extensive investigation by the FBI revealed, were murdered in 1965 by the Ku Klux Klan in Phila-
delphia, Mississippi, during Freedom Summer in 1964. Huie's 1970 book, *He
Slew the Dreamer: My Search for the Truth about James Earl Ray and the Murder
of Martin Luther King*, examines whether Ray really murdered Dr. King. Huie's
1967 novel, *The Klansman*, and the 1974 film based on it examine connections
between D. W. Griffith's 1915 film, *Birth of a Nation*, and the related 1905 novel,

The Clansman, by Thomas Dixon, to ponder their continuing and ongoing impact during the civil rights era. That we are now fifty years beyond the publication of this bold novel is just one reason that it seems important to reflect on the continuing significance of his legacy.

While investigative work in journalism and detective work can share strategies, their uses frequently differ. The work of investigative journalism is typically designed to inform, while detective work typically centers on uncovering information related to criminal cases. Because the cases in which Huie frequently got involved were also related to trials that were criminal in nature, he in effect blurred these lines in his practice as a journalist. In effect, he wore his detective hat in researching the Till case—and in investigating Milam and Bryant—not only because of its criminal character, but also because his research as a journalist uncovered and divulged information to the public that the main investigation failed to reveal. In a way, it would be more precise and useful to think of what he did as a kind of "detective journalism," for his methods also went beyond those typically associated with investigative journalism in light of their legal implications and import for civil rights cases. He took on bold assignments and did work on high-profile legal cases that put his life at risk in the hostile and racist climate of the Jim Crow South. Because of routine failings to treat blacks with fairness under the law during the Jim Crow era, Huie's interventions as a white man invested in protecting black civil and human rights were genuinely radical, exceptional, and heroic.

Indeed, the nature of Huie's work made him a pariah and target of threats by organizations such as the KKK, and he and his family experienced cross burnings because he produced a deconstructive critical discourse on whiteness. The artist William Christenberry's extensive body of sculptures and watercolors has highlighted ironic images of the Klan body disciplined and contained in many of the very postures that symbolize its historical victimizing of the black racial body. With the exception of Christenberry's project, Huie has surrendered one of the boldest, most subversive, and most direct artistic treatments of Klan ideology ever. He was also likely targeted because in his life he assumed postures that the theorist and activist Noel Ignatiev, one of the foundational scholars in the field of whiteness studies, has identified with the "race traitor": someone who, as part of the commitment to dismantling systems of white supremacy, recognizes and makes efforts to renounce white privilege, engages in a willful disloyalty to such interests at a social and political level, and, assuming the mantle of abolitionists, commits to abolishing whiteness as an ideology.

Huie is significant in part for having worked to dismantle systems of white power and repression that were staunchly entrenched during the era of segregation. Huie used his whiteness subversively and strategically in the interests of civil rights. In Huie's fictitious *The Klansman*, the character Breck Stancill is a white man who is the last remnant of a wealthy cotton farming dynasty. He uses his wealth to help impoverished blacks in the fictive Atoka County, Alabama, and gives them refuge on his mountain. In Huie's novel *The Revolt of Mamie Stover* (1951), Jimmie Madison is a journalist and screenplay writer reminiscent of Huie whose advice and continuing support help the title character, a prostitute from Mississippi, achieve wealth and social prominence after migrating to Hawaii and circumventing a system that would have otherwise kept her in subordination and poverty during World War II. He similarly exhibits disloyalty to white supremacy by challenging racial and class oppression.

The example of Huie is one on which we might draw to expand the epistemologies on the US South within whiteness studies, a field that is and continues to be intellectually impoverished to the extent that it fails to recognize the ideological significance of the US South within a national context, and increasingly, the role of the South in global contexts in the contemporary era. Indeed, the contemporary turn in southern studies toward transnational and postcolonial epistemologies on the US South, which have unsettled the conventional emphasis on its status in relation to or as an alternative to the prevailing nation-state, is a fecund and necessary context in which to ponder the role of the region in constituting politics of race.

Alongside race, Huie's writing also recurrently addressed gender inequality. He frequently emphasized female subjectivity and highlighted black and white female characters, as well as forms of female victimization such as domestic violence and rape. In his repertoire of fiction, including *Mud on the Stars* (1942) and *The Revolt of Mamie Stover*, along with *The Klansman* and several lesser known works, Huie's strategies of engaging and at times juxtaposing black and white female subjects reflected his effort to produce a visionary and revisionist discourse on race, nation, class, gender, and sexuality, alongside an anti-essentialist discourse on whiteness. Interrogating racism and sexism in his fiction was a foundation for some of his most significant activist work in civil rights.

The Southern Literary Trail's commemoration of Huie's centennial birthday in 2010, which was launched at the University of Alabama and culminated in his hometown, was a landmark moment that paid tribute to Huie's important legacy and exposed newer generations to his work. However, in spite of his prolific work, Huie's legacy deserves far more recognition and study than it has received in recent years. In the field of southern studies, my own effort to engage Huie began several years ago in my treatment of *The Klansman* and the related film (Richardson, "'The Birth of a Nation 'Hood'"). When my essay was published in the journal *The Mississippi Quarterly* in 2003, I received a very moving letter from Martha Huie, William Bradford Huie's widow, thanking me for it and expressing gratitude. We kept in touch regularly until her death in 2014. Her response underscored all the more the importance of reconsidering and reclaiming William Bradford Huie's lost legacy and recognizing his vigilant activism in civil rights.

Huie's 1956 book, *Ruby McCollum: Woman in the Suwannee Jail*, was the culmination of his little known collaborative investigative work a few years earlier with African American author Zora Neale Hurston. It profoundly demonstrated his investment in the detective genre and similarly reflected his inclination to deal with provocative topics and to unsettle racial boundaries during the era of segregation. *Ruby McCollum*, which was, significantly, published the same year that Huie investigated the murder of Emmett Till, focuses on the case against a married black woman accused of killing her white lover, a physician in Live Oak, Florida, who was rumored to have fathered two of her children. Hurston became intrigued by the case and had felt that McCollum would not receive a fair hearing and would be sentenced to death by electric chair without more probing to get at the complex truth. She eventually called on Huie because she felt that he was a white man sympathetic to her cause who would be able to garner more information in interviews among local whites than she had been able to as a black woman, whose color alone made her suspicious and even vulnerable in light of the delicacy of the case.

As Valerie Boyd observes in her monumental 2003 biography of Hurston, "Realizing that there were certain angles to the story she could not reach as a black woman in a white-run town like Live Oak [Florida], Hurston interested white Alabama journalist William Bradford Huie in the case, which was appealed to the Florida Supreme Court" (*Wrapped in Rainbows* 417). In Huie's words:

> I went to Live Oak because a Negro woman named Ruby McCollum was in jail there, under death sentence for killing a white man, an ambitious doctor-politician, Dr. Clifford Leroy Adams. The Negro author, Zora Neale Hurston, who had covered the trial for the *Pittsburgh Courier*, had asked me to establish the truth. (*Ruby McCollum* 7)

Suwannee is, of course, the location that Hurston herself chose as the setting for one of her best known literary experiments in which she attempted to unsettle the conventional wisdom about race and African American authorship in the novel *Seraph on the Suwanee,* with its characters who are all white. Huie's legacy is all the more interesting in light of his collaboration with Hurston, one of the most revered and prolific writers in African American literary history. Hurston's training as an anthropologist and folklorist accustomed to doing field work in these areas, sometimes as a participant-observer, made her an ideal comrade for Huie, given his investigative reporting and the lengths to which he sometimes went to get at the truth.

In recent years, the publication of Tammy Evans's study, entitled *The Silencing of Ruby McCollum,* has revisited this famous case and drawn on archives of both Huie and Hurston to underscore its continuing significance. Evans, who grew up in the town where it unfolded, developed her project to address the "silences" that shape the case, then as now: "I aim to challenge the silences that for far too long have gone unbroken, and somehow I know that Ruby McCollum—and all of us—deserve at least that much" (xxxii). Evans's work also makes a valuable contribution in its aim to probe race and gender in even more nuance than Huie's study of the case, with the goal of expanding epistemologies on it in southern studies. In her words:

> Huie's book describes my hometown as a place ruled by unscrupulous men and riddled with racism, violence, and hypocrisy. And I don't quarrel with his description; even as a child I sensed powerful enforced dichotomies among black and white, male and female, rich and poor. What compels me to write about McCollum, however, is the lack of attention on her and the fact that today they continue to perpetuate acts of silence on local, national and international levels. (Evans xxv)

Similarly, John Cork's 2015 documentary film, *You Belong to Me: Sex, Race and Murder in the South,* produced and filmed on location in north and central Florida, has revisited the Ruby McCollum story in recent years. The film is valuable in illustrating that forms of sexual abuse, violence, and subjection experienced by black women at the hands of white men rested in a continuum with the institutionalized violence, rape, and abuse of the black feminine body within slavery. This film draws on Huie's book related to the case, which the state of Florida prohibited from being sold after its release in 1956. The film incorporates both filmic dramatizations and interviews. The actress Denise Durette, a native of Clearwater, Florida, portrays McCollum. Brad Rogers, one of the sources interviewed for the film, reports that even after he bought the rights to the book from Huie for a $1 many years later, uneasiness about Huie's work lingered, and "many in the area did not want Huie's words published all those years later" (Filmore).[1] It is significant that the film recollects the impact of Huie's documenting this pivotal case, an achievement that would have been inconceivable without his work and the foundational contributions of Zora Neale Hurston. McCollum died in a Florida nursing home in 1992.

Alongside his body of work, Huie's representations in literature merit more critical attention. Above and beyond the body of work that Huie produced in journalism, literature and film, Thulani Davis's compelling characterization of him in her play that draws on this case, *Everybody's Ruby* (2000), points to how much he has become a legend in his own right and infiltrated the cultural and literary imaginary. The two signal articles on the Emmett Till case that he produced for *Look* magazine in 1956 and 1957 first introduced an audience in the national mainstream to Huie's work and incorporated the investigative strategies that characterized his journalism and inflected his writing in fiction and nonfiction genres. The book that he released on Ruby McCollum during this same period reflected additional interventions that he made at the outset of the modern civil rights movement in cases that involved black victims and that were linked to high-profile trials. This essay examines the portrayal of Huie in Davis's play focused on the case related to McCollum, a construction that significantly also evokes detective formulas in scripting him. In her play, which stands at the vanguard of twenty-first century African American literature and foregrounds drama in shaping the field, Thulani Davis has helped to restore and recollect his voice alongside Hurston's in relation to one of the most important and provocative legal cases of the twentieth century. Acknowledging the relationship of Huie's work to classic detective formulas and his foundational work on the Ruby McCollum case alongside Hurston is all the more important given how mystifying and controversial it continues to be, and the increasing interest that it has drawn in both literature and in popular film, in addition to ongoing research.

This line of inquiry also seems useful at this point in an era when the state of Florida—in part because of the controversial "Stand Your Ground" law enacted by the Florida legislature in 2005—authorizes individuals to use deadly force, instead of retreating, on anyone perceived to be a threat. In the years since, the justification of the murder of seventeen-year-old Trayvon Martin in Sanford, Florida, at the hands of George Zimmerman in February 2012, has been linked to this legislation. Because of their status as teens and the ways in which their deaths were justified by scripting them as black male youth through stereotypes of black masculinity as violent and threatening to potential white victims, this case has frequently been compared to the murder of Emmett Till. Just as the death of Till served as a catalyst in launching the modern civil rights movement, the death of Martin led to the emergence of the new activist and civil rights movement Black Lives Matter in the wake of Zimmerman's acquittal for his murder, a movement that has been mobilized to address multiple incidents of deadly police violence used against unarmed blacks. Similarly, the murder of the teen Jordan Davis by a white man named Michael David Dunn at a filling station in Jacksonville, Florida, in February 2012, was initially justified through an invocation of "Stand Your Ground" and mobilized activists around the nation.

Even as it has been invoked in attempts to vindicate whites who claimed to have found blacks threatening, the racial double standard in the application of "Stand Your Ground" was evident in the sentencing of a black woman named Marissa Alexander to twenty years in prison in 2012 for firing a warning shot to protect herself from her abusive husband, who had attacked her and threatened to kill her. National movements from Black Lives Matter to #SayHerName have brought attention to the case, which was also significant because it invoked "Stand Your Ground" and was prosecuted by Angela Corey, the same Florida state prosecutor who had been involved in the case involving Zimmerman, whose vindication was widely perceived as an assault on black civil rights and a miscarriage of justice. The case involving Alexander most directly recalls the McCollum case, while the one related to Martin recalls Till. Decades after Huie's work, it is most significant that these cases in Florida in the twenty-first century have been instrumental in launching major civil rights movements at the national level. All of these cases are the kinds about which Huie deeply cared; they serve as a reminder of the work in social justice that remains to be done.

Thulani Davis brings the Ruby McCollum case to life compellingly in her *Everybody's Ruby*, which was produced by George Wolfe at the Joseph Papp Theater in New York, directed by Kenny Leon, and featured Phylicia Rashad and Bill Nunn. In a section entitled "'Ruby' Rules" that prefaces the published version of the play, the author reviews the postures and social customs in the Jim Crow South that will be important for actors to remember and perform in the course of the play, such as "Zora and Huie would not sit together on a public bench. If they want to have food or drink together, they go to a black establishment, or a black home. To brush her teeth, she'd have to find a 'colored' sink" (7). Davis not only makes Huie a salient character, highlighting a rationale behind Hurston's appropriation of the prosthesis of his whiteness, but also stages his willful support of the McCollum defense, and friendship with Hurston, against the backdrop of a metaphysical conflict in him related to heritage, family lineage, and by extension, notions of racial purity. Significantly, these issues play out and work implicitly to unsettle and critique a social context in which issues such as interracial sex and miscegenation further complicate a legal case that is already heavily charged in terms of race. In a new millennium during which, simultaneously, postracial and postblack discourses that belie the continuing impact of racism have become increasingly pervasive, along with white nationalism and populism, it is all the more crucial to recognize the subversive critiques of race that this drama recollects at the dawn of the twenty-first century. Davis's fictive script of Huie is also valuable for its powerful and insurgent figuration of a white and masculine subject committed to challenging forms of antiblackness during the era when Jim Crown reigned.

Detective fiction has been a relatively marginal genre in African American literature. The impact of the former on the latter is not widely known or understood. Walter Mosley is perhaps detective fiction's best known, most popular, and most successful practitioner in the present era. Chester Himes is among the most renowned predecessors. Stephen F. Soitos points out that "an important aspect of popular culture transformation was contained in African American creations using detective motifs and formulas. By using a white Euro-American popular culture form, black authors created important new tropes in black detective fiction" (xi). Soitos goes on to observe that "black detective writers use African American detective tropes on both classical and hard-boiled detective conventions to create a new type of detective fiction," and identifies four primary tropes in its development, including black detective personas, double-consciousness detection, black vernaculars, and conjuring.

The genre of African American drama has experienced a revival through a host of award-winning stage productions in recent years. Yet it remains relatively marginal as a genre in African American literature. Drama shares status with detective formulas in being closer to the margins than the center in African American writing. Davis's embrace of both genres in developing *Everybody's Ruby* imaginatively registers the performative qualities inherent in the dynamic collaboration between Huie and Hurston, and its framing at the intersection of these genres makes it all the more significant and groundbreaking. It is developed as a production to be witnessed by public audiences. Davis provides a performative platform on which to rehearse, verbalize, and speak the silences that shadow this painful history. She grounds this work in a genre in which Hurston had also written, casting herself as an heir of this writing tradition in black literature. Furthermore, she recollects dramatic narrative strategies on which Huie relied in the journalistic stories on Till that first brought Huie (and Till) to national public attention. At the same time, Davis's play unsettles the silence and mystery surrounding Ruby McCollum as a figure by scripting her as a character and according her a voice.

Hurston did not embody the classic white and male detective hero. Yet her presence as a character challenges this conventional raced and gendered masculinist prototype. Similarly, by framing Huie as a white and masculine figure who stands in as a detective in this drama, Davis both expands and unsettles representational strategies related to race and gender in African American detective fiction that primarily foregrounds black and masculine protagonists, including their characteristic heroism.

In Davis's *Everybody's Ruby*, the character William Bradford Huie is introduced in act 2, scene 1, wearing a summer suit and a briefcase, and clearly surfaces as the play's most developed character, after the one modeled on the author Zora Neale Hurston. The character Hurston, who has been denied an interview with McCollum by the judge, is hopeful that Huie will make some headway in the investigation. While he admits that he is reluctant to get involved, Huie immediately begins to play along with Hurston's agenda, and—to avoid arousing suspicion—lies to the librarian that he is on vacation and just passing through the town, an implicit sign that he is aware of the facade that the work demands and of the importance of winning the trust of local whites even as he hopes to uncover information that will help McCollum's difficult case. Finally, Huie agrees to remain for two days, and his commitment to the case becomes more and more evident as his stay is extended and as he pours financial resources into the formidable investigation. With an understanding that Huie will likely make more progress in dialogue with the judge and of the difference that his race might make, she urges Huie to "talk to him, white man to white man" (*Everybody's Ruby* 44). It is significant that the dialogue in the play reveals Hurston's awareness of Huie as a man who is likely to be faithful to her cause and willing to engage in acts of racial subterfuge by passing as a white man who is naively interested in hearing about the facts of the case while in actuality is carrying out a far more radical agenda (45).

The plan backfires, as Huie is recognized almost immediately by the judge. Infuriated by the denial of his right of access as a reporter, Huie denies the Judge's suggestion that he is an "outsider" or an "agitator." "You call me an outsider? Nine generations of my folks are lying in a cemetery in Georgia. You just came from Missouri in 1906. I checked. Compared to me, you're the outsider." When Huie threatens to take the case to the Supreme Court if McCollum is denied the opportunity to talk to a reporter, he is jailed, an incident that makes him all the more passionate about and committed to the case and determined not to be intimidated by the town's power structure.

If Huie's remarks to the judge suggest his pride in his lineage and knowledge of its social worth, Hurston's comments to Huie before arrival bespeak her awareness of these sentiments: "By the way, I tell you we might be cousins? There's some Hurston from outta your county, Huie, I'm just kidding you. I know you're very serious about your family tree." As the prefatory notes in Davis's play suggest, both characters are intensely aware of the lines that divide them, as well as of the ties that bind, and underlying tensions in their collaboration are patently evident, even over as basic a matter as whose story it is, and by extension, over the larger question of Ruby McCollum, a woman claimed and thought known by all in the town for various motives, as the title, *Everybody's Ruby*, suggests. Tensions between Huie and Hurston come to the fore in Huie's inquiry about where he might secure laundry services.

That the African American mechanic asks Hurston and Huie suspiciously, "You all usually travel around like this together?" suggests the extent to which their public interactions are charged and to which both occupy outsider status in the Live Oak community. These layers suggest the potential of the collaboration between them to recollect the relationship of McCollum and the doctor in the minds of some local residents. When Huie flashes money to the mechanic, a strategy that is in keeping, of course, with the strategies of checkbook journalism for which Huie increasingly became known in his lifetime, it becomes apparent, to the ire of Hurston, that he even has the edge, due to his financial means, to extract information from local blacks that would not be surrendered otherwise. As Hurston remarks, "I've been coming here begging for information and this cracker shows up with money and you're shooing me out the yard" (52).

Tensions between Hurston and Huie further intensify before the appointment that he has made with the druggist, and his advice to her to just be "sweet and dumb"—the very suggestion that she gives him before the talk with the judge to ensure that their exchange would be revealing—takes on quite a different meaning in light of her race and gender. Ultimately, both the characters Huie and Hurston play the role of trickster in the play in keeping with conventions of African American folklore. Huie's deft investigative strategies reveal that money and a complex undercover operation is at the heart of the relationship among Ruby, her husband Sam (who runs an extremely lucrative numbers operation in the town), and the doctor. That Huie is always suspect as a race traitor is clear, however, when his hotel room is burglarized to determine how much information he has uncovered about the scheme. Ultimately, in the interests of the case, Hurston turns over all of her notes to Huie, because it is clear that he has the edge because of his identity and connections. As Hurston points out, "It's very simple. Huie, you're Ruby McCollum's best chance. You can get this job done. I can't. [Holding out notebook] This is what I have to offer. Let it be my investment in Ruby's case. Take it. You can deliver" (69). That the story is in Huie's hands is underscored by the fact that Huie claims the final words of the play, in monologue form, as Hurston freezes.

Huie informs us that "Zora's papers got me credentials and Ruby McCollum some new lawyers. They got her sentence set aside because her mental health declined" (78). However, the final sentences reflect on Hurston and himself:

> She didn't tell me about the hard times she came upon after the trial. I didn't even hear when she passed, because by then, we never heard her name anymore. She was living on welfare in a little Florida hamlet. All of her books and plays disappeared too. Hell, I became right obscure as well. All 20 books out of print. As Zora would say "Many a man thinks he is making something when he's only changing things around." (79)

The final comment reflects Davis's efforts to illustrate the common ground that Huie and Hurston share, in spite of their obvious differences, as prolific writers whose legacies became obscure, a factor that further sutures the bonds across racial lines that were established between them in life. For all of Huie's investigative acumen, the truth about Hurston evades him and remains a mystery. The kind of support that both he and Hurston provided McCollum was not there for Hurston.

The irony of this situation suggests the racial and cultural barriers that continued to separate them, in spite of their productive collaboration just a few years earlier. In some ways, he and Hurston remained strangers, even as their relationship unsettled the color line and subverted the boundaries associated with Jim Crow. However, Davis's play reminds us that Huie's investigative agenda prioritized and impacted black women subjects as much as black men, and also holds valuable implications for black feminist discourses.

Though the US South has historically yielded epistemologies of race that have frequently been appropriated and nationalized, the region itself has paradoxically remained marginal and excluded as a topic of conversation in contemporary whiteness studies. These are critical issues and problems that the example of William Bradford Huie allows us to engage with focus. That there is a continuing need for whiteness studies in the contemporary era is clear in a growing national climate of political reaction in which a purist, nativist, and antiforeign ideology of American identity gained ground during the presidential campaign of Donald Trump, and has proliferated all the more in the wake of his election, which precipitated a measurable increase in hate crimes and a resurgence in the KKK. Whiteness studies needs southern studies when dealing with the discourses of race in the United States, including the contemporary theoretical work in the field that reflects turns toward the global and the postcolonial.

The sustained critical effort to deconstruct the concept of race within poststructuralist thought, including an interest in illustrating the status of whiteness as a social construct, challenged and debunked essentialist notions of race and challenged its conventional definitions sanctioned by science. Similarly, in the field of whiteness studies, Richard Delgado, Jean Stefancic, Ruth Frankenberg, Noel Ignatiev and others have suggested the importance of denaturalizing and denormalizing the category "white," though the critical enterprise was taken to task by a range of critics who suggested that it ultimately recentered and prioritized whiteness within an academic climate that had begun to increasingly emphasize difference and otherness in terms of race, class, gender, and sexuality. With the exception of studies of the rural and white racial stereotypes, it is ironic that the scholarly enterprise of whiteness studies has largely overlooked southern studies, even as some of the most viable and enduring epistemologies of whiteness and ideologies of white supremacy—which have frequently undergone nationalization—have had their roots in the US South. The abstraction of D. W. Griffith's *Birth of a Nation* early in the twentieth century is just one example of this phenomenon. It is evident in the continuing, if typically unspoken, reliance in the contemporary political climate on reactionary strategies that have their roots in the notorious Southern Strategy of the 1960s.

Huie was ahead of his time in some respects, to the extent that his work has not always garnered the recognition that it deserved. In a way, we might say that if Huie's writing as a journalist and novelist was his main work, he frequently moonlighted as a de facto detective, and kept one foot solidly in that world as well. Thinking and talking more about his contributions at that level will help us gain a deeper understanding of the serious and extreme risks that he took in doing his work, along with the passion, courage and dedication that he brought to it, a perspective that will help us appreciate his contributions all the more. Huie's connections to Hollywood provided him a national and global platform and enabled his ideas to circulate widely. At the same time, the silence and evasion surrounding his most controversial and incendiary projects, including his work related to McCollum, have sometimes mirrored that of the victims whom he aimed to help out and for whom he spoke up. Yet silence and mystery are qualities that reinforce his detective aura all the more. They challenge new generations to reflect on the truths that he uncovered and to think about joining the business themselves.

NOTE

I dedicate this essay to the memory of Martha Huie and to her dear friend Cynthia Denham.

1. See also Brad Rogers, "Ruby and Me," *Ocala Star Banner*, 12 Apr. 2015.

WHITENESS UNDERCOVER

Racial Passing and/as Detection in Black Like Me *(1964)*

JACQUELINE PINKOWITZ

INTRODUCTION

In 1960, a few months after the civil rights sit-ins began in Greensboro, North Carolina, Howard Griffin temporarily darkened his skin and enacted the geographic and racial movement Elaine Ginsberg claims is embodied in acts of racial passing, crossing the seemingly intransigent color line into both blackness and the Deep South to discover "what it is like to be a Negro in a land where we keep the Negro down" (3). A serialized account of Griffin's journey into the South disguised as a black man appeared in *Sepia*, the African American periodical where he worked as a staff writer; the novel *Black Like Me* was published the next year, following the start of the Freedom Rides. At the time, readers and black and white critics praised Griffin's undercover detective work for exposing the "secret face" of white southern racism and the harsh realities of black oppression (in the South), thereby contributing to cross-racial understanding and the integrationist goals of the civil rights movement (Hathcock 109). Four years later, the ultrasmall-budget, independently produced and distributed film adaptation of *Black Like Me,* directed by Carl Lerner and starring James Whitmore as the renamed John Finley Horton, was released just ahead of Freedom Summer in May 1964.[1] In contrast to the novel's positive reception, the film version of Griffin's passing was met with scathing reviews and outright condemnation, sneeringly dismissed as misguided, "cliché-filled, often crude and even at times embarrassing" before being largely forgotten (Walker 18). While *Black Like Me* is considered the "most influential" example of the less common phenomenon of white-to-black racial passing, and the novel has been relatively well examined by scholars, the film adaptation remains woefully understudied (Pittenger 158).[2] When mentioned, it is often dismissed as an earnest yet problematic failure, an awkward footnote in Griffin's blackface experiment in racial tolerance and the history of black cinematic representation. The film is almost never discussed beyond the context of racial passing.

With its journalist-as-detective protagonist and its racial masquerade-as-undercover-disguise conceit, *Black Like Me* productively reveals the intersections of the racial passing and detective traditions as well as their relationship to the dominant social order and capacity for social critique. Though not often explicitly discussed in relation to each other, tropes of detection and criminality figure centrally in many historical, literary, and filmic narratives of (primarily black to white) racial passing. And while it defies strict or easy generic categorization as a detective film, *Black Like Me* functions as what might be called a racial-passing detective story. As such, it offers an interesting counterpoint and expansion to most conceptualizations of the detective film while its white-to-black masquerade and regional and racial investigations productively trouble conventional understandings of racial passing in America. For like Griffin, the film's Horton temporarily passes as black in order to investigate what can be considered the Jim Crow South's insidious "crime culture," working to uncover the region's racial/racist crimes and collect "proof" of white southern racism and black oppression (Leitch 13–14).

However, subject to the limits of cinematic representation and its liberal white passing experiment, *Black Like Me* ultimately fails to interrogate the national implications and scope of such critiques; it employs a strategy of regional containment that investigates the horrors and debasements of segregationist "crime cultures" only within the abjected, nationally-segregated spaces of the Deep South. Additionally, despite its earnest and realist attempt at regional exposé, by the early 1960s, both detective and passing films had faded from the mainstream and passing itself become increasingly suspect as the nation shifted towards Black Power and "Black is Beautiful" sentiments. Thus, though it dealt more directly with the nation's increasingly urgent "race question" than most Hollywood films, *Black Like Me's* passing detective plot and cinematic engagements ultimately failed to connect with the shifting racial discourses and civil rights politics of the mid-1960s.

DETECTION IN RACIAL PASSING & RACIAL PASSING AS DETECTION

Literary and filmic depictions of racial passing—which most often concern light-skinned, mixed-race black Americans passing for white to attain the cultural, economic, and political privileges of the dominant racial group—share many of the detective film's overriding thematic concerns, including truth, knowledge, and power (Ginsberg 3). Furthermore, because racial passing is a "movement that interrogate[s] and thus threaten[s] the system of racial categories and hierarchies established by social custom and legitimated by law," its narratives have been centrally preoccupied with themes of deception, concealment, disguise, proof/evidence, and the transgression of legal and social boundaries, which also mark detective and crime stories (Ginsberg 2). Indeed, passing for white—or rather, mixed-race Americans' claiming of their whiteness—became a criminal act through legislation like the 1924 Virginia Act to Preserve Racial Integrity (Sollors 254). Such legislation buttressed other laws and customs perpetuating the "sharp inequality" and "asymmetries of privilege and power" between black and white upon which racial passing depends, including the infamous "one-drop rule" and the "separate but equal" premise upheld in *Plessy v. Ferguson* (1896) and undergirding Jim Crow segregation (Sollors 248).

Passing engenders "possibilities of racial transgression," as Elaine Ginsberg argues, and "opportunities for challenging, appropriating, or unveiling" dominant investments in the color line (6). However, while passing narratives, like detective stories, carry the power to expose and challenge dominant social and racial orders, they can also uphold such ideologies, much as passing itself individually and conservatively flouts racial structures while leaving them intact. As mobilized in literary and filmic narratives of nonwhite passing, the tropes of detection and criminality have tended to come at the cost of the black passer, who was portrayed as betraying their own people, deceptively claiming a "fraudulent" white identity, and living under a "disguise," "camouflage," or "counterfeit" (Ginsberg 2–3; Sollors 249, 253). In particular, the myth of the often-female "tragic mulatto" depicted mixed-race people as doomed to madness, despair, and death while casting their passing (for white) as transgressive acts of deception and betrayal for which they ultimately suffered and were spectacularly punished (Sollors 249, 253). Though some Harlem Renaissance–era black-authored novels, like Jesse Fauset's *Plum Bum* (1928) and Nella Larson's *Passing* (1929), used passing to show the pain and cost of a segregated society, such stereotypes still permeated their work and continued to dominate cultural understandings of mixed-race identity and passing when replicated in Hollywood films like *Imitation of Life* (Stahl, 1934; Sirk, 1959), *Show Boat* (Whale, 1936; Sidney, 1951), *Duel in the Sun* (Vidor, 1946), and *Pinky* (Kazan, 1949).

Yet black passing itself has also explicitly functioned as a form of detection for exposing and critiquing white racial prejudice and structures of inequality. Such actions were originally undertaken by light-skinned African Americans who (re)positioned black passing not as criminal deception but as a conscious disguise enabling the critique and subversion of dominant racial orders. For instance, in the 1920s, future NAACP Chairman Walter White passed for white while investigating lynchings and riots in the South to both gain freer admittance of white racism and protect himself from retaliatory white violence (Sollors 147).

White men, too—for it is very often men—have historically undertaken racial passing in the name of antiracist intervention, though in so doing, they have overwhelmingly avoided the negative and criminal characterizations punishing non-white passers (Wald, *Crossing* 16). Despite this legacy of black investigatory and radical passing, Ginsberg explains that white passing narratives "embrace the efficacy of passing as a means of tearing down racial prejudice and establishing avenues of 'cross-racial' understanding" while stories of black passing "draw on metaphors of concealment and disguise to highlight the compromised agency of the subject who 'crosses over'" (Ginsberg 16). For instance, directly anticipating Griffin's racial disguise, in 1948 white journalist Ray Sprigle tanned his skin, shaved his head, and travelled into the South with black civil rights leader John Wesley Dobbs to gain firsthand experience of the costs of racial inequality on its poor rural black communities (Pittenger 154–55). Such motivation also marks the iconic white-passing film (and novel) *Gentleman's Agreement* (Kazan, 1947), in which Gentile journalist Phil Green (Gregory Peck) passes as a Jew to expose anti-Semitism in New England, and by extension, the nation. Not bound by the visual logics of black and white facing Griffin/Horton, Green had only to temporarily change his last name to Greenburg to adopt his ethnic disguise.

Sprigle's *In the Land of Jim Crow, Gentleman's Agreement,* and Griffin's novel reflect the way in which, throughout the postwar era, narratives of passing provided a "means for raising and responding to questions about the place" of marginalized groups within American society, in flux after WWII and amid the burgeoning civil rights movement (Pittenger 154–55). In Hollywood, a cycle of visually dark, *noir*-styled social problem films—reflecting what Thomas Cripps called the "conscience-liberal" trend that would end by the late 1950s— interrogated American race relations and white prejudice. Two of these films— *Lost Boundaries* (Werker, 1949) and *Pinky*—used black passing in both the North and the South to respond to the nation's increasingly contentious "Negro question" and critique white prejudices born of the color line (Cripps 7). *Lost Boundaries, Pinky,* and *Gentleman's Agreement* all use passing to stage racial and social critiques; yet though *Gentleman's Agreement* shares with *Pinky* the *noir*-influenced deep shadows and high contrast between black and white that visualize its racial message and politics—and its neo-realistic pretensions—it differs from its postwar fellows and directly prefigures *Black Like Me* in its use of racial passing as detection and its deployment of a white man going undercover to investigate white prejudice.

As such, both *Gentleman's Agreement* and *Black Like Me* function as what Baz Dreisinger has termed the "white-passing skin-dye" subgenre of passing narratives (519).[3] While it is easy to dismiss white passing as cooptation, blackface minstrelsy, or racial masquerade—as Norman Mailer's "White Negro" hipsters or the appalling *Soul Man* (Miner 1986) make painfully clear—*Black Like Me's* use of white passing as a form of antiracist intervention and regional critique necessitates a contextualization beyond the framework of blackface. As such, Dreisinger's category productively theorizes the whiteness (and power) at the heart of skin-dyers' passing, which fundamentally differentiates them from black passers, while still allowing for the racial-regional commentary it enables.

Because of their membership in the dominant racial group, skin-dyers, whose racial disguises are inherently temporary, have not generally been characterized as deceptive in the way their black counterparts have, nor are they narratively subjected to the same processes of racial detection. For while Horton's disguise enables the film to expose the structures of detection (and policing) meted out against those with black skin, white skin-dyers—in contrast to mixed-race people—pose no fundamental threat to the boundaries of whiteness or dominant racial categories. Like Griffin and Horton, they provisionally take on blackness "as experiments and/or lessons learned," after which they remove their racial disguise and return safely to the spaces and privileges of whiteness, having been personally bettered for the experience (Dreisinger 534). Ultimately then, as Dreisinger argues, because their racial signifiers are impermanent and such passing eschews the mixed-race bodies of black passing, skin-dye narratives often conservatively maintain and reinforce an "essentialized white identity" and the binaristic ideologies of racial difference which passing itself productively deconstructs (534).

THE PASSING PRIVATE EYE: SITUATING *BLACK LIKE ME* AS A DETECTIVE FILM

The crime film has proven troublingly amorphous in its scope and generic definitions, with scholars attempting to establish its most basic qualities around what Nicole Rafter describes as its general preoccupation with "crime and its consequences," or more simply, the "problems of law," as Frank Krutnik defines it (Rafter 5; Krutnik 128).[4] Yet its precise generic boundaries are less important here than its general interrogation of themes of law and order, justice, and society, which align closely with this civil rights–era film's interrogation of the laws and customs surrounding and maintaining southern segregation, white racism, and black oppression. More specifically, *Black Like Me* resonates particularly with elements of the detective film, a subgenre within the larger umbrella category of the crime film that channels many of these same concerns through a focus on the detective figure (Rafter 8). As a racially undercover figure, Horton epitomizes what Steve Neale describes as the detective film's central "agent of investigation" as well as its "emphasis on detection" as he interrogates the inhumanity of Jim Crow segregation while championing both federal integrationist laws and universalist laws of human equality (72).

Film noir—including *Double Indemnity* (Wilder, 1944), *The Big Sleep* (Hawks 1946), *Out of the Past* (Tourneur 1947), and *Kiss Me Deadly* (Aldrich 1955)—is perhaps cinema's most iconic engagement with the detective tradition. Characterized by chiaroscuro lighting and visual and thematic preoccupations with darkness and night, these films take place in the modern city's seedy underbellies and back alleys.[5] Though this cycle cathartically channeled the gender, racial, and existential anxieties of postwar America and influenced many non-detective films, including postwar social problem films, by the late 1950s the golden age of noir was over.[6] This left a major gap in mainstream cinematic engagements with the investigative figure until the late 1960s–early 1970s, when a "more critical" and cynical tradition emerged in the detective genre, and in American film more generally, that "pick[ed] up and revise[d], update[d] and subvert[ed] the motifs and themes" of earlier detective films (Nicol 18). *Black Like Me* provides an opportunity to explore the less overt ways popular film continued to utilize the detective figure in this gap while examining the possibilities and limits of blending racial passing and detection in the service of racial, regional, and social critique.

While his cinematic predecessors "traverse[d] the labyrinthine spaces of the modern urban American city," the blackfaced Horton passes through the Deep South's country roads and small towns, suffering the exclusions and debasements of Jim Crow laws and amassing a series of indignities and humiliations at the hands of his fellow white southerners (Nicol 7). Like the protagonists of the private eye film, a subgenre of the detective film that proliferated in the noir era, Horton's investigator "cannot be dissociated from his environment," and *Black Like Me* "continually explores the relation between the detective and the world he investigates" (Nicol 18). As he journeys deeper into both this southern environment and a state of racial(ized) degradation and despair, Horton becomes increasingly consumed and overwhelmed by the landscape. Kudzu and Spanish moss—those ubiquitous signifiers of southernness and regional decay—increasingly dominate the mise-en-scène until, towards the end of the film, Horton slips down an overgrown roadside when thrown out of a white man's car, nearly tumbling into the wild, jungled landscape in a way that visually mirrors his descent into racialized abjection and hatred.

Shot in the grainy black and white cinematography and documentary (neo) realist style necessitated by its low budget and inspired by the era's television news footage and "authentic"-coded independent "race films," such southern spaces atmospherically convey the region's fecund racism and moral bankruptcy.[7] In this way, the South—insistently othered via the abject-coding modifier "Deep," its separateness continuously asserted through repeated descriptions of "down here"—represents what Thomas Leitch describes as the crime film's presentation not of a singular criminal act, but of a larger "crime culture," one that "depends upon normalizing the unspeakable, a place where crime is both shockingly disruptive and completely normal" (13–14). For like the criminal underworld of 1930s Warner Brothers's gangster films or the morally vacuous Los Angeles of 1940s crime films, *Black Like Me*'s Jim Crow South represents a space of pervasive, racialized crime and degradation that has been wholly naturalized yet remains "shockingly disruptive" and destructive for its black citizens, a world which Horton's passing detective struggles to move through in his search for truth and justice.

In this sense, Horton has more in common with the hard-boiled private eye than the narrative patterns of most crime films and novels: he exhibits what Bran Nicol calls the private eye's "existential engagement" with the geographic, cultural, and moral landscape around him, rather than the cognition and puzzle-solving of his more literary "armchair" counterparts (21). Indeed, the film lacks the central crime, mystery, or "enigma" which has canonically defined both the crime and detective film, as indicated in Philippa Gates's definition of the genre as one wherein "a crime must be committed, a mystery must surround that crime, and a protagonist must investigate the crime and solve the mystery" (22). Instead, *Black Like Me* reflects what Jon Tuska describes as the detective film's shift, with the influence of the hard-boiled tradition, away from individual criminals towards "society itself," which forms the detective's main "opponent" and object of investigation (xviii). For unlike Detective Virgil Tibbs, the "first notable black detective-hero" played by Sidney Poitier in *In The Heat of the Night* (Jewison 1967), who indirectly discovers the horrifying and ongoing extent of southern prejudice and corruption while investigating the murder of a rich white man in Sparta, Mississippi, Horton's "detective-hero" investigates the more amorphous depths of the Deep South's white racism and "crime culture" in his quest to find out "how it felt to be a Negro in the South" (Orel 395–403).

INVESTIGATING JIM CROW'S "CRIME CULTURE"

Episodically visualizing the humiliations, abuses, and rejections which the temporarily black-skinned Horton experiences throughout his southern odyssey, *Black Like Me* presents a series of vignettes of southern racism that, while at times quite melodramatic and "preachy," amount to what Donald Bogle has described as "an earnest attempt to confront and expose racism in America" (Kauffman 26; Bogle, *Toms* 206). While the film strenuously works to regionally contain the national implications of its indictment of white prejudice, its depiction of Horton's investigation into Jim Crow's pervasive "crime culture" ultimately facilitates some of the same racial, social, and legal challenges enabled by both the detective and passing traditions. Specifically, through Horton's investigative passing, *Black Like Me* uncovers the visual logics of southern racial ideologies and the accompanying stereotyped, impersonal white view of blackness; the region's policing looks and social structures of racial surveillance; and the ordinary white racism and silence which maintain these dehumanizing—for both black and white—race relations.

Because of its focus on white southern "oppressors," the filmic Horton's investigative white passing neither detects nor claims to discover any reality of black subjectivity itself, but rather, the white (southern) view of blackness, what Mark Pittenger describes as the "white world's reactions to [his] visible blackness" (162). Unlike Sprigle, Horton's temporary skin-dye exposes the surface-level way that white southerners see those with black skin and place them within the region's racial hierarchies and segregated spaces. Often this manifests as racialized and sexualized stereotypes which debase and dehumanize the disguised Horton while revealing the "sexualized aspects of racism" (Wald 167). On no fewer than three occasions, Horton is subjected to the hypersexualized "black buck" or black rapist myth of black masculinity that historically justified the removal of freed blacks from the (post-)Reconstruction–era body politic, the policing of black (male) bodies, and the lynching of black men throughout the South (Richardson, *From* 3–4).

Yet beyond such relatively well-rehearsed tropes of white (southern) racism, these encounters also condemningly expose what Nelson Hathcock calls "the failure of the racist mind to see beyond the surface," beyond skin color and the racial difference it signifies within the region's—and nation's—visual logics and racial ideologies (109). Indeed, Horton laments having learned that "when you're a black man, it doesn't matter who you are or what you are, the color of your skin is all that matters!" Horton's passing reveals the dehumaniz-

ing white view of racial others to consist not only of sexualized stereotypes, but
a universalizing generalization that denies him any specificity or individuality
by identifying him solely through the subjugated racial group which his skin
color signifies. For instance, after being rejected for a so-called "white job"—
that is, not manual labor—despite his references and experience, the white man
adds roughly, "we don't want you people; we're gradually weeding you people
out." This generalization of the racial(ized) other—"you people"—follows Horton throughout the film, habitually marking his existence as a black man in the
white supremacist hierarchies and white-dominated spaces of Jim Crow through
what Albert Memmi has called the "mark of the plural," which projects colonized
and racialized peoples as "all the same" (Shoat and Stam 183).

Yet paradoxically, as Horton's visible blackness renders him individually, politically, and socially invisible, he also acquires the racialized hypervisibility that
places him within—and subjects him to—the region's visual logics and supporting structures of racial and spatial detection, surveillance, and policing, rooted
in plantation slavery and later segregation. Patricia Hill Collins explains that
while segregation sought to erase black individuality by rendering black people
interchangeable, its "racial etiquette" also subjected them to processes of white
surveillance meant to ensure that "Blacks would stay in their designated, sub-
ordinated places in white-controlled spaces" (Collins, *Fighting Words* 20). Since
passing itself is inherently about "specularity: the visible and the invisible, the
seen and the unseen," it inverts the legibility of racial signs to help black people evade these systems of surveillance and achieve the movement and mobility
which such processes and looks were meant to constrain (Ginsberg 2). Yet in
passing "down," Horton loses the "ubiquitous . . . invisibility" which Richard
Dyer says marks whiteness within Western cultures and acquires the racialized
hypervisibility which has systemically policed black bodies and movements and
subjected them to both "controlling images" and looks (Ginsberg 3; Collinss
"Mammies" 68).

Thus Horton's passing exposes the shocking degree to which racial legibility and emplacement depends on the visual. In encounters like this, the racial
component of Horton's generalized otherness is never explicitly stated, and apparently, does not need to be. Whites never verbally describe or insult him as
"black"; they merely see, then judge, place, and dismiss him. Such scenes further
reveal the unspoken social codes that circulate around and maintain the primacy
of visual signifiers of race while also cinematically conveying the power-laden
looking relations that detect and assign both race and racial difference, thereby
upholding the region's criminal culture of segregation and white supremacy. This

is all epitomized in one of the book and film's most iconic and much-discussed scenes: when Horton is subjected to the white "hate stare." As Horton attempts to purchase a bus ticket, the grandmotherly white clerk scowls fiercely at him, obstinately refusing to make change for his large bill and lying about a manager being unavailable. When Horton reasonably insists, despite the ferocious glare intended to keep him silent and in his proper "place," she angrily, silently hurls back his ticket and change. "Lady, do you know what you've got?" he asks her as she continues to stare resentfully, punishingly, incensed at his challenging of Jim Crow's unspoken visual and social codes; "We call it the hate stare. And I must say you've got the best one I ever did see." Through such primarily verbal and visual encounters, *Black Like Me* uses Horton's white passing to not only uncover the routine insults and threats facing southern blacks, but also to make visible the "'invisible' laws of looking" which enforce and uphold the region's culture of segregation and racial hierarchies (Wald, "Most" 166).

In particular, several public-set scenes throughout the film cinematically choreograph these looking relations to compellingly expose and condemn the "physical recognition and detection schemes" that emerged in the South after the abolition of slavery to define blackness and police its proper "place" in the racial, social, and geographic order (Sollors 141). As Horton sits down wearily on a public bench to eat lunch, a white man briskly passes by. Without so much as slowing down or even turning to directly acknowledge him, the fast-moving, cowboy-hatted stranger casually yells behind him, "You better find yourself someplace else to sit." He thus automatically and unthinkingly polices space according to the highly visual codes of racial difference and entrenched racial hierarchies, enforcing his region's segregationist logics and customs to deny this black man an equal or shared space among whites.

Scenes like this—which combine to form a damning indictment of white racism when laid end-to-end throughout the film—powerfully expose "the role of spectatorship in policing" race "and how [that] supervision is dependent upon hierarchy" and power (Wald, "Most" 166; Wald, *Crossing* 172). As such, *Black Like Me* uses Horton's detective-passer to condemn the "larger southern econ-omy of spectatorship" that upholds black-white inequality, with implications for nationwide racial politics and policies (Wald, "Most" 166). Scenes like this also facilitate Horton's interrogation of the relationship between "race and space" in a region where Jim Crow segregation "sought to organize race by physical space" (Dreisinger 528, 526). Cinematically, they reveal the degree to which the social, geographic, and bodily boundaries of race and place—which Horton himself crossed through use of his passing disguise—are policed, defended, and preserved by ordinary citizens of the dominant group. Indeed, this entirely non-melodramatic park scene is shocking for the cavalier and incredibly casual way the white man disciplines a perfect stranger, motivated by nothing more than the color of his skin.

Black Like Me's understated exposure of the ubiquity of racial hatred engendered by the color line and the ordinary nature of white southern racism remains one of its most salient critiques. Conveyed in realistic documentary-inspired stylings and production strategies—including being shot entirely on location in Maryland, Virginia, and Florida, and casting local black and white extras—Horton's investigative passing provides evidence of what Grace Elizabeth Hale calls "segregation as a culture," in which the "enactment of difference" between black and white was not only caused by legal structures, but also performed and maintained through everyday decisions, interactions, and encounters (xi). A medium-long shot fully captures the park scene with a sense of documentary-style objectivity and detachment, and the camera consciously lingers after the stranger has passed. In so doing, it exposes and condemns the other white men and women, seated on surrounding benches, who say and do nothing at this black man's public humiliation and exclusion. They quickly turn their heads away from his tired, imploring face as he helplessly looks at them for some defense or acknowledgement of their common humanity, what Griffin himself called everyone's "sameness under the skin" (qtd. in Wald, "Most" 154). Left unaided and unacknowledged by his (unknowing) fellow white southerners, Horton sadly puts away his half-eaten sandwich and leaves.

THE LIMITS OF RACIAL PASSING DETECTION: REGIONAL CONTAINMENT & CHANGING TIMES

Promoted through an exploitation-style campaign, the low-budget independent film was, surprisingly, a commercial success despite the contemporary industry dictate against race as box office poison and the difficulty it faced being booked into southern theaters. However, by the time the film adaptation was released in 1964, the white passing premise that had made Griffin's book and other "liberal universalist" texts powerful and popular racial commentaries in the 1940s and 1950s now came off as an uncomfortably presumptuous and painfully outdated way of advocating for black equality. Reviewers objected that the film was "both tardy and misguided," with Hollis Alpert of the *Saturday Review* complaining that "in exploring what is encountered by a quasi-Negro, [*Black Like Me*] has told us what we are already well aware of" (Gill 152; 25). His peer at *Newsweek* was even more blunt: "Horton's agonizing discovery of all the clichés of the past 300 years makes *Black Like Me* obscenely embarrassing" ("Cliché" 111). Black and white critics dismissed it for lacking the urgency, nuance, and realism which were now deemed necessary for filmic treatments of racial issues, not to mention the voices of African Americans themselves ("Dixie Shy"; "To Film"; Robe; Sieving 25, 32).[8] One reviewer protested that *Black Like Me* was more "surface-skimming than a treatise like this should be," while another lamented that "what may have started out as a seriously conceived cinematic version of Griffin's book wound up as a wishy-washy effort that will do the cause of integration little good" (Robe 6; Hartung 236).

Facilitated by the racial consciousness-building of the civil rights movement and other cultural changes of the era, the 1960s were marked by what Pittenger describes as a "growing sensitivity to the perils of trying to speak for the other and [a] heightened consciousness of the complexities of American identity," which fundamentally undermined the principle of investigatory passing (Pittenger 151). As such, the risk-averse studios had largely abandoned the conceit, along with most race-themed material, by the early to mid-1960s. The set of independent black-themed films which emerged in the gap to address/exploit the "controversial" subject of race largely avoided themes of passing—if not miscegenation—and the centering of whiteness which had prominently marked earlier social problem films (Canby; "Filmed 'Black'" 1). When passing did continue to provide cinematic source material, it was in cheap, lurid, and hypersexualized exploitation films like *I Passed for White* (Wilcox, 1960) and *The Black Klansman* (Wikels, 1966). This new industrial and cultural landscape left little hope for *Black Like Me*'s passing-as-detection conceit. One reviewer complained of Horton's racial disguise, "what this flamboyant trickery taught him—that he couldn't have otherwise learned—is not clear" ("Dixie Shy" 7). Southern blacks, too, were skeptical that (white) passing could any longer facilitate antiracist critique, with the film's producer Julius Tannenbaum reporting that one local "sneered at the idea, commenting, 'Well, I'm going to make a picture called 'White Like Me'" ("Dixie Shy" 7). Tied to a history of black caricature and erasure, Whitmore's blackface makeup inspired particular contempt: one reviewer wrote "there is no moment at which [Whitmore] even faintly resembles a Negro; indeed, he hardly looks human," while Alpert shamelessly described him as resembling "the rugged look of a Maine potato farmer who has wintered too long at Miami Beach" ("Cliché" 110; Alpert 25).

Seemingly anticipating such criticism amid the era's rapidly changing discourses and intensifying southern resistance to integration, the film works to distance itself from past incarnations of investigatory white passing and Griffin's own very public post-*Back Like Me* role as spokesperson and activist for black civil rights. Despite its exploitation-style tagline, which read "I changed the color of my skin . . . now I know what it feels like to be black!," the film insists that though his skin-dye enabled Horton to uncover much about Jim Crow society and white racism, it did not permit him to speak as the racial other (Wald, *Crossing* 151–53, 173). For instance, when Thomas (Al Freeman Jr.), the young black activist Horton meets at the end of the film, sneeringly asks him, "and you know what it's like [to be black], huh, after ten weeks?" Horton has the good sense to respond firmly in the negative. Furthermore, Thomas's father (P. J. Sidney) directly calls Horton out, plainly stating "that blackness on your face, it will come off won't it? You wipe that blackness off, they treat you like a man. We black in a white man's country, there ain't nothing we can do about that." While this statement reifies essentialized racial differences and the equation of race with skin color, it importantly testifies—from a black point of view—to the reality of racial inequality and prejudice facing black Americans not only in the South, but the nation as a whole.

Despite its civil rights motivations, *Black Like Me* positions Horton's investigative passing as a journey not into the dark heart of American racism and racial violence, but into the shadowy jungles and mossy backwoods of the Deep South. By criminalizing what Leigh Ann Duck has described as the "nation's region," the film perpetuates longstanding traditions of othering the "problem South" and disavowing national racial problems and legacies as isolatedly and distinctly southern (Griffin and Doyle). In so doing, the film actively contributes to the many historical and cultural "ways in which US nationalism has tended to code its investments in racial hierarchies as regional traits" and disavowed institutionalized racism, racial inequality, and white supremacy as truly American features (Duck, *Nations* 14). Cementing these conservative patterns of containment—themselves an iconic feature of crime and detective stories, which traditionally end by solving the mystery, punishing the "bad guy," and reestablishing the social order—the film concludes with Horton returning to his "proper" racial and geographic place, encouraged by Frank himself to "go on back home where you belong" (Leitch 13). Thus ultimately upholding a segregationist ethos and enacting the skin-dyer's "unambiguous rehabilitation to whiteness" after "questioning the injustice of racial lines," Horton crosses back over the dashed white line bifurcating the black highway (Driesinger 530, 522). Symbolically recrossing the color line, he leaves blackness and the South, along with any trace of his own or the nation's white criminality, safely behind.

CONCLUSION

Despite *Black Like Me*'s harsh reception and limitations, the bigger-budget, more mainstream films released at this time were often even more disappointing, evasive, and indirect in their treatment of the "race question." While a few independent black-themed films from both black and white producers—including *The Cool World* (Clarke, 1963), *Nothing But A Man* (Roemer, 1964), and *One Potato, Two Potato* (Peerce, 1964)—were beginning to challenge the limits of what Ellen C. Scott calls the cinematic "representability" of black civil rights, on the few occasions when the studios actually addressed the racial abuses occurring below the Mason-Dixon Line, like *Black Like Me*, they prioritized whiteness (Scott 3). Frequently centering on themes of crime, detection, law and order, and interracial solidarity, such Hollywood films highlighted idealistic white male savior types like Atticus Finch (Gregory Peck) in *To Kill A Mockingbird* (Mulligan, 1962) or the capacity of ignorant white men to learn tolerance from "magical Negroes," as epitomized by Tony Curtis's racist and Sidney Poitier's "ebony saint" in *The Defiant Ones* (Kramer, 1958) (Willis 3–4).[9]

Poitier, who himself experienced a similar shift in reception as black critics in the burgeoning Black Power era criticized him in the language of racial passing as a "Negro in white face," remained one of the only glimpses of blackness in the white sea of 1960s Hollywood film.[10] It wasn't until the Poitier vehicle *In the Heat of the Night* was released in 1967 that American film was able to send an actual black detective to the South to investigate its racial and other crimes.[11] Yet despite the passing of the Civil Rights Act (1964) and Voting Rights Act (1965) and the beginnings of desegregation in the South, racial equality and regional investigation remained so contentious that the production faced threats of white violence on its Tennessee shoot; such violence had been anticipated on *Black Like Me* and long been used by the studios—along with the loss of the mythic southern box office—as justification for avoiding race-themed films.[12] And though *Black Like Me*'s southern shoot was ultimately free of any such problems, the industry trade press credited this to its deployment of tactics of undercover disguise which mirrored Horton's and allowed the integrated cast and crew to evade white racism and violence: "subterfuge arose over subject matter of the film," which was shot "under cover," using a fake title—"No Man Walks Alone"— and falsely telling onlookers that its detective figure was from the FBI ("Filmed 'Black'"). In considering the white southern resistance which met even these films' qualified, compromised engagements with southern racism, black civil rights, and racial equality, the tremendous pressures and competing impulses

of the civil rights era become clear, as popular film struggled, often unsuccess-
fully, with how to engage the era's urgent and contentious racial, regional, and
national crises.

NOTES

1. *Black Like Me* was produced for $273,000 by Hilltop Productions, a partnership between pro-
ducers Julius Tannenbaum and Victor Weingarten and director Carl Lerner, and released through
the Continental Distributing arm of the Walter Reade company. See "$273,000 Budget."

2. Gayle Wald's "'A Most Disagreeable Mirror'" remains one of the most nuanced scholarly
essays on *Black Like Me* and insightfully explores the novel in relation to white passing. For more
background on *Black Like Me,* see Robert Bonazzi, *Man in the Mirror.*

3. Dreisinger also discusses Charles Chestnutt's novel "Mars Jeems's Nightmare" and Marvin
Van Peebles' film *Watermelon Man* (1970) as examples of the short story subgenre.

4. For an overview of the definition and critical study of the crime film, see Leitch pp. 52–78.

5. See Schrader, "Notes on Film Noir" and Place and Peterson, "Some Visual Motifs of Film
Noir."

6. See Place and Peterson; Root explains that "the major period of noir production is usually
taken to run from *The Maltese Falcon* in 1941 to *Touch of Evil* in 1958." pp. 305–11, 305.

7. Examples include the New York–set *The Cool World* (Clarke, 1963) and *Nothing But A Man*
(Roemer, 1964). See Sieving, *Searching.* pp. 12–13, 18, 27–28.

8. For the difficulty of booking *Black Like Me* into southern theaters, see "Dixie Shy," p. 58.

9. See also Graham.

10. Calypso singing sensation Harry Belafonte also rose to film stardom during this era, though
his political engagement and activism—and more overt sexuality—made him a riskier choice for
the studios.

11. The black detective or police officer would become a staple of Blaxploitation films in the
early 1970s; yet most of these films took place in urban northern cities like New York.

12. Director Norman Jewison explained that "the moment they [white southerners] found out
the movie was about a black detective and they saw Sidney Poitier in an expensive suit . . . it upset
people" (Harris 225).

CULTURE DETECTIVES

Contemporary Journalism, Creative Nonfiction, and the US South

ZACKARY VERNON

INTRODUCTION

Much southern-set, long-form journalism and creative nonfiction of the past three decades has remained outside debates over whether the US South still possesses an identifiable cultural distinctiveness, and works within this genre have diverged from scholarly conversations about southern cultural authenticity in ways that tend to reinscribe traditional and stereotypical notions of southernness. While the scholarly community has since the 1980s increasingly drifted toward ideas such as postmodern cultural simulacra and even postsouthernism, these theories have not gained purchase in the global popular imaginary, wherein the South all too often remains a distinct subculture within the United States.[1] Undergirding contemporary journalists' topics—which range from postplantation and postcolonial economies to homicidal antiques dealers, and from transatlantic racial identity formation to Florida orchid thieves—there is always a corresponding desire to locate the South or the "real South," to use the formulation deconstructed by Scott Romine. My analysis will highlight journalistic texts, in which the writers, always from outside the region and sometimes from outside the country, function as detectives attempting to understand and define the South. Some examples of texts written by these journalist-detectives include V. S. Naipaul's *A Turn in the South* (1989), John Berendt's *Midnight in the Garden of Good and Evil* (1994), Susan Orlean's *The Orchid Thief* (1998), and Gary Younge's *No Place Like Home: A Black Briton's Journey through the American South* (1999).[2]

While not many researchers have published on southern long-form literary journalism, there are a few notable exceptions, including Fred Hobson, Leigh Ann Duck, and Scott Romine. Examining Tony Horwitz's *Confederates in the Attic* (1998) and Naipaul's *A Turn in the South*, Romine argues that these works have a sort of "self-fulfilling intentionally" in that "the South sought is the South found" (61), and he suggests that this process is "archeological" (85). For instance, Naipaul has to strip away "layer upon layer" of southern simulacra— strip malls, mass marketing, and national and global franchises—before arriving at seemingly authentic cultural enclaves that are hiding below. Romine states, "For Naipaul, [. . .] the South of good roads merely requires closer inspection in order to ensure the legibility of the old frontiers and their identitarian effects" (82). While Romine's tendency to label these journalists "archeologists" is often fitting, this critical discussion could be extended by calling them "detectives." Thinking of detectives in the context of the South typically evokes images of Dave Robicheaux battling New Orleans crime in the novels of James Lee Burke, Ed Tom Bell pursuing Anton Chigurh in Cormac McCarthy's *No Country for Old Men* (2005), or Rust and Marty searching for a ritualistic mass murderer in *True Detective* (2014). However, journalists can also take on the role of the detective in that they are often attempting to solve various mysteries. At the same time, though, these journalists, when working in the South, are also detectives of culture, in that part of their quest becomes to locate the beating heart of the region. Thus, *culture detectives* is a fitting label, as these journalists set themselves up to search for and discover previously uncharted cultural terrain.

This terrain is, however, generally well trod already, and the culture detectives tend merely to reassert already-existing, and in many cases stereotypical, understandings of what "the South" means. Naipaul's South is mired in the hangover of southern and circum-Caribbean plantation slavocracies; Berendt's South, particularly Savannah, has achieved a degree of insularity that renders it completely cut off from popular culture; Younge's South, especially the African American South, is so authentic that it provides for him a sense of identity in an otherwise inauthentic world; and Orlean's South, specifically Florida, is "the last of the American frontier," full of wild and exotic peoples and landscapes (9). While some, if not all, of these scenarios are true, they are only partially true or true some of the time. The problem with culture detectives is one of forced cultural synecdoche. They locate part of the South, usually a relatively small part, and present it as the whole. Therefore, subculture becomes culture in the eyes of regional, national, or global audiences. This genre is particularly important to examine in southern studies because best-selling, nationally and internationally renowned authors often publish within it, and thus culture detectives have a profound effect on how the region is perceived and consumed.

SOUTHERN NONFICTION & THE RAGE TO EXPLAIN

In *Tell About the South: The Southern Rage to Explain* (1983), Fred Hobson demonstrates that the "radical need of the Southerner to explain and interpret the South" stems from the region's position within the nation as an unsuccessful, impoverished, grief-stricken, and historically burdened Other (3–4)—"an alien member of the national family, and [. . .] the most frequently analyzed member of that family" (9).[3] The "prototype" for this "rage to explain" is, of course, Quentin Compson of William Faulkner's *Absalom, Absalom!* (1936), who fervently attempts to interpret his native region for Shreve, his Canadian roommate at Harvard (5). While Hobson is concerned primarily with southerners writing about the South, he does note that non-southerners are also similarly obsessed with telling about the region: "In fact you do not have to be born there, as evidenced by several non-Southerners who have told about the South with as much comprehension, if not commitment, as have most native interpreters" (12). Romine echoes this point, saying, "If not being born there has rarely impeded the desire to read about the South, neither has it posed any special obstacles to telling about it" (61).

Romine provides a historical background that complements Hobson's work on southern nonfiction: "As a literary franchise, touring the South has been old business since the great travel narratives of the nineteenth century" (61). These journalistic texts, from the nineteenth century onward, have worked, according to Romine, "to *secure* an image of the South within the national imaginary" (61). For my own purposes, I would add to this a *global* imaginary, given that these works are often written by international writers and for international audiences.

Hobson's thesis that nonfiction writers have been obsessively telling about the South since the region became both identifiable and self-conscious in the 1840s and 1850s remains relevant to late twentieth-century and early twenty-first-century nonfiction. If southern "confessional literature"—namely autobiography and memoir—reached "epidemic proportions" between 1945 and 1970, with the school of shame and guilt increasingly surpassing the school of apologetic remembrance (Hobson 16), then what "school" carries the day after the 1970s? In the past few decades, nonfiction about the South, especially autobiography and memoir, has maintained popularity, with a range of best-selling and much-celebrated authors, from Rick Bragg to David Sedaris, and from Dorothy Allison to Janisse Ray. However, recent nonfiction about the South has also moved in another direction. No longer concerned with explaining and interpreting the region, either to defend or critique, nonfiction writers have instead been chiefly concerned with detecting an authentic South. This was not a concern for either Hobson's apologists or critics who took for granted, whether they loved or hated it, the existence of a real, identifiable South. Recent nonfiction writers, especially those from outside the region, tend to fall into a category I call the school of detection because of their ardent desire to discover authentic southern cultures in the midst of an increasingly homogenized, globalized world.

Contemporary non-southern nonfiction writers seem interested in the South as a "populist world," which Jon Smith, building upon Douglas B. Holt, defines not as the real world but one that serves identitarian desires due to its supposed authenticity and cultural purity. In other words, the populist worlds, precisely because they are "pre-, post-, or antimodern," offer "a sense that the merely modern self presents a lack (often of authenticity) to be filled elsewhere—on the farm or in the perfect pair of vintage earrings, in the Philippines or among the Hopi, up in the old, weird Appalachia or down in the Delta" (16). Furthermore, if there are no more Quentins, those obsessive native critics burdened by the region's history and desperate to interpret it, as Hobson suggests, then there are certainly still Shreves in the form of non-southern journalists obsessed with detecting the South.

CONTEMPORARY NONFICTION & THE SCHOOL OF DETECTION

Perhaps the first significant book within this subgenre of nonfiction is V. S. Naipaul's *A Turn in the South,* in which Naipaul describes his travels around the region and addresses a variety of topics including history, religion, tourism, and economy in the South. Naipaul's own nationality, ethnic identity, and personal past inflect his conception of the region. Born in Trinidad to parents of Indian descent and later educated and then dwelling in England, Naipaul focuses much of *A Turn in the South* on exploring the connections between Trinidad and the US South. In particular, Naipaul is fascinated by the parallels between plantations in the Caribbean and the South prior to the end of slavery, and he observes how post–Civil War whites in the South, more so than in the Caribbean, were and remain haunted by the past. The resemblance between the two reminds Naipaul, according to Leigh Anne Duck, of the fact that "these were plantation societies, shaped by similar experiences of heat, forced labor, and colonial management" ("Travel," 155). The African Americans whom Naipaul encounters and interviews are, not surprisingly, alienated from southern history, and yet he meets several white people who assert a deep attachment to this history, although they tend to divorce it from its legacy of racism. Duck states, "As he reveals this irrationality, he also seeks to historicize the southern past in more detail than is suggested by those who evoke the Civil War as a single and monolithic rupture" (160–61). As a way of working through this "irrationality," Naipaul shifts the narrative to focus on the southern "redneck," "who is purported to have a relationship to local space that is not compromised by history or change" (Duck 150–51). Naipaul locates, in his own mind at least, the "redneck," whom he describes as being like "an unusual bird or a deer" (213), precisely because he is a culture detective; the "redneck" is a "threatened species" that Naipaul, seemingly alone, has managed to discover in the region (213).

Naipaul's detection of the "redneck," a segment of the population disconnected from contemporary culture, is significant because earlier in the narrative he expressed a keen anxiety about whether he would be able to locate southern cultures that are distinct from national or global ones. Arguing that the "redneck" represents an exceptional and uncorrupted form of southern culture becomes untenable, however, if one considers the evidence presented to support this position. Duck succinctly asserts, "he finds the manifestations of this lasting pioneerism in cowboy boots, Graceland, and contemporary country music. Even the colossal classism and sexism of his account are exceeded by its ludicrousness: one simply cannot argue that such commodities, spectacles, and media productions separate people from modernity" (167). Therefore we recognize, even if Naipaul does not, that his "redneck" ultimately fails to fill the role of the authentic contemporary southerner because the "redneck" is also inextricably connected with popular culture and the globalized world.

If Naipaul signals the beginning of this phase of southern nonfiction, then it is John Berendt, former editor of *New York* magazine and writer for *Esquire,* who popularizes it with *Midnight in the Garden of Good and Evil,* a book that remained on the *New York Times* best-seller list for a record-breaking 216 weeks. Thus we might conclude that in addition to a desire on the part of subsequent writers to tell about the South, there may also be a desire to tell about the South in exchange for fame and money. The catalyst for Berendt's book is less self-consciously about the South than Naipaul's. Berendt suggests that the book materialized almost by accident, when he began taking weekend trips to Savannah. Berendt's early perceptions of Savannah come from reading *Treasure Island* (1883) and later *Gone with the Wind* (1936), as well as from the fact that the musician Johnny Mercer was born and raised there: "These, then, were the images in my mental gazetteer of Savannah: rum-drinking pirates, strong-willed women, courtly manners, eccentric behavior, gentle words, and lovely music" (27). These early imaginative encounters with Savannah undoubtedly inform the way he experiences the city. Moreover, Savannah is a city, it seems, that lends itself to romance. Berendt says, "An early-evening mist had turned the view of Monterey Square into a soft-focus stage set with pink azaleas billowing beneath a tattered valance of live oaks and Spanish moss" (9). Early in the book, Berendt notes that he was even warned against being "taken in by the moonlight and magnolias" (10). Berendt thus acknowledges that he must be ever-mindful of romanticizing the city, even when it lends itself so readily to romance. Despite this, though, Berendt's perception of the city is constantly marked by his preconceived notions about it, and he is undoubtedly romanced by it and in turn romanticizes it throughout the book. What Berendt seems to neglect is the fact that it is entirely possible to romanticize the "moonlight and magnolias" of the city as well as its seedier underbelly. In Berendt's account, Savannah's polished and grittier elements all thrive for precisely the same reason: the city is isolated, and willfully so, and thus has retained and augmented many exceptional elements of southern culture. This, of course, cannot be true, certainly not throughout the 1980s and probably was not true ever in the region's earlier history.

However, this is precisely the narrative that Berendt encounters constantly as he meets Savannahians, and this too is the narrative that he peddles throughout *Midnight in the Garden of Good and Evil*. Berendt's book takes place over a period of eight years, during which he lives on and off in Savannah, and it is set primarily in the city (with occasional side trips to Beaufort); and yet this focused location does not prevent him from zooming out at times and making sweeping generalizations about "the South." For example, Berendt remains confident that Savannah is "a rare vestige of the Old South" (36), and he sets himself up to be a culture detective able to penetrate this seemingly isolated and exceptional southern enclave. Within Savannah, Berendt detects and then catalogues an eclectic menagerie of characters, including: a transgender woman named Lady Chablis, who proclaims that "The South is one big drag show . . . ." (102); an ebullient but racist ne'er-do-well lawyer named Joe Odum who obsessively worries about the film adaptation that he assumes will follow Berendt's book; an eccentric inventor named Luther Driggers who possesses a poison powerful enough to kill all inhabitants of Savannah; and a nouveau riche antiques dealer named Jim Williams, who scandalizes the town's upper crust by killing a much younger man who was his lover.

The eccentricities of this cast of characters are all catalyzed or augmented, according to Berendt, by Savannah's purported cultural isolation. However, in at least one scene, Berendt highlights just how problematic this isolation can be. At a St. Patrick's Day parade, Berendt says that the "flavor" of the city, usually so charming, takes a "bitter turn," when a procession of men wearing Confederate uniforms enters the square where Berendt is standing (256). Berendt soon discovers that in a Confederate reenactor's horse-drawn carriage, there is a "chilling tableau" of a dead Union solider (257). Berendt asks Joe Odum why the South is still preoccupied with the Civil War, to which he responds with the rather tired view that Yankees past and present—and the latter includes Berendt himself—

should leave the South alone. While Berendt surely does not condone Odum's racism or appreciate his "bitter" evocation of southern separatist ideology, he does nonetheless perpetuate the isolationist myth of Savannah. Unlike the "tourists" who visit Savannah, he suggests that he possesses an insider's knowledge of the city: "The tourists would leave Savannah in a few hours, enchanted by the elegance of this romantic garden city but none the wiser about the secrets that lay within the innermost glades of its secluded bower" (386). This knowledge is afforded to him because he has succeeded in his role as a culture detective. He knows the city's "secrets," to which mere tourists do not have access. In the last paragraphs of *Midnight in the Garden of Good and Evil*, Berendt asserts one final time that Savannah's distinction derives from one overriding motive: "to preserve a way of life it believed to be under siege from all sides. [. . .] Savannah was not much interested in what went on outside Savannah. It had little enthusiasm for popular culture" (387). Like Naipaul, Berendt makes the same inaccurate argument—that somehow a city and even a region could remain outside of popular culture through the 1980s. Berendt clearly possesses a desire for a populist world: "For me," he contends, "Savannah's resistance to change was its saving grace" (388). Berendt suggests that his book tells the secrets and shows the underbelly of Savannah and the South, and Berendt implies to readers that they should trust him precisely because he can reveal an authentic South that remains unseen by outsiders who lack his skills of detection.

Another example of this type of nonfiction is Gary Younge's *No Place Like Home: A Black Briton's Journey through the American South*. He begins this book by describing Stevenage, the community outside of London where he was born and raised. Stevenage was created after World War II to be a "suburban Utopia thirty miles up the A1 from the capital—a concrete dream for London's poor who had been bombed out of their slums and were multiplying with gusto following the soldiers' return" (1). Younge's sense that his community is generic, malaise-riddled, and rootless explains his deep fascination with the US South. Growing up in Stevenage was particularly alienating for Younge both because he is black—one of four black students in a school of eight hundred (7)—and because he never felt at home either in Barbados, the home of his mother, or England, the place of his birth. Younge's mother seems to have contributed significantly to his childhood feeling of not belonging in either country because she taught him that Barbados was his true home, and she hoped knowledge of Barbados would instill in Younge a secure sense of racial identity; he states, "With her anthems, flags, maps and dates of independence, Mum had tried her best to ensure that we had a secure footing in our racial identity" (15). His great realization, though, is that "there was more to racial identity than nationality and that, in any case, [he] didn't have to cement [him]self in one identity and stay there for the duration of an entire conversation, let alone [his] whole life . . ." (12). Younge's negotiation of his racial identity eventually leads him to voraciously consume American popular culture, especially African American culture: "But America's dominance was especially strong among black Britons because our numbers were so few and our own reference points so well hidden. From the turntable to the fashion store, black America became our influence almost by default" (18).

Furthermore, Younge says that "it was the South that spoke to me urgently about the things I instinctively felt I was lacking—a sense of place and history, a feeling that the collage of insignificant experiences that made up my everyday life was in some way linked to a broader 'whole' that existed before me and would continue long after I was gone" (19). Thus Younge, like many other journalists, imagines the South as a populist world, as a source of identity because its inhabitants, as Jon Smith argues, seem to possess a grounding authenticity that consumers feel they lack (59–60).

Like Berendt, the way that Younge perceives the South—"the heartfelt affinity that both blacks and whites in the South seemed to have with their environment" (24)—is informed by film and fiction. While Younge is sometimes suspicious of this highly mediated relationship with the region, he is also guilty of perpetuating many southern clichés; for example, he says, "I ached for that all-immersion sensuality that came with a rich diet, hot sun and a passionate faith, delivered in deep tremulous tones, either from the pulpit or the soap box—or both. [. . .] [T]hese Southern characters spoke of rural beauty and sumptuous food in a rich and lyrical language" (24). Despite these stereotypes, Younge seems to genuinely believe that the people of the region played a vital role in his maturation process:

> They spoke of unbending resistance, uncompromising dignity and undeniable faith in a hostile world. They sang, danced preached and polemicized. Across the ocean, up the A1 and along SB5/15 route from the town-centre bus station they spoke to me—Gary Younge in Broadwater, Stevenage. (24)

In addition to exploring southern culture—which has so fascinated Younge since his childhood—he also undertakes his "journey" in order to retrace the route used in 1961 by the Freedom Riders, a group of civil rights activists, both black and white, who traveled throughout the region to test whether racial segregation was being enforced illegally among interstate travelers. Retracing the

Freedom Riders' trip from Washington, D.C., to New Orleans aboard a Grey-hound bus, Younge says that he was going to "familiar places to which I had never been. I 'knew' it as a land of lynching, blues and burning crosses. I had seen its battles unfold in black and white and heard its speeches and scream from over the Atlantic. [. . .] I wanted to breathe life into the legend of my for-mative years" (36). This passage provides a more complicated depiction of the South than previous ones that rely on more optimistic stereotypes than those propagated here. Additionally, it is important to understand that even in this pas-sage Younge admits that his perception of the region is informed by "legends"—be they a sunny South inhabited by happy, soulful blacks and whites, or a night-marish landscape peopled with subjugators and subjugated. In his analyses of the region, Younge often makes sound arguments—for example, when he states that "The South is not a place so much as a construct—a distinctive but undefinable fabric into which history, economics, culture, race, prejudice and cuisine have been woven" (42). However, Younge also tends to undermine such sophisticated claims by, in multiple passages, providing overly simplistic definitions of a region that is supposedly "undefinable."

Like Naipaul, Younge expresses a keen fear that the South in reality will not be as exceptional as the one created in his imagination, aided by a lifetime of consuming southern cinema, music, and literature. For Younge, as for Naipaul, this anxiety about a lack of southern authenticity is particularly acute when trav-eling on the region's interstates, where he suggests the South's exceptional sense of place has been erased by globalized capitalism: "As a result, travelling around the South, with its fair share of soulless malls, out-of-town cineplexes and sub-urban estates, can feel like travelling around anywhere else in the United States" (131). This fear that he is merely "anywhere" as opposed to *somewhere* suggests that Younge is more interested in the South as he hoped it would be rather than accepting that which he actually finds in the region (132).

Undeterred, this proves to be merely a bump in the road, and eventually Younge is able to detect what he believes to be the authentic South. For instance, when he arrives in Savannah, Georgia, Younge is quick to point out that it only takes five minutes "to know you could not be anywhere else" (164). Perhaps not surprisingly, Younge almost immediately brings up *Midnight in the Garden of Good and Evil*, which he says has turned Savannah into a "legend," transforming "the town from a minor outpost of Georgian eccentricity into a living cultural ar-tefact" (165). It is likely not a coincidence that Younge finds such an exceptional culture in the same place as Berendt; for one, Younge has already demonstrated that his perception of the region is heavily mediated by the film and literature he consumed prior to encountering the region. In addition, Younge (and his publisher) may have felt enthusiastic about a city like Savannah, which has been the topic of one of the all-time best-selling works of southern nonfiction.

The most significant thing that Younge detects during his journey through the region is an awareness of racial and ethnic hybridity that he suggests exists more readily in the United States, even in the South, than it does in England:

> So almost everybody in America lays claim to another identity. Almost everybody is entitled to a hyphen—Italian-American, Irish-American, Hungarian-American, African-American—and the hyphen qualifies their American identity but does not undermine it. (185)

Younge claims that his own cultural hybridity is not as readily accepted in England: "That is why a 'black Briton' does not come with a hyphen. They are two separate words relating to two very distinct and often conflicting identities" (185). However, that which is not accepted in his home country, Younge increasingly begins to accept in himself: "Identities suffocate if trapped in the narrow confines of a definition for too long" (168). Although this argument attains a certain level of complexity regarding race, Younge's approach to the South is less successful because he is constantly hampered by his expectations of the region. The South that Younge detects—one that he believes approaches racial issues more transparently than England—may not provide the comfort he anticipates. Younge's brief trip through the region enables him to shore up the populist world of his imagination in order to continue drawing upon it for identitarian purposes, without having to stay long enough to witness the ways in which the region, like his native Stevenage, can also feel hopelessly inhospitable and inauthentic.

A fourth and final example of the southern school of detection is Susan Orlean's *The Orchid Thief*, a text that has not received much attention in southern studies, despite the fact that it was a *New York Times* best seller and was the inspiration for Spike Jonze and Charlie Kaufman's film *Adaptation* (2002). *The Orchid Thief* is a productive text to study in the field because it demonstrates common tendencies of the journalist-detective, while at the same time deviating from the other texts explored here. Although Orlean's notion of southern exceptionalism is slightly less overt, it is present in *The Orchid Thief*, and while more subtle, it too has similar implications. Orlean's book began as a story for *The New Yorker* about John Laroche, a white man embroiled in a lengthy court case after stealing endangered plants, especially orchids, from Florida's Fakahatchee Strand State

Preserve, which is "sixty-three thousand coastal lowland acres in the southwest-
ern corner of Florida, about twenty-five miles south of Naples" (34). Prior to his
arrest for stealing orchids, Laroche had set up a nursery and orchid-propagation
laboratory for the Seminole Tribe on their reservation in Hollywood, Florida. Laroche, who Orlean describes as "lust[ing] only for orchids" (4), has an obsessive
preoccupation with the flower, and one of his life's chief goals was to cultivate
the *Polyradicion lindenii*, or ghost orchid. His plan, which went awry and led to
the court case, was to get three Seminole men to extract the orchids from the
swamp. Laroche was present and directed the men's every move in the extraction
process, but he never touched the orchids himself. The Seminoles, he believed,
could not be prosecuted and ergo neither could he because, as Orlean explains,
"Florida Indians were exempt from state laws protecting endangered species"
(26). The judge in the case ultimately ruled that Indian immunity to such laws
does not extend to non-Indian employees of the Seminole Tribe of Florida.

As captivating as this case is throughout *The Orchid Thief,* Orlean sometimes
cannot sustain her attention on Laroche and the ghost orchid. Instead, her focus
shifts, as it so often does in these types of narratives, and her ruminations turn
to the topic of Florida's unique cultures and landscapes. If Laroche is the orchid
hunter, then Orlean herself becomes the South hunter—a culture detective who,
like Naipaul, Berendt, and Younge, loses sight, at least at times, of her overarching project in order to attempt to make sense of the region. Orlean's obsession,
though, is not the South as a whole but south Florida specifically, that amalga-
mous liminal space between South and Caribbean.

Orlean explains that orchid hunters have, since the early to mid-nineteenth
century, chosen "lives that would take them to the corner pockets of the world
where they would see things maybe no one else ever would, things they thought
were more mysterious and different and beautiful than ever imagined" (67–68).
Orlean herself never makes the connection explicit between her relationship to
Florida and orchid hunters' exploration and even colonization of these "corner
pockets of the world"; however, this parallel is clear in how she portrays southern swamps. Orlean states that Florida "can look brand-new and man-made, but
as soon as you see a place like the Everglades or the Big Cypress Swamp or the
Loxahatchee you realize that Florida is also the last of the American frontier.
The wild part of Florida is really wild. The tame part is really tame" (9). Florida
causes Orlean to be "of a mixed mind," as she struggles to comprehend the peoples and places of a state she labels "exceptional and strange" (9). Later, Orlean
confesses, "A lot of the time I was in Florida I was in a bit of a daze, a kind of
stranger's daze that comes on when you hear and see and smell and touch so

many new things. [. . .] I felt as if I really was in some other exotic place where I didn't expect or want to recognize anything I'd see" (81). The phrase "want to recognize" here suggests what Orlean documents those things she desires to see, rather than recording only that which she actually encounters. Therefore, she desires to discover a version of Florida that adheres to her preconceived picture of it. The catalyst for this particular passage is not the wild swamps she had earlier described; instead, the source of the exoticism of south Florida is the collision of seemingly incongruous elements. The deepest, darkest swamps exist in Florida shockingly close to a "sushi bar in a strip mall that was alongside an Australian steakhouse, an Italian café, and Thai diner" (81). This collision of new and old, domesticated and wild, foreign and native, is one that Orlean cannot at first comprehend, which is precisely why the investigation of southern culture, in this case south Florida culture, eclipses the story of the orchid thief. Without realizing it, Orlean actually discovers what Smith, following Néstor García Canlini, identifies as "hybrid cultures" that "question the urban/rural binarism itself" (9). For Orlean, this hybrid culture is a source of dismay because she had anticipated a culture out of time and sheltered from the forces of a globalized world. While cultural hybridity is undoubtedly a positive and productive reality for the contemporary South, culture detectives such as Orlean see it as a negative if their intention is to unveil isolated subcultures for eager and expectant audiences.

CONCLUSION

The tendency to lapse into lengthy conversations about the state of the contemporary South goes beyond the mere literary desire to paint a vivid picture of the landscapes and customs of a particular place. Rather culture detectives seem unable to prevent their narratives from going off on long tangents assessing southern culture; throughout these journalists' books, there develops a narratological attention deficit disorder which precludes sustained attention to, for example, finding a murderer or determining the legitimacy of a legal case. Regardless of whether these writers self-consciously intend to search for the South, they invariably become sidetracked by the various delights and horrors of southern culture. Thus, instead of sticking to the story, these narratives, suffering from cases of southern-inspired attention deficit disorder, drift away from the previously determined subject and gravitate toward the South as subject.

On the one hand, the South seems somewhat unique in its ability to engender this kind of narratological attention deficit disorder. Southern-set journalism, after all, suffers from this condition more often than journalism set in other parts of the world. On the other hand, though, the emphasis on exoticism is typical of a journalistic or even anthropological and ethnographic draw toward difference. Remember, for example, Naipaul's anxiety over whether he would be able to "get beyond the uniformity of the highway and the chain hotel" (222). Citing Anthony Appiah's *The Ethics of Identity* (2005), Romine notes that researchers, regardless of field, can overemphasize differences, even relatively minor differences, because of a desire for the results of their fieldwork to appear more significant. Research, particularly in the poststructuralist vein, must yield something more than the conclusion that one's subject is similar to one's own culture (65–66). Thus journalists writing about the South try, and try desperately, to locate difference, both because their journalistic imperative is to find something new to offer to their readership and because their ability to sell books or articles is often determined by whether they can locate actual difference or, at the very least, perceived difference. The problem for journalists in the South is, of course, that as we persist in our increasingly homogenized late- or even postsouthern moment, locating difference becomes more difficult, and, as a result, contemporary culture detectives must go farther and farther afield, either wholly fabricating cultural authenticity or seeking it out in the most seemingly exotic locales of our ever-shrinking or deregionalized region.

Since the 1990s, there have been fewer popular travelogues and exposés about the South, especially those written by non-southern journalists. However, the obsession with uncovering contemporary southern identities certainly persists, and the ideological ramifications of these identities continue to be utilized in various and oppositional ways. Take, for example, two recent texts, Tracy Thompson's *The New Mind of the South* (2013) and Chuck Thompson's *Better Off Without 'Em: A Northern Manifesto for Southern Secession* (2012). Tracy Thompson, a self-proclaimed "Southerner" (with a capital S no less) (2), travels throughout her native region in order to discern what it means to be "Southern" today: ". . . writers and historians have been lamenting the death of Southern identity for fifty or sixty years now, though nobody can seem to get it to stay in its coffin" (7). Thompson's recorded perceptions of the region seem genuine, but they are also at times misguided; even while noting how "enigmatic" (16) and heterogeneous the region is, she often relies on outdated notions of southern exceptionalism in her attempts to define it: "The reason libraries are full of books by Southerners endlessly explaining the South is that, in truth, we *are* special" (14). Thompson tends to fall back on tired clichés about the South's deep sense of place and community in her attempts to explain why exactly it remains distinct. Conversely, Chuck Thompson, originally from Juneau, Alaska, approaches the region with a much more antagonistic attitude; and yet he too relies heavily upon southern stereotypes—largely negative as opposed to Tracy Thompson's unfailingly romanticized ones—in cultivating his argument that the United States would be more successful socially and economically if the South seceded. Like all the writers discussed in this essay, Chuck Thompson portrays himself as a culture detective, noting, for instance, his ability to discover the "traditionally more invisible parts of the South" (85). The conclusion of his investigation is particularly damning as he posits that "northern citizens might actually be better off without the ball and chain of the southern economy," given that the South tends to maintain exploitative labor practices, put corporate and foreign interests above that of its own people, and disregard or dismantle environmental protections (205). In the end, Thompson's perspective on the South is caustic and belittling, though his intentions seem aimed at social reform; he allows that "The majority of southerners are not loudmouthed, uneducated, redneck fuckwits flying Confederate flags from the backs of their Kia and Mercedes lynch wagons" (255), but at the same time he suggests that for the South to be a progressive and cooperative part of the nation, it must not let a regressive minority retain control of the region's cultural, political, economic, and educational systems.

Examining these two texts in conjunction with one another is instructive because of the stark contrasts between Tracy Thompson's romanticized exceptionalism and Chuck Thompson's Mencken-style critique. Most notably, these texts demonstrate the fact that the South can be mobilized for a range of ideological projects; they also reflect the increased bifurcation of the country—a schism that frequently plays out along sociopolitical and corresponding regional lines. Regardless of how much the region's complexities are flattened, though, works like these, as well as Naipaul's, Berendt's, Younge's, and Orlean's, will surely continue, as regional, national, and global interests in the South show no sign of waning. If this school of journalism persists in the future, the primary agenda will be to continue detecting the South as it was or is, or never was or never is.

NOTES

1. Beginning with Lewis P. Simpson's declaration in 1980 that we have entered a postsouthern era, academics in southern studies have debated about whether or to what extent southern culture is performed and commodified. Scholars such as Michael Kreyling, Scott Romine, and Martyn Bone have contributed to this critical vein, suggesting that southern identity was never coherent or mono-

lithic, and that it certainly is not today. In an analysis of southern cinema, Jay Watson provides a succinct summary of postsouthernism: "A postsouthern South is thus one that appears to rest on no 'real' or reliable foundation of cultural, social, political, economic, or historical distinctiveness, only on an ever-proliferating series of representations and commodifications of 'southernness'" ("Mapping" 219).

2. Other similar texts could include both southern and non-southern writers and their texts, such as Anthony Walton's *Mississippi: An American Journey* (1993), Denis Covington's *Salvation on Sand Mountain* (1995), Peter Applebome's *Dixie Rising* (1996), Tony Horwitz's *Confederates in the Attic* (1998), Randall Kenan's *Walking on Water* (1999), Edouard Glissant's *Faulkner, Mississippi* (1999), Elizabeth Gilbert's *The Last American Man* (2002), Paul Hendrickson's *Sons of Mississippi* (2003), Gerard Helferich's *High Cotton* (2007), John Jeremiah Sullivan's *Pulphead* (2011), Chuck Thompson's *Better Off Without 'Em* (2012), Tracy Thompson's *The New Mind of the South* (2013), and Kiese Laymon's *How to Slowly Kill Yourself and Others in America* (2013).

3. My use of Fred Hobson's work in framing this chapter should not signal to readers that I am somehow mired in "old southern studies." Attendant to Jon Smith's often withering critique of old southern studies—and he would likely put Hobson in this category—I prefer to build on both old and new southern studies, as I still find value in each.

WORKS CITED

"$273,000 Budget on Read-Sterling 'Black Like Me.'" *Variety*, 17 July 1963, pp. 3, 20.

Abbott, Megan E. *The Street Was Mine: White Masculinity in Hardboiled Fiction and Film Noir*. Palgrave, 2002.

"About." *The American Society of Cinematographers*, theasc.com/asc/about.

Adorno, Theodor. "Commitment." Translated by Francis McDonagh. *Aesthetics and Politics*, written by Adorno, et al. Verso, 2007, pp. 177–95. Radical Thinkers 13.

Alpert, Hollis. "SR Goes to the Movies: Mood Ebony." *Saturday Review*, 25 Apr. 1964, p. 25.

Altman, Rick. *Film/Genre*. BFI, 1999.

Alvarado, Karina O., et al. Introduction. *U.S. Central Americans: Reconstructing Memories, Struggles, and Communities of Resistance*, edited by Alvarado, et al. U of Arizona P, 2017, pp. 3–35.

Anderson, Eric Gary, et al., editors. *Undead Souths: The Gothic and Beyond in Southern Literature and Culture*, 2015.

Anderson, John. "Andy Griffith's 'What it Was, Was Football' Recorded." *This Day in North Carolina History*, North Carolina Department of Natural and Cultural Resources, 14 Nov. 2012, www.ncdcr.gov/blog/2012/11/14/andy-griffith-recorded-what-it-was-was-football.

———. "'Streetcar' Uncensored." *New York Newsday*, 29 Oct. 1993, pp. 59, 64.

Arias, Arturo. "Central American-Americans: Invisibility, Power and Representation in the US Latino World." *Latino Studies*, vol. 1, no. 1, 2003, pp. 168–87.

Arnold, Jay. "Filmmakers Stampeding Out of Hollywood to Greener Pastures in Other States." *New Orleans Times-Picayune*, 8 Dec. 1983, sec. 8, p. 7–Ca.

Arrizón, Alicia. *Latina Performance: Traversing the Stage*. Indiana UP, 1999.

Atkins, Ace. *Dirty South*. HarperCollins, 2004.

Bailey, Sarah Pulliam. "How nostalgia for white Christian America drove so many Americans to vote for Trump." *The Washington Post*, 5 Jan. 2017, www.washingtonpost.com/local/social-issues/how-nostalgia-for-white-christian-america-drove-so-many-americans-to-vote-for-trump/2017/01/04/4ef6d686-b033-11e6-be1c-8cec35b1ad25_story.html.

Baker Sotelo, Susan. *Chicano Detective Fiction: A Critical Study of Five Novelists*. McFarland, 2005.

Baldwin, James. *The Devil Finds Work: An Essay*. 1976. Delta/Dell, 2000.

Balio, Tino. *Grand Design: Hollywood as a Modern Business Enterprise, 1930–1939.* U of California P, 1995.

Baker, Vaughan B. "Mad, Bad, and Dangerous: Conceptions and Misconceptions of Louisiana's History and Heritage." *Louisiana History: The Journal of the Louisiana Historical Association,* vol. 42, no. 3, 2001, pp. 261–75.

Barker, Deborah. *Reconstructing Violence: The Southern Rape Complex in Film and Literature.* Louisiana State UP, 2015.

Barker, Deborah E., and Kathryn McKee. Introduction. *American Cinema and the Southern Imaginary,* edited by Barker and McKee, U of Georgia P, 2011, pp. 1–23.

Barnouw, Eric. *Tube of Plenty.* Oxford UP, 1990.

Baron, David. "'Big Easy' Is Fun for N.O. Audiences." *New Orleans Times-Picayune,* 21 Aug. 1987, sec. Lagniappe, p. 7.

Berendt, John. *Midnight in the Garden of Good and Evil: A Savannah Story.* Random House, 1994.

Bernard, Shane K. *The Cajuns: Americanization of a People since 1941.* UP of Mississippi, 2003. *ProQuest Ebook Central.*

Bodroghkozy, Aniko. *Equal Time: Television and the Civil Rights Movement.* U of Illinois P, 2013.

Bogle, Donald. *Primetime Blues: African Americans on Network Television.* Farrar, Straus and Giroux, 2001.

———. *Toms, Coons, Mulattoes, Mammies, and Bucks: An Interpretive History of Blacks in American Film.* 3rd ed., Continuum, 1996.

Bonazzi, Robert. *Man in the Mirror: John Howard Griffin and the Story of* Black Like Me. Orbis Books, 1997.

Bone, Martyn. *The Postsouthern Sense of Place in Contemporary Fiction.* Louisiana State UP, 2005.

Bourbon Street Beat. Warner Bros. Television, 1960.

Boyd, Valerie. *Wrapped in Rainbows: The Life of Zora Neale Hurston.* Scribner, 2003.

Brasell, R. Bruce. *Sweet Uses of Degeneracy: Southern Gothic, Genre-ship, and American Culture,* unpublished manuscript.

Breu, Christopher. *Hard-Boiled Masculinities.* U of Minnesota P, 2005.

Brinkmeyer, Robert H. *Remapping Southern Literature.* U of Georgia P, 2000.

Bronstein, Phoebe. "Failed Souths: Race, Gender, and Region in Bourbon Street Beat." *Quarterly Review of Film and Video,* vol. 33, no. 4, Mar. 2016, pp. 348–61.

Brooks, Ed. "On the Square." *New Orleans Times-Picayune,* 6 Aug. 1950, sec. 2, p. 8.

Brown, John Mason. "Southern Discomfort." Review of *A Streetcar Named Desire,* by Tennessee Williams. *Saturday Review of Literature,* 27 Dec. 1947, pp. 22–24.

Bruno, Giuliana. *Atlas of Emotion: Journeys in Art, Architecture, and Film.* Verso, 2002.

Burke, James Lee. *In the Electric Mist with Confederate Dead.* Hyperion, 1993.

Butt, John and Carmen Benjamin. *A New Reference Grammar of Modern Spanish.* 3rd ed., McGraw-Hill, 2000.

Cain, James M. *Three by Cain: Serenade, Love's Lovely Counterfeit, The Butterfly.* Vintage Crime, 1974.

———. *The Postman Always Rings Twice.* Vintage Crime/Black Lizard Edition, 1992.

Canby, Vincent. "Race to Film Race Issues: Indies React to Negro News." *Variety,* 17 July 1963, pp. 3, 20.

Capp, Rose. "Dead Man Walking in Frank Borzage's *Moonrise*." *Senses of Cinema,* vol. 31, Apr. 2004, sensesofcinema.com/2004/cteq/moonrise/.

Carpenter, Brian. Introduction. *Grit Lit: A Rough South Reader,* edited by Tom Franklin and Brian Carpenter, U of South Carolina P, 2012, pp. xiii–xxii.

Cassuto, Leonard. *Hard-Boiled Sentimentality: The Secret History of American Crime Stories.* Columbia UP, 2009.

Castille, Philip Dubuisson. "Too Odd for California: Incest and West Virginia in James M. Cain's *The Butterfly*." *Appalachian Journal,* vol. 23, no. 2, Winter 1996, pp. 148–62.

CBS, "WWL-TV . . . *new* New Orleans Favorite." *Sponsor: The Weekly Magazine Radio/TV Advertisers Use,* 28 Aug. 1961, p. 2, www.americanradiohistory.com/Archive-Sponsor -Magazine/1961/Sponsor-1961-08-04.pdf.

Chandler, Raymond. *The Big Sleep.* 1939. *Stories & Early Novels,* Library of America, 1995, pp. 587–764.

Chase, James Hadley. *No Orchids for Miss Blandish.* 1939. Avon Classic Crime, 1961.

Christian, Karen. *Show and Tell: Identity as Performance in U.S. Latina/o Fiction.* U of New Mexico P, 1999.

Classen, Steven D. *Watching Jim Crow: The Struggles over Mississippi TV, 1955–1969.* Duke UP, 2004. Console-ing Passions: Television and Cultural Power.

"Cliché Odyssey." *Newsweek,* 25 May 1964, pp. 110–11.

Cobb, James C. *The Selling of the South: The Southern Crusade for Industrial Development 1936–1990.* 2nd ed., U of Illinois P, 1993.

Cohen, Rich. "Can Nic Pizzolatto, True Detective's Uncompromising Auteur, Do It All Again?" *Vanity Fair,* 11 June 2015, www.vanityfair.com/hollywood/2015/06/nic-pizzo latto-true-detective-season-2-better-than-season-1.

Cole, Nat King. "Why I Quit My TV." *Ebony,* Feb. 1958, pp. 29–34.

"Collateral Damages." *Law & Order: Special Victims Unit,* season 17, episode 15, NBC, 17 Feb. 2016. *Hulu,* www.hulu.com/watch/906834.

Collins, Patricia Hill. *Fighting Words: Black Women and the Search for Justice.* U of Minnesota P, 1998.

———. "Mammies, Matriarchs, and Other Controlling Images." *Black Feminist Thought: Knowledge, Consciousness, and the Politics of Empowerment,* Routledge, 2000, pp. 76–107.

"Community Policing." *Law & Order: Special Victims Unit,* season 17, episode 5, NBC, 14 Oct. 2015. *Hulu,* www.hulu.com/watch/857498.

Connell, R. W. *Masculinities.* 2nd ed., U of California P, 2005.

"Coon, n." *OED Online,* Oxford UP, Dec. 2016, www.oed.com/view/Entry/41015.

Cooper, Stephen. "Sex/Knowledge/Power in the Detective Genre." *Film Quarterly*, vol. 42, no. 3, Spring 1989, pp. 23–31. *JSTOR*, doi: 10.2307/1212598.

Cooper-Clark, Diana. "Interview with Ross Macdonald," *Designs of Darkness: Interviews with Detective Novelists*, Bowling Green State U Popular P, 1983, pp. 83–100.

Corbin, Amy Lynn. *Cinematic Geographies and Multicultural Spectatorship in America*. Palgrave Macmillan, 2015. Screening Spaces. *ProQuest Ebook Central*.

"Cotton Patch is Needed for Movie Scenes." *Baton Rouge State-Times*, 11 Oct. 1956, sec. C, p. 7.

"The Cow Thief." *The Andy Griffith Show*, written by R. S. Allen and Harvey Bullock, directed by Bob Sweeney, CBS, 29 Oct. 1962.

Cox, Karen L. *Dreaming of Dixie: How the South Was Created in American Popular Culture*. U of North Carolina P, 2011.

Cripps, Thomas. *Making Movies Black: The Hollywood Message Movie from World War II to the Civil Rights Era*. Oxford UP, 1993.

Cunningham, David. *Klansville, U.S.A.: The Rise and Fall of the Civil Rights-Era Ku Klux Klan*. Oxford UP, 2012.

Davis, Thulani. *Everybody's Ruby*. Samuel French, 2000.

Dawson, Andrew. "'Bring Hollywood Home!' Studio Labour, Nationalism and Internationalism, and Opposition to 'Runaway Production,' 1948–2003." *Revue Belge de Philologie et d'Histoire*, vol. 84, no. 4, 2006, pp. 1101–22.

"Deadly Ambition." *Law & Order: Special Victims Unit*, season 14, episode 15, NBC, 6 Feb. 2013. *Hulu*, www.hulu.com/watch/458785.

Deleuze, Gilles. *Cinema 2: The Time-Image*. Translated by Hugh Tomlinson and Robert Galeta, U of Minnesota P, 1989.

Deliverance. Directed by John Boorman, performances by Jon Voight, Burt Reynolds, Ned Beatty, and Ronny Cox, Warner Brothers, 1972.

Derr, Mark. *Some Kind of Paradise*. U of Florida P, 1989.

Dexter, Pete. *The Paperboy*. Random House, 1995.

Dimendberg, Edward. *Film Noir and the Spaces of Modernity*. Harvard UP, 2004. Review of *Dirty South*. *Publishers Weekly*, 2 Mar. 2006, www.publishersweekly.com/978-0 -06-000462-0.

Dischinger, Matthew. "*The Walking Dead's* Post-Southern Crypts." Hinrichsen, Caison, and Rountree, pp. 259–76.

"Dixie Shy of 'Black Like Me.'" *Variety*, 17 Feb. 1965, pp. 7, 58.

Doane, Mary Ann. *Femmes Fatales: Feminism, Film Theory, Psychoanalysis*. Routledge, 1991.

Dodd, Donn, and Wynelle Dodd. *Historical Statistics of the South: 1790–1970*. U of Alabama P, 1973.

Dodds, Richard. "'Big' Means Small for Local Actors." *New Orleans Times-Picayune*, 21 Aug. 1987, sec. Lagniappe, p. 7.

Donaldson, Susan V. "Reimagining the Femme Fatale: *Requiem for a Nun* and the Lessons of Film Noir." *Faulkner and Mystery*, edited by Annette Trefzer and Ann J. Abadie, UP of Mississippi, 2014, pp. 139–61.

Dostoyevsky, Fyodor. *Crime and Punishment.* 1866. Translated by Richard Pevear and Larissa Volokhonsky, Vintage, 1993.

"Double Strands." *Law & Order: Special Victims Unit,* season 13, episode 4, NBC, 12 Oct. 2011. *Hulu,* www.hulu.com/watch/285093.

Dove, George N. *The Police Procedural.* Bowling Green U Popular P, 1982.

Dover, J. K. Van, and John F. Jebb. *Isn't Justice Always Unfair?: The Detective in Southern Literature.* Bowling Green State U Popular P, 1996.

Dreisinger, Baz. "Dying to Be Black: White-to-Black Racial Passing in Chesnutt's 'Mars Jeems's Nightmare,' Griffin's *Black Like Me,* and Van Peebles's *Watermelon Man.*" *Prospects,* vol. 28, 2004, pp. 519–42.

Duck, Leigh Anne. *The Nation's Region: Southern Modernism, Segregation, and U.S. Nationalism.* U of Georgia P, 2006.

———. "Travel and Transference: V. S. Naipaul and the Plantation Past." *Look Away!: The U.S. South in New World Studies,* edited by Jon Smith and Deborah Cohn, Duke UP, 2004, pp. 150–70.

Duggan, Lisa. *Sex Wars: Sexual Dissent and Political Culture.* Routledge, 2006.

———. *The Twilight of Equality: Neoliberalism, Cultural Politics, and the Attack on Democracy.* Beacon Press, 2004.

Dumont, Hervé. *Frank Borzage.* Translated by Jonathan Kaplansky. McFarland, 2006.

DuRocher, Kristina. *Raising Racists: The Socialization of White Children in the Jim Crow South.* UP of Kentucky, 2011.

Dussere, Eric. *America is Elsewhere: The Noir Tradition in the Age of Consumer Culture.* Oxford UP, 2014.

Duvall, John N. *Race and White Identity in Southern Fiction: From Faulkner to Morrison.* Palgrave Macmillan, 2008.

Dyer, Richard. *White: Essays on Race and Culture.* Routledge, 1997.

Earle, David M. *Re-Covering Modernism: Pulps, Paperbacks, and the Prejudice of Form.* Ashgate, 2009.

Edgerton, Gary. "The Film Bureau Phenomenon in America and Its Relationship to Independent Filmmaking." *Journal of Film and Video,* vol. 38, no. 1, Winter 1986, pp. 40–48. *JSTOR,* www.jstor.org/stable/20687705.

"Educated Guess." *Law & Order: Special Victims Unit,* season 13, episode 8, NBC, 16 Nov. 2011. *Hulu,* www.hulu.com/watch/300844.

"Elia Kazan Wanted to Be 'Honest': Why He Picked New Orleans." *New Orleans Times-Picayune,* 20 Aug. 1950, sec. 2, p. 10.

"Ellen DeGeneres' 86th Oscars Opening." *YouTube,* uploaded by The Academy of Motion Picture Arts and Sciences, 11 Mar. 2014, www.youtube.com/watch?v=HUmX6CiMoFk.

Eller, Ronald D. *Miners, Millhands, and Mountaineers: Industrialization of the Appalachian South: 1880–1930.* U of Tennessee P, 1982.

———. *Uneven Ground: Appalachia since 1945.* UP of Kentucky, 2008.

Evans, Beau. "Louisiana Tops Murder Rate Again, New FBI Data Shows." *The Times-Picayune*, 27 Sept. 2016, www.nola.com/crime/index.ssf/2016/09/louisiana_ tops_murder _rate_aga.html.

Evans, Tammy. *The Silencing of Ruby McCollum: Race, Class, and Gender in the South*. UP of Florida, 2016.

A Face in the Crowd. Directed by Elia Kazan, performance by Andy Griffith. Warner Brothers, 1957.

Faulkner, William. *Sanctuary: The Corrected Text*, edited by Noel Polk and Joseph Blotner, Vintage, 1985.

Fiedler, Leslie A. "Pop Goes the Faulkner: In Quest of *Sanctuary*." *Faulkner and Popular Culture*, edited by Doreen Fowler and Ann J. Abadie, UP of Mississippi, 1990, pp. 75–92.

Fillmore, Andy. "Familiar Faces in New Documentary." *Ocala Star Banner*, 8 Apr. 2015, www.ocala.com/article/LK/20150408/News/604142345/OS/.

"Filmed 'Black' in South under Cover of 'Story of FBI.'" *Variety*, 12 Feb. 1964, pp. 1, 3.

"Filming New Orleans Scenes." *New Orleans Times-Picayune*, 8 Dec. 1949, sec. 1, p. 12.

"Fire in the Hole." *Justified*. FX. 16 Mar. 2010.

"Fire on the Frontier." *Yancy Derringer*, written by Mary Loos and Richard Sale, directed by Richard Sale, CBS, 2 Apr. 1959.

Fitzhugh, Louise. *Harriet The Spy*. Harper & Row, 1964.

Flores, Antonio, et al. "Facts on U.S. Latinos, 2015: Statistical Portrait of Hispanics in the United States." *Pew Research Center*, 18 Sept. 2017, www.pewhispanic.org/2016 /04/19/statistical-portrait-of-hispanics-in-the-united-states-trends/.

Flynn, Gillian. *Gone Girl*. Crown, 2012.

———. "I Was Not a Nice Little Girl . . ." *Medium*, 17 July 2015, medium.com/@Powells /i-was-not-a-nice-little-girl-c2df01e0ae1.

Flynt, Josiah, and Francis Walton. "Found Guilty." *The American Rivals of Sherlock Holmes*, edited by Hugh Greene, Penguin, 1976, pp. 86–99.

"Forgiving Rollins." *Law & Order: Special Victims Unit*, season 16, episode 10, NBC, 7 Jan. 2015. *Hulu*, www.hulu.com/watch/734284.

Forman, Murray. "Employment and Blue Pencils: NBC, Race, and Representation 1926–1955." *NBC: America's Network*, edited by Michelle Hilmes, U of California P, 2007, pp. 117–34.

Forter, Greg. *Murdering Masculinities: Fantasies of Gender and Violence in the American Crime Novel*. New York UP, 2000. Sexual Cultures Series.

Foster, Frederick. "Filming 'The Fugitive Kind.'" *American Cinematographer*, June 1960, pp. 354–55 and 379–82.

Franco, Jean. "Gender, Death, and Resistance: Facing the Ethical Vacuum." *Critical Passions: Selected Essays*, edited by Mary Louise Pratt and Kathleen Newman, Duke UP, 1999, pp. 18–38.

Franklin, Ruth. "Morbid Longings." *The New Republic Online*, 2 Jan. 2003, newrepublic. com/article/66655/morbid-longings.

Friend, Craig Thompson. *Southern Masculinity: Perspectives on Manhood in the South Since Reconstruction.* U of Georgia P, 2009.

Friend, Craig Thompson, and Lorri Glover, editors. *Death and the American South.* Cambridge UP, 2014.

———. Introduction. Friend and Glover, pp. 1–14.

"Friending Emily." *Law & Order: Special Victims Unit,* season 14, episode 6, NBC, 31 Oct. 2012. *Hulu,* www.hulu.com/watch/419205.

Gach, Gary. "John Alton: Master of the Film Noir Mood." *American Cinematographer,* Sept. 1996, pp. 87–92.

Gaitely, Patricia. "Robicheaux's Revenants: The Use and Function of the Revenant in James Lee Burke's Dave Robicheaux Novels." *CLUES: A Journal of Detection,* vol. 28, no. 2, Sept. 2010, pp. 77–86. *ProQuest Literature Online,* doi: 10.3172/CLU.28.2.77.

Gallagher, Gary W. Introduction. *The Myth of the Lost Cause and Civil War History,* edited by Gallagher, Gary W., and Alan T. Nolan, Indiana UP, 2000, pp. 1–10.

"A Game of Chance." *Yancy Derringer,* written by Mary Loos and Richard Sale, directed by William F. Claxton, CBS, 5 Feb. 1959.

García, María Cristina. *Seeking Refuge: Central American Migration to Mexico, the United States, and Canada.* U of California P, 2006.

Garnier, Caroline. "Temple Drake's Rape and the Myth of the Willing Victim." *Faulkner's Sexualities,* edited by Annette Trefzer and Ann J. Abadie, UP of Mississippi, 2010, pp. 164–83.

Gates, Philippa. *Detecting Men: Masculinity and the Hollywood Detective Film.* State U of New York P, 2006.

Geherin, David. *John D. MacDonald.* Frederick Ungar Publishing Co., 1982.

Gelly, Christophe. "De William Faulkner à James Hadley Chase: appropriation et mutation du genre policier." *E-rea: Revue électronique d'études sur le monde Anglophone,* vol. 2, no. 1, 15 June 2004. *OpenEdition,* doi: 10.4000/erea.482.

Gennis, Sadie. "7 Reasons Why Women Love *Law & Order: SVU* so Much." *TV Guide,* 4 Nov. 2014, www.tvguide.com/news/reasons-women-love-svu-1088704/.

Giddens, Anthony. *Emile Durkheim: Selected Writings.* Cambridge UP, 1972.

Gill, Brendan. "The Current Cinema: Danger! Virtue at Work." *The New Yorker,* 23 May 1964, pp. 151–52.

Ginsberg, Elaine K. Introduction. *Passing and the Fictions of Identity,* edited by Ginsberg, Duke UP, 1996, pp. 1–18.

Goddu, Theresa. *Gothic America: Narrative, History, and Nation.* Columbia UP, 1997.

"Goes to the Movies." *TV Radio Mirror,* vol. 51, no. 5, Apr. 1959, p. 15. *Library of Congress,* archive.org/details/radiotvoomac.

Golsan, Richard J. "Interview with James Lee Burke." *South Central Review,* vol. 27, no. 1–2, Spring/Summer 2010, pp. 167–70. *JSTOR,* jstor.org/stable/40645937.

Goodman, Paul. "Reflections on Drawing the Line." *The Paul Goodman Reader,* edited by Taylor Stoehr, PM P, 2011, pp. 34–40.

Gotham, Kevin Fox. "Destination New Orleans: Commodification, Rationalization, and the Rise of Urban Tourism." *Journal of Consumer Culture*, vol. 7, no. 3, Nov. 2007, pp. 305–34. *SAGE Publications*, doi: 10.1177/1469540507085254.

Graham, Allison. *Framing the South: Hollywood, Television, and Race During the Civil Rights Struggle*. Johns Hopkins UP, 2003.

Graham, Allison, and Sharon Monteith. "Southern Media Cultures." *The New Encyclopedia of Southern Cultures, Volume 18: Media*, edited by Graham and Monteith, U of North Carolina P, 2011, pp. 1–30.

Gray, Richard. "*Sanctuary*, 'Night Bird,' and Film Noir." *Sanctuary*, edited by Michel Gresset and André Bleikasten, PU de Rennes, 1996, pp. 83–88.

"Great Expectations." *Law & Order: Special Victims Unit*, season 18, episode 11, NBC, 8 Feb 2017. *Hulu*, www.hulu.com/watch/1035829.

Griffin, John Howard. *Black Like Me*. New American Library, 2003.

Griffin, Larry J., and Don H. Doyle. Introduction. *The South as an American Problem*, edited by Griffin and Doyle, U of Georgia P, 1995, pp. 1–9.

Grimm, Andy. "Hollywood South Movie Tax Credit Trial Wraps." *New Orleans Times-Picayune*, 24 Apr. 2015, nola.com/crime/index.ssf/2015/04/arata_hoffman_movie _tax_trial.html.

Grundmann, Roy. *Andy Warhol's Blow Job*. Temple UP, 2003.

Gustafson, Henrik. "A Wet Emptiness: The Phenomenology of Film Noir." *A Companion to Film Noir*, edited by Andrew Spicer and Helen Hanson, John Wiley & Sons, 2013, pp. 50–66, *ProQuest Ebook Central*.

Guttman, Sondra. "Who's Afraid of the Corncob Man? Masculinity, Race, and Labor in the Preface to *Sanctuary*." *Faulkner Journal*, vol. 15, nos. 1–2, 1999–2000, pp. 15–34.

Halberstam, J. Jack. *In a Queer Time and Place: Transgender Bodies, Subcultural Lives*. New York UP, 2005.

Hale, Grace Elizabeth. *The Making of Whiteness: The Culture of Segregation in the South, 1890–1940*. Vintage Books, 1998.

Hall, Stuart. "Cultural Identity and Diaspora." *Identity: Community, Culture, Difference*, edited by Jonathan Rutherford, Lawrence & Wishart, 1990, pp. 222–37.

———. "The Whites of Their Eyes: Racist Ideologies and the Media." *Gender, Race, and Class in Media, A Text-Reader*. 2nd ed., edited by Gail Dines and Jean M. Humez, Sage, 2003, pp. 89–93.

Hamilton, Nora, and Norma Stoltz Chinchilla. *Seeking Community in a Global City: Guatemalans and Salvadorans in Los Angeles*. Temple UP, 2001.

Hannah, Barry. "Dark Harvest." *Oxford American*, vol. 55, Winter 2006, pp. 50–53.

Harari, Yuval Noah. *Sapiens*. 2011. Translated by Yuval Noah Harari, John Purcell, and Haim Watzman. HarperCollins, 2015.

Hare, David. "Great Expectations." *TheGuardian.com*, 26 Oct. 2001, theguardian.com/books /2002/oct/27/ fiction.features.

Harkins, Anthony. *Hillbilly: A Cultural History of an American Icon*. Oxford UP, 2005.

Harris, Mark. *Pictures at a Revolution: Five Movies and the Birth of the New Hollywood*. Penguin, 1998.

Hartung, Philip T. "The Screen: Like Who?" *Commonweal*, 15 May 1964, pp. 236–37.

Harvey, David. *The Condition of Postmodernity: An Enquiry into the Origins of Cultural Change*. Blackwell, 1990.

Hathcock, Nelson. "'A Spy in the Enemy's Country': *Black Like Me* as Cold War Narrative." *American Studies*, vol. 44, no. 3, Fall 2003, pp. 99–119.

Hay, Stephen. *Bertrand Tavernier: The Film-maker of Lyon*. I.B. Tauris, 2000.

Hinkson, Jake. "Night and the Country: A History of Rural Noir." *Mystery Scene*, vol. 133, 2014, pp. 34–36.

Hinrichsen, Lisa, et al. Introduction. Hinrichsen, et al., pp. 1–23.

Hinrichsen, Lisa, et al., editors. *Small-Screen Souths: Region, Identity, and the Cultural Politics of Television*. Louisiana State UP, 2017.

Hirshberg, Edgar W. *John D. MacDonald*. Twayne Publishers, 1985. Twayne's United States Authors Series.

Hobson, Fred. *Tell About the South: The Southern Rage to Explain*. Louisiana State UP, 1983.

Holben, Jay. "Southern Gothic." *American Cinematographer*, Dec. 2000, pp. 58–67.

Holmlund, Christine. "Sexuality and Power in Male Doppelganger Cinema: The Case of Clint Eastwood's *Tightrope*." *Cinema Journal*, vol. 26, no. 1, Autumn 1986, pp. 31–42. *JSTOR*, doi: 10.2307/1224985.

"Home Invasions." *Law & Order: Special Victims Unit*, season 13, episode 14, NBC, 15 Feb 2012. *Hulu*, www.hulu.com/watch/329157.

Horsley, Lee. *The Noir Thriller*. Palgrave Macmillan, 2009.

Hughes, Alex. "'Law & Order: SVU' Is an Alternative Reality Where Assault Survivors Are Taken Seriously." *Vice.com*, 10 June 2016, www.vice.com/en_us/article/law-order -special-victims-unit-offers-women-justice-and-thats-why-i-love-it.

Huie, William Bradford. *He Slew the Dreamer: My Search for the Truth about James Earl Ray and the Murder of Martin Luther King*. Delacorte P, 1970.

———. *The Klansman*. Delacorte P, 1970.

———. *Mud on the Stars*. New York: Signet Books; 2nd ed., 1956.

———. *The Revolt of Mamie Stover*. New York: Signet, 1954.

———. *Ruby McCollum: Woman in the Suwannee Jail*. E. P. Dutton & Co., 1956.

———. *Three Lives for Mississippi*. UP of Mississippi, 2000.

Huyssen, Andreas. *After the Great Divide: Modernism, Mass Culture, Postmodernism*. Indiana UP, 1986.

Ignatiev, Noel. *How the Irish Became White*. Routledge, 1995.

Ignatiev, Noel, and John Garvey, editors. *Race Traitor*. Routledge, 1996.

"Info Wars." *Law & Order: Special Victims Unit*, season 19, episode 20, NBC, 31 Jan. 2018. *Hulu*, www.hulu.com/watch/1214676.

Irons, Glenwood. Introduction. *Feminism in Women's Detective Fiction*, edited by Irons, U of Toronto P, 1995, pp. ix–xxiv.

Irwin, John T. *Doubling and Incest/Repetition and Revenge: A Speculative Reading of Faulkner*. Rev. ed., Johns Hopkins UP, 1996.

Jameson, Fredric. *The Political Unconscious: Narrative as a Socially Symbolic Act.* Cornell UP, 1981.

———. *Postmodernism, or, The Cultural Logic of Late Capitalism.* Duke UP, 1991. Post-Contemporary Interventions.

———. *Raymond Chandler: The Detections of Totality.* Verso, 2016.

Johansen, Emily. "The Neoliberal Gothic: *Gone Girl, Broken Harbor,* and the Terror of Everyday Life." *Contemporary Literature,* vol. 57, no. 1, Spring 2016, pp. 30–55.

Kapur, Jyotsna, and Keith B. Wagner. Introduction. *Neoliberalism and Global Cinema: Capital, Culture, and Marxist Critique,* edited by Kapur and Wagner, Routledge, 2011, pp. 1–16. *ProQuest Ebook Central.*

Kauffman, Stanley. "The Fire This Time." *The New Republic,* 23 May 1964, pp. 24–27.

Kaufman, Boris. "Filming 'Baby Doll.'" *American Cinematographer,* Feb. 1957, pp. 92–93+.

Kelly, Erin. "Why We Are All in the Grip of the Suburban Noir," *The Telegraph,* 4 Oct. 2014, www.telegraph.co.uk/culture/film/11138933/Why-we-are-all-in-the-grip-of -suburban-noir.html.

Kelly, R. Gordon. "The Precarious World of John D. MacDonald." *Dimensions of Detective Fiction,* edited by Larry N. Landrum, Pat Browne, and Ray B. Browne, Bowling Green State U Popular P, 1976, pp. 149–61.

"Knock on Any Tombstone." *Bourbon Street Beat,* written by Sig Herzig and Charles Hoffman, directed by William J. Hole Jr., ABC, 25 Jan. 1960.

Kreyling, Michael. *Author and Agent: Eudora Welty and Diarmuid Russell.* Farrar, Straus and Giroux, 1991.

———. *Inventing Southern Literature.* UP of Mississippi, 1998.

———. *The Novels of Ross Macdonald.* U of South Carolina P, 2005.

Krutnik, Frank. *In a Lonely Street: Film Noir, Genre, Masculinity.* Routledge, 1991.

Laberge, Yves, and Merril D. Smith. "Films, U.S." *The Encyclopedia of Rape,* edited by Merril D. Smith, Greenwood, 2004, pp. 76–78.

Lehman, David. *The Perfect Murder: A Study in Detection.* Free P, 1989.

Leier, Mark. "From Rebel to Reactionary: Class and the Politics of Travis McGee." *Journal of American Culture,* vol. 21, no. 3, 1998, pp. 89–101.

Leitch, Andrew. *Crime Films.* Cambridge UP, 2002.

Lester, Cheryl. "'Same as a Nigger on an Excursion': Memphis, Black Migration, and White Flight in *Sanctuary.*" *Faulkner Journal,* vol. 26, no. 1, 2012, pp. 37–56.

Lightman, Herb A. "'Reflections in a Golden Eye': Viewed Through a Glass Darkly." *American Cinematographer,* Dec. 1967, pp. 862–65+.

Lindop, Samantha. *Postfeminism and the* Fatale *Figure in Neo-Noir Cinema.* Palgrave Macmillan, 2015.

Lirette, Christopher. "Something True about Louisiana: HBO's *True Detective* and the Petrochemical America Aesthetic." Review of *True Detective. Southern Spaces,* 8 Aug. 2014, southernspaces.org/2014/something-true-about-louisiana-hbos-true-detective -and-petrochemical-america-aesthetic.

Lloyd-Smith, Alan. *American Gothic Fiction: An Introduction.* Continuum, 2004.

London, Jack. "Pinched." 1907. *Vital Ideas: Crime,* edited by Theresa Starkey, The Great
  Books Foundation, 2011, p. 32.

"The Long Bright Dark." *True Detective,* written by Nic Pizzolatto, directed by Cary Joji
  Fukunaga, HBO, 12 Jan. 2014.

"Loot from Richmond." *Yancy Derringer,* written by Irving Wallace and Mary Loos, directed by William F. Claxton, CBS, 20 Nov. 1958.

Loren C. Scott & Associates. "The Economic Impact of Louisiana's Entertainment Tax
  Credit Programs." *Louisiana Office of Entertainment Industry Development,* Apr. 2013,
  louisianaentertainment.gov/assets/ENT/docs/2013_OEID_Program_Impact_Report
  %20_FINAL.pdf.

Lott, Eric. "The Whiteness of Film Noir." *American Literary History,* vol. 9, no. 3, Autumn
  1997, pp. 542–66. *Oxford Journals,* doi: 10.1093/alh/9.3.542.

Louisiana Motion Picture Incentive Act (480). R.S. 47:1121–1128/H.B. 2104. 18 July 1990,
  State-Times [Baton Rouge, LA], 3 Aug. 1990.

Louisiana Act 894. R.S. 47:6007/H.B. 252. 8 July 1992, *State-Times* [Baton Rouge, LA],
  3 Aug. 1992.

MacCannell, Dean. "Democracy's Turn: On Homeless *Noir.*" *Shades of Noir,* edited by Joan
  Copjec, Verso, 1993, pp. 279–97.

MacDonald, John D. *The Brass Cupcake.* Gold Medal Books, 1950.

———. *Bright Orange for the Shroud.* Gold Medal Books, 1965.

———. *Cinnamon Skin.* Harper and Row, 1981.

———. *Dead Low Tide.* Gold Medal Books, 1953.

———. *Deep Blue Good-By.* 1964. Ballantine Books, 1995.

———. *The Dreadful Lemon Sky.* Gold Medal Books, 1974.

———. *Dress Her in Indigo.* 1969. Random House, 2013.

———. *The Drowner.* Gold Medal Books, 1963.

———. *The Empty Copper Sea.* J. B. Lippincott, 1978.

———. *The Executioners.* Gold Medal Books, 1957.

———. *The Girl in the Plain Brown Wrapper.* Gold Medal Books, 1968.

———. *The Long Lavender Look.* Gold Medal Books, 1970.

———. *Pale Gray for Guilt.* Gold Medal Books, 1968.

Macdonald, Ross. *The Blue Hammer.* Vintage Crime/Black Lizard, 1976.

———. *Sleeping Beauty.* Knopf, 1973.

———. *Stories of Suspense.* Knopf, 1974.

———. *The Underground Man.* Knopf, 1971.

Malraux, André. "A Preface for Faulkner's *Sanctuary.*" *Yale French Studies,* vol. 10, 1952,
  pp. 92–94.

"The Manhunt." *The Andy Griffith Show,* written by Jack Elinson and Charles Stewart,
  directed by Don Weis, CBS, 10 Oct. 1960.

Marcus, Laura. "Detection and Literary Fiction." *The Cambridge Companion to Crime Fiction,* edited by Martin Priestman, Cambridge UP, 2003, pp. 245–67.

Mark, Rebecca. "Ice Picks, Guinea Pigs, and Dead Birds: Dramatic Weltian Possibilities in

'The Demonstrators.'" *Eudora Welty, Whiteness, and Race,* edited by Harriet Pollack, U of Georgia P, 2013, pp. 199–223.

Marrow, Helen B. *New Destination Dreaming: Immigration, Race, and Legal Status in the Rural American South.* Stanford UP, 2011.

Marrs, Suzanne. *Eudora Welty: A Biography.* Harcourt, 2005.

Marrs, Suzanne, and Tom Nolan. *Meanwhile There Are Letters: The Correspondence of Eudora Welty and Ross Macdonald.* Arcade, 2016.

Mason, Walter Scott. *The People of Florida as Portrayed in American Fiction.* George Peabody College for Teachers Bureau of Publications, 1949.

Mayer, Vicki. *Almost Hollywood, Nearly New Orleans: The Lure of the Local Film Economy.* U of California P, 2017. *Luminos,* doi: 10.1525/luminos.25.

McCabe, Janet, and Kim Akass. Introduction. *Reading Desperate Housewives: Beyond the White Picket Fence,* edited by McCabe and Akass, I.B. Tauris, 2006, pp. 1–14.

———. "Sex, Swearing, and Respectability: Courting Controversy, HBO's Original Programming, and Producing Quality TV." *Quality TV: Contemporary American Television and Beyond,* edited by McCabe and Akass, I.B. Tauris, 2007, pp. 62–76.

McCarthy, Anna. *The Citizen Machine.* New P, 2010.

McMahand, Donnie, and Kevin Murphy. "'Remember right': Disenfranchised Grief and the Commemoration of Queer Bodies in Welty's Fiction and Life," *Eudora Welty Review,* vol. 6, Spring 2014, pp. 69–82.

McNay, Lois. "Self as Enterprise: Dilemmas of Control and Resistance in Foucault's *The Birth of Biopolitics.*" *Theory, Culture & Society,* vol. 26, no. 6, Dec. 2009, pp. 55–77. *SAGE Publications,* doi: 10.1177/0263276409347697.

McPeek Villatoro, Marcos. *Blood Daughters.* Red Hen P, 2011.

———. *Home Killings.* Arte Público P, 2001.

———. *Minos.* Justin, Charles & Co., 2003.

———. *A Venom beneath the Skin.* Justin, Charles & Co., 2005.

McPherson, Tara. *Reconstructing Dixie: Race, Gender, and Nostalgia in the Imagined South.* Duke UP, 2003.

Means Coleman, Robin R. *Horror Noire: Blacks in American Horror Films from the 1890s to Present.* Routledge, 2011.

"The Member of the Funeral." Review of *Clock without Hands,* by Carson McCullers. *Time,* 22 Sept. 1961, pp. 118, 120.

Merivale, Patricia, and Susan Elizabeth Sweeney, editors. *Detecting Texts: The Metaphysical Detective Story from Poe to Postmodernism.* U of Pennsylvania P, 1999.

———. "The Game's Afoot: On the Trail of the Metaphysical Detective Story." Merivale and Sweeney, pp. 1–24.

Merrill, Hugh. *The Red Hot Typewriter: The Life and Times of John D. MacDonald.* Thomas Dunne Books, 2000.

Metress, Christopher. "Living Degree Zero: Masculinity and the Threat of Desire in the Roman Noir." *Fictions of Masculinity: Crossing Cultures, Crossing Sexualities,* edited by Peter F. Murphy, New York UP, 1994, pp. 154–84.

Milian, Claudia. *Latining America: Black-Brown Passages and the Coloring of Latino/a Studies.* U of Georgia P, 2013.

Mittell, Jason. *Genre and Television: From Cop Shows to Cartoons in American Television.* Routledge, 2004.

Mohl, R. "Globalization, Latinization, and the *Nuevo* New South." *Globalization and the American South,* edited by J. Cobb and W. Stueck, U of Georgia P, 2005, pp. 66–99.

Moody, Nickianne. "Crime in Film and On TV." Priestman, pp. 227–43.

Moonrise. Directed by Frank Borzage, Republic Pictures, 1948.

Moore, Leonard N. *Black Rage in New Orleans: Police Brutality and African American Activism from World War II to Hurricane Katrina.* Louisiana State UP, 2010. *ProQuest Ebook Central.*

Moore, Lewis D. *Meditations on America: John D. MacDonald's Travis McGee Series and Other Fiction.* U of Wisconsin P, 1994.

Muller, Eddie. *Dark City: The Lost World of Film Noir.* St. Martin's Griffin, 1998.

Mulvey, Laura. "Visual Pleasure and Narrative Cinema." *Feminism and Film Theory,* edited by Constance Penley, Routledge, 1988, pp. 57–68.

Murphet, Julian. "Film Noir and the Racial Unconscious." *Screen,* vol. 39, no. 1, March 1998, pp. 22–35. *Oxford Journals,* doi: 10.1093/screen/39.1.22.

Mustian, Jim. "Innocent Man or 'Gangster with Badge'?: Racially Divided New Iberia Not Sure about Acquitted Sheriff." *Advocate* [Baton Rouge, LA], 5 Nov. 2016, theadvocate.com/acadiana/news/crime_police/article_7b126ca8-a237–11e6–8296–6bcde7e37d36.html.

Naipaul, V. S. *A Turn in the South.* 1989. Vintage, 1990.

Naremore, James. *More than Night: Film Noir in Its Contexts.* U of California P, 1998.

———. *More than Night: Film Noir in Its Contexts.* Rev. ed., U of California P, 2008. *ProQuest Ebook Central.*

Nathan, George Jean. "The Streetcar Isn't Drawn by Pegasus." Review of *A Streetcar Named Desire,* by Tennessee Williams. *New York Journal American,* 15 Dec. 1947, p. 20.

Neale, Steve. *Genre and Hollywood.* Routledge, 2000.

Nevins, Francis M., Jr. *Cornell Woolrich: First You Dream, then You Die.* Mysterious P, 1988.

Newcomb, Horace. "From Old Frontier to New Frontier." *The Revolution Wasn't Televised: Sixties Television and Social Conflict,* edited by Lynn Spigel and Michael Curtin, Routledge, 1997, pp. 287–302.

"New Orleans' 'Forbidden Past,'" *New Orleans Times-Picayune,* 4 Feb. 1951, sec. *Dixie Roto Magazine,* p. 9.

Nicol, Bran. *The Private Eye: Detectives in Movies.* Reakton Books, 2013.

O'Brien, Geoffrey. *Hardboiled America: Lurid Paperbacks and the Masters of Noir.* Expanded ed., Da Capo P, 1997.

Odem, Mary E., and Elaine Lacy, editors. *Latino Immigrants and the Transformation of the U.S. South.* U of Georgia P, 2009.

"Old Dixie." *Yancy Derringer,* written by John Hawkins and Richard Sale, directed by Richard Sale, CBS, 25 Dec. 1958.

"Old Homes Alluring to Tourists." *New Orleans Times-Picayune,* 2 Mar. 1958, sec. 3, p. 8.

Oliver, Kelly, and Benigno Trigo. *Noir Anxiety.* U of Minnesota P, 2003.

"Opie and His Merry Men." *The Andy Griffith Show,* written by John Whedon, directed by Richard Crenna, CBS, 30 Dec. 1963.

Orel, Harold. "The American DetectiveÐHero." *The Journal of Popular Culture,* vol. 2, no. 3, 1968, pp. 395–403.

Orlean, Susan. *The Orchid Thief.* Random House, 1998.

Osteen, Mark. "Dark Mirrors: *Sanctuary's* Noir Vision." *The Faulkner Journal,* vol. 28, no. 1, 2014, pp. 11–35.

"Padre Sandunguero." *Law & Order: Special Victims Unit,* season 16, episode 12, NBC, 21 Jan 2015. *Hulu,* www.hulu.com/watch/740490.

Palmer, R. Barton. *Shot on Location: Postwar American Cinema and the Exploration of Real Place.* Rutgers UP, 2016.

Palmer, R. Barton, and William Robert Bray. *Hollywood's Tennessee: The Williams Films and Postwar America.* Austin: University of Texas Press, 2009.

"Panic in Town." *Yancy Derringer,* written by Cole Trapnell and Mary Loos, directed by Richard Sale, CBS, 12 Feb. 1959.

"Patrimonial Burden." *Law & Order: Special Victims Unit,* season 17, episode 7, NBC, 4 Nov. 2015. *Hulu,* www.hulu.com/watch/866515.

Pendarvis, Jack. "Fiction and Bullshit: An Interview with Ace Atkins." *Lent Mag,* 7 June 2014, lentmag.com/fiction-and-bullshit-an-interview-with-ace-atkins/.

Pepper, Andrew. "The American Roman Noir." *The Cambridge Companion to American Crime Fiction,* edited by Catherine Ross Nickerson, Cambridge UP, 2013, pp. 58–71.

Phillips, K. J. Review of *Figures of Division: William Faulkner's Major Novels,* by James A. Snead, *International Fiction Review,* 1987, pp. 104.

Pittenger, Mark. *Class Unknown: Undercover Investigations of American Work and Poverty from the Progressive Era to the Present.* New York UP, 2012.

Place, Janey, and Lowell Peterson. "Some Visual Motifs of Film Noir." *Film Noir Reader,* edited by Alain Silver and James Ursini, Proscenium, 1996, pp. 65–76. Originally published in *Film Comment,* vol. 10, no. 1, 1974, pp. 30–35.

Polchin, James. "Selling a Novel: Faulkner's *Sanctuary* as a Psychosexual Text." *Faulkner and Gender,* edited by Donald M. Kartiganer and Ann J. Abadie, UP of Mississippi, 1996, pp. 145–59.

Pollack, Harriet. *Eudora Welty's Fiction and Photography: The Body of The Other Woman.* U of Georgia P, 2016.

Pope, John. "State Shoots for the Stars. *New Orleans Times-Picayune,* 15 Jan. 1984, sec. 1, p. 8.

Porter, Carolyn. *William Faulkner.* Oxford UP, 2007.

Porter, Denis. "The Private Eye." *The Cambridge Companion to Crime Fiction.* 2003, edited by Martin Priestman, Cambridge UP, 2013, pp. 95–113.

Portes, Alejandro, and Rubén G. Rumbaut. *Legacies: The Story of the Immigrant Second Generation.* U of California P, 2001.

Prédal, René. "Bertrand Tavernier: Qu'est-ce que la mise en scène?" *Jeune Cinéma*, vol. 322, Spring 2009, pp. 6–14. *ProQuest Performing Arts Periodicals.*

Prenshaw, Peggy. *Conversations with Eudora Welty.* UP of Mississippi, 1984.

Priestman, Martin, editor. *The Cambridge Companion to Crime Fiction.* Cambridge UP, 2003.

Rabinowitz, Paula. *Black & White & Noir: America's Pulp Modernism.* Columbia UP, 2002.

———. "Tupperware and Terror: The Rise of 'Chick Noir.'" *The Chronicle of Higher Education*, 8 Jan. 2016, www.chronicle.com/article/TupperwareTerror/234716.

Rafter, Nicole. *Shots in the Mirror: Crime Films and Society.* 2nd ed., Oxford UP, 2006.

Rash, Ron. *One Foot in Eden.* Picador, 2002.

———. Personal interview. 10 May 2017.

Read, Herbert. "The Paradox of Anarchism." *Anarchy and Order: Essays in Politics*, Faber & Faber, 1954, pp. 129–37.

Reddy, Maureen T. *Traces, Codes, and Clues: Reading Race in Crime Fiction.* Rutgers UP, 2003.

———. "Women Detectives." Priestman, pp. 191–207.

"Return to New Orleans." *Yancy Derringer*, written by Mary Loos and Richard Sale, directed by Richard Sale, CBS, 2 Oct. 1958.

Rich, B. Ruby. "Dumb Lugs and Femmes Fatales: Films Such as *Pulp Fiction* and *Devil in a Blue Dress* are Film Noir." *Sight and Sound*, vol. 5, no. 11, 1995, pp. 6–10. *ProQuest Performing Arts Periodicals.*

Rich, Nathaniel. "The Preacher and the Sheriff." *New York Times Magazine*, 8 Feb. 2017, nytimes.com/2017/02/08/magazine/the-preacher-and-the-sheriff.html.

Richardson, Riché. "'The Birth of a Nation 'Hood': Lessons from Thomas Dixon and D. W. Griffith to William Bradford Huie and *The Klansman*, O. J. Simpson's First Movie." *The Mississippi Quarterly*, vol. 56, no. 1, Winter 2002–2003, pp. 3–31.

———. *From Uncle Tom to Gangsta: Black Masculinity and the U.S. South.* U of Georgia P, 2007.

Rieger, Christopher. *Clear-Cutting Eden: Ecology and the Pastoral in Southern Literature.* U of Alabama P, 2009.

———. "Don't Fence Me In: Nature and Gender in Marjorie Kinnan Rawlings's *South Moon Under*." *Mississippi Quarterly*, vol. 57, no. 2, 2004, pp. 199–214.

Robe. "*Black Like Me*: Movie Review." *Variety*, 20 May 1964, p. 6.

Roberts, Diane. "The South of the Mind." *South to a New Place: Region, Literature, Culture*, edited by Suzanne W. Jones and Sharon Monteith, Louisiana State UP, 2002, pp. 363–73.

Rodriguez, Ralph E. *Brown Gumshoes: Detective Fiction and the Search for Chicano Identity.* U of Texas P, 2005.

Rogin, Michael. "'The Sword Became a Flashing Vision': D.W. Griffith's *Birth of a Nation*." *American Culture Between the Civil War and World War I*, special issue of *Representations*, no. 9, Winter 1985, pp. 150–95.

Römers, Holger. "'The Moral of the *Auteur* Theory': Frank Borzage's *Moonrise* (and Theodore Strauss' Source Novel)." *Senses of Cinema*, vol. 42, Feb. 2007, sensesofcinema.com
/2007/the-moral-of-the-auteur-theory/auteur-theory-moonrise/.

Romine, Scott. *The Real South: Southern Narrative in the Age of Cultural Reproduction.*
Louisiana State UP, 2008.

Root, Jane. "Film Noir." *The Cinema Book.* 3rd ed., edited by Pam Cook, BFI, 2007, pp. 305–11.

Ross, Scott. Foreword. Linda Thurman, *Hollywood South: Glamour, Gumbo, and Greed.*
Kindle ed., Pelican, 2016.

Rothfeld, Becca. "*Gone Girl's* Feminist Update of the Old-Fashioned Femme Fatale." *New Republic*, 8 Oct. 2014, newrepublic.com/article/119743/gone-girl-has-offered-feminism
-new-hero.

Rothstein, Richard. *The Color of the Law: The Forgotten History of How Our Government
Segregated America.* Liveright, 2017.

Rowe, Anne E. *The Idea of Florida in the American Literary Imagination.* Louisiana State
UP, 1986.

Rozzo, Mark. "First Fiction." Review of *One Foot in Eden*, by Ron Rash. *Los Angeles Times*,
29 Dec. 2002, p. R10, articles.latimes.com/2002/dec/29/books/bk-rozzo29.

Ruble, Raymond S. *Round Up the Usual Suspects: Criminal Investigation in Law and Order,
Cold Case, and CSI.* Praeger, 2009.

Rzepka, Charles J. *Detective Fiction.* Polity P, 2005.

Sayre, Katherine. "Louisiana's Movie Tax Credits Attracted Corruption along with Film
Industry." *New Orleans Times-Picayune*, 11 Mar. 2014, nola.com/business/index.ssf
/2014/03/louisianas_movie_tax_credits_a.html.

Scaggs, John. *Crime Fiction.* Routledge, 2005.

Schiller, Mark Daniel. "Gothic Horror Revived with *Sister, Sister*." *American Cinematographer*, Mar. 1988, pp. 69–76.

Schlotterbeck, Jesse. "Non-Urban Noirs: Rural Space in *Moonrise, On Dangerous Ground,
Thieves' Highway*, and *They Live By Night*." *M/C—A Journal of Media and Culture*,
vol. 11, no. 5, Oct. 2008, journal.media-culture.org.au/index.php/mcjournal/article
/view/69.

Schmidt, Pete [posted by Steve Scott]. "When John D. Met the Movies and McGee." *The
Trap of Solid Gold*, Blogger, 14 Dec. 2015, thetrapofsolidgold.blogspot.com/2015/12
/when-john-d-met-movies-and-mcgee.html.

Schrader, Paul. "Notes on Film Noir." *Film Noir Reader*, edited by Alain Silver and James
Ursini, Proscenium, 1996, pp. 53–63. Originally published in *Film Comment*, vol. 8,
no. 1, Spring 1972, pp. 8–13.

Schulman, Michael. "Why *The Paperboy* is a Camp Classic." *The New Yorker*, 28 Jan. 2013,
www.newyorker.com/culture/culture-desk/why-the-paperboy-is-a-camp-classic.

Scott, A. O. "Harriet the Spy." *The New York Times Online*, 3 Nov. 2002, nytimes.com
/2002/11/03/books/harriet-the-spy.html.

Scott, Ellen C. *Cinema Civil Rights: Regulation, Repression, and Race in the Classical Hollywood Era.* Rutgers UP, 2015.

Scott, Robert Travis. "Movie Tax Credits Could Pay for Condos, Golf Courses." *New Orleans Times-Picayune* blog, 30 May 2007, blog.nola.com/times-picayune/2007/05/movie _tax_credits_paid_for_con.html. *Nola.com.*

Sedgwick, Eve Kosofsky. *Between Men: English Literature and Male Homosocial Desire.* Columbia UP, 1985.

Sepinwall, Alan, and Matt Zoller Seitz. *Two Experts Pick the Greatest American Shows of All Time.* Grand Central Publications, 2016.

Shandley, Robert R. *Runaway Romances: Hollywood's Postwar Tour of Europe.* Temple UP, 2009.

Shohat, Ella, and Robert Stam. *Unthinking Eurocentrism: Multiculturalism and the Movies.* 2nd ed., Routledge, 2014.

Sieving, Christopher. *Soul Searching: Black-Themed Cinema from the March on Washington to the Rise of Blaxploitation.* Wesleyan UP, 2011.

Simpson, Amelia S. *Detective Fiction from Latin America.* Cranbury, Associated U Presses, 1990.

Simpson, Lewis P. *The Brazen Face of History: Studies in the Literary Consciousness in America.* Louisiana State UP, 1980.

Slotkin, Richard. *Gunfighter Nation: The Myth of the Frontier in Twentieth-Century America.* U of Oklahoma P, 1998.

Smith, Imogen Sara. *In Lonely Places: Film Noir Beyond the City.* McFarland, 2011.

Smith, Jon. *Finding Purple America: The South and the Future of American Cultural Studies.* U of Georgia P, 2013.

Smith, Kevin Burton. "Ross Macdonald." *The Thrilling Detective,* www.thrillingdetective .com/trivia/kenmillar.html. 27 May 2018.

Smye, Rachel. "The McConaissance." *The New Yorker,* 16 Jan. 2014, www.newyorker.com /culture/culture-desk/the-mcconaissance.

Sobchack, Vivian. "Lounge Time: Postwar Crises and the Chronotope of Film Noir." *Refiguring American Film Genres: Theory and History,* edited by Nick Browne, U of California P, 1998, pp. 129–70. *EBSCOhost.*

Soitos, Stephen F. *The Blues Detective: A Study of African American Detective Fiction.* U of Massachusetts P, 1996.

Solà-Morales Rubió, Ignasi de. "Terrain Vague." *Anyplace,* edited by Cynthia C. Davidson. MIT P, 1995, pp. 199–223.

Sollors, Werner. *Neither Black nor White yet Both: Thematic Explorations of Interracial Literature.* Oxford UP, 1997.

Souther, Jonathan Mark. *New Orleans on Parade: Tourism and the Transformation of the Crescent City.* Louisiana State UP, 2006. Making the Modern South.

"Southern Variety." Review of *Search for a Hero,* by Thomas Hal Phillips, *Ghost and Flesh,* by William Goyen, and *The Courting of Susie Brown,* by Erskine Caldwell. *Time,* 25 Feb. 1952, pp. 102, 104.

Spicer, Andrew, and Helen Hanson, editors. *A Companion to Film Noir.* John Wiley & Sons, 2013. *ProQuest Ebook Central.*

Spigel, Lynn. *Make Room for TV: Television and the Family Ideal in Postwar America*. U of Chicago P, 1992.

Spill, Frederique. "Amy's Men, or Wounded Masculinity in Ron Rash's *One Foot in Eden*." *Babel: Litteratures plurielles*, vol. 31, 2015, pp. 103–30.

"Spiraling Down." *Law & Order: Special Victims Unit*, season 13, episode 10, NBC, 7 Dec. 2011. *Hulu*, www.hulu.com/watch/306861.

Stabile, Carol. *Black and White and Red All Over: Women Writers and the Broadcast Blacklist*. U of Illinois P, forthcoming.

———. *White Victims, Black Villains: Gender, Race, and Crime News in US Culture*. Routledge, 2006.

"Star-Struck Victims." *Law & Order: Special Victims Unit*, season 17, episode 16, NBC, 24 Feb 2016. *Hulu*, www.hulu.com/watch/909638.

Stevenson, Joe. "The People Speak." *The Chicago Defender*, 22 Feb. 1958, p. 10.

The Story of Temple Drake. Directed by Stephen Roberts, Performances by Miriam Hopkins, Jack La Rue, and William Gargan, Paramount, 1933.

Stransky, Tanner. "*Desperate Housewives*: Housewives Confidential." *Entertainment Weekly*, 23 Mar. 2012, ew.com/tv/2012/03/23/desperate-housewives-housewives-confidential/.

Strauss, Theodore. *Moonrise*. The Viking Press, 1946.

Sweeney, Susan Elizabeth. "'Subject-Cases' and 'Book Cases': Impostures and Forgeries from Poe to Auster" Merivale and Sweeney, pp. 247–72.

Tapley, Heather. "The Making of Hobo Masculinities." *Canadian Review of American Studies*, vol. 44, no. 1, 2014, pp. 25–43.

Tartt, Donna. *The Little Friend*. Vintage Books, 2002.

Tavernier, Bertrand. *Pas à pas dans la brume électrique: récit de tournage*. Flammarion, 2009.

Thompson, Chuck. *Better Off Without 'Em: A Northern Manifesto for Southern Secession*. Simon & Schuster Paperbacks, 2012.

Thompson, Tracy. *The New Mind of the South*. Free P, 2013.

"To Film Hot 'Black Like Me.'" *Variety*, 23 Jan. 1963, pp. 3, 6.

Tomasello, Michael. *A Natural History of Human Morality*. Harvard UP, 2016.

Tompkins, Jane. *West of Everything: The Inner Life of Westerns*. Oxford UP, 1992.

Torres, Sasha. *Black, White, and in Color: Television and Black Civil Rights*. Princeton UP, 2003.

"Travel the River Road Fantasy Land." *Advocate* [Baton Rouge, LA], 14 Apr. 1974, Vacation and Travel Special Edition, p. 34.

Trouard, Dawn. "Diverting Swine: Magical Relevancies of Eudora Welty's Ruby Fisher and Circe." *The Critical Response to Eudora Welty*, edited by Laurie Champion, Greenwood, 1994, pp. 335–55.

Tuska, Jon. *In Manors and Alleys: A Casebook on the American Detective Film*. Greenwood P, 1988.

Urgo, Joseph R. "Temple Drake's Truthful Perjury: Rethinking Faulkner's *Sanctuary*." *American Literature*, vol. 55, no. 3, 1983, pp. 435–44.

"V as in Voodoo." *Yancy Derringer*, written by Mary Loos and Richard Sale, directed by Edward O. Denault, CBS, 14 May 1959.

"Valentine's Day." *Law & Order: Special Victims Unit*, season 13, episode 17, NBC, 18 Apr. 2012. *Hulu*, www.hulu.com/watch/351629.

Van Dover, J. K., and John F. Jebb. *Isn't Justice Always Unfair?: The Detective in Southern Literature*. Bowling Green State U Popular P, 1996.

Vanderschelden, Isabelle. "Quand Bertrand Tavernier filme en noir." *Panorama mondial du film noir*, special issue of *CinémAction*, edited by Delphine Letort, vol. 151, 2014, pp. 117–24.

Vickery, Olga W. *The Novels of William Faulkner: A Critical Interpretation*. Louisiana State UP, 1995.

Vieira, Mark A. *Sin in Soft Focus: Pre-Code Hollywood*. Abrams, 1999.

Wager, Jans B. *Dangerous Dames: Women and Representation in the Weimar Street Film and Film Noir*. Ohio UP, 1999.

Wald, Gayle. *Crossing the Line: Racial Passing in Twentieth Century U.S. Literature and Culture*. Duke UP, 2000.

———. "'A Most Disagreeable Mirror': Reflections on White Identity in *Black Like Me*." *Passing and the Fictions of Identity*, edited by Elaine K. Ginsberg, Duke UP, 1996, pp. 151–77.

Walker, Jesse H. "'Black Like Me' Opens in Some 60 Theaters." *New York Amsterdam News* [New York City, NY], 23 May 1964, p. 18.

Walton, Priscilla L. "Bubblegum Metaphysics: Feminist Paradigms and Racial Interventions in Mainstream Hardboiled Women's Detective Fiction." *Multicultural Detective Fiction: Murder from the "Other" Side*, edited by Adrienne Johnson Gosselin, Garland Publishing Inc., 1999, pp. 257–79.

Ward, Jason Morgan. "'A Monument to Judge Lynch': Racial Violence, Symbolic Death and Black Resistance in Jim Crow Mississippi." Friend and Glover, pp. 229–49.

Warner, Michael. *The Trouble with Normal: Sex, Politics, and the Ethics of Queer Life*. Harvard UP, 1999.

"Warner Sets Up Own Syndication Unit." *Sponsor: The Weekly Magazine Radio/TV Advertisers Use*, 7 May 1962, pp. 12. *Library of Congress*, archive.org/stream/sponsormaga zine-1962–05/Sponsor-1962–05-1#page/n11/mode/2up.

Watson, Jay. "The Failure of Forensic Storytelling in *Sanctuary*." *Faulkner Journal*, vol. 6, no. 1, 1990, pp. 47–66.

———. "Mapping out a Postsouthern Cinema: Three Contemporary Films." *American Cinema and the Southern Imaginary*, edited by Deborah E. Barker and Kathryn McKee, U of Georgia P, 2011, pp. 219–52.

Welty, Eudora. "The Alterations." ca. 1987, MS. Eudora Welty Collection, Mississippi Department of Archives and History, Jackson, MS.

——. *The Collected Stories of Eudora Welty*. Harcourt Brace Jovanovich, 1980.

——. *Delta Wedding*. Harcourt Brace, 1946.

——. *Early Escapades*. Compiled and edited by Patti Carr Black, UP of Mississippi, 2005.

——. *The Eye of the Story: Selected Essays and Reviews*. Random House, 1977.

——. *Losing Battles*. Random House, 1980.

——. "The Night of the Little House." ca. 1937, MS. Russell and Volkening records, Manuscripts and Archives Division, The New York Public Library. Astor, Lenox, and Tilden Foundations.

——. *One Writer's Beginnings*. Harvard UP, 1984.

——. "The Reading and Writing of Short Stories." *Atlantic*, Feb. and Mar. 1949, pp. 54–58 and pp. 46–49.

——. *The Robber Bridegroom*. Doubleday, 1942.

——. "The Shadow Club." ca. 1975, MS. Eudora Welty Collection, Mississippi Department of Archives and History, Jackson, MS.

——. *A Writer's Eye: Collected Book Reviews*. Edited by Pearl McHaney, UP of Mississippi, 1994.

Wenska, Walter. "'There's a Man with a Gun over There': Faulkner's Hijackings of Masculine Popular Culture." *Faulkner Journal*, vol. 15, nos. 1–2, 1999–2000, pp. 35–60.

Whalen, Terence. *Edgar Allan Poe and the Masses: The Political Economy of Literature in Antebellum America*. Princeton UP, 1999.

Whitehouse, Lucie. "Our Growing Appetite for Chick Noir," *The Telegraph*, 16 Jan. 2014, www.telegraph.co.uk/culture/books/booknews/10574425/Our-growing-appetite-for-chick-noir.html.

Wilhelm, Randall. "'A Boxed and Stilled Forever': Vision, Death and Affect in the Work of Ron Rash." *Summoning the Dead: Essays on Ron Rash*, edited by Randall Wilhelm and Zackary Vernon, U of South Carolina P, 2018, pp. 83–98.

Williams, David E. "Forging Future Noir." *American Cinematographer*, Aug. 2007, pp. 34–37.

Williams, Linda. *Playing the Race Card: Melodramas of Black and White from Uncle Tom to O.J. Simpson*. Princeton UP, 2001.

Williams, Linda Ruth. *The Erotic Thriller in Contemporary Cinema*. Indiana UP, 2005.

Williams, Raymond. *Marxism and Literature*. Oxford UP, 1977. Marxist Introductions Series.

Williamson, J. W. *Hillbillyland: What the Movies Did to the Mountains and What the Mountains Did to the Movies*. U of North Carolina P, 1995.

Willis, Sharon. *The Poitier Effect: Racial Melodrama and Fantasies of Reconciliation*. U of Minnesota P, 2015.

Winders, Jamie. "New Americans in a New South City? Immigrant and Refugee Politics in Nashville, Tennessee." *Latino Immigrants and the Transformation of the U.S. South*, edited by Mary E. Odem and Elaine Lacy, U of Georgia P, 2009, pp. 126–42.

———. "Placing Latino/as in the Music City: Latino Migration and Urban Transformation in Nashville Tennessee." *Latinos in the New South: Transformations of Place,* edited by Owen J. Furuseth and Heather A. Smith, Ashgate Publishing Co., 2006, pp. 167–89.

Wolff, Robert Paul. *In Defense of Anarchism.* Harper & Row, 1970.

"Wondermen of the Westerns." *TV Radio Mirror,* vol. 52, no. 1, June 1959, pp. 42–47. *Library of Congress,* archive.org/details/radiotv00mac.

Wood, Amy Louise. *Lynching and Spectacle: Witnessing Racial Violence in America, 1890–1940.* U of North Carolina P, 2009.

Woods, Gregory. *A History of Gay Literature: The Male Tradition.* Yale UP, 1999.

Wray, Matt. *Not Quite White: White Trash and the Boundaries of Whiteness.* Duke UP, 2006.

Wright, Richard. *Black Boy: A Record of Childhood and Youth.* Harper & Brothers, 1945.

———. *Eight Men.* 1961. Thunder's Mouth Press, 1987.

———. "Inner Landscape." Review of *The Heart Is a Lonely Hunter,* by Carson McCullers. *New Republic,* 5 Aug. 1940, p. 195.

Yaeger, Patricia. "Black Men Dressed in Gold." *PMLA,* vol. 124, no. 1, Jan. 2009, pp. 11–24. *JSTOR,* doi: 10.1632/pmla.2009.124.1.306.

———. *Dirt and Desire: Reconstructing Women's Writing, 1930–1990.* U of Chicago P, 2000.

Yakir, Dan. "Painting Pictures." Interview with Bertrand Tavernier. *Film Comment,* vol. 20, no. 5, 1984, pp. 18–22. *ProQuest Performing Arts Periodicals.*

Yarbrough, Scott. "The Dark Lady: Temple Drake as Femme Fatale." *Southern Literary Journal,* vol. 31, no. 2, 1999, pp. 50–64.

Younge, Gary. *No Place Like Home: A Black Briton's Journey through the American South.* 1999. UP of Mississippi, 2002.

Zavattini, Cesare. "Some Ideas on the Cinema." Translated by Pier Luigi Lanza. *Monthly Film Bulletin,* vol. 23, no. 2, Dec. 1953, pp. 64–69. *ProQuest Performing Arts Periodicals.*

Žižek, Slavoj. *Sublime Object of Ideology.* Verso, 1989.

CONTRIBUTORS

MEGAN ABBOTT is the award-winning author of eight novels, including *Dare Me* and *You Will Know Me*. Her work has won or been nominated for the CWA Steel Dagger, the International Thriller Writers Award, the Los Angeles Times Book Prize and five Edgar awards. She is also the author of *The Street Was Mine*, a study of hard-boiled fiction. She received her PhD in American literature from New York University.

JACOB AGNER is a PhD candidate in English literature at the University of Mississippi. His dissertation is titled *Moonshine and Meanness: Country Noir and the Rural Undergrowth of the American Crime Tradition in Fiction and Film, 1930–1960*. He has published essays on Eudora Welty, Cormac McCarthy, and film.

ACE ATKINS is the *New York Times* bestselling author of twenty-one novels, including *The Fallen* and Robert B. Parker's *Little White Lies,* both from G.P. Putnam's Sons in 2017. Atkins has been nominated for every major award in crime fiction, including the Edgar three times and twice for novels about former US Army Ranger Quinn Colson. A former newspaper reporter and SEC football player, Ace also writes essays and investigative pieces for several national magazines including *Outside* and *Garden & Gun*. He lives in Oxford, Mississippi, with his family, where he's friend to many dogs and several bartenders.

DEBORAH E. BARKER is professor of English at the University of Mississippi. She is the author of *Reconstructing Violence: The Southern Rape Complex in Film and Literature* and *Aesthetics and Gender: Portraits of the Woman Artist*. She coedited, with Kathryn McKee, *American Cinema and the Southern Imaginary*.

R. BRUCE BRASELL is the author of *The Possible South: Documentary Film and the Limitations of Biraciality* and articles in *Cinema Journal, Film History, Journal of Film & Video, Wide Angle, Jump Cut, Mississippi Quarterly,* and several anthologies. He has taught film and media studies at New York University, Sarah Lawrence

College, Vassar College, Brooklyn College, Hunter College, Manhattanville College, the University of Alabama, Birmingham, and Oklahoma State University.

PHOEBE BRONSTEIN is assistant teaching professor and the Director of the Culture, Art, and Technology Program at University of California, San Diego's Sixth College. Her work has appeared in the peer-reviewed publications *Camera Obscura, Quarterly Review of Film and Video,* and *JumpCut.* She is currently working on a book project that focuses on the intersections of race, masculinity, and the South in television's network era.

GINA CAISON is associate professor of English at Georgia State University where she teaches courses in southern literatures, Native American literatures, and documentary practices. She is the author of *Red States: Indigeneity, Settler Colonialism, and Southern Studies* and coeditor of *Small-Screen Souths: Region, Identity, and the Cultural Politics of Television.* In addition to these projects, Caison's work has appeared in journals including *The Global South, Mississippi Quarterly, The Simms Review,* and *PMLA,* and she is producer and host of the podcast *About South.*

CLAIRE COTHREN is an Upper School English teacher at The Hockaday School in Dallas, Texas. Her dissertation explores the evolution of the southern gothic as a literary mode that emphasizes connections between constructions of race, gender, and region in the American South.

JAMES A. CRANK is associate professor of English at University of Alabama. He is a National Humanities Center Summer Fellow and the co-host of the podcast *The Sound and the Furious.* His work has appeared in *south: an interdisciplinary journal, Global South, Southern Literary Journal, Mississippi Quarterly, Southern Studies,* and collections such as *Agee Agonistes: Essays on the Life, Legend, and Works of James Agee ,* and *Southerners on Film: Essays on Hollywood Portrayals Since the 1970s.* His books include *Understanding Sam Shepard, New Approaches to Gone with the Wind, Race and New Modernisms,* and *Understanding Randall Kenan.*

DOMINIQUA DICKEY is the author of "God's Gonna Trouble the Water," one of the thirteen stories featured in Akashic Books' critically acclaimed *Mississippi Noir.* She received an MFA in Creative Writing from The University of Mississippi and a fellowship from the New York State Summer Writers Institute at Skidmore College. She teaches at her alma mater, UCLA, and is currently writing a novel that explores more noir, Elnora May Hardin, and Grenada, MS.

LEIGH ANNE DUCK is associate professor of English at the University of Mississippi, where she edits the journal *The Global South*. Her published essays examine literary and visual representations of the US South as well as comparative approaches to Jim Crow segregation and South African apartheid. Her book, *The Nation's Region: Southern Modernism, Segregation, and U.S. Nationalism*, was published in 2006. She is currently working on a manuscript, *On Location in Hollywood South: An Aspirational State in Uncertain Times*.

GREG HERREN is the award-winning author of over thirty novels and editor of twenty anthologies. He has won two Lambda Literary Awards (out of 14 nominations), and has been shortlisted for the Shirley Jackson, Macavity, and Anthony Awards. He writes two private eye series set in New Orleans, the most recent of which is *Garden District Gothic*. His young adult fiction has won two medals from the Independent Press Moonbeam Awards` for Children and Young Adult Fiction.

BOB HODGES is a PhD candidate in literature and critical theory at the University of Washington. His dissertation covers nineteenth- and early twentieth-century transatlantic detective and artist fictions. He is coediting the collection *The Weird and the Southern Imaginary*. His contributions have appeared or are forthcoming in the journals *ESQ, Poe Review*, and *Clues* and the collections *Horror through History* and *Portable Prose: The Novel and the Everyday*.

SUZANNE LEONARD is professor of English at Simmons University in Boston. She is the author of *Wife, Inc: The Business of Marriage in the Twenty-First Century*, *Fatal Attraction* and coeditor of *Fifty Hollywood Directors*.

SARAH LEVENTER is visiting assistant professor in Film and New Media Studies at Wheaton College in Massachusetts. She is currently completing her book project, *Beasts of the Southern Screen: Race, Gender, and the Global South in American Cinema since 1963*.

KRISTOPHER MECHOLSKY is a faculty member in the Residential Colleges Program at Louisiana State University, where he earned his doctorate in English in 2012. His first book (co-authored with David Madden) is a critical overview of the crime fiction author James M. Cain. He has published essays on film, crime fiction, and the South with Scarecrow, McFarland, Palgrave, and Salem Presses, as well as with *South Atlantic Review*, the *Baker Street Journal*, the *Faulkner Journal*, and others.

YAJAIRA M. PADILLA is associate professor of English and Latin American and Latino Studies at the University of Arkansas, Fayetteville. She is the author of *Changing Women, Changing Nation: Female Agency, Nationhood, and Identity in Trans-Salvadoran Narratives* and has published articles in *Latin American Perspectives*, *Latino Studies*, the *Arizona Journal of Hispanic Cultural Studies*, and *Studies in 20th and 21st Century Literature*, among others.

JACQUELINE PINKOWITZ is a doctoral candidate in Media Studies at the University of Texas at Austin. Her dissertation, *Reel South: Race, Region, and the American Film Industry in the Era of Black Civil Rights (1955–1975)*, examines the co-construction of blackness, whiteness, and the US South across a range of industrial sectors and generic film cycles. Her work has been published in the *Journal of Popular Film and Television*, the *Journal of Transformative Works and Cultures*, and the *Quarterly Review of Film and Video*. She previously served as Co-Managing Editor of *Flow* and on *The Velvet Light Trap* editorial board.

HARRIET POLLACK, affiliate professor of American Literature at College of Charleston, is the author of *Eudora Welty's Fiction and Photography: The Body of The Other Woman*. She is the editor and director of the UPM series, *Critical Perspectives on Eudora Welty*; the series inaugural volume, *New Essays on Eudora Welty, Class, and Race*, is forthcoming. Her previous edited and coedited volumes include *Eudora Welty, Whiteness, and Race*, *Emmett Till in Literary Memory and Imagination*, *Having Our Way: Women Rewriting Tradition in Twentieth-Century America*, and *Eudora Welty and Politics: Did the Writer Crusade?* She received the Phoenix Award for outstanding contributions to Eudora Welty scholarship in 2009 and has twice served as president of the Eudora Welty Society.

RICHÉ RICHARDSON is associate professor of African American literature in the Africana Studies and Research Center at Cornell University. Her essays have been published in *American Literature*, *Mississippi Quarterly*, *Forum for Modern Language Studies*, *Black Renaissance/Renaissance Noire*, *TransAtlantica*, the *Southern Quarterly*, *Black Camera*, *NKA*, *Phillis*, *Technoculture*, and *Labrys*. Her first book, *Black Masculinity and the U.S. South: From Uncle Tom to Gangsta*, was highlighted by Choice Books as one of the "Outstanding Academic Titles of 2008." Since 2005, she has served as coeditor of the New Southern Studies book series at the University of Georgia Press.

THERESA STARKEY is the associate director of the Sarah Isom Center for Women and Gender Studies at the University of Mississippi, where she also teaches as an instructional assistant professor for the program. Her writing has appeared in the *Oxford American, Mississippi Review,* and elsewhere.

ZACKARY VERNON is assistant professor of English at Appalachian State University. His teaching and writing focus on American literature, film, and environmental studies, and he has an abiding interest in the material and cultural histories of Appalachia and the US South. His research has appeared in a range of scholarly books and journals including *Mississippi Quarterly, Southern Cultures,* and *Journal of American Studies.* He is coeditor with Randall Wilhelm of *Summoning the Dead: Essays on Ron Rash* and the editor of *Ecocriticism and the Future of Southern Studies.*

RANDALL WILHELM is assistant professor of English at Anderson University. He is the editor of *The Ron Rash Reader,* coeditor of *Conversations with Robert Morgan,* and coeditor. with Zackary Vernon. of *Summoning the Dead: Essays on Ron Rash.*

INDEX

abject, 70–71, 121, 238, 256, 264–65, 291–92

Adorno, Theodor, 28–29

African Americans: absence of in *Home Killings,* 245–46; and authenticity, 101–3; in *Big Easy, The,* 87; black feminist discourse, 284; Black Lives Matter, 279; and blues, 60, 98–99, 100, 104, 107, 309; in *Brume,* 93; in detective fiction, 3, 8, 280–281; drama, 280; in *Moonrise,* 58–62; in *In the Electric Mist,* 95; and hip-hop, 98–102; and history of lynching, 161; and mistreatment of by whites, 161–166; in noir, 59, 81; in *Panic in the Streets,* 83; passing as black, 12, 286–99, 300n2; and plantation narratives, 180–181; postracial, 31, 280; #SayHerName, 279; stereotypes of black masculinity, 212, 278–279, 293; twenty-first century literature, 278. *See also* civil rights movement; Jim Crow; masculinity

AIDS, 65–66

Akashic Books, 4

Akass, Kim. *See* McCabe, Janet

Alton, John, 43

American Cinematographer (magazine), 41, 42–48

anarchism, 9–10, 187, 195–97, 200–202

Andy Griffith Show, The, 183, 184n3, 207–20

Angel Heart, 85

Anthropocene, 187, 191, 196, 202. *See also* ecology

antihero, 53–54, 69

Appalachia, 51, 54, 59, 60, 62n1, 214, 223, 227, 228, 230, 304; Appalachian noir, 230, 235. *See also* hillbilly; mountain

Archer, Lew, 144–45

Atkins, Ace, 5, 138; *Dirty South,* 7–8, 96, 97–103, 105–7, 109–10

authenticity, 8, 85, 96, 98–101, 106–10; blackness, 103; noir, 4–5, 103–4; Louisiana, 96–97, 107–8; New Orleans, 99–101, 103–4, 109; southern, 97, 99, 109–11. *See also* commodification

auteur, 46, 48, 89. *See also* Borzage, Frank; Pizzolatto, Nic

Baby Doll, 40, 43–45, 46

Baby Face, 38

Baldwin, James, 85

Barker, Deborah, 3, 13n2, 30, 32, 34, 111n1, 222, 255, 256–57, 258

Bass, Ernest T., 209, 212–16

Berendt, John, 302, 308, 311, 314; *Midnight in the Garden of Good and Evil,* 301, 305–7, 309

Big Easy, The, 7, 86, 88, 94

Birth of a Nation, 172, 178, 180, 183n1, 184n2, 184n8, 185n13, 273–74, 284

Black Like Me (film), 12, 286–300. *See also* Griffin, John Howard

Black Mask, 27, 143

Blade Runner, 43; future noir, 43

blood, 70, 98, 147, 150, 159, 223, 232; bad, 58–59; as genealogy, 72

blues, 60, 98–99, 100, 104, 107, 309. *See also* Guy, Buddy

Bogle, Donald, 293

Boorman, John. *See Deliverance*

Borzage, Frank, 6–7, 52, 54, 56–62. *See also Moonrise*

Bourbon Street Beat, 9, 173, 178, 182, 183, 183–84n1, 184n11, 185n12

Breaking Bad, 50, 74

Brume, 82, 89–90, 93–95. *See also In the Electric Mist* (film)

Burke, James Lee, 92, 302; *In the Electric Mist with the Confederate Dead,* 7, 81–82, 90

Burnett, W. R., 31, 145

Cain, James M., 6, 29, 39n3, 39n5, 40; *Butterfly*, 6, 49, 54–55, 63n4; *Postman Always Rings Twice, The*, 28, 49, 50. See also *Double Indemnity*; noir: mountainnoir

capitalism, 79, 85–86, 88–89, 186–87, 197, 202, 309; neoliberalism, 66, 92, 120–21, 125

Capote, Truman, 45, 137

Chacón, Romilia. *See* Villatoro, Marcos McPeek

Chandler, Raymond, 27, 29, 33, 39n5, 96, 144, 145, 199; *Big Sleep, The*, 33

Chase, James Hadley, 38

chiaroscuro, 6, 30, 34, 291

Christie, Agatha, 137, 145

cinematography, 6, 30, 41–48, 292; noir, 6

civil rights movement, 4, 9, 173–74, 177–78, 180, 181, 183–84n1, 184n6, 207, 273–76, 278–79, 286, 287, 289, 290–91, 297–300; Freedom Riders, 308–9

Civil War (U.S.), 3–4, 89, 92, 103, 176, 178, 183–84n1, 304, 306–7; as analogy for corporate invasion, 140; in film, 81

civil war (Central America), 238, 244, 248–49; in Guatemala, 240; legacy of, 246

Classical Hollywood, 48, 49, 83

cliché, 7, 12, 22, 32, 34, 43, 82, 85, 89–90, 259, 268, 286, 296–97; southern, 19, 308, 313–14

Clover, Carol, 77

Collins, Patricia Hill, 294

commodification, 3, 7, 82, 85, 102, 186–87, 314–15n1; of authenticity, 4–5

consumption, 4–5, 87–88, 117, 239–40, 302, 308; mass, 39n5, 68–69; public, 79

cowboy, 67, 68–71, 76, 177–79, 183; boots, 305; hat, 60, 295; southern detective as, 67

creative nonfiction, 301–5, 307, 310

Cronenweth, Jordan, 43

Dallas Buyers Club, 64, 65–66, 68, 74–75, 79

Dans la brume électrique. See Brume

degeneracy, 45, 47–48

Deleuze, Gilles, 89, 90, 92

Deliverance, 55, 223

Desperate Housewives, 8, 112–18, 120, 125

Dexter, Pete, 307

Dickey, James. *See* Deliverance

Doane, Mary Ann, 35–36

domesticity, 112–18, 124–25, 208, 215, 216, 219

Double Indemnity, 49, 129, 132, 222

Drowning Pool, The, 85

Duck, Leigh Anne, 7, 64, 78, 159, 264, 298, 301, 304, 305

Duggan, Lisa, 65–66, 80n3

Dyer, Richard, 162, 179, 294

ecology, 9–10, 82, 145, 187, 190–94, 196–97, 201–2

Edward Scissorhands, 115, 116

Eggleston, William, 5–6, 22–25

Ellison, Ralph, 151–52

Evers, Medgar. *See* civil rights movement

Faulkner, William, 4, 5, 9, 20, 42, 45, 47, 73, 135–36, 190; *Absalom, Absalom!*, 17, 73, 303; influence on the detective genre, 1–2, 6, 17–18; *Intruder in the Dust*, 17, 20, 121, 43–44; *Sanctuary*, 2, 6, 26–39

Fearing, Kenneth, 27, 39n5, 145

femme fatale, 27, 51, 57, 64, 132–33; in suburban noir, 112–13, 116, 118, 121, 123–25; Temple Drake as, 6, 26, 29, 35–39, 39n2

Florida, 9–10, 68, 72, 73, 186–87, 191, 193, 194–96, 198, 202, 257, 273, 276, 277–79, 283, 296, 302, 310–12; Everglades, 201, 311; as southern, 188–91

Flynn, Gillian, 112, 118; *Gone Girl*, 8, 112–14, 118–25

freak (figure of the), 57, 58

Freedom Riders. *See* civil rights movement

Friend, Craig Thompson, 161, 178

Fugitive Kind, The, 44, 45, 46

gender, 6, 8, 10, 17; black feminist discourse, 284; chick noir, 112–116; femininity, 112, 124, 175, 185n13, 265; feminism, 155, 254–55; heteronormative, 7, 31–33, 67, 72–3, 75, 70–80, 88, 115; heterosexuality, 7, 8, 32–33, 37–38, 66–67, 72–73, 114, 125; homosexuality, 6, 26, 29, 31–35, 74, 75; homonationalism, 66; homonormativity, 65–66; homosocial, 75, 80n4; lesbian characters, 137–38; postfeminism, 8, 112–13, 120–23; queer/ing characters, and suburban noir, 112–128; #SayHerName, 279. *See also* masculinity genre, 1, 2–3, 10–11, 26, 39n2, 69, 80n1, 85, 96, 143, 168, 221–22, 267, 280; versus style, 40–41, 44–46; Welty's transformation of, 157, 158n7. *See also* noir; Western (genre)

German Expressionism, 6, 43

Gift, The, 48, 49

gothic, 6, 10, 41, 42–43, 46, 85, 109, 117, 119–21, 124, 222; and noir, 45. *See also* southern gothic

Graham, Allison, 174, 177, 179, 184n5, 184n7, 300n9

Gray Ghost, The, 9, 172–73, 180, 182

Great Recession, 113, 118, 120

Greene, Graham, 27, 28, 145

Griffin, John Howard, 286–87, 289, 296, 298

Griffith, Andy, 213, 217–18; *Andy Griffith Show, The,* 10, 183, 207–20

grit lit, 2, 5, 10, 12

Grundmann, Roy, 71

Guy, Buddy, 93

Harrelson, Woody, 74–75

Halberstam, J. Jack, 115

Hall, Stuart, 181, 240

Hammett, Dashiell, 26–27, 28, 33, 39n5, 50, 96, 144, 145, 156

HBO, 2, 50, 74–75, 78, 105, 107, 110, 111n3, 111n4

heterosexuality, 7, 8, 32–33, 37–38, 66–67, 72–73, 114, 125; heteronormativity, 7, 31, 66, 67, 75, 79, 88, 115; normative, 87

hillbilly, 7, 54–56, 59, 60–61, 63n3, 109, 213, 214–15, 228. *See also* Appalachia

Himes, Chester, 3, 280; "He Knew," 27; "His Last Day," 39

Hinrichsen, Lisa, 255–56, 257, 267

hip-hop, 98–100, 102

homosexuality, 6, 26, 29, 31–35, 74, 75, 138; gay male gaze, 139, homonationalism, 66; homonormativity, 65–66; homosocial, 75, 80n4. *See also* queer(ness)

Houghton Mifflin, 155

Huie, William Bradford, 11, 273–85; *He Slew the Dreamer, My Search for the Truth about James Earl Ray and the Murder of Martin Luther King,* 273; *Klansman, The,* 273, 275–76; *Mud on the Stars,* 275; relationship with Zora Neale Hur-ston, 11, 276–83; *Revolt of Mamie Stover, The,* 275; *Ruby McCollum, Woman in the Swannee Jail,* 11, 273, 276–83; *Three Lives for Mississippi,* 273

Hurricane Katrina, 7, 95, 111n3, 139–40

Huston, John, 45–46

In the Electric Mist (film), 7, 81–95. *See also Brume;* Burke, James Lee; *In the Electric Mist with the Confederate Dead*

Jameson, Fredric, 29, 39n2, 89

Jim Crow, 19, 169, 184n6; and black women, 129, 283–84; and criminal culture, 287, 291–95; cultural values, 131, 160, 163, 279–80; era, 274–75, 279–80; and lynching, 160–62,169, 257–58; and southern rape complex, 146, 149, 151, 257–58; and visual logic, 295–98

journalism, 40, 278, 312–13, 314; checkbook, 273, 282; investigative, 11, 274; investigative journalist, 68, 72, 240, 273–76, 284, 289; long-form, 301

Justified, 50, 183, 213, 230

Kaufman, Boris, 44, 46

Killer Joe, 64, 67

King, Dr. Martin Luther, 174; murder of, 273

Kreyling, Michael, 145, 155, 314–15n1

Ku Klux Klan, 173–74, 212, 273

LaLaurie, Madame, 134

Latino, 11, 239, 240, 243; Central Americans, 238, 245–250; as cop, 242; in the South, 237, 239, 241, 244

Laroche, John, 310–11

Laveau, Marie,134

Law & Order: Special Victims Unit, 11, 252–69

Losing Battles, 144, 157

Louisiana, 2, 7, 50, 74–76, 78, 96–99, 107–8, 110, 111n2, 111n3, 111n4; noir, 81–95. *See also* New Orleans

lynching, 10, 31, 37, 38, 89, 92, 161–62, 169, 171n2, 173–74, 176, 288–89, 293, 309, 314

MacDonald, John D., 9–10, 186–89, 191–94, 196–200, 202; *Brass Cupcake, The,* 187, 192;

MacDonald, John D. (*continued*)
Bright Orange for the Shroud, 194, 201; *Dead
Low Tide,* 189; *Deep Blue Good-By,* 192, 198;
Dreadful Lemon Sky, The, 192, 195; *Dress Her
in Indigo,* 202; *Drowner, The,* 192, 199; *Empty
Copper Sea, The,* 192; *Executioners, The,* 192,
199; *Girl in the Plain Brown Wrapper, The,* 195;
Long Lavender Look, The, 202; *Pale Gray for
Guilt,* 192, 194
Macdonald, Ross, 9, 143–45, 199; *Blue Hammer,
The,* 144; *Great Stories of Suspense,* 145; *Sleeping
Beauty,* 145; *Underground Man, The,* 144–45.
See also Welty, Eudora
MacLeod, Chanse, 9, 136, 138–39
Magic Mike, 64, 67, 68–69, 79
Mailer, Norman, 71, 290
Marigny District, 135, 137
marriage, 56, 72, 93, 112, 113–14, 116, 119–20,
124–25, 131, 144, 157, 221, 236n2
Marrs, Suzanne, 143, 144, 158n4
masculinity, 67, 69, 76, 78, 84–85, 88, 227; avoidance of, 259, 269n2; hard-boiled, 9, 13, 29, 31–
38, 96; homosocial, 75; instability of, 84, 88,
143, 211–12, 216; and misogyny, 254; in neo-
noir, 86; in noir, 35, 76–77, 85; queer, 32, 67,
69–72; stereotypes of black masculinity, 212,
278–279, 293; and Western cowboy, 76, 179,
183; white, 31, 82–83, 163, 173, 178–83, 215;
white southern; 173, 177–78, 184n11, 280–81,
299; in works of Ron Rash, 236n4. *See also*
southern rape complex
masochism, 70–72
Mayberry, 10, 207–8, 210–13, 215–16, 218–19
McCabe, Janet, 74, 116
McConaissance, 66–67, 79
McConaughey, Matthew, 7, 64–79, 110; relationship with Woody Harrelson, 74–75. *See also*
McConaissance
McCullers, Carson, 42, 45, 47, 48; *Heart Is a
Lonely Hunter,* 42
McGee, Travis, 9–10, 139, 187, 191–202, 203n1
McKee, Kathryn, 3, 13n2, 111n1, 222, 255, 256–57
McPeek Villatoro, Marcos, 11, 237–39, 243–44,
245–46, 250n6; *Home Killings,* 237–50; *Minos,*
237, 239, 244–46; *Venom Beneath the Skin, A,*
237, 250n3

Merivale, Patricia, 168, 228
Millar, Ken, 144–45. *See also* Macdonald, Ross
Millar, Margaret, 144–45
Mississippi Blues, 91
Mississippi Sissy. See Sessums, Kevin
Missouri, 3, 38, 50, 113, 118–21, 281. *See also*
Ozarks
modernism, 26–29, 38, 39n2, 39n5, 142, 156–57
Moonrise, 6–7, 50–63. *See also* Borzag, Frank;
Strauss, Theodore
Mosley, Walter, 3, 280
mountain, 7, 50–51, 52– 56, 59–61, 212–14,
216–18, 221, 275; girl, 227; mountaineer, 51,
54, 58, 60, 209, 214–15, 228, 233–34; Stone
Mountain, 184n8. *See also* noir; mountainoir

Naipaul, V. S., 12, 301–2, 304–5, 307, 309, 311,
314; *Turn in the South, A,* 301, 304
Naremore, James, 4, 28, 39n5, 54, 81
narratology, 29, 42–46, 312–13
New Orleans, 4, 7–8, 9, 82–87, 93–95, 134–41,
173, 175–81, 302; Noir/"No-Orleans," 8, 96–111
New York, 1, 3, 11, 41, 118, 120–21, 130, 137, 144,
173, 252–65, 300n7, 300n11
noir, 1–12; and African Americans, 59, 81, 83,
103; Appalachian noir, 230, 235; Akashic
Books, 4; and blackness, 29–31, 38, 59, 69–72,
101–4; color noir, 40–44, 48; future noir, 43;
and gothic, 64, 72, 64, 72–73, 80n1; and Louisiana, 81–95; mountainoir, 6–7, 50–55, 58–
62; neo-noir, 22–23, 43, 48, 65, 76, 85–88, 93,
125, 223; rural, 3, 6, 50–55, 58, 62n1, 109–10;
Noir/"No-Orleans," 96–111, 221; and *Sanctuary,* 6, 26–39, 39n1, 2; spacial logic, 93–94,
227–28; southern gothic noir, 7, 64, 74, 80n1;
southern noir, 4–7, 67; suburban noir, 8, 112–
28; urban noir, 1, 4, 51, 77, 96, 114, 130, 227;
visual style, 43–44, 59, 83–84, 221–23, 289.
See also femme fatale; southern gothic
North Carolina, 114, 212–13, 217, 286
North(ern), 68, 124, 175, 188, 189, 190, 191, 252,
253, 260, 262, 264–66, 268–69, 289, 314;
audience, 9, 67, 78, 172, 183n1; characters, 1,
175, 180, 189; imaginary, 67; urbanity, 256–59,
300n11
Notorious Sophie Lang, The, 38

O'Connor, Flannery, 39n5, 45, 48, 73, 76, 145
Orlean, Susan, 12; *Orchid Thief, The,* 301, 310–12
Out of the Past, 75, 291
Ozarks, 60, 113, 123–25

Pajarito, 242
Palmer, R. Barton, 45, 83
Panic in the Streets, 83
Paperboy, The (film), 7, 64–65, 67–73, 74, 77, 78, 79
performance, 86–88, 93, 209, 212, 215, 280; as detective, 233; ethnic, 239, 240, 244, 246, 249, 253; as femme fatale, 35, 36; feminine, 112; postfeminist, 120; queer, 65; of southerness, 77
Pizzolatto, Nic, 108–11. See also *True Detective*
plantation, 3, 29, 39n2, 57, 69, 77, 82, 84–85, 130, 164–65, 172–74, 176–83, 294, 302, 304
Poe, Edgar Allan, 1; "Gold Bug, The," 1; "Tell-Tale Heart, The," 153, 154
police procedural, 4, 8, 10–11, 143, 153, 154–55, 207–20, 222, 225, 228, 236, 252, 255, 258–60
postsouthern, 301, 313, 314n1, 315
poverty, 54, 122–23, 164, 170, 227; southern, 5, 113, 123, 139, 214, 221
"Poverty Row," 51–52
production codes, 28, 37, 38
Puar, Jasbir, 65–66

queer(ness), 7, 9, 32, 74, 79, 80n3, 137; and blackness, 67–68, 70–72; co-opting of, 65–66

Rabinowitz, Paula, 39n5, 81, 113
rape, 18, 114, 117; abuse of black women, 277; antirape activism, 88; in *Law & Order: SVU,* 254, 256–59, 262–65, 275; male as victim; 28, 35, 55; in *Sanctuary,* 28–29, 32–38. See also southern rape complex
Rash, Ron, 10–11, 221–36
realism, 78, 83, 287, 292, 297; "locative," 83; neo-realism, 83, 89, 292; magical, 96; social, 78, 79
Reconstruction, 161, 177, 178
Reddy, Maureen T., 254, 258–59, 267
Reflections in a Golden Eye (film), 46, 48

Richardson, Riché, 276, 293
Rieger, Christopher, 186, 189–90
Rountree, Stephanie, 255–56, 257, 267
rural, 1, 2, 5, 6, 19–20, 39n3, 50–52, 56, 60, 62, 73, 98, 104–6, 107, 109, 112–13, 188–90, 202, 210, 215, 256, 284, 289, 308; naturalism, 39n2. See also noir
Russell, Diarmuid, 155, 158, 158n3, 158n5, 153n6, 153n9

sadomasochism. See masochism
Sáenz, Diego, 240, 243, 246, 248
Sedgwick, Eve Kosofsky, 75
Seldes, Tim, 155, 158n3
Sessums, Kevin, 148–49
Shadow, The, 149
Shadow of a Doubt, 35, 129, 132
Sister, Sister, 48–49
social critique, 64, 73–44, 78, 94, 287, 289, 291
southern gothic, 3, 6, 8, 10, 40–49, 64, 67–68, 70, 72–74, 77–79, 110–11, 111n1, 159, 221; and noir, 64, 72, 64, 72–73, 80n1; southern gothic noir, 7, 64, 74, 80n1
southern imaginary, 3, 7, 12, 13n2, 64–65, 67, 71, 73, 76, 111n1, 113, 186, 222, 255, 256
southern rape complex, 146–52, 175, 257, 263–64
Stand Your Ground, 278–79
St. Louis Cemetery Number One, 134
Stepford Wives, The, 115, 117
Story of Temple Drake, The, 6, 30, 38. See also Faulkner, William: *Sanctuary*
Streetcar Named Desire, A (film), 40
Strauss, Theodore, 7, 51, 55–56. See also *Moonrise* (film)
suburbs, 8, 20, 50, 81, 98, 103, 115–17, 125, 307, 309. See also noir: suburban noir
Sweeney, Susan Elizabeth. See Merivale, Patricia

Televisual South, 173, 182–83, 184n3, 252–53, 255–57, 266–67
Tennessee, 239, 299; Chattanooga, 244, 245; Memphis, 4, 6, 29, 37, 96, 142, 245; Nashville, 2, 11, 237, 239–41, 246–47, 249
Texas, 3, 66–69, 76, 79, 136, 138–39
Thompson, Chuck, 313–14, 315n2

Thompson, Jim, 39n5, 94
Thompson, Tracy, 313, 314, 315n2
Tibbehah County, 5, 17, 20
Tightrope, 7, 86, 87–88
Times-Picayune, 83, 85–86
tourism, 82–87, 88–89, 93, 98, 103–4, 122, 134, 189–90, 193, 200, 202, 217–18, 304, 307
True Detective, 2, 7–8, 50, 64, 68, 73–79, 105, 107–11, 111n3, 302. *See also* Pizzolatto, Nic
Twain, Mark, 1, 269n4; *Pudd'nhead Wilson*, 1, 269n4; *Tom Sawyer, Detective*, 1
Twin Peaks, 114–15, 116, 117

urban, 84, 96, 108, 143, 256–57, 291; crime in, 1, 5, 6, 39n2, 256; Florida, 189; as inauthentic, 97; New Orleans, 96, 106, 109–10; northern locales, 255, 256, 259, 300n11; north v. south, 257, 258; southern poverty, 2, 4, 8, 104, 186; urbanization, 81, 186, 187, 189–90; versus rural, 109–10, 216, 217, 312. *See also* noir: urban noir

Vallée, Jean Mark, 65
Van Peebles, Melvin. *See Watermelon Man*
Virginia, 7, 51–53, 296; 1924 Virginia Act, 288
violence, 1, 2, 5, 9, 27, 28–29, 37, 39n2, 47, 49, 51, 54, 74, 94, 96, 111, 117–18, 131, 143, 148–49, 157, 161, 163–64, 169–70, 172, 174, 176, 179, 199–200, 216, 221, 230, 237, 239, 246, 247, 257–58, 259, 264–68, 275, 277, 279, 288–89, 298
voodoo, 3, 181, 185n12

Wald, Gayle, 293, 300n2; *Crossing the Line*, 289, 295, 298; "A Most Disagreeable Mirror," 295, 296
Walking Dead, The, 183, 264
Walmart, 18, 140
Watermelon Man, 300n3
Watson, Jay, 32, 315n1
Welty, Eudora, 9, 10, 49, 76, 142–58, 184n10; abuse as recurring plot element in her writing,

148, 157; "Alterations, The," 152–55, 158n6; *Cheated, The*, 155–56; *Curtain of Green, A*, 142, 55, 157; "Demonstrators, The," 144–45, 157, 158n1; draft of 1937 novel, 155; "Flowers for Marjorie," 143, 157; "Great Pinnington Solves a Mystery," 143; "Hitchhikers, The," 142, 157; homage to Richard Wright, 151–52; "Key, The," 143, 155–56; "Lily Daw and the Three Ladies," 155, 157; "Night of the Little House, The," 155–56; "Old Mr. Marblehall," 143; *One Writer's Beginnings*, 147; *Optimist's Daughter, The*, 145, 157, 158n4; "Petrified Man," 143, 157; "Piece of News, A," 143, 155–56, 157; "Powerhouse," 143; puzzle-text as signature form, 142, 143, 156; relationship with Ralph Ellison, 151–52; relationship with Ross Macdonald, 143–45, 148; "Shadow Club, The," 9, 143, 145–51, 158n6; "Whistle, The," 55, 57, 157; "Why I Live at the P.O.," 155–56
West Virginia, 6, 51, 54–55
Western (genre), 9, 69–70, 173–74, 177–79, 183, 184n3, 184n4, 217
white, masculinity, 31, 173, 179–83; passing as, 288–89; poor, 2, 51, 53–55, 58–62, 76, 166–67, 215; power, 161–62; privilege, 245, 274. *See also* masculinity
White Citizens' Council, 176, 180
"White Negro, The." *See* Mailer, Norman
Williams, Tennessee, 42, 45, 47, 136, 137; *Baby Doll*, 40, 45; *Fugitive Kind, The*, 44; *Streetcar Named Desire, A*, 40, 134
Woodrell, Daniel, 5, 50
Woolrich, Cornell, 27–28, 34
Wright, Richard, 39, 151–52; "[The Man Who Was] Almost a Man," 149, 151; *Black Boy*, 151; *Eight Men*, 151–52; "Inner Landscape," 42; "Man Who Killed a Shadow, The," 149, 151

Yaeger, Patricia, 76, 91, 159, 166
Yancy Derringer, 9, 172–83, 183n1, 184n3, 185n12
Younge, Gary, 12, 301, 302, 311, 314; *No Place Like Home*, 307–10